PRAISE FOR JAMES P. BLAYLOCK, Winner of the World Fantasy and Philip K. Dick Awards

"BLAYLOCK IS A MAGICIAN!"

—Michael Swanwick

"BLAYLOCK IS A TRUE AMERICAN ORIGINAL!"

—Bruce Sterling,
author of *Islands in the Net*

"BLAYLOCK is well on his way to taking a place among the first rank of American novelists."

—Lucius Shepard,
author of *Life During Wartime*

"BLAYLOCK makes you see a familiar world with fantasy eyes, until even time itself refuses to behave in a predictable fashion."

—Patricia A. McKillip

"BLAYLOCK'S prose is so rich it literally sings! . . . His vision . . . allows us to see our own world through his glasses, and realize that there are wonders all around us, as magical as in any tale . . ."

—Charles de Lint

"BLAYLOCK is better than anyone else at showing us the magic that secretly animates our world . . ."

—Tim Powers, author of *On Stranger Tides*

"BLAYLOCK has a deft touch."

—Fantasy Review

"BLAYLOCK [is a] gifted stylist."

Ace Books by James P. Blaylock

THE DIGGING LEVIATHAN
HOMUNCULUS
LAND OF DREAMS
THE STONE GIANT

From Ace Hardcover

THE LAST COIN

The Stone Giant

JAMES P. BLAYLOCK

ACE BOOKS, NEW YORK

This book is an Ace original edition, and has never been previously published.

THE STONE GIANT

An Ace Book / published by arrangement with the author

PRINTING HISTORY
Ace edition / June 1989

For information address: The Berkley Publishing Group, 200 Madison Avenue, New York, New York 10016.

ISBN: 0-441-28702-6

Ace Books are published by The Berkley Publishing Group, 200 Madison Avenue, New York, New York 10016.

PRINTED IN THE UNITED STATES OF AMERICA

10 9 8 7 6 5 4 3 2 1

To Viki, Johnny, and Danny
and to old Ahab, that rare and enviable dog

Escape at Bedtime

The lights from the parlour and kitchen shone out
Through the blinds and the windows and bars;
And high overhead and all moving about,
    There were thousands of millions of stars.
There ne'er were such thousands of leaves on a tree,
    Nor of people in church or the park,
As the crowds of the stars that looked down upon me,
    And that glittered and winked in the dark.

The Dog, and the Plough, and the Hunter, and all,
    And the star of the sailor, and Mars,
These shone in the sky, and the pail by the wall
    Would be half full of water and stars.
They saw me at last, and they chased me with cries,
    And they soon had me packed into bed;
But the glory kept shining and bright in my eyes,
    And the stars going round in my head.

—Robert Louis Stevenson

1

At Stover's Tavern

River fogs were by no means uncommon along the Oriel. When October came and the nights grew cool and wet, mist would rise along the river and creep ashore, stealing along the edge of the meadow, past the Widow's windmill, seeping between scattered houses at the edge of the village and down Main Street. The Guildhall and the market and Stover's Tavern would disappear behind a gray shroud, and nighttime noises—the footfalls of a late traveler, the hooting of an owl, the slow creak of tree limbs in the breeze—would sound unnaturally loud and ominous.

Anyone who had any sense, of course, would be abed, with their windows closed and curtains drawn, and the embers of the evening fire burning low and cheerful in the grate. There was something heavy and strange about a river fog, something that suggested it was the work of enchantment and not of nature. It was the sort of thing that was awfully fun to read about in books, especially if you had a glass of something at hand—ginger beer or a spot of good port—and if the fire hadn't burned down yet, and if the clock was ticking away low and comfortable on the mantel, reminding you that it was getting on time for bed.

But almost no one in Twombly Town would give you ten cents actually to be *out* in the fog—not after dark, anyway. It wasn't so much that there was anything in particular to be afraid of; it was that there was *nothing* in particular to be afraid of. Nothing but the humped shape of a bent tree with a limb hooked down over the road, looming dimly through the mist as if it were waiting there just for you, as if it were going to clutch at you and snatch off your hat. There were autumn leaves, drifting groundward, floating like paper boats on the wet night air and ridden, or so said the old stories, by henny-penny men in beards and hats and with enormous round eyes. There was the occasional traveler, out and about for no good reason at all, who would appear up the road like a ghost, slowly growing more distinct as he drifted toward you, but with his face veiled by mist. And you would wonder if he had any face at all as you listened to his footsteps, clump, clump, clump, echoing off the darkness and the moonlit fog. No, it was best to be indoors, reading in the lantern light, smoking a cheerful pipe.

The rising sun would burn the mists away, and by noon there would be nothing of the fog left but dew on the meadow grasses and scattered leaves. In the distance would loom a pale cloud-bank that lay low against the mountains, watching. There would be no enchantment involved anymore, just the solid scrape of your neighbor in a plaid shirt with the sleeves rolled up, hoeing weeds among turnips and string beans. Amos Bing would clatter past in a cart full of cheeses, bound for town, reining up at the crossroads so as not to hit young Beezle, who, on his bicycle, pedaled a carton full of groceries toward the Widow's house on the hill. Twombly Town, like all sensible villages, was mostly a daytime place. At night it slept.

All of that was irksome to Theophile Escargot. He much preferred the nighttime with its mystery and portent, when no one could say what mightn't be lurking just over there, beyond that copse or at the edge of that patch of shadow. If a man slept by day he had little time to work. That was a satisfying notion to Escargot. And he needn't be bothered to make tiresome small talk about the weather or radishes or the lamentable state of the river road between Twombly Town and Monmouth. So, unlike his fellows, he was fond of being abroad by night and abed by day—a fondness which led him into difficulty with his wife.

There were other things that led him into difficulty with his wife, especially his taste for pies. Apple pie was his favorite and lemon meringue next. Then came pumpkin and cherry and peach and blackberry and raspberry and apricot and sweet potato and just about anything at all, although he drew the line at salmonberry, which had an unnatural color and the flavor of thin soap. He could tolerate it with ice cream, but alone it wasn't worth eating. Unlike other foods, there was no right-time-of-the-day for eating pies, according to Escargot. And there is where he got into trouble with his wife. It was the last, in fact, of a long series of gettings-into-trouble.

His wife, a thin woman with elbows like broken sticks, believed in *slices* of pies, in the evening, and only after dinner had been dutifully consumed. If dinner was made up largely of brussels sprouts and boiled tongue—if it wasn't, in other words, dinner at all, but was a sort of joke dinner mucked up in the interests of health—then the pie would stay in the locked pantry, the key hanging on a piece of heavy thread around his wife's neck while Escargot poked at the sprouts with a fork, imagining the ghastly sour taste of the things, and staring sorrowfully at the pink and horrible tongue which seemed always on the verge of looking up at him and saying tsk, tsk, tsk. If Escargot was absolutely honest, he wouldn't be able to swear that there hadn't been moments when he felt the passing urge to grab that key and give the thread a bit of a twist.

But it had never come to that. His wife, he was certain, baked the pies to torment him, parsing out little slivers now and then to remind him of something. He couldn't, however, figure out what that something was. More often than not her pies were bound for church socials or camp meetings, to be consumed by any number of utter strangers. So and so, she would boast, ate *three* slices, and Escargot, who had missed out on the meeting because of a stomachache or a twisted shoulder, would miss out on the pie, too. So and so, it would turn out, had eaten the *last* three slices. Why, wondered Escargot, could another man eat multiple slices of pie with impunity, could turn it into a virtue, in fact, when Escargot's eating a single slice was at best something to be tolerated. It made him dizzy to think about it.

One night, after nearly two years of it, he pried the door off the pantry and ate a whole pie along with a cup of heavy cream. He could imagine his wife squinting at him as he poured the cream over the pie, commenting idly on his waistline, shaking her head sadly but with the air of someone bearing up. Mr. Stover, she would say, would find the behavior appalling. Gluttony is what it was, and Mr. Stover had told his congregation about gluttony more than once. Mr. Stover held meetings in the Guildhall every Tuesday night—more often if there was particular need for it. Escargot had resisted his wife's insistence that he attend in order to be clarified and uplifted. Besides Stover, only one man in the village was known to attend, and there was little doubt that he came only for the sweets. Escargot, despite his perpetual yearning for a slice of pie, had never been desperate enough to attend revival meetings for the sake of it.

It was one o'clock in the morning when he put the fork down. He lay the empty pie pan in the sink and filled it with water. It wouldn't do to let the remains harden on the pan; he was in for a tough enough time in the morning as it was. There was no sense in enduring a lecture on common kitchen courtesy to boot. Then, bucked by the pie and the excitement of having pinched it, he decided to take a stroll along the river. Perhaps he'd get in a couple of hours of night fishing. She'd awaken sometime early in the morning and find him gone, and the business with the key on the thread wouldn't seem half so clever to her. I'll show her, he thought to himself, stuffing two bottles of cold ale into his knapsack and pulling on a coat.

On his way out he poked his head into the baby's room, thinking to himself that if she were five years older he'd take her along, teach her a bit about fishing by lantern light. He saw little enough of her as it was. His wife, it seemed, was worried that he might be an "influence." If Annie had been awake, Escargot thought, she'd have helped him eat the pie. *She'd* have seen the virtue in it. But she wasn't awake, of course; she was asleep and had wiggled half out of the covers. So Escargot tucked her in before he tiptoed out.

By five o'clock in the morning, just before dawn, he had a brace of river squid in his sack and was fairly well satisfied with himself. He strolled along up the river road, past the woods that ran in a dark line along the meadow. The fog hovered dense and cool and with a sharp, metallic, morning smell that was worth having stayed awake for. Water dripped from the limbs of overhanging oaks, a drop now and then plunking down onto his neck. He pulled his coat tighter and quickened his pace, suddenly weary. Bacon and eggs and half a pot of coffee would go a long way toward reviving him. If he was lucky, he realized, his wife wouldn't have awakened in the night at all, wouldn't know he'd been gone, wouldn't yet have discovered the missing pie, the wrecked pantry door. Perhaps he could have a go at fixing the door, claim that he'd risen early and found it hanging, the pie gone, a window pried open. He'd pitch a half dozen jars of canned fruit under the house for good measure, to make it look as if the thief had filled his sack from the larder.

A rustling in the woods hurried him along. Probably just a rabbit, he thought, glancing over his right shoulder. Ten feet into the trees the fog thickened so as to hide everything but a few ghostly trunks, pale and twisted, with now and then a limb thrust out over the road, springing out of the mist, its few remaining leaves heavy with water. The rustling sounded ahead of him, closer to the road. There it was again, behind him now. On his left lay the riverbank; behind him lay deeper woods. All around was the impenetrable murk, masking the night noises. Why he'd gone so far downriver to fish he couldn't at all say—he'd been drunk, to a degree, on pie and cream. Twombly Town was a mile ahead of him, still sleeping in the early morning darkness.

A light glowed ahead, bobbing slowly on the path as if someone carried a lantern toward him. He wasn't certain he wanted to meet anyone, lantern or no lantern. But it wasn't lantern light; it was flames—a halo of weird fire dancing round the head of a waist-high, wizened little man. Beside him stood another, grinning, his hair standing up in a frizzle of thin spikes. Both were thin, almost skeletal, and wore clothes which hung from them like sacks. Both had sharpened teeth—not fangs or canine teeth, but flat, slab-like teeth that had been filed to points.

"Goblins," Escargot said, half aloud, and knew, as he said it, that more of the little men had stepped out of the woods behind him. The one with the flaming hair stretched his eyes until they seemed to be round as plates. He extended a thin, clawed finger and said, "Give us."

Escargot cocked his head. "Certainly," he said, supposing they meant the squid. It was better not to argue with goblins, after all, better not to get all clawed up saving a few squid when the river was full of them. Catching them was half the fun anyway. He opened his creel, pulled two of the squid from the bed of wet grass that lay within, and tossed them to the goblins. The creatures watched stupidly as the squids flopped onto the trail and sat there in the dirt.

The goblin with the burning head looked at Escargot in amazement, then leaped on the squids, poking his fellow goblin in the ear with his finger and pushing him against the trunk of an oak. A flurry of steps sounded on the path behind Escargot, and three more goblins, gabbling like raccoons, rushed past, throwing themselves onto the first goblin, who swatted at them defiantly, half a squid protruding from his mouth. He held the other in his hand, and as the quickest of his brethren rushed upon him, he flailed at the creature with the rubbery squid, effecting nothing but the squid's ruination. He champed down on the squid in his mouth, razoring it in half with his filed teeth, the protruding bit falling onto the road and vanishing beneath all five of the shrieking goblins, two more of whom had managed, in the struggle, to catch fire. Escargot tiptoed past. There was no weapon like a squid, apparently, for defeating a party of goblins. For good measure he pitched three more of the leggy beasts in among them, then took to his heels, dodging round bends that appeared suddenly in the fog, leaping over a fallen tree that he'd remembered from the journey out four hours earlier.

The gabbling receded behind him, and he slowed to a walk, gasping in lungfuls of fog, looking over his shoulder and listening between breaths for the sound of pursuit. It wouldn't do to stop. This was no time to rest; he had a quarter mile of woods to get through before he'd be onto the relative safety of the meadow. The meadow was close to the lights of town, and goblins, like wolves or trolls, hadn't any use for towns.

A twig snapped above him. He lurched and sprawled forward, tumbling onto the roadway, yanking at the thing that had landed suddenly on his back. It shrieked inhumanly into his ear, gabbling out a continual stream of gibberish. The goblin's tiny hands were around his throat, scrabbling after something, tugging at the drawstring of Escargot's pouch. The little devils were trying to rob him! It hadn't been squid at all they were after. He rolled toward the river, crushing the little man beneath him, half dislodging the thing as it whooped and gibbered. It peered around into his face, grinning past pointed teeth, eyes whirling like pinwheels. Escargot got a hand round the goblin's neck and jerked the thing loose. He grabbed its skinny leg with his other hand, hefted it over his head, and threw it headlong into the river.

His pouch was safe. His creel, however, was a ruin. The spindly willow basket was crushed almost flat, and the head of one doleful-eyed squid had been forced out through a split in the bottom. Escargot snatched the creel open, yanked out the half dozen flattened squid that remained, and scattered them over the path, leaping away toward the village as the first party of goblins rushed toward him, their flaming heads advertising their appearance like beacons. Escargot pounded along for all he was worth, his creel and fishing pole tossed away into the river grasses. Within five minutes he was clear of the woods and free of goblins. The fog was lightening with the morning, and he could smell on the breeze the smoke of pruning fires and chimneys from the village ahead.

The church bell rang six when he trudged up the path to his house, thinking to slip in at the back door and have a go at falsifying the utterly obvious evidence that his wife would find, at any moment, in the kitchen. He found the back door padlocked. A note on the front door invited him to leave and not to return. There was no use pounding and railing; his wife had gone to Stover, who knew about morality and the law both.

For a week he slept by day in the abandoned Widow's windmill. By night he fished and wandered through the autumn streets, holding imaginary conversations with his wife and developing the suspicion that she was never going to give him the satisfaction of actually carrying on one of those conversations. Protestations through the locked windows effected nothing. His wife was gone far more often than she was in.

On more than one night, very late, when the fog had risen and obscured the oaks and the hemlocks that ran down out of the foothills and lined the road, Escargot slouched along, hands in his pockets, and fancied that he heard in the distance someone coming along toward him, tapping along the road with a stick, feeling his way through the fog. The sound seemed to be carried on a breath of cool air. Always it faded into nothing, as if the stroller were walking away from him, an odd thing altogether. For whoever it was hadn't passed him; the tap, tap, tap of the stick on the road simply started up out of the mists and echoed its way into nothing.

Escargot told himself it was a woodpecker of some nocturnal

variety, tapping holes in the bark of trees to hide acorns. But he didn't half believe it. And more than once he heard the titter of laughter somewhere off in the fog. It was as if someone were laughing at *him*, an unsettling notion altogether, and one which led him to keep an eye out for goblins, although it did seem unlikely that any of the little men would leave the darkness of the woods. There was no good in being careless, though, it had already been made very clear to him that goblins wandered by night farther up the Oriel River valley than most villagers liked to believe.

His thoughts always returned home, however, even though he'd never cared much about such things before. A home had simply been shelter, and one shelter was as good as another. A man ought to have any number of them, he told himself, so that if one wore out he could move on to another. He wouldn't grow too fond of any that way and go moping about through the silent evening streets if his house burned down or was blown away in a hurricane or if he was pitched out of it for eating a pie with cream. Perhaps it was the same way with children. It mightn't have been a bad idea to have a couple in reserve. But he hadn't any except little Annie, had he?

After a week of such nights he found his clothes and books and assorted odds and ends in a heap on his front porch, or on *her* front porch, such as it was. He left most of them. It was then that he began to feel very sorry for himself. It was all very well to be tramping about in the foggy darkness when one knew that just over the hill lay a bed with a feather comforter, a fireplace loaded with last year's oak logs, and a waiting family. But it was another thing when just over the hill lay nothing at all but more hills.

Perhaps it *had* been his fault. He'd been hasty, compounding the pie crime by leaving without a word. What had happened, he wondered, to his marriage. He wasn't prime husband material; that was certain. When it came to being husband material, he was pretty much tangled together out of old rags. He liked fishing a little too much, and he believed that work was something a man did when he had to. He had always been able to get along well enough without it, especially for the last couple of years. A little bit of barter at just the right moment would keep things afloat—a squid clock, perhaps, for a pair of boots; the boots for a brass kaleidoscope and a penknife with a bone handle; the knife for a hat and the hat for a coat and the kaleidoscope rented out for a penny a glimpse. A man could keep busy forever, couldn't he?

It made him tired to think about it, but not half as tired, apparently, as it had made his wife, who had pointed out that he was "too heavy for light work and too light for heavy work." Escargot's defense—that he had an artistic temperament suited more to philosophy than to work—had rung false even to him. He had no excuse; that was the truth of the thing. But why should a man go about with an apology on his lips? Why, in fact, did a man have to beg to eat his own pie? The thought of pie reminded him somehow that the nights were getting longer and colder, and he slipped once again into remorse. He took to hanging round the old house in the mornings, careful not to be seen but half hoping that he would be, as if by magic something would appear to make everything all right again.

What appeared was Gilroy Bastable, heading along very officiously toward town, happy with himself. Bastable shook his head. Everyone in the village, by that time, was familiar with Escargot's fate, and sympathy, said Bastable, was pretty much on the side of the wife, lamentable as it might seem. Stover had preached an entire sermon on it. It was something in the way of a lesson, wasn't it? And this business about stealing pies . . .

"Pie," said Escargot.

"Pardon me?" asked Bastable amiably.

"There was only one pie involved. And stealing doesn't enter into it, does it? A man's own pie, after all, made of peaches from his own well-tended garden."

Mayor Bastable cast a glance toward Escargot's weedy orchard with its overgrown trees. He widened his eyes and shrugged, as if to say that he'd only been passing on what he knew about the case. "You shouldn't have walked out on her, old man."

"I went fishing," said Escargot, forgetting in a rush everything he'd convinced himself of only moments before. "She pitched me out without a backward glance. Two years of bliss up the flume. Women are mad is what I think. Chemistry is what it is. I've . . ."

Bastable put a hand on his shoulder and shook his head, a

set smile on his lips. "We know just how you feel," he said, as if such a thing might be vastly calming. "We all of us hope you'll come to terms with this little sadness."

"We!" cried Escargot, shrugging off his friend's hand. "Terms! Damn all terms!" And with that Escargot stormed away toward the village, his teeth set with determination. He'd leave; that's what he'd do. There were grand places in the world. He'd go to the coast, to the Wonderful Isles. Twombly Town could writher in its own slime; that's what. He smiled grimly. He rather liked that last bit. *Writher* was a good word—if it was a word. If it wasn't, it should be, he decided, slowing down and angling toward Stover's Tavern.

The tavern was almost empty. It was early, after all. Candles burned in wall sconces, throwing cups of sooty yellow light up the plaster walls. A half hour earlier the floor had been covered with sawdust and shavings and littered with nut shells and sausage rinds and greasy newspaper. It was swept clean now, though, and the tavern maid, Leta, was scooping up heaps of debris with a broad, flat shovel and emptying it into a bucket. A lock of dark hair had fallen across her forehead, and she shoved at it, pausing to poke it in under a red bow at the top of a heavy braid. Immediately the lock mutinied and fell back across her forehead. She looked up and frowned at Escargot, who stood in the doorway gaping at her.

He'd seen her for the first time a month earlier at Professor Wurzle's lending library. They'd both been after the same book, or at least books by the same author: G. Smithers of Brompton Village. There was nothing Escargot liked to do more than to lie up with a book and a pipe in the afternoon heat, under an oak if one was handy, or beneath the docks along the river Oriel. He couldn't much read at home. The interruptions set him crazy. There was always something to do—trash to be hauled away, weeds to be pulled, boxes to be got down off closet shelves, a roomful of furniture to be rearranged a dozen ways, only to end up back where it started. His wife would say something to him from another room in a voice calculated to carry about eight feet. What! he'd shout, knowing that he was expected to drop the book, frivolous thing that it was, and trot round to lend a hand—to squish a harmless bug most often, a bug that was minding its own business, looking for a quiet place to read a bug story and put its feet up, but finding instead the business end of a shoe. Escargot had been the unwilling accessory to countless murders. But he was being petty. He had promised to catch himself if he was in danger of becoming petty, especially out loud. That sort of thing made a person tiresome.

He watched Leta shove the bucket out the back door and pick up a fat gunny sack. She dumped shavings from it onto the cleaned floor, kicking them under tables with her feet. At the lending library she'd found a book about the harvest festival at Seaside, and Escargot, catching sight of the title, had said truthfully that he'd always wanted to visit Seaside, days away down the Oriel, for the yearly festivals held at the time of the autumnal equinox. She had been to more than one. She'd been born in the foothills above Seaside, on the eve of the festival, and so was a harvest maid, even though she wasn't a dwarf. She was about five feet ten inches tall, only an inch shorter than Escargot.

He'd made her promise to bring the book back quickly, certain at the time that his interest would appear feigned and that she would think he was being fresh. He wasn't, though. He was married, wasn't he, and had been for two years, and although some might say he was lazy and thought of himself as often as he thought of anyone else, he had his code. He hadn't had his fingers crossed when he'd promised to be true to his wife. But he had found himself worrying that Leta would think his attentions at the library less than sincere, and then he had worried about being worried, because the worry seemed to throw a cloud of doubt over the code he prided himself in having. Fat lot of good all the worrying had done him. He might as well have tossed all codes out the window for good and all. But he knew he couldn't do that, even now. He was *still* married, even if he *was* living in an abandoned windmill and eating fish and berries. Who could say, the condition might prove to be temporary.

He sat down at a table against the wall and smiled at Leta when she looked up at him. She pulled a pocket watch out of her leather apron and gave it a look. "It's an hour before we open," she said.

"Of course," said Escargot, taken aback. Did she think he was after a glass of ale at that hour? This is an unfortunate start, he thought, and realizing as he did so that he *had* been after a glass of ale at that hour and that he hadn't ought to be intending to "start" anything. He grinned—foolishly, it seemed to him. "I was just wondering how you liked the book. I was passing by and saw you through the open door, so I thought I'd come in out of the fog and keep you company."

"Which book was that?"

"*Harvest Moon*, by G. Smithers. From the Professor's. Remember?"

"I remember having told you I liked it very much, just days ago. Next to the melon bin at Beezle's market." She looked at him strangely, as if beginning to suspect he was either stupid or up to something.

"Of course," he said. "Of course. I've been a bit . . . upset, I suppose is the word for it." He started to go on, to explain things, but he caught himself and stopped. There was no use boring anyone. "I'm about halfway through it. I always have a hard time with Smithers. I can't tell what's true and what's not. A few years ago, before the Professor took over the library, old Kettering had Smithers filed under history. The Professor says that Kettering was an idiot, that Smithers is full of tall tales. But that wasn't the way Kettering saw it. I figure that half of what anyone says is nonsense, including Professor Wurzle—*especially* Professor Wurzle. And including G. Smithers, for that matter."

Leta scattered one last handful of shavings under a corner table, hefted the half-empty sack onto her shoulder, and set out toward the back of the tavern. Through the leaded glass of one of the front windows, Escargot could see that the fog was thinning. Pale sunlight shone through it, turning the mist white, as if the windows were glazed with milk glass. The appearance of the sun, for some reason, made him feel almost contented for the first time in two weeks. He pulled his pipe from his coat pocket and pushed tangled tobacco into it, wondering idly if it wouldn't be a good idea to mix a few shavings of aromatic cedar into the tobacco, just to give it a try. Probably not, he decided. It would likely blaze up like a torch and burn the whole pipe. Leta would be certain he'd gone mad.

She appeared again, rolling up her sleeves. "So which half is true and which half is made up?" she asked, pulling a handful of pint glasses out of a sink full of clear water.

Escargot shrugged, eyeing the glasses. "Have you read the Balumnian books?"

"Only one. *The Stone Giants*. Do you know it?"

"Yes," said Escargot. "That's just the one I want to ask you about. I've been having the most amazing dreams. Foolish, of course, like all dreams, but different too. There's this sort of face, you see, watching the dreams. And it's not my face. That's the peculiar part. Take a look at these."

Escargot removed his coat. Slung around his left arm and neck hung his pouch on a long leather thong. He yanked his arm through the thong, and without pulling the bag from around his neck, emptied into his hand agate marbles—blood-red and big as cats' eyes.

"Marbles?" asked Leta, raising her eyebrows at Escargot as if she didn't share his peculiar enthusiasm.

"I'm not at all sure. There was a bunjo man through a month or so back. You might have seen him around the village hawking whales' eyes. I bought one of those too. Massive thing in a jar. When I saw it I told myself, this is just the thing you've been waiting for. They weren't cheap, but my wife's got a pile of the gold stuff. She's pretty much swimming in it, though it's precious little of it that she lets me on to." Escargot caught himself. Here he was speaking in the present tense. As if he *had* a wife in any real sense. Leta had gone back to washing glasses. "Anyway," he said, gazing out the window at the dwindling fog, "ever since then I've had these dreams, like I said. I don't think the whale's eye had anything to do with it, because I traded it away to Gilroy Bastable a week later for Smithers' White Mountains books. All twenty-five of them. The first volume is signed and there's a page of manuscript laid in."

"Really?"

"Yes indeed," said Escargot proudly, noting that mention of the Smithers books had seemed to warm Leta up a bit.

"Would you like a pint?" she asked, raising a glass. "It's close enough to eleven to warrant it, I suppose."

"No he would not like a filthy pint!" shouted a voice from the back, and Stover, bent and scowling, strode in and slammed his fist onto the first handy tabletop. Stover, who doubled on Sundays as a church parson and tripled on Saturdays as a judge, was taller by a head than anyone else in the village. But he was opposed on moral grounds, in spite of his owning a tavern, to eating and drinking, or at least to eating, and so was astonishingly thin. The weight of his head seemed to have bent him almost double, as if he were always looking along the ground for some lost object—a penny, perhaps. His eyes, to balance things, rolled upward and half disappeared under his eyebrows, which beetled out over his nose like the eaves of a house. He leaned against the table and glowered at Escargot.

"That *dear* woman . . ." said Stover, wrinkling an acre of forehead and scowling slowly and deliberately.

Escargot thought at first that Stover was referring to Leta, who rolled her eyes, set down the glass she was holding, and walked past Stover toward the rear of the tavern. A door slammed shut. Stover heaved with exertion. What in the world, wondered Escargot, did the nitwit suppose was going on?

"The great shame of it," cried the tavern keeper, raising a finger aloft and twirling it in a tight little circle, "is that the law hasn't a cage to pitch you into."

Escargot looked over his shoulder, wondering briefly if there wasn't someone else in the room who had so excited Stover. But there was no one. Escargot raised his eyebrows theatrically and pointed at himself, cocking his head in a questioning way.

"Laugh if you will!" shouted the enraged Stover, squinting and pounding again on the table. "But let it be known to you, sir, scoundrel that you are, that that dear, poor woman and her precious baby child are a dozen times better off alone than they were two weeks past. It was a charitable thing you did, abandoning them that night. Robbing your own wife blind while she slept. Lying up in a drunken stupor until dawn, then stumbling home, intent, no doubt, on some further mischief. But that sort of charity, sir, will . . ."

Escargot stood up slowly, interrupting the innkeeper. I'll have to hit him, he thought, taking a step forward. He was struck suddenly by the notion that there might easily be more to the affairs of the previous weeks than he'd known. Stover trod back, gaping at Escargot in fear and surprise, and groped in his own coat pocket, unearthing a silver flask. He unscrewed the lid, tilted the bottle back, and swallowed three times, his Adam's apple bobbing like a fishing float jerked by a trout.

"Medicine," Stover gasped, wiping at his mouth with the

back of his hand. He stepped back, fumbling at a chair as if to use it as a weapon. Sweat stood out on his forehead.

A door slammed and Leta reappeared, stopping abruptly at the sight of the scowling Escargot, who had slipped the leather thong from around his neck and was slapping the heavy bag full of marbles into the palm of his hand. "Eleven o'clock," she said, pulling out her pocket watch and twisting the stem in order to force the issue. "Time to open. Put that away," she said to Escargot. "Don't turn yourself into more of a fool than you already are."

"Listen to the little lady," croaked Stover, pulling at the top button on his shirt.

"Shut up," said Leta, giving him a look. She stepped across to the keg and drew a pint of ale, knocking off the head with a wooden ruler and sliding the glass across the bar in Escargot's direction.

"I won't serve his kind here!" cried Stover, working himself up again.

"I know," said Leta, "that's why *I* did it. But that's the last pint I draw, old man, so you'll serve everyone else. You paid me yesterday evening. You don't owe me a thing for this morning."

"You can't!" began Stover, but he found himself storming at nothing. Escargot glanced through the window at Leta disappearing through the thin fog, walking briskly up Main Street in the direction of Beezle's market. "You'll have to pay for that pint," said Stover weakly, sliding in behind the bar. He fumbled out his flask one more time and had another go at it. Escargot stared at him, drained the glass, set it on the nearest table, and dropped a coin into the dregs. He turned and walked out without a word—very cool, it seemed to him. Once on the street, though, he set out at a run.

"Wait!" he shouted, catching sight of Leta's red blouse a half block up. She stopped, gazing in through a shop window until he puffed up behind her. "Perhaps I can buy you lunch." He took off his hat and gave it a nervous twist, grinning at her. Then it struck him that the grin looked foolish, so he wiped it off and looked serious instead.

"I don't think that would work, would it?"

"Wouldn't it?"

"Give it a while," she said, smiling just a bit. "Maybe I'll see you at Wurzle's."

"Maybe you will," said Escargot, watching her fade into the fog for the second time in five minutes, having no idea on earth what to make of her.

2

The Appearance of Uncle Helstrom

Late one afternoon, three and a half weeks after he'd been pitched out by his wife, Escargot caught sight of himself in the big window in Beezle's store, and realized with a start that he looked like a tramp, that his jacket was torn and his trousers needed soap. His shirt, which he'd owned long before he'd developed the temporary madness that had led to his getting married, had turned thin. The elbows resembled muslin or, worse yet, spiderweb.

He was on his way to Wurzle's lending library. He'd given up pretending that he was only after a book. He had a stack of G. Smithers—all of the White Mountains books he'd traded out of Gilroy Bastable—hidden away in the Widow's windmill, and hadn't half read through them yet. He was going to Wurzle's to find Leta; that's what he was doing. So far he'd had no success. Just look at me, he thought to himself, staring at his sad reflection in Beezle's window. A month earlier if he'd looked like that he wouldn't have cared. Caring wouldn't have crossed his mind. He would have *prided* himself in it, to a degree—laughed at Beezle in his starchy shirt and tie, tiptoeing around mud puddles and dusting off chairs before he sat down. Who in the world did a man like Beezle intend to impress? Grocery shoppers? Old fatheads who complained about spots on the apples and argued about the price of dried beans? A month ago Escargot would have grinned to think about it. He had had no one but his wife to impress, and. . . Well, he thought, looking at his ill-shaven face in the store window, perhaps he hadn't done as well at that as he might have. The door of the market opened and Beezle's head shoved out, round and grinning and with its pale hair greased up like a fence.

"Theophile," said Beezle, half grinning and half saddened, as if he'd seen his friend looking better, perhaps, or as if he didn't entirely fancy seeing Escargot at all.

Escargot gritted his teeth. He detested being called by his first name, which no one in the world, apparently, could pronounce. He forced himself to grin at Beezle, though. Nothing would be accomplished by his going about town flying into rages. Heaven knew what rumors had been circulated about his run-in with Stover, especially since Stover was the only one who would have done any rumor circulating. Leta didn't at all seem to be the sort who would go in for telling tales, even though her version would be closer to the truth.

"I say, old man," Beezle said, screwing his face into a wide grin. "This is a delicate sort of subject, I know, but I was watching you there in the window a moment ago, and you seemed . . . you seemed . . . out of sorts, if you follow me." With that Beezle looked Escargot up and down as if contemplating the cut of his coat. Escargot waited, befuddled. "What I mean to say, don't you know, is simply this. Would a spot of work help? Sweeping and dusting? Deliveries? This window, it strikes me now, could use a washup." His face brightened, as if he were about to say something really clever. "It could well be," he finished, eyes widening, "that half of what you were looking at is the fault of the window, couldn't it?"

Escargot began to nod silently, as if in agreement with Beezle's last comment. But then he shook his head and smiled back. If there was nothing else to be done, at least he could out-smile him. "I'm not up to it today, Evelyn," he said, deliberately using Beezle's first name, which was about eight times as foolish as his own. "But I'll keep my eyes open. If I see any of the village lads lounging about, doing nothing, I'll send them your way. That spot on your tie appears to be strawberry jam, doesn't it? My wife, bless her heart, used to tell me by the hour about how that sort of thing stains. Soak it in cold water first; that's what *she'd* tell you. Then smear soap on the stain before you go after it with the washboard."

Escargot tipped his hat and set out, leaving Beezle to study his tie. He was happy enough with the exchange. Beezle had meant well, to be sure. He was just thick-headed—a blessing, no doubt, in a man who set such lofty goals for himself. At least Professor Wurzle wouldn't rag him about his fallen state. Wurzle seemed to appreciate the art of doing nothing almost as much as did Escargot. The Professor had turned it into a study. He'd pluck up a lot of leaves when he was out strolling in the forest and pretend that the *purpose* of the stroll was to collect those leaves. Then he'd tack labels on them and put them in a box and mutter now and again about opening a museum of natural history. His lending library was an excuse to sit in a stuffed chair and read and smoke all day.

But when Escargot arrived at the library, the Professor wasn't, in fact, reading and smoking. He was out with a net after salamanders, said his young assistant. Escargot wondered aloud if the assistant had, perhaps, seen the young lady who was so fond of Smithers books. Not for a week, said the youth, grinning at Escargot as if the two of them shared an unspoken joke. Rumor had it she'd left town. Old Stover, they said, had fired her, and she'd gone back to Seaside. She had been renting a room over the tavern and had left the same night as the altercation. The young man winked familiarly at Escargot, then seemed to take a long look at him, as if suddenly noticing something that he hadn't seen a moment before. Escargot straightened his shoulders abruptly and gave the youth a sidewise glance.

"Did she *say* she was going back to Seaside?"

"Now how would I know?" asked the youth, bending over the counter to have a look at Escargot's shoes. "She didn't say *nothing* to me, did she? Though that don't mean she wouldn't have. She said plenty to me before."

"Did she," said Escargot flatly, shaking his head and turning to leave. He was suddenly tired of trekking around town in worn-out clothes and with nothing to do but carry on maddening conversations with whomever he was unfortunate enough to bump into. That was one of the drawbacks of having no real business to attend to. If he were Beezle, pedaling groceries up the hill, he could shout incoherencies at people without offending them. He'd be respected because he was busy. Being busy was a virtue; being idle was a vice. That was one of life's vast mysteries.

On the way out the door he nearly bumped into Professor Wurzle, who everyone referred to as "the Professor" even though he was only three years out of the university and had never been, as far as Escargot could tell, a teacher of any sort. Escargot himself had attended the university, for a time anyway. It gave one—what was it?—a certain respectability when one was pursuing a monied wife. Wurzle carried in either hand a fat salamander, speckled and wide-eyed.

"Look at these specimens!" he cried happily at Escargot.

"Very nice indeed."

"First of the season, sir. First of the season. You don't get many of this stature, not east of the mountains."

"I don't suppose you do," said Escargot, stopping for a moment to admire the beasts. Then, almost under his breath, he asked, "Haven't seen Leta around, have you? The dark-haired girl who reads Smithers?"

"Who?" asked Wurzle, wrinkling up his forehead. Then he looked hard into the face of one of the salamanders, as if it had been the salamander that had spoken to him, or as if he suspected that the creature knew the answer to Escargot's question.

"I already told him all there is to know!" shouted the young man from within the store. "He don't want nothing but trouble!"

"Say," said Wurzle, brightening up. "I've built a cage for these two that I'm rather proud of—potted plants, little caverns, bit of a pond. Care to take a look at it?"

"Thanks," said Escargot, backing off down the boardwalk, "but I've got to be off. Got to check the lines before dusk. Perhaps later?"

"Certainly," said the Professor, already stepping into the library and looking again into the face of his salamander. "Anytime at all. I'm always here, or at least the boy is." His voice evaporated as the door swung shut behind him. Escargot trudged away down the street, heading for the harbor, watching the toes of his shoes kick up little sprays of pebbles, his mind revolving and yet thinking about nothing in particular, but lost in a salad of thoughts about his daughter and his wife and Beezle's window and Leta and Stover and the silly fat salamander that Professor Wurzle held in such high esteem. It was entirely conceivable that Twombly Town wasn't big enough to hold the lot of them. And if Leta *had* left for Seaside, then perhaps it was high time he did the same.

The evening promised to be cool and wet. The black oaks across the Oriel were dark with dampness and twilight, and already the fog covered the ground around them like a gray, cottony blanket. Escargot sat on a fallen tree, staring across the river into the woods and thinking of nothing. Tied to scattered branches along the tree were heavy fishing lines that angled out into the shadowy water, trailing away downstream in the current. Clumps of waterweeds clung to the lines where they entered the water, and now and then some bit of debris—a tangle of twigs and leaves or a half-submerged piece of driftwood—came floating along to bump into one of the lines, spinning away and taking most of the waterweeds with it.

The river was rising. It seemed to be hurrying along toward the sea, as if more anxious by the day to arrive at its destination. Escargot had begun to fancy the idea of destinations himself. It struck him that it might as easily be *him* swirling away down the river toward the coast. It seemed to him that he had somehow been wasting his time for years.

Destinations—that was the secret. It didn't much matter what they were. There was something frightening about staying overlong in the same place, about "settling down." You could too clearly see the end, perhaps—all the gray years laid out end to end like paving stones and winding up at a last carved stone standing upright in a weedy cemetery. Movement, Escargot thought, squinting into the dark trees, would somehow bend and twist the path so that a person couldn't tell finally where he'd started and where he was likely to finish. That was appealing—to be always heading somewhere, bartering a bit along the road in order to stay in tobacco: washing the occasional window if it was absolutely necessary and whistling while you were at it; pinching the odd pie that was cooling on a windowsill, and leaving for it a willow flute or a handful or marbles or a grass basket full of salted fish.

While the sensible villager huddled in his house at night wondering at the scrape and swish of branches in the wind and half fearing the humped shadows of tangled berry vines out in the dark yard, Escargot would be abroad, *living* among the shadows. It would be *his* feet that would crunch past on the gravel at midnight and cause the villager to sit upright in his bed, listening, shivering, cocking his head. Perhaps he'd sail to Oceania and fall among pirates or tramp downriver to seek out treasure in the Goblin Wood.

Perhaps—perhaps he'd start by going to Seaside and looking up Leta. That was a good enough destination for the moment. In a week, when Halloween was past and the nights were a bit emptier of enchantment, they would hold the harvest fair in Seaside. Escargot could picture himself among the crowds—bonfires burning in the streets, men and elves and linkmen milling among the Seaside dwarfs, an occasional band of goblins hooting with idiotic laughter and scuttling away down an alley after having terrorized an innkeeper or having pulled the hair of a poor old woman in the street. There would be Leta, little realizing who it was that stood behind her. He'd tap her on the shoulder. She'd turn, surprised. He'd smile and say something to her, something witty. What would it be? He'd have to think about it. That was the sort of moment he'd want to be prepared for; otherwise he'd spend a lifetime regretting having said something foolish.

Escargot was startled by a splash twenty feet out into the river, and he grabbed the line near his right ear, thinking that a river squid had taken the glowworm on the end of it. The fog had crept higher. Only ghostly branches could be seen across the water. The docks in Twombly Town Harbor were invisible fifty yards distant, and the evening was silent and still. The muted hooting of an owl drifted like a disembodied voice out of the woods. There was nothing on any of the lines.

Out over the river, sculling along some four or five feet above the water and angling in toward where Escargot sat on his log, a spiney, round-headed fish glowing like a lantern swam leisurely through the foggy air. It drew up to within five feet of him before blinking and changing course. "Fogfish!" whispered Escargot, slowly standing and peering round for his net. There was something odd about the fog—about the heavy, lazy nature of it, about the way it seemed to have crept out of the forest instead of having risen from the river. It felt like enchantment, the product of the season, of the approach of Halloween. Fogfish never appeared in a common fog. Escargot was certain of that much.

Two minutes earlier he couldn't have sworn that fogfish ever appeared at all. You heard stories, of course, stories told on the same late and festive evenings that produced tales of great river squid that dragged fishing boats to a watery doom in the Oriel River delta above Seaside, tales of mermaids in the shallows off Monmouth Point and of drowned sailors who piloted ghostly sloops far beneath the surface of the river, hauling along toward unknowable destinations. There were stories that the Oriel River was the magical counterpart of another vast river in a faraway and magical land. When the night was particularly full of misty enchantment, or so the stories went, boats and fish and heaven knew what sorts of deepwater creatures wandered out of one river and into the next.

G. Smithers was full of such stuff—tales of a land known as Balumnia, illustrated maps tracing just such a river, a river strangely like the Oriel with similarly situated towns and a vast haunted woods not at all unlike the Goblin Wood that stretched along the river south of Hightower Village. Escargot had always had curious notions about G. Smithers and his maps. Professor Wurzle had insisted that Smithers, living in Brompton Village on the Oriel itself, would naturally have used a river he was familiar with as a model. All writers, insisted Wurzle, were bound by the familiar, by what they knew. They were slaves to it. But Professor Wurzle was too full of what passed for common sense to satisfy Escargot. There was nothing common sensical about fogfish.

Escargot crouched on the bank, clutching his net. All was silent but for the occasional, distant tap, tap, tap of something, of a woodpecker, perhaps. Night had drifted in with the fog, and both had thickened until the dark river disappeared, all but the still water along the bank at Escargot's feet. The glow of another wandering fogfish shone briefly offshore like a windborne jack-o'-lantern, then another drifted past, even farther out, slanting briefly in, then disappearing with a muted splash into the river.

Minutes passed, one by one, Escargot listening in the silent night, watching, thinking that even the dirt floor of the Widow's windmill and the sorry little heap of late berries and pickled fish that awaited him there had begun to look awfully warm and cozy. There were nights to be out and about in, it seemed to him suddenly, and there were nights to leave alone. He yanked one last time on his lines, then turned toward the meadow, thinking to hide his net in a hollow beneath the log.

Before him, revealed by suddenly thinning mist, stood an

old woman, bent with age, her eyes the color of moonlit fog. She leaned on a crooked stick, looking at nothing. Then she turned slowly and hobbled away into a dense wall of gray, disappearing utterly. The tapping began again, closer this time, each tap just a fraction sharper and clearer than the last, as if it were the tapping of a blind man feeling his way across cobbles. The breeze stirred the meadow grasses, swirling clouds of fog into a little wind devil.

Then, in a wink, as if she had appeared out of the vapors, out of the breeze itself, Leta stood before him on the meadow. Beside her stood a dwarf in a slouch hat and carrying a staff, a broad grin on his face. In his mouth was a long pipe. Thick smoke, strangely aromatic, curled from it, disappearing at once into the fog. The smoke was heavy with the curious smell of waterweeds and river mud and the dusty odor of powdered, dry bone. The dwarf winked slowly and put a finger to the brim of his hat.

Escargot found that he couldn't speak. Here was Leta, on the one hand, miraculously restored to the village, and here was a night full of portent and mystery on the other, a night of blind old ladies strolling along the river road, of dwarfs in slouch hats winking and grinning and smoking odd pipes. He found that despite the wet air his lips and throat were dry. He croaked out a hello, which made Leta smile, as if she thought it was funny that she had surprised him there on the meadow.

"I'd like to introduce my uncle to you," she said, gesturing at the dwarf. "Mr. Abner Helstrom, of Hightower Village. I've been downriver, staying with him."

"Glad to meet you, sir," said Escargot dubiously, shaking the cold hand of the dwarf. He patted his pocket, suddenly wishing for the company of a familiar lit pipe.

"Like to try a pipe full of my blend, Mr. . . . what was it again?"

"Escargot. Theophile Escargot, sir, at your service." He grinned at Leta while waving away the open pouch of tobacco that the dwarf thrust in his direction. "Too exotic for my tastes, I'm afraid. I have common tastes in tobacco. Very common." He looked into the open mouth of the pouch, just as the dwarf pushed it shut, and was certain he saw curling up out of the tangled leaves either the tiny tentacle of an octopus or the pink tail of a pig. He couldn't say which. The dwarf winked at him and patted him on the arm. Then, leading him by the elbow, the little man set off up the meadow, angling across toward the windmill. Leta followed along behind.

"My niece tells me you've fallen on hard times."

"Tolerably hard times," said Escargot, wondering why on earth his troubles would concern this winking uncle. Maybe Leta had more of an interest in him than she'd let on. That was it. He was suddenly certain of it. Her abrupt disappearance and now her return—what could it mean but that she'd been disturbed by his bad luck? He turned and smiled at her. She smiled back and nodded, as if having read his thoughts. "A man has to bear up, though," said Escargot staunchly, pushing open the plank door of the windmill.

The dwarf gave him a hearty slap on the small of his back. "That's the spirit!" He looked about the octagonal little room, nodding over the bit of rag stuffed into knotholes and the sad pine needle bed. "Bearing up," he muttered, shaking his head sadly, as if genuinely sorry for Escargot's plight. "Plan to winter here, do you?"

Escargot cast Leta a look, suddenly ashamed of his borrowed quarters. "No. I've got a few things to do. A man can't sit idle, can he? Since you know the short of it anyway, the long of it is that I'm waiting for this business with the house to be settled. My house, that is. Or at least it *was* mine. I've been led to understand that I'm likely to lose it. Public opinion hereabouts favors my wife, who, with the baby and all, needs a place to live. And I'm not one to argue with that, am I? I'm not one to raise questions about why the child shouldn't just come along downriver with me. For that matter, why Annie and I shouldn't have the house and the *wife* leave. It was her idea, wasn't it? Not mine." Escargot stopped himself. This was no one's trouble but his own. And here was Leta, looking sorrowful, strangely silent. It suddenly occurred to him that he ought to bring up the wife and child less often around her. Why had she sought him out, anyway? Certainly not to listen to him carry on about his troubles. Should he offer them a seat on the floor, he wondered, wishing that it weren't too late to stroll into town. But the only tavern left open at that hour would be Stover's, and that wouldn't do.

"Have you spoken to the judge?" asked Uncle Helstrom, tamping his pipe and squinting up at Escargot.

"I almost hit him in the eye. Leta was there. There's not much need for judges in Twombly Town, actually, so they just ask for volunteers. A man named Stover holds office now, and has for three years. No one else wants the job. What decent man would? Put his neighbor in a cell for taking an extra drink. Take a man's child away from him because this judge, mind you, has an eye toward the man's wife and wants the child into the bargain. No, I didn't talk to the judge."

"Well," said the dwarf, shaking his head knowingly, "I don't hold any particular sway in these parts, but I have certain—what can I call them?—methods, let's say, which I can bring to bear. Do you follow me?"

"I suppose so," replied Escargot, not wanting to look foolish. His opinion of the uncle was growing. Here was a man who saw things clearly, who went to the nub. Had he come all the way upriver from Hightower Village to lend another man a hand? Escargot found himself smiling at Leta again. She nodded and winked, as if to say that here, in this little man, lay Escargot's hope, perhaps both their hopes.

"Now, sir," said the dwarf. "I didn't come all the way upriver from Hightower Village entirely on a mission of mercy. I wish I could say I did, because if it was true, it would make me a better man than I am. And there isn't one among us that wouldn't profit—morally speaking, of course—from being a better man than we are, is there?"

Escargot agreed that there wasn't. Uncle Helstrom's humility and wisdom seemed suddenly boundless to him.

"And at the same time I can see, with my own eyes, and I know, in my own heart, flawed as it is, that a good man shouldn't be living like this, bearing up or no. Not when his rightful house and property sit waiting for him up the road. No, sir. He should not. He *must* not. And so your business, I'm trying to say, must take precedent over my own."

"Uncle!" cried Leta, in such a fearful tone of voice that Escargot jumped. The girl seemed on the verge of tears—as if there were something in her uncle's generosity that spelled ruin for the little man, as if the dwarf were so wholeheartedly charitable that another man's good fortune *was* more precious to him than his own. Escargot, for the second time that evening, could barely speak.

"Quiet, girl," said the dwarf, whacking his stick against the dirt floor in a spirit of righteous determination. The end of the staff, shod in brass, struck sparks from the dirt, to the amazement of Escargot, and the sparks seemed to lend a spiritual force to his decision, whatever that decision had been. Escargot was bound, of course, to find out. He reminded himself of his code.

But he couldn't let himself be out-virtued by Uncle Helstrom. At least it must appear as if he struggled against it. Here was Leta, after all, hoping, perhaps, that Escargot himself was the equal of her uncle, that in Escargot lay unmined depths, laden with emeralds of good will, rubies of self-sacrifice. "My business," said Escargot stoutly, "will have to hold until morning. Late morning. Our man Stover isn't an early riser. So let's hear about your business, sir. I'm entirely at your service."

The dwarf stood for a moment as if contemplating, wrestling with his better instincts, then nodded. "My niece has spoken of you often, young man." He paused for a moment and looked into the lit bowl of his pipe, grinning slightly as if happy to have seen Escargot's face brighten at the mention of his niece. "You share, she says, a number of—what shall we call them?—common interests, perhaps, and that you've held earnest conversations about things artistic and philosophic."

Escargot nodded, happy to hear himself referred to as a philosopher. This was a decidedly superior uncle. His odd appearance was merely eccentric. And there was nothing at all wrong with eccentricity. Escargot liked to think of himself as something of an eccentric.

"She mentioned, my good fellow, a certain bag of marbles. Red agate marbles. A bit above the average in size—of the type, in fact, that a child might refer to as a 'shooter.' I believe she said you'd gotten them from a wandering bunjo man."

"Right as rain," said Escargot, vaguely troubled at this unexpected turn. He inadvertently patted the bulge under his coat.

"I feel duty bound to tell you that those are very valuable marbles, young man. Very valuable marbles. Guard them well,"

"Thank you," said Escargot, doubly puzzled and leaping just a bit with surprise when he discovered Leta standing beside him, outlined in the open door of the room. The fog had thinned outside, and it swirled by now in patches on the wind.

For a moment the moon shone through it in sudden silver illumination like a fogfish disappearing beneath the surface of the Oriel, and made Leta's dark hair glow with misty, reflected light. It seemed, for that one moment, that her skin was almost transparent, that she was a wraith or a delicate porcelain doll so finely wrought that the porcelain was like frosted glass. Then the fog settled in again and the moon winked out and Escargot found that Leta's arm was around his shoulder and that she was gazing at him meaningfully. He grinned at Uncle Helstrom and looked down at his feet, noting with horror that the tongues of both shoes had betrayed him and protruded from beneath their laces and that the cuff of one of his trouser legs had come unstitched and had fallen out.

"What my uncle means to say . . ." Leta began earnestly.

"Leta, my girl," interrupted Uncle Helstrom in a voice full of doubt. "I really don't . . ."

"What he means is that those marbles would be of particular use to him at the moment. He is engaged in certain experiments, certain very vital experiments, and for reasons that baffle me, those particular marbles are of monumental importance to him."

"Absolutely," put in Uncle Helstrom, his face taking on a serious look.

"In fact," Leta continued, "not three months ago those were *his*. They were stolen from his laboratory above Hightower Village and perhaps were sold or traded to the bunjo man you told me about in the tavern that day."

"Oh, I say," said Escargot, not knowing entirely *what* to say beyond that.

"I went off downriver, if you want to know the truth, to alert Uncle." With that, Leta began crying and buried her face in her hands.

"There, there," said Escargot, putting his hand around her shoulders now and giving her a squeeze. Uncle Helstrom looked into his pipe bowl again.

"A man can't just stroll in and make demands, can he?" continued the uncle. "You've bought the marbles, fair and square, and, as I say, their value is inestimable, especially to a man of science like myself. Where do you have them, by the way, in a vault?"

"Why no," began Escargot, feeling the lump of the marble

bag against his chest. "Not entirely. That is to say, I had thought of making some such arrangement, but to be absolutely truthful, with this recent business and all . . ."

"Of course, of course, of course," said Uncle Helstrom. "I understand utterly. Haven't lost them though?"

"Oh, no. No. They're safe. Here they are, as a matter of fact. Excuse me." And with that Escargot wrestled off his coat, cringing at the sight of his elbow thrust through the sleeve of his worn-out shirt, and hauled the marble bag off from around his neck. "They're yours, sir. Take them. What I payed for them was a pittance. And anyway, I don't fancy myself a man of property anymore."

"You're too good," said the dwarf, waving his hand at the marbles, "but you haven't got any reason to be so generous."

"And you hadn't any reason for your generous offer to speak to Mr. Stover in the morning, had you?"

Uncle Helstrom shrugged. "I'll tell you what, lad. I'll make you an offer. I admire your contempt for property—there is nothing more admirable, as far as I can see. But a man has to eat, hasn't he? And a man doesn't like to sleep on pine needles, does he? Because it doesn't matter how much you mash the things down, there's still a half dozen pricking you through your clothes all night long. And what's this?" he asked, pointing with his foot at the little earthen bowl of pickled fish that sat on a stone next to the pine-needle bed, "Dinner?" He shook his head sadly. "It looks as if it might have been alive once, doesn't it? What was it, fish? The goblins wouldn't eat it, would they? No, sir, a man can give up property. Damn all property. But he can't give up his health, can he? He can't give up—what is it that he can't give up?—the civilizing influences of a good meal and a glass of ale. Here, sir; here are enough gold pieces to see you through the winter. Keep the marbles against hard times. That's what I advise. If you're shrewd, you can do well with them. I'll get by. I quite likely won't see the end of my experiments anyway. I . . . Hush, child," he said to Leta, who had begun to weep again, then he heaved a sigh, heavy with the weight of unexpressed weariness.

"Take the marbles, for heaven's sake!" cried Escargot. "They just give me nightmares anyway. What in the world am *I* going to do with them, catch fish? I'll just trade them away for trinkets. And this gold, sir, there's really no need . . ."

"Of course there's need. If I were down and out and came to you, what then? Would you give me a handful of gold and then take it back? No you would not. The gold has nothing to do with the marbles. It can't have. The marbles can't be valued so. They're enchanted, I don't mind saying. Money can't buy enchantment—not that sort anyway. But I *will* take the marbles—on loan. Yes, I insist. There will be no discussion of it. You'll have them back in a week. And in the meantime, as collateral, you'll take this."

Uncle Helstrom reached into his cloak and pulled out a bag of his own, tied off at the top with a leather thong. "This, my boy, is a truth charm. If it's the truth you need, this'll give it to you. In spades."

Escargot took the bag from him and tugged at the thong, wondering what a truth charm might look like. He imagined windup chattering teeth of the sort you'd buy at a joke shop and leave on your wife's pillow as a lark.

"Don't open it here," cried Uncle Helstrom, putting a hand on his wrist. "Avoid opening it at all. It's very powerful magic that lies within that bag, and magic like that oughtn't to be meddled with unless it's desperately necessary. Do you grasp my meaning?"

Escargot nodded, handing over the marbles and hanging the truth charm in its place. "Collateral isn't at all necessary, actually, not between friends."

"I'm rather a businessman in my own way," said the dwarf shrewdly. "Business, as they say, is business, and friendship is another thing altogether. I've studied, my boy, in the school of regret." And with that he shook his head and gave Escargot a look—the look a teacher might favor a student with when he's reached a really solid and weighty conclusion.

"Are these the Smithers books?" asked Leta, having regained her composure.

"Yes they are. Take a look at the top copy—*The Man in the Moon*."

"Ooh," said Leta, flipping it open to the frontispiece. "Here's the page of manuscript laid in. And an inscription, too. Aren't you the lucky one."

"Would you like to have it?" asked Escargot, filled suddenly with generosity.

"Oh I couldn't."

"Of course you could. Just don't set it back down. Who knows, perhaps you'll let me visit it sometime."

"Anytime you'd like," said the girl, smiling and closing the book.

Escargot nearly pitched over. This is more like it, he thought to himself, remembering Leta's cool and sensible rebuff on the street just days earlier. He must have had a more pronounced effect on her than he'd thought. Uncle Helstrom nodded and grinned, happy, it seemed, to see his favored niece treated so.

"In a week, then, let's say, I'll return this bag of marbles. But I'll look you up in town, then—won't I?—and you'll be in a position to stand me to a glass of ale. Then I'll do the same for you." With that he drew a pocket watch out of his cloak and looked at it with evident surprise. "Late, late, late," he said, clicking his tongue. "We've got to be off, haven't we? Come along, niece. And by the way, by ten o'clock tomorrow morning your man Stover will have heard from me. I'd pay him a visit if I were you and beard him on the issue of the settlement. I think I can guarantee you he'll see reason."

Together the dwarf and the girl stepped out into the night and without a backward glance strode away through the fog, carrying his marbles and his signed Smithers, and leaving Escargot standing in the doorway, conscious of the fact that the three of them had been standing all along, that he had been reduced to such a state that he couldn't even offer a friend a chair. He looked at his pocketful of gold coins, then picked up his bowl of fish and pitched it out the door and onto the meadow. He'd see Stover in the morning, all right. He'd take a room at Stover's tavern is what he'd do, and he'd drink up a pint or two of Stover's ale with Stover's scowling face to flavor it. And if Stover complained, maybe he'd pop him one on the beezer, just for good measure.

He lay down on his pine needles, wrapped his blanket around his feet, and pulled his jacket tight, then watched the three candles burn themselves into little heaps of wax. Finally he drifted toward sleep, thinking of Leta and of last laughs, his thoughts swirling together into mist. Hovering within the mist was a vaguely familiar face, watching him, leering, perhaps. Before he could rouse himself enough to identify it, to focus on it, he was asleep, untroubled at last by nightmares.

3

Stover Has His Way

Escargot awoke to a clear dawn sky. The mists of the night before had fled, the distant hills had shrugged off their mantle of fog, and the sun rose hot and enormous in the east. It was a perfect day for doing nothing, for bathing in the river—a perfect day, that is, if a man had nothing better to do with his time and no better place to take a bath. A man with a pocketful of gold, though, a man who was a friend of Mr. Abner Helstrom, *that* man could make better use of his time.

"Time to pitch the bed out," Escargot said aloud, and then handful by handful he hauled pine needles out of the little room and scattered them over the meadow. Then he lay his blanket out over the ground, piled all but one of his Smithers books into the center of it, gathered the corners, and heaved the whole thing over his shoulder before setting out toward the river. It seemed, taken all the way around, that it was time to move to better quarters.

At the river he pulled in his lines, twisting them one by one around a fat stick, securing each hook and shoving the stick in with his net beneath the log. Then he sat in the sun with his back against the log and opened Smithers' *The Stone Giants*. He thumbed through, stopping at each illustration, until he got to the part where the Moon elves and the stone giants battle for power over the land of Balumnia, and the Moon elves, riding in sky vessels, perform desperate and dangerous incantations. The ground heaves, mountains crack asunder, and the giants are swallowed by the earth and crushed, droplets of giant blood splashing into the river and solidifying into little globes like water-cooled obsidian.

Escargot was particularly fond of stories that took place eons in the past, in a past so distant that anything might have happened. Then the air was so full of magic that the wind sang when it stirred the leaves on trees or blew through willows along a river. The Moon was still close enough to the Earth so that with a really long ladder—the sort, perhaps, that the linkmen use to pick fruit in their orchards—a man might climb high enough to touch it. Smithers was full of that sort of thing. It didn't matter where you started reading Smithers books, really. They were like one vast history that began in mist and hadn't yet ended, and it didn't make a nickel's worth of difference whether you started in at chapter twelve, which chronicles the arrival of the armies of the field dwarfs at the battle of Wangley Bree, or in chapter forty-two, in which the light elves sail to the Moon in a flying machine to explore the emerald caverns of the Green King. In short, there was no end to adventures in Smithers, and in the three hours that Escargot had before it was time to visit old Stover, he could look into only a smattering.

But he was anxious to pay Stover a visit. As ten o'clock drew near and passed, he found himself checking his watch again and again, certain that more time had gone by than really had and making up and discarding conversations that he was likely to have with the tavern keeper. At last he stood up, put Smithers into the blanket, slung it all over his shoulder, and set out toward town, whistling a higgledy-piggledy tune.

Stover stood on the boardwalk outside the tavern door, slapping whitewash onto the wooden siding and scrubbing it off with a brush whenever he slopped it across the stones of the foundation. Escargot watched him from across the street. There was something oddly satisfying in the scowl on Stover's face. It was a scowl that seemed to suggest that there was nothing he loathed more than whitewashing. He could, of course, hire any of a number of village boys or girls to do the whitewashing for him, for a fee. But the idea of fees turned Stover purple—they were worse than whitewashing, worse than anything. Escargot strolled across the street, still whistling.

"Whitewashing is it?" he said cheerfully.

The old man gave him an up and down look. "If I've got

any left after I finish here I'll give you a coat of it too. But don't count too heavily on success, sir, for it'll take a bucketful at least to hide the grime that covers the likes of you."

Escargot hadn't been prepared to be insulted. His imaginary conversations that morning had involved his insulting Stover, and Stover wringing his hands and politely apologizing. He forced himself to stretch his grin. "Leta still renting the room upstairs then?"

Stover stared at him and shook his head—not by way of answering, but as if Escargot's question were so foolish that no answer would work.

"I'm not at all surprised, actually," said Escargot. "I suppose she's had her fill of Stover's Tavern. But I rather fancy it, myself. I've been thinking that a man like me might elevate himself if he was to study a man like you, a pillar, as they say, of the village."

"Go away," said Stover.

"I'm very serious. If Leta's moved out, I'll take her room."

"I haven't any room to rent, not in the tavern I don't. I *do*, however, have the power to let you into a room in Monmouth Prison, very cheap. And they'd give you a fresh set of clothes along with it. Abandonment, sir, is worth a year under the law. Civil disruption, of course, is worth a month or two more. And if you're inclined toward violence, which I haven't any doubt you are, then we can make it a round five and have you hung into the bargain. My advice to you is to pack your bag and go."

The conversation had gone awry. Perhaps the uncle hadn't yet spoken to Stover. "My agent, I assume, hasn't contacted you yet?"

"What in the world are you talking about?"

"You haven't spoken, this morning, to Mr. Abner Helstrom, my attorney?"

"Damn Mr. Abner Helstrom. I've spoken to no one. It's inconceivable that anyone with such a name as that could exist. And it's late to think of hiring attorneys, even imaginary attorneys. They can't save you. Nothing can save you now. Your life is a ruin and you've only your own sloth to thank. Mr. Abner Helstrom! Why not Mr. Abner Maelstrom? If you're going to invent names, brigand, invent good ones. Get away from me now! Slink off and leave me to my work."

"I'll buy a pint of ale first," said Escargot through his teeth. It was just eleven o'clock. He'd have a pint of ale out of Stover or wring his neck. He'd have a pint of ale and *then* wring his neck.

The old man looked at him, his face suddenly saddened. "I fear that the price of a pint of ale is rather dear this morning," he said, shaking his head. "I've been forced to steepen things just a bit—far beyond your means, if I'm any judge of a man's means."

"You're not." Escargot dug the gold out of his pocket, a dozen coins in all, and scattered them at Stover's feet. They lay glinting in the sunlight in a very satisfying way. Then, strangely and slowly, they began to shift and shudder, for all the world as if they were waking up and setting in to walk away. The golden glow dimmed, and Escargot could see the planks of the boardwalk through the coins. In another instant they were gone and a dozen black beetles scrabbled roundabout Stover's feet, the old man hopping and dancing and crushing bugs. Escargot stood astonished, watching the display, unable to summon up the precious last laugh that he'd anticipated all morning long. "Goblin gold," he muttered.

"What!" cried Stover. "Get out of here, I tell you! Your money is worth as much as your miserable soul, apparently. Now be gone, or by heaven I'll thrash you with this brush and have you jailed."

Escargot backed away, not out of fear but out of lingering astonishment. The gold was gone. The bugs were crushed on the planks of the boardwalk. Who *was* this Uncle Helstrom? He turned and set out slowly, back the way he'd come, his rage having suddenly abandoned the shouting Stover and settled on the dwarf uncle. Goblin gold, was it? Truth charms. Vital experiments. He'd show someone a vital experiment with a club.

"Wait!" shouted Stover, stepping off into the street.

Escargot turned, glaring, his face set like stone. Stover stepped back onto the boardwalk as if ready to bolt into the tavern and shut the door.

"Tomorrow," said the old man triumphantly. "You can come round to Mr. Smeggles' office on Pine Street. You'll be paid for a third of the house and property, less money for repairs and for the child's education, of course. You deserve nothing.

But the woman you abandoned insists—as long, that is, as you agree to have nothing more to do with the child. Not a thing."

Escargot stared at him. "We'll see who agrees to what."

"*You'll* see the inside of a jail cell!" Stover shouted after him as Escargot trudged back toward the meadow, his plans all gone to smash, his marbles gone. First goblins, then goblin gold. It made sense, didn't it? Abner Helstrom! Stover was right. Escargot had made a fool of himself. He hadn't any doubt that half the village had been watching just now—gaping out of windows, cupping hands to their ears. And what of Leta? That had been the worst bit of foolery of all. Had the entire thing been layed out weeks ago, from before the first time he'd seen her at Wurzle's? Stover would say, if he knew anything about it, that the entire mess was the consequence of sin, of Escargot's roving eye, of his watery soul. And maybe Stover would be right.

It took about a minute and a half for Escargot to decide otherwise. Whatever the truth was, Stover didn't have it. Stover was a shriveled toad, a bug, a viper, an officious, petty, and bent man who, unfortunately, *could* have Escargot pitched into Monmouth Prison. Never see his child again! They'd pay him off, would they? He kicked a clump of meadow grass, and the effort of it dislodged the blanket full of books. Copies of G. Smithers sailed out all over the meadow, bumping down with pages fluttering, scattered atop what was left of the pine-needle bed.

Escargot set in to give the clump of grass another kick, just for good measure. If the books had been anything but Smithers, he would have danced on them and kicked *them* to bits, then dumped the lot of them into the river, just for having betrayed him. Why, he wondered, hadn't he gone into Beezle's store first and spent his gold on a suit of clothes and a pair of shoes. It was the sunlight that had turned the goblin gold back into the stuff it was made out of. Inside the store it would have remained gold. Then it would have been Beezle's problem. He'd been too anxious to see Stover squirm; that was the truth of it. Fine adventurer *he'd* make—fleeced by a dwarf in a slouch hat, taken in by a pretty face, chased from town by a tavern keeper, and tossed, for goodness sake, out of his own house by a wife who had driven him mad with pies for two solid years.

He bent to pick up the fallen books, laying them once again atop the blanket. When he stood up, the leather sack with the truth charm in it bumped against his chest. He bundled up the blanket and books and hurried into the windmill, pulling the door shut behind him. Magic or no magic, he'd have a go at the charm. It was probably worthless. Of course it was worthless. It couldn't be anything else. It probably *was* a set of clacking teeth. Leta and her false uncle were quite likely gasping with laughter at that very moment. He wiggled loose the thong that tied the bag and dumped the heavy charm out into his hand. It was a rock—a round, grayish lump of stone shot through with lines of amethyst and quartz crystal and with a lidded eye carved into the top as if it were about to wink at him.

It certainly *looked* like a charm; there was no denying that. There was the possibility, of course, that it was some sort of goblin charm, made up simply as a lark. It might even be dangerous. But why, he wondered, would either Leta or the dwarf want to harm him? What they wanted, it seemed, was to steal his marbles, for purposes he couldn't fathom. At least he hadn't had any nightmares the previous night, only the remnants of the face. The dwarf—that's whose face it had been. The curious Uncle Helstrom. Of course it had. The thought was just a little bit frightening. What was this uncle, some sort of magician, perhaps, with his waterweed tobacco and his metal-shod staff that struck sparks out of dirt? His signed Smithers! Damnation! Leta had made away with his signed Smithers, and he'd been left with a carved rock.

He set the charm on the sill of the little window in the wall that faced the river. Outside, the vanes of the windmill revolved slowly in the breeze, one by one going past. "Tell me, truth charm, whether the books of G. Smithers are truth or lies." The truth charm sat there, washed in sunlight. Escargot tried again. "What is Abner Helstrom's true name?" Nothing happened. "What is the color of my shirt?" asked Escargot. "It's right in front of you, truth charm." The charm was silent. "I'm a worthless fool," said Escargot to the charm. "I've lost everything I've owned and wanted, and if *you* want to know the truth, half of it can be laid to vanity. More than half. That's where the fault lies."

He picked the charm up and slipped it back into the bag.

He'd been left with a worthless, dead piece of rock. He would carry it around his neck forever, he decided, in order to remind himself of the fruits of vanity. He would become a holy man, wandering the river road, getting thin, living on grubs, heaping burning trash on his head. The picture of it struck him suddenly as funny. Even the tongues of his shoes were hilarious, waggling out like that, giving him the raspberry. Shambling old Stover and his prayer meetings, his wife and her precious pies, Wurzle and his salamanders—the lot of them, himself included, were evidently born into the world to cut ridiculous capers for the amusement of the gods. Or, Escargot thought grimly, of the Uncle Helstroms. Well he'd cut no more. He'd be off downriver is where he'd be, just as soon as he got the money from Smeggles the lawyer. Perhaps he'd take Annie with him, fly in the face of the law. They could chase him if they chose, but they'd find it a warm chase indeed. And if he ran into Uncle Helstrom, magician or no magician, he'd tweak the dwarf's nose.

He hung the sack round his neck, buttoned his shirt over it, and set out toward the forest after fresh pine needles. Halfway there he abandoned the plan. He wouldn't bother with sleep tonight. He'd spend the night planning. Then tomorrow he'd have the money out of Smeggles, buy a horse and supplies, and ride down the river road toward Hightower Village and put up at an inn. If anyone *had* heard of Abner Helstrom in Hightower, then Escargot would have a go at the dwarf straightaway. If not, then the whole business was a lesson well learned, wasn't it? He dug out *The Stone Giants* and headed for the river.

The weather that evening wasn't all it might have been. The sun, which had set out so gloriously that morning, had become thin and distant, and once again before dusk the fog rose off the river and the evening grew watchful. When Escargot found himself squinting to see, and cocking the book this way and that to catch the feeble light, he gave up. Once again he could feel something in the air. Maybe it was just autumn; maybe it was Halloween drifting nigh. The moon crept up over the tree line, appearing and then disappearing through breaks in the fog. And once, when Escargot chanced to look into the sky, something sailed across the face of the moon—a bat, perhaps.

But it hadn't looked much like a bat; it looked more like a witch aloft.

Escargot wondered about it for a moment, but his mind drifted back to the problem of little Annie. He could slip into the house and bundle her away. Damn his wife's padlocks. She would be nothing to carry along downriver, and she was fond enough of his cooking to stay plump. Escargot smiled to think of how she hadn't cared a rap when there'd been lumps in the oatmeal. And she'd grow up with calluses on her feet and an eye sharp as a hawk's eye. She'd be able to tell time by the wind and understand elfin tongues and make sense of the gabbled laughter of goblins. What would come of her if she grew up in Twombly Town under the watchful eye of Stover the high and the mighty? Escargot didn't want to think about it. He'd have to steal her. There were no two ways about it.

Of course it mightn't be easy on her at first, little as she was. Some rough roads lay ahead of him, after all, and danger—no little bit of it. What would he do if halfway to Hightower Village he ran headlong into the dwarf, or perhaps into the same party of goblins that had set upon him a week past? He'd have to move quickly, and with a child in his arms it was quite likely that he wouldn't move quickly enough. What would he do, stow her under a bush like a hedgehog? What if she fell into the hands of goblins while her father lay bleeding on the road? What then?

Escargot couldn't fathom it. There were too many whats. He sat with his chin in his hand, looking out over the dark river. The water still flowed along toward the sea, oblivious to him, caring nothing for the troubles of the people along the bank. It was out in midstream that he ought to be, floating along with it. It was his destiny, perhaps, to be alone. A quick breeze, cool and sharp, blew across the back of his neck. He shrugged his coat tighter around him, but the cool air seemed to pass right through it, as if it weren't a breeze at all but the presence of something—or of someone—standing behind him in silence. He sat frozen, half expecting a touch on his shoulder, the wisp of cold breath on his cheek. "Aah!" he shouted, whirling around and leaping from the log onto the slippery bank. He slid toward the river, grasping at a branch, falling down onto one knee in the mud of the bank. There was nothing there—

no old milk-eyed woman with a stick. Whatever it was that had thickened the atmosphere a moment ago had disappeared.

He found that he was shaking, and when he grabbed at his cap to pull it down tighter over his forehead, he succeeded only in batting it off into the weeds. What, he wondered grimly, would have happened if there *had* been someone there—worse yet, if he'd had Annie along. In his fright, he would have pitched her into the river.

Through the fog appeared the glow of lantern light, out on the meadow. Escargot blinked, thinking at first that a fogfish had wandered over the bank. But it wasn't a fogfish. It was bright as Christmas and coming from the Widow's windmill, and yet no one, as far as he knew, used the abandoned windmill except himself. He watched the light for a moment, waiting for it to waver or move. Maybe it was someone walking on the meadow, looking into the windmill—looking, perhaps, for him. Could it be Uncle Helstrom, he wondered, narrowing his eyes. All things considered, Escargot hadn't any real enthusiasm for running into the dwarf on a foggy night.

But he'd have to see, wouldn't he? If it was a band of robbers, say, or marauding goblins, then he'd have to alert the village. He crawled across his log and crept up the grassy slope toward the windmill, hunkered down and squinting through the mist. He could hear the slow creak of the latticework windmill vanes turning aimlessly in the breeze, disconnected from the gear mechanism that had rusted and fallen to bits years earlier. The light seemed to flicker and dance, as if the lanterns had no shades, or as if it weren't lantern light at all but was the light of about a hundred candles all guttering in the breeze blowing through the broken window.

A gust of wind scoured across the meadow, blowing the fog clear for an instant. Escargot dropped to his chest on the wet grass, partly hidden by the rise of the hill. He could see just for a moment the eastern sky, paled to morning purple, a scattering of stars winking out with the coming dawn. Slowly, before the mists settled back in and obscured the mill, he pushed himself up on his hands to have a look. There was a good chance he'd see someone through the window. If it was Uncle Helstrom, he'd . . . Well, he didn't quite know *what* he'd do. But the only thing visible in the window was the broad, glowing face of a lit jack-o'-lantern, grinning out at him through the hovering fog. The long vanes swished across in front of it, whoosh, whoosh, whoosh, so that the candlelight glowing through the mouth and eyes seemed chopped to bits. Why it faced the meadow was a puzzle. Unless it was meant to attract someone. Was it a beacon, a signal? Escargot decided to keep a sharp eye out for things lurking in the night. He crept toward it, masked again by fog.

A low murmur issued from within the mill. A cackle of laughter erupted, then was hushed and the murmuring continued, now rising in volume, now falling away into silence. It was impossible to tell how many voices in all were murmuring and laughing—at least three or four. And just when Escargot was sure they were the voices of men, low and throaty and rough, he'd change his mind and decide they were the voices of women—witches, perhaps. One voice, though, was a bit higher. It was a familiar voice—very pretty, actually.

Escargot stiffened. He knew whose voice it was. He'd *have* to take a look through the window. There was another window higher up on the second floor, but there was no way to climb the slippery, shingled sides of the mill—no handholds or footholds unless he clambered up one of the vanes. The noise of it, though, would give him away. They'd catch him at it, halfway up and utterly defenseless. At least if he was discovered on the ground he could make a run for it.

He crept forward, thankful that the grass and leaves on the meadow were heavy and silent with fog. He cupped an ear to the wall below the windowsill, but all was silent save for a low and rhythmic chanting in a guttural language he had no desire to understand. When he turned up toward the window, there on the sill, next to the glowing pumpkin, a black cat sat peering out into the night. Escargot crouched below, staring up at it. It wouldn't do to frighten it. Perhaps it wouldn't do to be *seen* by it. The cat seemed to be watching the vanes turn in the breeze, fascinated with it as it might be fascinated by a bit of dancing yarn.

Then it leaped across the four feet that separated it from the revolving vanes, lit against the ragged lattice and scrabbled its paws through, holding on as the blade swept upward into the mist. Escargot watched the vanes whoosh back down—one, two, three, four, five, and then he was counting the same vanes over again. The cat was gone—perhaps searching the upper story for mice.

Escargot edged past beneath the window, conscious of the turning blades behind him. It wouldn't do to have one of them crack him in the head. He pulled himself up on the sill, wafered against the damp, dark shingles, and peered in at the window. A half dozen jack-o'-lanterns burned round the walls. Three witches kneeled on the dirt inside, casting a pair of enormous ivory dice across a carven board. Leta wasn't among them. Yet Escargot had been certain that it was her voice he had heard above the murmuring. Near the shut door of the mill an iron cauldron sat on a heap of burning kindling. The smoke from the fire mingled with steam from the cauldron, hovering in the air in a pink cloud before condensing and falling back into the cauldron like bloody raindrops. Four broomsticks leaned against the door.

One of the witches was enormously fat, with a fleshy face that nearly hid her eyes. She crouched there on the floor, an overstuffed, robed doll, her fingers working like pudgy snakes over the tumbling dice. Next to her lay a leather bag—Escargot's leather bag. Marbles spilled out of the mouth of it.

"Hey!" cried Escargot in sudden surprise, astonished to see the bag and determined to get it back. The fat witch grinned up at him, as if she were happy that he'd dropped by, as if she'd been expecting him. She plucked up one of the marbles, held it up briefly in the light of a glowing jack-o'-lantern, and flipped it into the cauldron which hissed and smoked and sent a reeking cloud of vapor swirling about the little room, smelling sickeningly of blood.

Escargot lurched backward, pushing the pumpkin on the windowsill into the room. He heard it thud against the dirt just as one of the vanes swung round toward him, skiving across the back of his head, brushing his ear. The next vane, whipped round in a sudden gust of wind, snatched the back of his coat, and the ragged lattice tangled itself like fingers into his collar and hair.

Before he had time to cry out he found himself swept around in a broad arc, into the air, following the path of the cat. He clawed at the air behind him, clutching for a hold on the rickety vane. Surely his weight would stop the thing's turning—either that or simply snap it off. He'd find himself rolling down the hill with a broken neck. He managed to hook one foot into a slat and to grab hold behind his head with his right hand. It wouldn't be too difficult to disentangle his coat, but he wasn't at all sure he wanted to do that, not until he was a shade closer to the ground.

So he held on, the vanes spinning faster as he dropped, then climbed again, the sound of cackling laughter ringing out from within the mill. Wood snapped. His heel broke through the spindly lattice, jammed against another, and snapped through that. His coat ripped and he slumped an inch, his stomach lurching up into his throat. Again the vane crested the top and plummeted toward the meadow. Escargot shouted involuntarily, waiting to smash into the ground. Then he sailed upward again in an increasing rush, as if the wind had turned suddenly into a gale. The fog blew round his face, thinning and evaporating as he spun faster and faster, round and round, the meadow and the woods and the hills and the red glow of dawn racing past in a blurred whirligig. Finally, dizzy and hanging, his jacket crammed up round his shoulders and neck, he swung to a stop at the top of the mill, facing the upper window.

Crouched on its haunches on the floorboards was the cat. A fat mouse cowered between its paws. The cat batted at the mouse, dropping it, snatching it up in its teeth, peering out suddenly at the dangling Escargot, who watched horrified, understanding that the jack-o'-lantern in the window below *had* been meant to attract someone—him. The cat seemed to shimmer and waver, to grow and shrink and then, in a blink, it was Leta who crouched on the floorboards, holding in her hands his signed G. Smithers, shredded and stained, the binding hanging by a half dozen stretched threads. Then she was a cat again shaking with silent laughter, the mouse in her teeth. Once again the vanes revolved, and when they came back around there was Leta, grinning out at him, red dawnlight reflecting off her eyes. She shimmered once again, metamorphosing into a hunched, cat-like shadow and then into the old, bent woman with milky eyes and hair like cobweb.

The jacket ripped one last time, and Escargot jerked downward, the vane warping with his weight. He lurched sideways for a handhold, his heel skidding through brittle slats. He fell, banging against the blade below and sliding along it before tumbling down onto the meadow. Then he was up and running.

He angled across toward the river road and the comfortable lights of Twombly Town aglow in the distance. He had no desire to look back, perhaps be turned to stone, but ran straight on to Smeggles' door, pounding away on it until old Smeggles, his white hair in a frazzle and he wearing a nightshirt and cap, threw the door open with a curse.

"It's tomorrow," gasped Escargot. "Give me my money."

4

The Smashed Hat

Before his head stopped whirling, Escargot was miles down the river road, cantering along on an uncooperative horse he'd bought too hastily and for too much money. The woods on his right were solemn and dark, the ground beneath the oaks and hemlocks covered with red-brown leaves and rotted stumps. The sun drifted in the sky as if it were tired and heavy and about to plummet into the river, and slow clouds sailed across in front of it now and again, casting the afternoon into deep shadow.

Escargot was hungry. Even the pickled fish he'd tossed onto the meadow—when was it, only the night before last?—had begun to appeal to him. He stopped twice to gather berries, but it was late in the season, and most that were left were withered or small—good, perhaps, for warding off starvation, but they did little for simple hunger. There were mushrooms aplenty sprouting from the decaying vegetation of the forest floor, and if he'd had a little butter, maybe, and garlic . . . But he hadn't any butter, any more than he had the urge to nibble the funguses raw. What he wanted was steak and potatoes, or a meat pie and a bowl of gravy.

For weeks he'd thought of leaving Twombly Town for a dozen reasons. And here he was being *chased* out, or at least it seemed so, and chased out hungry to top it off. When he finally began to consider it, it made little sense. It was every bit as possible that he was being chased *into* something. That was the result of all the chasing, anyway. The witches had done a first-rate job of frightening him off, but where had he fled?—

straight down the river in the wake of the dwarf and the old woman, or Leta, or both, or all three. It had become a confused mess.

Something in him couldn't believe that Leta was a witch, that she and the old blind woman were one and the same. But what he'd seen through the window rather argued in that direction. It might quite likely be vanity, he thought, that explained his doubts. He'd obviously rather believe that he hadn't been the victim of a hoax, that Leta's rare but wonderful attentions had been genuine.

He carried with him a thrown-together bundle of clothes and supplies, bought with a bit of the house money. He'd given his Smithers books to the Professor. Escargot had come across him early in the morning in town. He'd been downriver, the Professor had, collecting waterweeds for his aquaria, and had discovered clumps of homunculus grass in a little backwater two miles below the village. Not a lot of it, to be sure, but some half dozen of the sprouts had gone to seed, and through the papery walls of the seed pods could be seen the first vague outlines of polywog-like henny-penny men. Wurzle had gathered enough to study, and then, on the road, had bumped into a curious dwarf in a slouch hat. The dwarf had paid handsomely for the homunculus grass and had insisted facetiously that he intended to grind up the little men inside and smoke them in his pipe.

Professor Wurzle displayed a bag of gold coins, which he offered to trade Escargot for the Smithers books. But Escargot was fairly sure that the coins, once removed from the bag, would be of use to no one but Stover, who might relish the exercise involved in tramping on bugs. So he gave the books to the Professor on loan, all but *The Stone Giants*, and rode away toward Hightower, feeling that the morning air was still too full of enchantment for him to sit idle. He overtook no one on the river road, and by late afternoon he joggled along, shifting from side to side on the saddle and thinking dark thoughts.

If he rode hard enough he could be in Seaside for the harvest festival. He would find nothing there, quite likely, to solve any mysteries, but it was enough just to have a destination. He no longer had a home. That much had been made very clear to him. When he got back to Twombly Town—*if* he got back to Twombly Town—little Annie wouldn't know who in the world he was. It had been a matter either of stealing her away or letting her go. Letting her go had been wisest. Of course it had. There was no doubting it, was there? The open road was no place for a child, a baby. And as for her becoming a creature of nature and learning to tell time by the wind, it might just as easily be true that creatures of nature were ignorant and dirty and had twigs in their hair. A child needed a school and playmates and a story before being tucked up in bed. That was the truth of it, wasn't it?

Or was the truth of it that Escargot didn't entirely want her? He'd never make it to Seaside in time for the festival if Annie was riding along. And where might his travels take him after Seaside? To the Wonderful Isles? Into the White Mountains? There was business to be done—*that* was the truth of it, and Annie wouldn't be an asset to business. Escargot wished there weren't quite so many truths. The more there were, the more boggled up things got.

So the idea of a destination had become solid, had become more substantial to him than the idea of his home on the hill above the village, which had, in the past weeks, already begun to change like goblin gold into something hazy and unfamiliar. His only real link with Twombly Town were the Smithers books he'd loaned Professor Wurzle. Someday he'd have to come back after them. And when he did, he would wear an eyepatch and a beard and be dressed in exotic rags and a cocked hat, and he'd look up Annie and see how she was getting on.

For the moment, though, it was Seaside that attracted him. There, if nothing else, he might get some glimpse of just how much of G. Smithers' account of the festivities was accurate. He couldn't imagine that they *really* burned witches. That sort of thing was hardly likely. But then any number of things that were hardly likely had come to pass in the past month.

Sometime after four in the afternoon the air grew chill and the shadows long and deep and a wind blew up off the river cold enough to set Escargot's teeth chattering. A road sign announced that he was twenty miles yet outside Hightower Village, and that a mile inland, on the road to McVicker, lay an inn. "Lodging at The Smashed Hat" the sign read, and below it, dangling from brass hooks, was an ill-carven broad-brimmed hat with a hatband painted around its dented-in crown. The inn it advertised was a mile out of the way. The alternative, though, was to spend the night on the ground—hungry, and with one eye open all night for goblins.

Escargot yanked on the reins and trotted away up the trail, telling himself that at the very least he'd get a bed and a bottle of ale for his trouble. When he clopped up to the inn at sunset he found that he couldn't throw his leg over the horse to climb down. Both his legs had apparently petrified during the ride. He nodded seriously at the waiting stable boy, a pudding-faced youth in an altogether suit and with feet the size of pot lids. He had an unpleasant, frowning countenance, like he just that moment remembered the time he'd drank a glass of turpentine by mistake, thinking it was soda water.

Escargot made an effort to throw his right leg back over the horse. It was impossible. His right leg, like his left leg, had gone stiff. He leaned off over the lawn until the gravity hauled him down.

The stable boy smirked and nodded, as if he'd expected some such thing. The horse stepped forward with an eye toward a patch of clover in the lawn. Escargot sat up, feeling very foolish. "I wouldn't get round behind her if I was you," said the boy, holding the horse by the bridle.

"What's that?" asked Escargot, wondering how he was going to "get round" anywhere ever again. He was stiff as yesterday's fish and convinced that he'd have to eat supper that night standing up.

"Don't get round behind her, where she can kick you."

"Kick me? Why on earth would she want to kick me?"

"They kick for sport, horses do." And with that the boy patted the horse on the side of the head, happy, perhaps, with an animal that kicked for sport. "She'd kick you right in the ear, and you'd be deader'n a corpse."

Escargot crept a few feet across the grass. It felt as if he'd just bounced down a hillside on his rear end. "Why don't you just lead her around to the stable then, my man, instead of across in front of me like that?"

"There wouldn't be nothing you could do about it neither. Can't persecute a horse."

"You mean prosecute," said Escargot. "Just take the thing away. That's what you're paid for, isn't it? Or are you the lad that hands out advice on the lawn?" He stood up, shakily and out of patience, and dusted off his knees, then hauled his bags off the horse and slung them over his shoulder as the horse and the stable boy disappeared toward the back of the inn.

Escargot stepped across toward the inn itself, a tall house full of eaves and gables and balconies. It sat almost sideways on the weedy lawn, and one corner had slumped across a crumbling and sunken stone foundation. The entire house seemed to be tilting toward the river, and the windows and doors all sat askew in their frames so that the wind whistled merrily past them above and below. Tattered curtains hung across most of the windows, and even from below on the lawn they appeared to be so dirty that it seemed likely they hadn't been washed in twenty or thirty years, probably around the time the place had gotten its last coat of paint. A faded sign hung across the front of the porch; "The Smashed Hat," it read—an oddly appropriate name for the place.

There was something about it that ran counter to the cozy, ivy-covered inn that Escargot had pictured. If there were any other travelers at the inn they kept themselves well hidden. They certainly weren't sitting in the willow chairs on the porch—possibly because the chairs hadn't any seats to sit on, just a few rotted fragments of willow cane.

The bell on the front porch had no clapper in it, but the door itself was ajar, so Escargot, after shouting a hello through the crack, grabbed the rusted doorknob and gave it a push. The door was jammed against the sill and wouldn't budge. He pushed again, rattled the knob, and shouted, then gave the door a half dozen kicks on the bottom of the stile where it had jammed, inching it forward a scrape at a time until it sprang inward with a lunge. Standing at the foot of a stairway that tilted steeply away overhead was an almost chinless man in a white apron. He wore a ragged and thin little mustache that looked as if it had been bought at a fire sale.

"Here now," he said, grimacing at Escargot, "we don't want none of that."

"Door was stuck and the bell didn't work. I hollered, but I guess no one heard."

"I heard, didn't I? Here I am, standin' here in front of you. This ain't the city, friend."

"Pardon me?" asked Escargot, feeling embarrassed for having kicked the door.

"I say this ain't no rush, is it? This ain't no bow and scrape. This is the country, isn't it? I'm a poor man."

"That's right. Sorry and all that. No rush at all. Not a bit of it."

"All right, then," said the man in the apron. "Want a room, do you?"

"And some supper, if I could."

"Supper too, is it?"

"Both," said Escargot, looking around him at the disheveled interior of the inn. Dust coated everything, including the man in the apron. On second look, the man was coated in baking flour, and he held a dough-covered spoon in his hand. Escargot looked at the spoon favorably. "Mixing up dough, are you? Making a pie perhaps?" He smiled at the man. There was no use being belligerent about the whole affair. The man was right, anyway. Here they were miles from anywhere. It wasn't like in town where a person could trot over to Beezle's market for a new bell when the clapper fell out from rust. This was the country, the open road.

"A pie?"

"That's right—with the dough and all. I thought maybe a pie . . ."

"Rats," said the man, looking at the spoon, then back at Escargot. "I'm mixing up a batch of poison flour to use as bait. I can't stand rats." He shook suddenly, as if he'd had a quick chill. "Walls are full of rats. They ate the corner off the porch, ate my chairs. There's nothing they don't eat, including you and me."

Escargot nodded slowly, looking around him once again. "Forget the pie. Anything at all will do for supper. Don't have a spare bottle of ale, do you?"

"Not a one, more's the pity. Not a one. There's cider, though, if you're a cider man. Traveling far?"

"Seaside for now. And cider is fine. I'll just put my bags away, perhaps, before I eat."

"Care to deposit any valuables in the vault? It's the safest thing. No telling who might put up at an inn like this. Lonesome road and all. You can have my affidavit on anything you put in. Safe as a baby."

"Thanks anyway," said Escargot. "*Is* there anyone else besides me staying here? The road seems to be empty."

"Not another living soul. That's just what I mean. It's not hardly safe to travel anymore, is it, not with the goblins and all. And highwaymen. They just hung three of 'em up at McVicker last Tuesday, but that ain't half the gang. Who knows but what you ain't one of 'em? That's why I have the vault. The way I see it, if you put your valuables in my vault, then you won't leave with *mine*. But a man who don't want to take advantage of such a thing, he might be one of your thieves, gone in the morning along with the silver. Do you follow me?"

"That's clever," said Escargot, nodding his head. "And I wish I *had* something to put in that vault of yours. I'd sleep easier if I knew I had something in a vault, but I'm not the kind of traveler they make vaults for. Give me a room and a bite to eat and I'm gone in the morning when the sun comes up. I'm happy enough to settle the bill tonight."

"Good," said the innkeeper, turning away down a narrow hall. "First unlocked room off the second-floor landing."

The second-floor landing was a ruin of warped floorboards and cracked plaster, and the rooms fronting the open stairwell were in pretty much the same shape. Escargot stepped into one, then stepped back out again when an enormous rat scuttled across the corner of the floor and winked through a rathole gnawed in the floor moulding. The next room was a copy of the first, except that the floor mouldings were ungnawed, so he threw his bag onto the bed and then sat next to it, wondering if destinations weren't just a little less grand when you arrived than they had seemed when you set out.

He bent down and peeked under the bed, then sat back up, relieved to find no rats. He stepped across to a cracked and dusty window, hung with cobweb, and looked out onto the rear yard where his horse munched grass next to a tumble-down barn. Directly behind the barn was a woods, dark and silent in the gathering evening. Cider. He might have known it. A man rides along the open road from dawn to dark until he'd kill for a bottle of ale—even a bottle of the sort of ale sold by an inn like The Smashed Hat—and what does he find, dusty and weary as he is, his throat dry as an old rock? Cider and a poison pudding for rats that live in the room next door.

He flopped back onto the bed and stretched out. He was tired enough so that if he fell asleep, there'd be no need to bother with supper at all—probably a good thing, taken all around.

But somehow he wasn't inclined to let the innkeeper get away with feeding him nothing, so he promised himself he'd just doze for a moment, then go back downstairs and choke down some cider.

It was a half hour later that he lurched awake in the darkness, jackknifing up into a sitting position, his boot thrashing out into the footboard and kicking loose the corner post, which fell to the floor with a bang. It seemed as if he'd heard something—a noise, a rattling on the doorknob. But there was nothing now. It was just as likely that he'd jostled the footboard in his sleep and rattled himself awake—a good thing, since if he hadn't, he'd have slept till noon the next day. He instinctively felt for his pouch, where his money and his truth charm hung together in their leather bag. They were safe—far safer than they'd be in the innkeeper's vault. An affidavit indeed. That's all he'd have had in the morning; his truth charm would be gone along with his money, and he'd have an affidavit.

He lit the oil lamp by his bed and reached into his shirt, plucking out the truth charm. As he stared at it he began to feel like a fool. How could a carven stone, for goodness sake, tell the truth about anything? How could it *tell* anything at all? It hadn't any mouth. But it did look like a truth charm, or some sort of charm anyway. Perhaps, he thought, in a sudden fit of inspiration, it was never expected to tell anyone anything. Perhaps it answered only specific sorts of questions—questions with yes or no answers. What had he asked it before? To elaborate on the validity of G. Smithers. Of course it hadn't answered. What had he expected, a treatise?

He set the charm on the little deal table, under the lantern. The yellow light seemed to sink into the stone like water into a brick; the eye peered up at him, regarding him, waiting. He cleared his throat. "Should I have brought little Annie?" he asked, steeling himself for an answer he didn't half want to hear. The stone, however, sat silent in the lamplight. "Is Leta a witch?" Nothing happened. Was it the eye that told the tale? Would it wink, perhaps, when he'd stumbled upon the truth? "What . . ." he began, when the door burst open and the innkeeper strode through, a carving knife in his hand.

Behind him, leering in the open door, stood the pudding-faced stable boy, his cuffs rolled up halfway to his knees and his teeth set in determination. Escargot snatched at the charm in order to thrust it into his pocket, but he knocked it off onto the floor instead and it rolled toward the window. He leaped after it, away from the bed. His heel kicked the fallen bedpost. He stooped, snatched up the heavy, turned post, and menaced the innkeeper, who endeavored to circle round behind so as to trap Escargot between himself, the bed, and the stable boy.

"We're a-going to rob you!" shouted the innkeeper, strangely honest. "We rob nearly everyone who stops here, we do. Then we beat them silly. The last one we rode up to McVicker and said he'd tried to rob *us*, and they hanged him, they did, as a thief. They'll hang you too. See if they don't."

Escargot watched the man in amazement, and held his post like a ballbat, wondering at the man's speech. "I deserve it," he found himself admitting. "That and more. I've abandoned my daughter to her horrible mother and a bent-up hypocrite of a preacher and there's not a thing I can do about it but run. Do you understand what that means?"

The innkeeper nodded. Apparently he understood very well what that meant. The stable boy nodded too, stepping into the room and crossing to the bed, as if to creep across it and confront Escargot from the other side. "I *wanted* that horse to kick you out on the yard today," he offered, squinting at the astonished Escargot. "A horse like that kicked me once. More than once. Kicked the stuffing out of me. But it didn't hurt, not until the next day. I hate horses."

"I don't hate horses," said Escargot, "but I can't stand my wife. And it's not just for the pies, either. She was after me every minute. Do this; do that. There was no such thing as peace."

The innkeeper lunged at him with the carving knife. Escargot lurched backward, folding up in the middle so that the knife swished past his belly, ripping his shirt. He swung the bedpost, clipping the innkeeper in the shoulder. The stable boy shouted and rushed at him, but Escargot thrust the end of the post into his chest and knocked the wind out of him. The stable boy collapsed in a heap on the floor, gasping and wheezing.

"That hurt!" cried the innkeeper, clutching his shoulder and staggering back, the knife angling ceilingward past his ear. "I had a wife once and she left with a traveling hat salesman in the night. So I followed them down toward the river and I bashed him and bashed him and bashed him and all his hats until they run off down the river road howling like tea kettles. Them two did, I mean to say, not the hats. And I come back and changed the name of this inn and swore I'd bash some more people before I was through. That's what I did.''

The stable boy had crawled back a foot or two, leery of the bedpost and of the look of resolve in Escargot's face. ''I'm a-going to leap on you!'' he shouted, throwing himself at Escargot's legs. The innkeeper, seeing his chance, loomed in with the knife upraised, his lip curled back, his eyes screwed half shut like pig eyes.

Escargot swung his club at the stable boy's head, but the post was too long for close work, and he managed only to bounce it off the floor before going over backward in a tangle of arms and legs. He slid his left hand down the post and whipped it up into the looming face of the innkeeper, catching the plunging knife midway between his own two hands. The force of the blow pushed the post down against the back of the stable boy's neck, wrenching the knife away from the innkeeper. Escargot rolled onto his back, banging himself clumsily in the knee with the bedpost, then wedging it against the throat of the stable boy, who bit wildly at his shoulder, grinding his teeth into a mouthful of jacket.

''I hates you!'' cried the lad, letting loose. ''I hates everyone!''

Escargot jerked the bedpost away, surprised to see the knife still dangling from it. The innkeeper lunged for the knife, caught the blade instead of the handle, and shrieked with surprise and pain. Escargot slid away under the window, his elbow cracking down on the escaped truth charm. ''I'll club you senseless!'' he shouted, waving the bedpost. The innkeeper, grasping his hand through his shirt, fell back in horror.

''On him, Grimes!'' he hollered.

''No!'' hollered the stable boy.

''I've wanted to murder you in your bed for years!'' shrieked the innkeeper.

''Don't think I haven't robbed you blind ever since I came to this filthy inn!'' the stable boy hurled back at him.

''I'll bash anyone who gets in my way,'' said Escargot, striding purposefully toward the door. He snatched up his bag, turned one last time to threaten the two with his bedpost, then leaped out of the room, shouting over his shoulder as he hurtled down the stairs, "Do yourself a favor and shave your mustache!" In a trice he was in the yard, clambering into the saddle on legs renewed with fear and excitement and listening for the sound of pursuit. But the only sounds were of the two shouting at each other, still on the second floor. Escargot cantered toward the road, leaving his bedpost on the lawn. There was a last cry from above, followed by a crashing and a long howl cut off abruptly.

Escargot flicked at the reins, kicking the horse into a gallop and scouring through the night until he angled round onto the river road and away toward Hightower. It seemed to be a good night for traveling after all—certainly a better night for traveling than for putting up at inns. He found that he was shaking so thoroughly that he could hardly take the truth charm out of his pocket.

It had been a weird fight, to say the least. Obviously it had been the innkeeper who had awakened him—probably trying to sneak into the room and slit his throat while he slept. It was puzzling that the man had thought it necessary to announce all his intentions in a loud voice. Why, when it came to that, had Escargot seen fit to drag little Annie into the conversation? And why had they compared notes on their wives? He looked again at the truth charm in his hand, its eye glowing dully in the moonlight. A truth charm—of course. It had nothing to do with the sort of truth he'd been trying to draw out of it. It worked the other way around; it had drawn the truth out of *him*, and, of course, out of the other two, who had fallen under its spell when they'd stepped into the room. He slipped the stone into his pouch and hunkered down in the saddle, drawing his coat around him. It would be a weary three or four hours yet into Hightower, and then there wouldn't be an inn with a light left lit.

5

The Harvest Festival

Escargot slept that night in a boat in Hightower Harbor, and breakfasted, wrinkled and sore, on steak and eggs in Hightower Village. No one had heard of any Abner Helstrom—not a living soul. But they knew the dwarf in the slouch hat well enough to steer clear of him when they heard him tapping along the road. He dwelt, they said, in the stone castle on Hightower Ridge. But he'd been gone for a month nearly, and no smoke had issued from the tower chimneys. If there was any such thing as luck, said one old man in the cafe, the dwarf would be gone for good.

As for Leta, no one knew the first thing about her. Witches, on the other hand, were a dime a dozen, especially at that time of the year. It was Halloween, wasn't it? The air at night was full of them, and no one with both oars in the water would be out and about after dark.

Escargot grinned at the idea. He rather fancied running into one or two, he said, but he knew when he said it that it was partly an idle boast. There was part of him that wanted to run into nothing at all, that longed for a wainscotted parlor and a hearth and locked and shuttered windows. Another part of him, though, longed to be away, riding beneath the moonlit sky, pressing on downriver toward the sea.

Four days later he was almost there, cantering through drizzling rain, the Oriel delta stretching away on either side. There was salt on the breeze, the smell of spindrift and tar and oyster beds and the musty, smoky smell of autumn. The road was full of people on foot, and rattling along in carts and on horseback, all of them bound for Seaside and the harvest fair. Parties of light elves hummed along down the river in long, cylindrical canoes, paddles dipping wildly and the canoes skimming wonderfully fast as if they raced on skids atop a frozen river. Early in the afternoon, when his horse tramped wearily up a long, slow rise, there lay Seaside, spread out far below him and running down into the endless gray ocean.

It was a walled city, prodigiously old, that wrapped around the swerve of shore like a quarter moon. Off toward the western edge the steep wall dropped almost forty feet into the bay, where the salty ocean mingled with the water of the Oriel River. The wall had crumbled here and there, and heaps of stone and scree lay tumbled on the mud flats of the bay. A party of dwarfs, wielding trowels, crept along like bugs on precarious scaffolding that dangled from the top of the wall, and more dwarfs on the wall above lowered hods of mortar and stone down to them for the purpose of patching the crumbled sections of seawall.

From where Escargot sat on his horse atop the rise, the city seemed to be an illustration from G. Smithers book, all turreted and alley-crossed and with the seawaves crashing beyond along the rocky, open shoreline and long washes of cloud-drift blown across the afternoon sky. Standing out to sea was a swell-tossed galleon, riding at anchor, its sails furled. It wasn't hard to imagine a fleet of such ships on a moonless night, flying the skull and crossbones from the mast, the cannon exchanging shot for shot with the long guns mounted in the high seawall of the city.

The streets of Seaside spread out like the spokes of a cartwheel from the central palace, disappearing and then reappearing from beneath arched stone bridges, full of milling people. Smoke rose from a thousand cooking fires, and even from his aerie a mile above the city Escargot could catch on the wind the grease and charcoal smell of roasting sausage and the sharp, hoppy tang of breached kegs of dark ale.

He flicked the horse's reins, but the beast needed little urging. In minutes they'd descended the rise, and the city disappeared behind another, lesser, hill in front of them. Then there rose into view directly ahead a massive arched gate in a wall of hewn granite blocks. He filed through the open gate along with a half dozen other travelers—men from Monmouth and the City of the Five Monoliths, and in moments he was swallowed by the crowds of people and the old, tilted houses, the shouts of sidewalk vendors, and the cries of reeling seabirds.

Now he had arrived at his destination. There was nothing in front of him but the sea, and though its shifting mystery was part of what had drawn him down the river road, it hadn't yet become the object of his journey. There was the harvest festival to see to first, that and a month's explore along the coast. The place names on the maps of the coastline below Seaside were almost magical in themselves: Thrush Haven, Manatee Head, Emerald Bay. It would be a shame not to have a look at them. After that, he'd quite likely have enough gold left in his pouch to book passage on a sloop bound for Oceania. And in the tropics, it seemed to him, a man might get by on nothing.

He clip-clopped into the city, swept up in the spirit of the fair. Despite the cool of the evening, windows were thrown open in almost all of the houses that lined the street, and people leaned out, shouting and gesturing, appearing and disappearing. The sidewalks were jammed with chairs and tables, and front porch stoops were littered with sleeping people. It struck Escargot suddenly that there would be little chance of finding an inn. Food and drink he'd already found in plenty, but it was moronic to think that a bed would be left unspoken for in the middle of such a crowd of people. Why hadn't he thought of that? He didn't much fancy a front porch stoop. And what would he do with his horse? If he put up at an inn he'd have a place to stable her. But if he merely tied her to a lamppost and wandered away, the next person who walked past would climb onto the beast and ride off. He'd sell her; that's what. What did he want with a horse? He'd arrived, hadn't he? He could easily travel the coast road on foot, after all.

Selling the horse turned out to be an easier thing than he would have guessed. It didn't take five minutes, once he put his mind to it, to find a willing buyer: a gyroscope salesman who'd walked downriver from Stooton for a week and a half to get to Seaside, but who didn't half fancy walking another week and a half upriver to get home. It was a sad business, he found, selling the horse, but he'd come too far already to let sentiment stand in the way of getting on, so he patted her once or twice on the flank, threw his bag over his shoulder, and let her go, wealthier enough only to regret how much he'd spent on her in the first place, but lighter in step for having one possession the fewer.

"Say," he said to the man, yanking his bags back off his shoulder, "what do you do, sleep on the sidewalk?"

"That's just what I do. And a hard sidewalk it is, after a few days. But if I put up at an inn, there ain't no profit in it. I might as well stay home. This ain't a pleasure trip."

"Of course not. I'm not putting up at an inn myself. What would you say if I left my bags with you? I'll be back around tonight, maybe, or tomorrow. I'll make it worth your while."

The fellow scowled at Escargot, as if he half supposed that Escargot were up to something. But it didn't seem so. Here he was being given a man's bags. "What's in 'em?"

"Nothing but clothes," said Escargot. "See for yourself. I just don't want to be cluttered up, you know. I've been carrying that stuff for two weeks and I aim to be rid of it for a night. What do you say?"

"How much?"

"A silver half crown?"

"Yep," said the man, holding out his hand. Escargot immediately regretted having offered so much. The man had accepted more readily than he ought to have accepted. But Escargot could afford it. Why be a cheapskate? There was the spirit of the festival to think of. In the end he left the bags with the man and set out, carrying only his pouch and his copy of *The Stone Giants*. He hated to go anywhere without something to read, just in case.

He spent the late afternoon walking, savoring the idea of having no place to go, of finding himself on a street corner with no earthly reason to turn right rather than left. A man on foot might travel six miles in a day, if he was leisurely: stopping here to sleep for an hour in the sun, dawdling there over a glass of ale. On horseback he could do better, of course. But he might easily ride past that spot of sunshine, or feel less inclined to climb down and open his book. And what did it matter if he wandered along six miles of coastline in a day or if he hurried past twenty? He hadn't seen *any* of it yet. He was getting a grip on this business of time; that's what he was doing. And here on the sunset streets of Seaside, faced with doing nothing, or, rather, with doing anything in the world he pleased, it seemed to him that never before had he felt so certain that he had time by the neck.

The events of the past weeks had been trying, to be sure. And if he was given the chance to have it all back again—his house, his wife, Annie, Twombly Town, his net and lines still hidden beneath the log along the river—he'd jump for it. Or at least for some of it. He could always buy new fishing tackle, though. There was a rock reef running out into the ocean just below Seaside—he'd seen it when he'd paused on the rise above the city two hours earlier—that would be full of some fairly amazing pools and channels. Heaven knew what sorts of fish he'd find there. As for Annie . . . That was behind him now.

Before him stretched a long avenue full of dancing people. A trio of dwarfs tooted on long horns, and an elf in a pointy cap fiddled away at an enormous stringed instrument that emitted a flurry of rising and falling notes. The music set the entire street mad, and even the tall houses that tilted away overhead seemed to be swaying and jigging in time. The sun dropped toward the seawall, faster and faster as it was chased out of the sky by evening, and the orange-red glow of sunset seemed to set the street afire. Foghorns moaned offshore, distant and lonesome when the music fell, as if to remind the revelers of something they'd been working hard to forget. And then a flurry of ascending notes swallowed the low sigh of the foghorns, and the street swept once again into dance.

Around a distant corner, already partly invisible in rising fog, bobbed a dozen enormous wooden puppets at the head of a capering procession of people. The heads of the things were painted and leering, and they bowed and swiveled and canted over to peer in a wild rush into second-story windows and balconies. Escargot pushed up onto the sidewalk along with the dancers to let the procession pass, and he watched in fascination the clacking wooden jaws of the things and the flapping ears and revolving eyes. Dwarfs and elves hunched inside, working furiously to manipulate arms and legs and to squeeze away at inflated bladders that squeaked out a ceaseless oratory of inhuman speech, utterly random and wild, but seeming in the early evening mists to signify some deep, portentous thing. Escargot fell in behind the throng, clapping and stamping and hooting and surrounded almost immediately by countless revelers including the four musicians, who continued to toot and fiddle as if abandoned to madness. People danced roundabout, and in half a minute Escargot found himself dancing with them, finding and abandoning partners in a blind rush of music and lights and the bursting of firecrackers.

They angled up toward the palace, the procession growing by the moment and stretching away finally almost to the seashore. People appeared from doorways carrying sheafs of wheat and corn bound in red ribbon. An enormous cornucopia clattered up a parallel avenue, appearing and disappearing across the ends of alleys and cross streets. In its upturned mouth was a strange collage of pumpkins and squashes and scarecrows knitted out of corn husks, all of it tangled into what seemed to be the legs of tumbled furniture: broken, upturned chairs and smashed tables, and the carcass of a grandfather clock, built for a giant, that thrust crazily through the tangle. The dying sun reflected off the cracked glass of the moon-faced clock, and it seemed to Escargot that the hands of the clock whirled around and around as if years were spinning away in moments.

The procession danced beneath an arched bridge made of cut stone that wheeled around into a high, crenellated wall, and for the space of five minutes the cornucopia vanished. When it hove once again into view, there, among the throng that danced behind it, was Leta. He was certain of it.

He pushed along toward the sidewalk, jumping and craning his neck to see. An enormous woman with a feathered hat grabbed him by the wrists and whirled him away. He yanked loose, bumped against a trio of circling pipe players, and nearly went down. "Here now!" cried one, hopping for a moment and grabbing the toe of his shoe. Escargot shouted an apology to the wind as he leaped into a brief clearing. He sprinted toward a tiny cobbled alley, pushing through an almost solid, writhing mass of revelers who blew in time on paper flutes. In a moment the way was clear. There was just enough sun left. In five minutes he'd have to trust to torchlight to illuminate the crowds, and the task of finding Leta would become monumental.

Ahead, winding up the hill, labored the cornucopia, flanked by scores of marchers clad in great circular masks, painted like rouged baby faces, all of them whirling round like tops, revealing at one moment a hideous grin, at the next a weeping frown, and amid them, looking hither and thither as if lost, stumbled Leta. Escargot shouted. He waved his arm. But she was oblivious to him. She couldn't conceivably hear him above the noise. She angled away to the right, disappearing for a moment behind the lurching cornucopia, then appeared again, stepping into the gloom of an alley, running now, as if pursued. Escargot followed. It was impossible that she was running from him. She couldn't know he was there.

In the shadow of the alley he slowed. He could hear footfalls ahead, scraping against cobbles. But the sun was gone and the alley was shrouded in ocean mist. He had forgotten in his haste and in his desire to see a familiar face that Leta wasn't what she seemed. He recalled, suddenly, the sight of her in the windmill, crouched on her haunches like a great cat and changing with the rising sun into the stooped, blind crone. And his ruined Smithers—he recalled that too. Their paths, he reasoned in a sudden fit of courage, seemed destined to cross; they might just as well cross now, while he was the pursuer and not the pursued.

The alley curved down the hill, past countless overgrown backyards, and evening slipped by the moment into night. The fog thickened. Escargot slowed, then stopped and listened. The sure tread of Leta's footfalls had been replaced by the dim, measured swish and scrape of someone walking slowly, almost wearily—toward him now. He took a step back, quelling the urge to cut and run. He'd see this out, he told himself. Come what may he'd wrestle with these devils so that he could get on with things. He couldn't have them continually popping up at him out of every alley he passed.

The fog before him swirled and parted, as if stirred by an unfelt breeze, and out of it, looming toward him, shuffling along slowly and inexorably, hunched the witch, leaning on her stick and twisting her head back and forth as if she knew someone were there, watching her. Escargot smashed himself against a fence and waited.

A clatter of footfalls arose in the fog, as if a company of people were running toward them down the alley. Shouts rang out. Escargot stepped along into the shadow of an entryway, feeling for the knob with his left hand. It was unlocked. If it came to it, he'd slip the door open, enter the house, and lock the door after him. He'd be pitched out, for sure, as a drunken reveler, but better that than . . . what? He didn't at all care to find out.

The old woman shuffled along past him, hurrying, it seemed, tapping the cobbles with her stick. The lace of her shawl hung like wet cobweb and the bones of her cheeks and forehead seemed to twitch with anticipation. The shouts and footfalls grew louder, and the lights of wavering torches hovered in the fog. Then Uncle Helstrom appeared, running out of the mist, pursued by a torch-carrying mob that waved hayforks and coils of rope. In his mouth burned his curved pipe, packed, no doubt, with the smoking, brittle bones of henny-penny men.

Uncle Helstrom, chased! Here was an interesting turn. But then it was clear that no one was chasing the dwarf. They were following him, pursuing the old woman. They closed in on her, snarling and yelling and shoving. She croaked a single protest before they were upon her. She was borne down, tied, then hoisted onto the shoulders of two men, who, at the urging of the dwarf, hauled her along at the head of the mob, up the alley toward the festivities. Her stick clattered to the cobbles and was trod to fragments by a hundred stamping feet. Escargot followed, awash with surprise and confusion.

The cornucopia had been pulled into a great square. Above sat the palace, its gray stone half lost in the hovering fog. The light of countless torches danced and flickered, and the streets, running off away from the square like spokes from the hub of a wheel, were packed with people, pushing forward, dancing in time to foggy rhythms that were the strangely melodic product of a thousand separate musicians. Escargot elbowed along behind the mob from the alley as the crowd parted before them. They were destined, it was clear, for the center of the square, and it had begun to dawn on Escargot why that was. He didn't at all like it.

From the shadow of the palace stepped four of the wooden puppets that had led the revelers earlier in the evening. One, quite clearly, was intended to be a dwarf, with a waggling beard and an axe in its belt. Another was an elf, thin and grinning and in a pointed cloth cap. A third was a jolly, long-legged linkman, a basket of summer fruit on his back. The fourth was a man in leather boots and a shop coat and spectacles. Appearing behind them, its cornsilk hair afire, a goblin jerked along, its eyes opening and shutting as it bent forward at the waist and then straightened again, bowing to the assembled masses.

The first four plucked long torches from the palace wall and lurched toward the cornucopia, which, as Escargot drew closer, seemed to be almost rectilinear—all angles and joints like a weirdly winding stairway that led to a spiral cavern full of strange autumnal debris. The torches dipped and rose, spilling burning oil onto the dry and brittle wood. The goblin puppet reached into the tangle and wrenched at a great wooden chair built of tree branches. Scores of pumpkins cascaded out onto the roadway, breaking open and scattering candies and coins across the square. People shouted and scurried. A hatch midway back in the side of the cornucopia fell open on hinges, spilling no end of stuffed pumpkins and spraying the night with elf-stars that burst into momentary light when they struck the ground and bounced.

In moments the wooden hulk of the cornucopia was aflame. The goblin puppet straightened, and looked about itself through oddly lit glass eyes. It seemed to see the blind witch, bound, mute, and held up as an offering. It stooped, plucked the witch out of the hands of the cheering crowd, and set her atop the enormous chair as if she were a stuffed doll. The witch's head swiveled, empty eyes regarding the flames. Escargot slid between hooting men so that he stood directly before the pyre. The flames crept upward, and the hem of the witch's dusty robe sparked and flickered. Her face was lit in a horrid glow that made it seem as if the milky glaze of her blindness evaporated, and for one repellent moment she gazed down at Escargot through sighted eyes, eyes full of weary despair and longing.

Escargot staggered back. Smithers hadn't lied. Not a bit. Everything had been there: the lurching puppets, the torchlight, the odd, enchanted music piping in the fog, the burning sheaves of wheat, the upturned, firelit faces of countless people watching half in wonder, half in fear. Smithers had seen all of it, all but one, last, inexplicable horror: the witch seemed to shimmer behind the curtain of heat, to fade and then grow distinct again, until staring down at him, ringed by fire, sat Leta, bound and helpless.

Escargot leaped. He hadn't thought about leaping; he simply

leaped, grabbing hold of an iron-shod cartwheel and clambering up toward the fire. The heat staggered him. Someone grabbed his foot from below, and he looked back and kicked the man in the face. He jerked loose and pulled himself onto the underside of the cornucopia itself, reaching into the gathering flame. Yanking himself forward and grappling for a foothold, he hauled himself up until he got an elbow over the edge, inches away from one of the front legs of the chair. Above him dangled a leg—Leta's leg. He reached for it, shouting incoherently into the flames, grabbing an ankle. He lurched upward to get a better grip and felt himself grasped from behind. The wizened, bespectacled face of the shopkeeper puppet looked into his own, and from behind it came a disembodied voice that shouted, "Give off!" then "Let go, will you!"

It was someone inside, yelling at him. Escargot held onto the ankle. If they hauled him off they'd haul her too. The lot of them would smash into the street, but that was better than letting Leta incinerate. "Pull!" he shouted into the puppet's face, and then he felt himself falling, carrying with him a single, smouldering shoe.

He landed on a mess of flailing people, and for a moment he lay trapped beneath the torso of the puppet. He could hear the dwarf inside cursing him and pounding on the wall of his temporary prison. The cornucopia burned above him. In the wild glow it was impossible to say what sat in the chair, but it seemed, just as two chair legs slumped into the burning mass of debris, that there was nothing at all in the chair but an almost transparent, leathery bag of wind encircled by a halo of flame. Then the ropes that had bound the witch fell slack and the chair was empty.

Escargot was suddenly free of the puppet. He leaped up, hoping that in the general melee he wouldn't be recognized, but he found himself peering into the down-bent face of the goblin puppet, its hair by now burnt to a frazzle. It reached for his neck with hands that seemed to be constructed of wired-together human bones, and in the split second that it took for him to shake off this new horror and run, he saw, peering out at him through the thing's open mouth, the grinning face of Uncle Helstrom.

Escargot shouted. A man beside him clutched at his arm. Escargot turned and swung at the man's face with a fury born of sudden terror, then ducked through the straddled legs of the puppet and ran. He heard cries of pursuit and the pounding of feet as he was swallowed by the blessed fog, rebounding off people who loomed suddenly up before him. He had no idea where he was going—only that he had no intention of stopping until he got there.

The square gave out onto a broad thoroughfare and a thinner crowd, most of the people having pressed along farther to watch the burning. Running, Escargot could see, was attracting attention. It was better, to be subtle, to slow down and become a part of the crowd again, rather than a hunted man who flew in the face of it. He was winded anyhow. He could circle back around and rejoin the crowd at the square—no one there had the foggiest notion who he was; no one but the dwarf, anyway. But it was late, and he was in no mood for further revelry, so in the end he decided to hunt down his man with the gyroscopes and fetch his bags, then set out in search of a doorway in which to spend the rest of the night.

Twice as he walked he heard the sound of hurrying feet. He ducked into the safety of a dark alley the first time; then, five minutes later, he was forced to take refuge behind a cart. In each case it was a party of dwarfs in uniform, striding along. Leading the first party and chattering breathlessly was the man whom Escargot had hit. In the midst of the second, tapping along purposefully in dignified silence, was Uncle Helstrom.

This wasn't, apparently, going to be as easy as it had seemed. The crime he'd committed by meddling with the sacrifice had quite clearly been more grand than one would think, either that or the dwarf carried with him some of the authority he'd boasted of two weeks back on the meadow. Rats, thought Escargot, edging along toward the river gate. He'd hoped to extend his stay in Seaside a bit. And here he was a hunted man not ten hours after he'd ridden in. What a fool he'd been to sell his horse! It hadn't occurred to him that he'd want to leave the city quick. He'd fancied a walking tour of the coast, not desperate flight from the local guard.

He hadn't any real notion of direction, only that the coast road wound around to the river gate. So as long as he chose alleys and byways that ran down toward the ocean or bay he'd get there right enough. The darkness and the fog were his allies for once, and when he thought about it, there was a certain relief in knowing that the old woman wouldn't come looming out at him, that she'd been burned to nothing on the pyre.

The problem, as he saw it, was that he'd been trusting entirely to destinations—to the notion that mere wandering would somehow free him from becoming entangled in the cobweb of other people's lives. But that very apparently wasn't the case. He'd managed to leave Twombly Town far behind him, or most of it anyway, but he'd simply blundered deeper into the affairs of Uncle Helstrom.

The only hope lay in walking purposefully in the other direction. If he'd ridden *upriver* out of Twombly Town, Uncle Helstrom would be little more than a shadow in his memory, and he wouldn't be hunted through the late night streets like a criminal. He'd leave straightaway then—walk up the coast road, sleep by day for a week until he'd put a few miles between himself and Seaside. It was simple as pie, really, all but one thing: the hunted look he'd seen in Leta's eyes when she'd fled down that misty alley, running from what, from whom? It was pretty clearly the case that she'd metamorphosed into the old woman, but why had Uncle Helstrom led the mob that ran her down? There were too many uncomfortably loose threads dangling about the mystery to entirely satisfy him.

But he wasn't a detective, was he? He had no stake in the mystery, had he? Cut and run, that was the smart thing. If he nosed deeper into the affairs of the curious Uncle Helstrom, he'd quite likely have *his* nose tweaked. Leta or no Leta, it was high time to move on. It was true that he'd like to have his marbles back, especially since they seemed to be as valuable as the devious Uncle Helstrom had claimed they were. But they weren't worth spending a few months in a dwarf prison. And it was entirely possible that they'd been pitched into a cauldron long ago and turned into some sort of bloody soup.

He strolled with his hands in his pockets out of a skinny alley and onto the High Street, just a block up from the coast road. He'd been two hours sauntering up and down the maze of Seaside avenues. It was time to collect his gear and be gone; there weren't enough hours left to the night to make it worth sleeping. The fog had risen and had blown on onshore winds up the hillside, and the moon had risen over the sea and hung now amid a wash of stars like an opal among diamonds. People slept everywhere: on benches and lawns, on wagons and front porch stoops. The wares of vendors still littered the curbs and sidewalks, but were covered with tablecloths and newspapers and blankets to keep out the wet and the prying eyes of late night passersby. Now and again people would approach, usually stumbling, and Escargot would give them the street, sinking back into moonshadow and waiting until their footfalls had echoed into nothing before stepping out into the open.

Ahead of him rose the north wall and the river gate. One sleeping guard sat slumped on a chair before it, his hat having tumbled off, his axe leaning against the timbers of the gate beside him. All was quiet. There lay his gyroscope vendor, his devices stowed in the steamer trunk next to which he slept, the trunk cutting the sea wind and shading his face from moonlight. Beside him were Escargot's bags. It would be an easy enough thing to pluck them up and be gone.

He tiptoed past the sleeping vendor and grasped the bags, then turned and reached into his shirt for his pouch. The leering face of the gyroscope man hovered a foot from his own. In the man's hand was a club.

6

The Flying Scud

''My stuff,'' began Escargot, nodding toward the bags slung over his shoulder.

''That's the man!'' cried a figure that crouched out from under a cart at the curb. Escargot spun round to face him. It was a tall man with a bruised cheek—the man he'd hit that evening. Three dwarfs in uniform sat up in the bed of the wagon, shrugging off the tarpaulin beneath which they'd been waiting.

Escargot leaped atop the trunk, swinging his bags at the gyroscope trader. The man waded into them, tangling his stick into the straps and pushing forward in an effort to topple Escargot onto the ground. The dwarfs clambered off the wagon, shouting to wake the street, and ran round to cut off his escape. Escargot yanked his bags, hoping at first to pull the stick from the man's hands, then hoping merely to free the bags. He felt himself going over backward. The gyroscope man grunted at him, flailing away with the trapped stick like an eggbeater.

Damn the bags, thought Escargot, landing in a crouch. One of the dwarfs was upon him, brandishing an axe.

''Cease!'' the dwarf cried.

Another hopped toward him from the other side, grinning smugly. The gyroscope man tugged his stick free, dropped Escargot's bags, and backed away, leaving Escargot to the guards. But Escargot had had enough of the guards—the guards meant being hauled deeper into inexplicable plots, a sudden end to his new life as a wanderer. The dwarf to his right dropped his axe and reached into his tunic, hauling out a set of manacles. Escargot grabbed the bill of the dwarf's circular hat and yanked it down over his eyes, then jumped past him. He heard the rush of air from the hurriedly swung axe of his companion, and stormed into the face of the third dwarf who sailed in, axe upraised.

Escargot jumped onto the front stoop of a row house, grabbed a long, wooden flowerpot full of geraniums, and hurled them into the faces of all three dwarfs as they swarmed up the several stairs. Two went over in a heap, the third pressed himself against the stone bannister and then came on again, just as Escargot, his luck with him this time, wrenched the door open and leaped in, smashing the door shut on the hand of the pursuing dwarf, then opening it for the instant it took for the hand to be jerked free. He threw the bolt and spun round to confront a wizened little man in a nightshirt.

There was no time to exchange histories. "Sorry," said Escargot, pushing past him and running down a long, low hallway. "Quite," shouted the man after him, almost apologetically. The end of the hallway opened onto a kitchen, and the kitchen onto a walled backyard. Escargot was out through the kitchen door even as he heard the clatter of feet behind in the hall. He loped across a cropped lawn, jumped onto a wooden table, and boosted himself onto the stone pilings of the wall, ready to leap down onto whatever it was that lay on the other side. But what lay on the other side was a rocky beach, forty feet below. Already the three guards shouted on the lawn, scrambling toward the table. The dwarf in the nightshirt held his back door open, watching the melee in wonder. Escargot bent onto his knees, reached down, and hauled the table up the wall, nearly losing his grip, then swinging it up and over, not stopping to watch it sail down onto the beach. He was off, loping along the top of the wall, watching the copings and the flying backyards on his left.

The wall was broad enough, certainly. It was like running along a road. But he avoided looking off the edge to the right anyway. He would put some distance between him and the guards, then find his way—where? Out of the city? They'd watch the gate for a week. He was a doubly desperate criminal now that he'd beaten the guards with a planter box and broken into an innocent man's house. A glance back over his shoulder betrayed the running forms of the three dwarfs, but they rapidly fell away. In a moment they'd give off the chase and set out to alert their companions. Ahead of him lay a good two miles of seawall, then the coast road gate. He could reach it before the news of his flight could; there was little worry about that. But what would he find there? Uncle Helstrom, perhaps. Something cluttered the wall a hundred yards down—machinery of some sort. It was the scaffolding of the masons who had been working at the face of the seawall the day before.

Escargot looked back; no one pursued him. The beach below was dark and empty, and the galleon still tossed on the moonlit ocean offshore. A long rowboat pulled along just beyond the breaker line, as if it had launched from the galleon. But it couldn't conceivably have anything to do with him. His way lay clear. He stepped out onto the scaffolding, looping one of the safety ropes under his arms and tying it in a bowline. Then he unlatched the ratchet catch and played out line. The scaffold jerked toward the sand a foot at a time. He cast one look downward, just to keep an eye on the rising beach thirty feet below, then twenty, then fifteen. The scaffold dropped once again and hung there, the rope going slack in his hand. He slouched out from under the noose round his chest, crawled from beneath the safety net that stretched around the perimeter of the scaffold, latched onto the wooden boards, and jumped, falling with an ankle-twisting scrunch into the soft sand.

He rose to his feet and hobbled a few steps, unsure of his ankle but finding that the pain disappeared with each step. He set out to the west, intent on clambering across the rocks on the seaward side of the gate and fleeing up the coast. The rowboat had run up through the surf, and half a dozen men clambered out, hauling it up onto the sand. One of the men waved at him as the six of them trudged up the beach. Escargot waved back. There was no need to be uncivil—or to seem suspiciously hasty, for that matter. Although, heaven knew, lowering himself as he had down the seawall in the middle of the night must seem suspicious enough.

The men on the beach seemed pleasant sorts; they were grinning, anyway. One wore a billed captain's hat, and was limping and bearded. He waved his pipe in Escargot's direction.

"Have you got a fill of tobacco, lad?" he asked from ten feet off. "Mine fell into the drink when we come in through the surf, and none of these lads can help. I'd be happy if you'd got just enough for a fill."

Escargot stopped. Of course he had enough for a fill. A man shouldn't be tobaccoless at that hour of the morning. He looked back toward the wall, half expecting to see an army of dwarfs scouring along the copings. But there was no one. They'd wait for him at the gates. It would be hours yet before they realized that their scaffolding had been messed with. By that time he'd be gone, and the captain would have had his smoke. "Certainly," he said to the smiling captain, pulling his pouch from his coat. He smiled back, offered up the pouch, and was bashed on the head from behind. He saw the gray-brown sand rushing up at him, then saw no more.

He awoke in the hold of a ship. It was dark as coal dust: neither day nor night, just black. The ship heaved on the swell, nosing up so that Escargot nearly slid down the deck into the stern, then plummeting down the back face of the swell so that when Escargot tried to stand, holding onto the back of his head to keep the throbbing from cracking his skull in two, he pitched forward onto his hands and knees, nearly somersaulting into a heap of gunnysacks.

He'd been shanghaied. That was the long and the short of it. The galley offshore had been after crewmembers, and had put in at Seaside thinking that there'd be no end of drunken revelers to haul away to sea. And they were right, all except for the drunkenness, anyway. It had happened just like it might have happened in a G. Smithers book. He should have seen it coming. But how could he have? A man offers another man a fill of tobacco and gets bonked on the conk. It wasn't the most predictable thing in the world, was it? At least he was safe from the guard and from the clutches of Uncle Helstrom.

There was something unsatisfactory in the rolling of the ship. Each rise and fall seemed to tug on whatever it was that connected his stomach to his throat. And the closeness of the hold—the smell of bilgewater and mildew and rot—lent an air of desperation to his plight. He was sick, or was going to be. There were no two ways about it. He stumbled forward, cracking into a post, then held on as the ship heeled to starboard in a plunging rush.

It was air he needed—air and wind in his face. He'd be all

right if he could feel ocean air on his forehead. It was just possible to walk, if he planted his feet wide and swayed to and fro as if striding along on either side of a stream. His stomach, all of a sudden, seemed to come unstuck from its moorings inside him and go sloshing away as it pleased, and just then the ship listed again to starboard. He lost his hold on the post, lurched along in a crouched run through the darkness, and sailed into a little hillock of burlap sacks, stuffed and stitched. He crawled up onto them and lay curled on his side.

Would the filthy crew that shanghaied him leave him to starve? He certainly hoped so. Starvation seemed to him suddenly to be a wonderful thing in light of his sausages and ale. How could he have consumed sausages and ale? They'd obviously poisoned him. He flopped onto his back momentarily, then folded up like a jackknife. It was hours later before he was awakened in the darkness.

"Bit of biscuit for you," said a voice, and he felt a hand on his arm.

"Good grief," he managed to croak, then shook the arm off.

"Best to have something in the hold. Ballast, it is. Something dry to settle you out."

Escargot mumbled. His head didn't throb half so lively as it had earlier, but he could feel a bump where the back of it was pressed against burlap. "Lamp?" he asked hopefully. His eyes felt as if they'd been screwed shut. The utter darkness was beginning to wear on him, and it seemed to him suddenly that he might stand a better chance of negotiating with his captors if he could see them.

"No, no. No lamp. These here biscuits ain't half as good in the light. Six weeks ago when we put out o' Hailey there wouldn't have been nothing like lamplight to sort of set them off. But not now. The captain ain't an epicure."

"I don't feel much like a biscuit," Escargot admitted, forcing himself to sit up, then flopping back onto his sacks in a single rhythmic movement.

"Best eat 'em before you go up. Sharp's the word on deck. We been chased for three hours by deep-sea pirates. In another hour they'll be all over us."

"Give them my best," said Escargot, clutching his stomach.

"I'll be up tomorrow. Leave the door ajar so I can find it. And don't wait dinner for me. Let the captain have my biscuit."

"Now, laddie, there ain't no room aboard the Flyin' Scud for slackers. It's all hands on deck now, isn't it? So if you don't want this bit o' biscuit, I won't hold it against you. If you'd seen it in the light o' day you wouldn't want it half so bad, yet. But my orders is to bring you up, and bring you up I will. Do you come on yer feet, or on my back?"

Escargot, in the darkness, had no way of knowing whether his benefactor was sizable enough to carry out his threat, but the man spoke in the tone of someone used to being obeyed. Escargot's stomach, right then, spoke in very much the same tones. He was in no shape either to resist or to follow. All he could do, it seemed to him, was groan and pitch from side to side.

"Here now!" cried the sailor, hauling on Escargot's arms. "If you soil the captain's tea bags it'll go bad. It's the open sea, is what it is, that'll put you right. Off the stern. An hour o' watchin' the horizon drop and you'll be all of a piece again. Come along, quickly now. That's it." And with that encouragement he tugged Escargot from his bed of tea leaves and steadied him as they lurched toward the door.

Escargot found that the sea had calmed. He no longer pitched this way and that with each passing swell. Now it was just a broad, continual rolling, so that he seemed to be walking uphill one moment, then downhill the next, not knowing exactly when it was he'd reached the crest, and dangling there waving a foot in the air for a bit before rolling away again. He could walk right enough, it seemed, but his stomach still hadn't gotten the word and it rose and fell so giddily that it seemed to spend about half its time hovering in his throat.

Sunlight nearly blinded him. A sharp wind blew out of the northwest, scouring the sky clean of clouds and mist and chopping the surface of the sea. The galleon sailed before the wind, sails rigged, slanting past a rocky headland—the tip of what appeared to be a long, mountainous island. The wind bit Escargot's neck and ear. He yanked his cap lower and turned up the collar of his coat, then looked about him at the casks and flotsam and coils of line that littered the deck. A grizzled sailor sat in his shirtsleeves mending a heap of dirty sail, and two others methodically stacked cannonballs in wooden troughs beside a half dozen wheeled cannon that were lashed to the deck.

"Toyon Island off to starboard there," said the sailor with the biscuit. He was a small man, as it turned out, lean and craggy and burnt a deep brown-ochre from years at sea. He wore a Leibnitz cap, and, like the sailmender, wore no coat. "We're beating up for the Isles with a load of tea and silk, and then it's back we'll come with rum and cinnamon and nutmeg."

Two shrill whistles sounded from the crow's nest, followed by a thump of feet in the companionway off to Escargot's left. The wind and spray had revived him enough so that he was mildly interested to see the captain burst out, his face purple, followed by two men in mismatched uniforms—officers, quite likely. The second of the two staggered in a way that had nothing to do with the rolling of the ship.

"Fill of tobacco?" asked Escargot of the captain as the man pushed past him.

"Shut yer gob!" came the reply.

Escargot watched the three men disappear into the stern. He wondered exactly what it was he'd been commissioned to do. Haul on the bowline, perhaps, or lay about him with the marlinspike. Everything he knew about ships and sailing he'd learned from G. Smithers. In fact, it was becoming clear that almost everything that he knew about the world beyond Twombly Town he'd learned from G. Smithers, or from some writer or another who had made up the stories he'd written. Most of it had been lies, in other words, just like Professor Wurzle had insisted.

"Don't press it," said his companion, gesturing toward the stern.

"Pardon me?"

"I say don't push the captain there. He ain't safe to push even when there *ain't* pirates in his wake. He's like to pitch you overboard himself when there is. If he weren't in such a blamed hurry he might have."

Escargot leaned out over the rail and peered behind them. The ocean was empty. "Pirates?" he asked.

"Deep-sea pirates, like I said. Them two whistles means they was sighted. They ain't on no pleasure cruise. For my money they'll come up on us when we pass the headland there and wrap round off the lee shore. The captain'll run for the shallows and blast away with the ten-pound guns."

"Good man," said Escargot.

"Dead man," replied the sailor, spitting overside. "They won't let us nowhere near the shallows. We'll give the ship over or they'll ram her, and we'll all be swimmin' 'mongst the sharks. There's a little port on the far shore o' the island. Ships put in there often enough. I'd make for that if I was you."

"Would you?" asked Escargot, surprised. "When?"

"Hold on till we angle in through the gap there, then go over the starboard side and strike out for the rocks. That there headland wraps up into the hills and there's a cut through the mountains that drops down the far side into town. It ain't much, but you'll be off the island in a month, one way or another."

Escargot studied the man, who stood with his feet planted and smoked his pipe, gazing out toward the island. It was hard to believe that after having helped shanghai him the man was advising him about effecting an escape. It could simply be that the sailor was an honest man who did as he would be done by, but one didn't expect to run into such a man, not after being hauled feetfirst off a beach. "I don't get it," said Escargot.

"If I was them pirates I'd sink this tub. That's what I'd do. What does a pirate need with eight tons o' tea wrapped in burlap? They might use the silk—trade it, maybe. But the tea ain't worth a penny, not to deep-sea pirates it ain't. They can't transport it. For my money they lays us by and demands the cargo. Then they finds out it's tea, and down we go."

"For no reason beyond that?" asked Escargot.

"Bloodthirsty lot, pirates. Especially this lot. Stove in the side of a dwarf galley off Picaroon Bay down south of here, because they weren't carrying nothing but pepper. Only so much a man can do with pepper. Down she went, and all hands aboard her. She was too far off the bay to swim for it. Most of 'em drown, the rest of 'em was eat by sharks."

"Sharks!" Escargot exclaimed, looking out over the water. Suddenly the sailor's plan seemed ill-advised.

"Do you want to swim a quarter mile through 'em or two mile? Like I say, if *I* was them pirates, I'd lay us to off the headland there when we wraps around. Then I'd board us and find out there weren't nothing aboard to amount to nothing. And then I'd ask if there weren't men aboard the ship that wants to go a-pirating. Half of 'em steps forward then, you see, because they was commissioned with a marlinspike just like you was. But they don't need 'em all, do they? They don't need but half a dozen, maybe, to take over for dead men. The rest goes overside or goes down. It won't matter a hair to the pirates which it is. Then they'll back off a half mile and come on full tilt, bam, and lay open the starboard side. Then again, they might just smash us to bits for sport, and never mind the tea. Captain of that 'ere ship never give anyone quarter. Not him. That's Cap'n Perry, is who that is. There now. There's the p'int. We ain't never going to be so close to any bit o' land as we are now, 'less it's the sea bottom."

"Come along," said Escargot, noticing suddenly that the crew of the galleon seemed to have been suddenly sent mad. The captain shouted orders from the poopdeck. Sails were unfurled in a rush of plummeting canvas. The ship came about, angling in toward the calm waters of the leeward side of the island. Three cannon from the starboard side were unlashed and wheeled across toward the port. The sailor nodded meaningfully toward shore.

"I ain't much of a hand in the water," he said. "And I got three months pay coming to me and a triple share. I always did like to play the odds. Goin' over is a sure thing—all but the sharks—and a lubber like you, just gettin' out among it, is better off by a sight with the sharks than with the cap'n here."

Escargot looked back toward the stern, where he could just see the shoulders and head of the captain, who barked orders, now at the men in the crow's nests, now at the pilot, now at the dozen men shoving shot and powder into the cannons. The shore of the island slipped past, the rocks on the beach shadowed by cliffs above. The water looked powerfully cold. But the sailor was right. It wouldn't be any warmer or shallower a mile out to sea.

"Jump for it, mate."

Escargot hesitated.

"Jump now. There's a current wraps round the p'int there that'll sweep you out to sea if you wait. Jump and strike out hard for the beach. The captain's too busy with his pirates to give a flying damn. Now jump!"

And Escargot jumped. He put both hands on the rail and vaulted over, sailing feetfirst into the sea and plunging in a rush of bubbles into the green depths. His jacket was shoved up around his chest and his pants around his knees. He thrashed and kicked and shot out into the sunlight gasping for breath.

"There he goes, by heaven!" thundered a voice from above, and Escargot spun round to find the galleon looming overhead, and the sailor whose advice he'd taken leaning out over the rail and shouting. Another man joined him, and then a third. This last carried a gun with a barrel that opened out into a sort of cone, and he rammed shot into the end of it with a singleness of purpose that sent Escargot diving once again beneath the surface.

His clothes and shoes made swimming cumbersome, but they also seemed to make the chilly water bearable. His head felt as if it were being squeezed between two frozen rocks. He surfaced again and at once heard the sound of an explosion followed by a curse. He'd fallen away astern, and it was the captain he saw now, shaking a fist at him, as his benefactor hopped along toward the captain, wrestling the gun away from the third sailor, who loaded it wildly, hoping to get in another shot. The biscuit sailor threw the stock to his shoulder and fired off a shot that zinged into the water ten feet to Escargot's left, and as Escargot dove again, determined to stay under until he was out of range of the weapon, he heard the captain shout, "Blast! . . ." something or other. But whether he was generally blasting his ill-shooting crewmembers or was exhorting them to blast away again with the gun, Escargot never learned, for when he surfaced again the *Flying Scud* was pulling fast away and the island swept by at what seemed suddenly to Escargot to be a remarkable distance.

He'd swum often enough in the Oriel River to know what it was to swim against a current, and he knew that in a lake, say, or in the still water of the marshes below Stooton Slough, he could easily cover a mile of open water in a half hour and have wind enough left to swim back again. There was a rhythm to it; that was all. But in the ocean, with the cold brine slapping against the side of your face and with your jacket and shoes tugging you down, and with your mind on whatever it might be that swam in lazy circles beneath you, covering half that distance was another thing altogether. Just to *see* the island he was forced to swim with his head out of the water, and half his effort seemed to be spent keeping afloat. His beach, visible only because of the beetling cliffs over it, seemed to be edging away sidewise. He'd wind up, if he was lucky, somewhere to the west, among the rock reefs that made up the tip of the headland. Whether those reefs were visible only because of a low tide was an interesting question—one which Escargot pondered for only a moment. There was no profit in studying his fate, only in taking another stroke.

A shivering chill had gotten in under his clothes, and each stroke and kick surged a cold wash of seawater across him. He stopped to tread water and negotiate. There was the *Flying Scud*, a mile off the point and beating round in order to angle up the island. His beach was hopelessly lost to the east, and even as he sculled in place, kicking to stay afloat, he was swept along in the wake of the ship, as if doomed to catch her again. He struck out afresh toward shore. It mattered little where he ended up, as long as it was solid ground. He looked about himself and wondered at the play of shadow and light on the tossing ocean, thinking about sharks and whales and eels and wanting not to. But they kept swimming round and round in his mind as if to hurry him along, to force him not to quit again.

The island, in minutes, was dropping away behind him. He was in the current that the sailor had warned him against and would be swept out to sea, food for the fishes. A half hour earlier he'd been sick at his stomach aboard a galleon bound for the Wonderful Isles; now his stomach wasn't sick at all—it was tip-top—and he was afloat in the open ocean bound for nowhere. Even his gunnysack tea bed had been a positive comfort in comparison. He found that his teeth were chattering and the ends of his fingers were numb. He seemed to be able to move only very slowly, as if the cold water were coagulating his blood.

Little clusters of exposed rock drifted past to his right, one by one, shrinking in size as they fell away to sea. There was one last cluster, weedy and angular, looming toward him. He swam for it, plunging along with deep, purposeful strokes, holding his head above the chop, correcting his course as the reef drifted alarmingly away, out of reach. He wouldn't catch it.

He found himself swimming straightaway in toward shore, hauled along sideways in the current. Black shadows swept beneath him—angular shadows like the black bulk of waiting sharks—best not to think about it at all. He stopped again and drifted with the current. Maybe it would drop him somewhere on the leeward side of the island. Of course he'd be drowned and eaten by then.

He kicked himself upright, banging his heel against something sharp. "Shark!" he shouted, certain for one desperate moment that his swim had drawn to a fateful end. He thrashed, turning in a ragged circle, feeling in his pocket for his foolish penknife and promising himself that he'd buy a real knife if only he'd be spared to. It would have a blade eight inches long. A foot long. He'd buy a knife and a sword and he'd carry a leather sap full of lead beads. He lived in a world that required such a thing, apparently. Water rushed about him. A swell humped up and pushed him toward the island but dropped him again before it had done any good. No shark appeared, only more shadows.

A tendril of leafy kelp wrapped round his legs and arm, and he pulled and kicked at it until he was lifted by another swell, clear green with the afternoon sun shining through it. He found himself dragging across barely submerged rocks, and he scrabbled for a handhold among tufts of eel grass, ripping loose handfuls of the slippery weed when another swell swept him along, off into deep water again. He bumped across a narrow ledge, caught a thick kelp stalk and held on, washing on the surge up onto yet another rocky plinth, knee deep in water.

He stood up on shaky legs and collapsed immediately, tumbling off, struggling back onto the shelf, cutting his hands on the rough edges of the rock. The ocean dropped away and he was lying on a bit of exposed reef, watching as a new swell humped up and surged across him, tearing him loose and dumping him headfirst into the ocean once more and then pushing him into a farther ledge where he fought again for a handhold. He struggled upright, forcing his numb and shaking legs to cooperate, to carry him along toward a higher shelf.

When the next swell washed over the rocks he was only ankle deep and he held onto handfuls of waterweeds, feet planted, then stepped delicately away when the ocean fell off. He crossed from rock to rock toward what had been the last exposed bit of the headland. There he would rest. He could dry himself in the sun. He could spend the night there and hoof it for shore at low tide the next day. It wasn't exactly the Widow's windmill, but it beat The Smashed Hat all to bits if hospitality was the issue.

He struggled one last time with a swell, letting it lift him along the edge of the rock, then caught and held when it dropped him, hauling himself up the edge, higher and higher until the next wave lapped past below him, then higher yet until he collapsed atop the rock, shivering with his face to the sun and his head in dried weeds. The boom of cannon fire jerked him upright.

For one fearful moment he assumed they were shooting at him—that the captain had seen his deliverance onto the reef and had decided to blow him off his perch with the ten-pound guns. But it wasn't so. There lay the *Flying Scud*, wallowing in the leeward calm and the rising swell. Smoke and brimstone belched from the guns along her starboard side. She seemed to be firing at nothing. From his rock, Escargot could see little geysers of water sailing skyward in the direction of the island, but there was no pirate ship to be seen; there wasn't a thing besides the sunlight glinting on little wavelets and the scattered rocks in the shallows.

Yes, there was something—what was it? There was a shadow on the surface of the sea. Escargot stood up and shaded his eyes with his hand, shivering in the afternoon breeze. The thing in the water seemed to be a whale, lolling in the shallows. But why was the captain taking potshots at whales when there were desperate pirates about?

The ship tacked before what little wind there was, making away up the island, perhaps toward the village at the far end. The shadow in the water seemed to drift after it, out of the turquoise of the shallows and into the deep green of the open ocean. Cannonballs hailed roundabout it, volley after volley, and more than once, echoing over the sea with a resounding bong, one of the balls apparently struck home, bouncing skyward with the impact and falling harmlessly into the sea.

Escargot could see the thing's eye as it dropped away into the deep. It glowed like lantern light, unblinking, and a row of phosphorescent circles like portholes shone along its flanks. The *Flying Scud* gave off its firing and slanted along miserably slowly in the wind. The biscuit sailor had been wrong, apparently; they were round the headland and beating up island.

Before nightfall they'd reach a safe port and be drinking rum out of casks. Escargot had, apparently, gotten into the habit of taking bad advice. He wondered if he was lucky or just the opposite. He'd taken the advice of a man who'd helped assault him on a beach and had been caught up in the very current the man had assured him he might avoid. But then he'd washed up onto the rocks just when he'd given himself up for drowned, in time to watch the ship he'd sailed on, back when he was warm and dry and had a biscuit at hand, making away toward civilization. And where was *he*? On a weedy rock, contemplating a dinner of raw periwinkles and limpets. He plucked a periwinkle off the rock and peered into it, wondering how many of the little things he'd have to crack and eat before they'd do him any good. They wouldn't need any salt anyway.

There was the distant boom of cannon fire and a sploosh of water, out to sea now. The *Flying Scud* had come round into the wind and was booming away, shot after shot. He could hear, between explosions, whistling from the crow's nest and the shouting of the captain on the poopdeck. The sun lay almost on the sea, setting fire to a long orange-red avenue that ran right along to the foot of Escargot's rock. But it was a cold sort of a fire. And all at once, as if someone had drawn a curtain, evening seemed to rise out of the ocean in the east, carrying a chill along with it.

Escargot could do nothing save wait it out. He wouldn't freeze, surely, out there on his rock. The tide had risen enough to cover half the rocks that had been high and dry a half hour before. An attempt to gain the shore would mean thrashing across the current again, an obviously futile business. There would be another low tide sometime in the early morning. If the moon was cooperative, perhaps he'd try for the island then.

He peered across the hundred yards of broken water toward the shore, then jerked around in the direction of the galleon at the sound of a tearing crack, monstrously louder than the occasional explosions of cannon fire. The *Flying Scud* listed crazily, as if she had no ballast in her hold, and her mizzenmast and a tangle of rigging lay sprawled across the tilted deck. She seemed to be going down even as Escargot watched, spinning lazily around so that the bowsprit swept past the island, pointed briefly at Escargot, then angled skyward as the stern settled beneath the waves. Sailors crowded the bowrail, hanging off and dropping into the sea. A half dozen seemed to be working at the fallen mizzenmast. They chopped away with axes at lines that secured the mast onto the deck until it fell with a splash into the water and swung round, drifting away from the settling hulk. A dozen men jumped after it, grabbing hold of the floating mast and hanging on.

Escargot could hear shouts and cries and curses drifting over the water, and he watched in numbed horror. The galleon, perhaps, had struck a reef. Only the bow was visible, sinking quickly now, settling into the sea like the sun. It slid away, the bowsprit saluting the heavens for a quick moment before the ship was gone. It was as if he were watching a play, seated as he was atop his rock. So distant was the tragedy that it seemed staged, and only the memory of the biscuit sailor made it seem that the sinking ship had any connection with him. Luck was with Escargot after all. He hoped mightily that his benefactor was one of the sailors clinging to the mast, but even in the deepening twilight Escargot could see that the mast, a floating bit of flotsam now on the sea, was drifting away across the dark, empty ocean, leaving the island in its wake.

Below him the cold tide swirled against the reef. Finger kelp and eel grass that had lain limp against exposed rock ten minutes earlier washed now with the surge. It occurred suddenly to Escargot that the periwinkles and limpets that crept across his rock were waiting for something; they hadn't simply trudged up out of the ocean on holiday. And what they were waiting for lapped and splashed a bare foot from the top of the rock with each surge. Between him and the shore there were no rocks visible. The evening might have obscured one or two, but it didn't seem so. It seemed, to the contrary, that Escargot's lucky streak, short as it was, had ended.

A dark wave humped up out of nowhere and rolled straight across the top of the rock, filling his shoes. Another appeared, big enough this time to feel the shallow reef beneath it and break across the rock rather than roll past. Escargot dropped and clutched a kelp holdfast, thinking optimistically that there hadn't been much to the wave after all. He could stick it, he told himself. The tide would peak and then fall away. He looked up, shaking the water out of his face, and stared straight on into a rushing hillock of ocean. He sucked in a quick breath, then sailed over backward with the force of the wave, onto his back on the rocks before being lifted and tossed into deeper water.

He was afloat again, gasping, kicking away from the rocks where another wave broke and roiled, a mass of tumbling white foam against the dark sky and ocean. Escargot swam into it, hoping that the force of the wave would push him toward the island, up onto the next reef, perhaps, where there'd be a chance of being swept even farther. But the wave lost its fury abruptly when it passed him, and he found himself once again in the current, sweeping offshore. He swam, but swimming did nothing but tire him. And if he was destined to drown, it seemed to him he'd be a happier drowned man if he hadn't tired himself out first with a lot of futile swimming.

7

Captain Perry and His Men

Escargot drifted in the current, dead tired, his legs kicking feebly and his arms sculling in quick, ineffective little jerks. He'd shed his jacket and trousers and shoes when they threatened to drag him under. Beneath his shirt hung the truth charm pouch, a few coins, and the maps torn from the front of *The Stone Giants*. It had been difficult to part with Smithers, but a few hours soaking might quite likely turn the book to mush anyway, and, as was true of books, there was more than that one copy in the world.

He lay on his back and rested more and more often, watching the slivered moon pole its way up the sky like a rocking gondola, floating lonely and cold amid the far-flung stars. The long shadow of the island had edged entirely into view, and when he bobbed over the crest of a passing swell he could see a scattering of lights away off in the distance—the village, no doubt, that would have to get by without his company.

His floating wasn't worth much. It seemed less and less possible to steady himself, and after a minute or two of dipping to port or starboard he'd find himself with a mouthful of seawater, and he'd be sputtering and floundering and gasping. How long *could* a man float on the ocean? Until morning? Another hour was pushing it. And what good would morning do him anyway?

The water brightened around him, as if the moon had slipped in closer to the earth to see what manner of thing it was that floated there on the ocean. He could see his feet all of a sudden, treading below him, and beyond them the shadows of two plate-size fish kicked away into the depths as he watched. The light wasn't coming from the moon; it was coming from below. A wash of fine bubbles burst on the surface, and the ascending light shaped itself into two spheres—the eyes of the deepwater creature that had so confounded the cannon fire from the *Flying Scud*.

The thing surfaced beneath him—not in a rush, but in a lazy drift, an enormous shadow in the green depths. There was nothing to do but wait for it, for the opening of ponderous jaws as the beast flopped over onto its back to feed, thrashing for a brief moment in its silent journey through the seas. Luck was a fickle thing indeed.

The beast stopped. It hovered there. In the clear water it might have been twenty feet down or it might have been ten. A score of angular dorsal fins rose along its spine, disappearing in the depths, and wide pectoral fins undulated slowly behind its glowing eyes. It drifted closer, eyeing him. Escargot braced himself. He watched horrified, unable to look away, needing to know the precise moment that doom would overtake him.

He peered into the thing's face. The front of its head between its eyes seemed curiously transparent. He could see straight into it. Things moved in there. My heaven, thought Escargot, there's a man afloat in the beast. It's consumed the crew of the *Flying Scud*, and it's cruising about, looking for survivors. It's a sea monster, a thing part serpent and part whale, and it's swallowed the men whole.

Alive, he realized abruptly. The man inside seemed to be looking out at him, though the surface of the sea was too full of chop for him to be sure. He shoved his head under and opened his eyes, but that just made it worse—nothing but blurry lamplight and shadow confronted him. Then he cupped his hands across his forehead and blew them full of air, peering through the bubble into the face of the scowling, black-haired man, who piloted the thing, not a sea monster at all, but an undersea boat.

A moment later the craft was afloat, bobbing on the moonlit ocean. A hatch popped open amidship and a head poked out—not the head of the pilot, but of a short man with whiskers and wearing a striped stocking cap. He hauled a wooden ring out from within the ship and flung it at Escargot, nearly banging him atop the head. Escargot held onto the ring and to the rope it was tied to and was dragged to the boat, which had, it seemed fairly certain now, been the demise of the *Flying Scud*. The biscuit sailor had been right: deep-sea pirates, he had called them, accurately enough.

If they'd given the galleon and her crew no quarter, then what could Escargot expect but death at their treacherous hands? But better that than to drown. He half clambered and was half dragged up the side of the craft, and he hadn't strength enough left to haul himself into the open hatch when he arrived at it. It felt as if he'd metamorphosed into some sort of jellyfish—a very cold jellyfish. His hands and feet were worthless to him. The whiskered man cursed him roundly and yanked on his arms, tumbling him head foremost into the hatch. He clutched at the iron rungs of the ladder, then collapsed all of a heap on the deck below, lying there like soggy old newspaper. The whiskered man strode away down the dimly lit companionway, leaving Escargot alone. In a moment, when the warmth of the interior of the vessel had begun to thaw him out and his feet had begun to feel like electrified sponges, he flopped over and pulled himself up to sit against the wall.

The companionway was aglow with the light of a thousand tiny stars—chips of fire quartz mined by dwarfs beneath the Emerald Cliffs on the edge of the White Mountains. Escargot had read about it in Smithers. And in the university at Monmouth there'd been an entire chandelier strung with it that lit the Hall of Geology. It burned, or so said Smithers, for close on to five hundred years once it was exposed to the atmosphere or was dropped into water, but it was wonderfully rare, most of it trafficked by light elves. Only occasionally did a crystal fall among men. Below the chips of fire quartz was a frieze of jade and copper, running the length of the companionway. It was all elf runes, depicting heaven knew what sort of story. Perhaps, thought Escargot, it was instructions—on how to open the hatch, say, or what to do in case an octopus climbed in at the window. The vessel, clearly, had been built by elves. It was laden with magic. The very contrivances that propelled it had to have been the product of enchantment.

He became aware of a low hum deep in the hull of the craft somewhere. It sounded for all the world as if it were coming from miles off—a sound carried on wind. He stood up and tested his pincushion legs, then slogged along toward the door through which the whiskered man had disappeared. It wouldn't be at all a bad idea, he decided, to confront the captain of the ship, to inform him of the men on the mast, who might quite easily still be saved. There was profit in it. The captain could sell the lot of them into slavery in the Wonderful Isles.

There was no latch or knob on the circular copper door. Escargot poked at it, effecting nothing. Then he knocked and hallooed, but it was such a solid contrivance that it was like knocking on stone, so he gave off and sat back down. Almost immediately the door slid open and a face peered through; not the whiskered man this time, but a lean, squinting face with tarred hair and a long scar down its cheek. "What?" said the face.

"I'd like to talk to the captain," said Escargot stoutly, nodding at the man as if he meant business.

The head disappeared and the door slid shut. Escargot sat in silence for a time, then banged on the door once more. Again it opened and the same face thrust through. "What now?"

"About talking to the captain . . ." Escargot began, but the man interrupted him.

"You can't talk to the captain," he said. "No one talks to the captain. The captain talks to you. He talks; you listen."

"There's a half score of men from the galleon, afloat on the mizzenmast. They were drifting east when the sun set, and so was I. They can't have drifted much farther or faster than I did, so they're probably roundabout. We . . ."

"We don't do nothing but sail on. We're bound for the Isles. Your men on the mast are all dead."

"Dead?"

"Every blessed one. Eat by sharks, the whole lot of 'em. Nothing left of 'em now but trash for the smelts to pick over."

Escargot sat staring. "Murderers," he said thickly.

"Complain to the captain," said the man, and started to shut the door.

"By heaven I will!" shouted Escargot, leaping up. "Let me at him!"

"No one talks to the captain. Didn't I tell you that? Are you deaf, mate, or stupid? If I was you I'd shut up; that's what I'd do. I'd shut up and keep shut up."

And with that the door closed. No amount of hollering and threats would open it again. Escargot was awakened hours later and led toward the stern, where another door opened onto a wide room. A suit of clothes hung over the back of a tooled leather chair, and a plate full of food sat on a table. He was left without a word. The clothes fit well enough, and the food was good. He feared at first that it might be poisoned, but what sensible pirate would save a man from drowning and then poison him?

He was quite clearly in the captain's quarters. Books lined the walls, thousands of them, tilted and stacked and braced with great gemstones and with corked specimen bottles in which floated tiny sea creatures. There were shelves of nautical books and of geology and geography and chemistry. Great, dusty atlases lay heaped on the floor, and Escargot recognized G. Smithers among the novels. A bank of lamps dangled from the arched, ebony joist that spanned the ceiling, each lamp a chunk of fire quartz dangling from a brass chain. The floor was wood—pegged rosewood and oak, from the look of it, inlaid with ivory and jade and silver and emerald. Much of the marquetry was lost beneath chairs and cabinets, but it seemed to depict the ocean bottom, aswarm with odd fishes and lorded over by a weedy, pale sea god leaning on a trident and casting four golden coins onto a shelf of rock.

In the middle of his peering at the floor, he heard what sounded like organ music. At first it blended with the deep and sonorous hum of the engines, but when he cocked his head and listened, it was quite clearly something else. It seemed for all the world to be coming from an adjacent room.

The door to that room, he discovered, had a knob, which turned easily. The door swung open to reveal a room very nearly the size of the one in which he stood. One of the long walls was windowed with broad portholes, which looked out on the dark and silent ocean. A pipe organ stood against another wall, and sitting at it, moaning away on the keys, was an elf, his black hair combed back theatrically, his hands and arms hovering and dancing and sweeping back and forth with exaggerated intensity.

Escargot watched respectfully, looking around him at the oceanic wonderland of bottled specimens that lined the second long wall. There were squids in jars and the carcasses of dried devilfish. A collection of eyeballs of decreasing size was clustered on one shelf—the first eye big around as a hat brim, as if it had been plucked from a nautical behemoth, and the last eye so small as to be invisible. There were jellyfish and chitons, octopi and urchins—the creeping denizens of tidal pools and the phosphorescent monsters of deep-sea grottoes.

The organ music gave off abruptly. The elf sat as if listening to the echoes of his playing, echoes that resounded in his mind. Escargot cleared his throat. Very slowly the elf turned on his stool, cocking an eye and screwing up his face. He ran the fingers of both hands through his hair in a gesture of tired despair, and then waved roundabout him, first with one hand, then the other.

"With whom am I about to be acquainted?" he asked Escargot, very formally but in a high, piping voice that was utterly at odds with his black hair and dramatic mannerisms.

"Theophile Escargot. And you are Captain . . ."

"Perry. No more nor no less than Captain Perry of the *Omen*, my good fellow, cast off from the great mass of human misery and degradation in an undersea boat, and there to carry out a private struggle against all that smacks of the treachery of the surface world."

Captain Perry's eyes had an odd look in them, as if he'd just then seen some stupefying and terrible thing, crawling up the wall, maybe, right behind Escargot's head. Escargot smiled, not knowing whether to look over his shoulder or to wait for Captain Perry's fit to pass. He glanced around him, but there was nothing to explain the look, the rolling of the captain's eyes. When he looked again into the face of his host there was only silent amusement painted across it. The elf winked at Escargot and nodded toward the bottled eyeballs.

"These are my children," he said, gesturing widely.

"Of course they are," agreed Escargot, edging back toward the door.

"A man would guess that the greatest of them, the eye of the great, oceanic narwhal, is the one which pleases me most, the gem of my collection." He raised his eyebrows as if to allow Escargot to respond.

"Of course," said Escargot, "of course. The great narwhal. It had quite an eye on it, didn't it? Big as anything."

"But a man is a fool," cried the elf, squinting fiercely. "This, sir, this is the prize!" And with that he clambered precariously up onto a chair and snatched down the last of the jars. "This, I say, is the purpose of my odyssey through the seas." He held the jar out for Escargot to inspect. In it was nothing at all, it seemed, beyond a scattering of sand grains on the bottom.

"What do you make of it?" asked the elf, almost whispering.

Escargot cleared his throat and bent toward it squinting. The elf waited. Here was another Professor Wurzle, thought Escargot, stark raving mad for salamanders and weeds. "Fine specimen," he said, nodding wisely. "You don't see many like that one."

"Phaw!" cried the elf, waving the sloshing jar in Escargot's face. "You don't see anything at all, do you? Admit it!"

"Well, now that you mention it," said Escargot, peering uncomfortably into his pipebowl.

"Hah! That's because, my land-lubberly friend, to your half-blind eyes there is nothing at all in this jar. Nothing! But I can see it. It's vast as the ocean to me, vast as the heavens that are nothing but fish, fish, fish! The beast I plucked from the sea was himself almost invisible. A gummidgefish, it was, that I searched half a year for. And if it weren't for my powers of observation, I wouldn't have found it either. I'd be searching still. But I excised its eye, didn't I? When I say I'm a man who searches after trifles, you'll know what I mean by it, won't you?"

Escargot nodded sagely.

"Hah!" cried the elf, as if to imply that Escargot's nodding was worth nothing to either one of them. He put the jar back and climbed down off his chair.

"Captain," said Escargot, "there is a grave matter which I'd like to discuss with you if I might. Some few crewmembers of the *Flying Scud*, the galleon you sank off the island yesterday evening, were alive and floating on their dislodged mast. They could still be alive. Your man with the pigtail tells me that they were eaten by sharks, but I find it unlikely that he could be certain of such a thing. Now I have no understanding of your purpose in staving in the side of the galleon, but surely there is no profit in letting those men drift until they slip from their perch and drown. We must find them without delay, sir."

"Sharks is it!" cried Captain Perry, slamming his fist into his open palm. "There's precious little difference, my uninformed friend, between the common oceangoing shark and the thing that walks upright on the land with an eye toward murdering his brothers. No sir, not a thing. They're creatures of a kind, mast or no mast. Drink?"

"Thank you," said Escargot, accepting a snifter of brandy. "What I mean to say . . ."

"What you mean to say is that you understand nothing, sir. Not one blessed thing. My vow is to look upon the faces of men no longer, and it makes little difference to me if the faces sit astride a drifting mast or peer past spectacles in a haberdashery. And you, my fine, drowning gentlemen, must steel yourself for the same fate. Do you follow me?"

"No," said Escargot. "Will you save the lives of those men?"

"What men is that?" asked Captain Perry, giving Escargot a look.

"Why the men off the island! The crew of the *Flying Scud*!"

"Sounds rather like a cow, doesn't it? I haven't seen a cow nor any other land creature for half a lifetime." Captain Perry heaved a sigh and shook his head, as if remembering.

"Listen to me!" shouted Escargot, in a sudden rage. "*Will* you search for those men?"

"Off the island, do you say?"

"Off the filthy island! Afloat on the mizzenmast!"

"Impossible, sir. That island is two score leagues to westward in an ocean vast as the aether. We're bound for islands smaller yet. For islands tiny as the eye of the gummidgefish. And any man that goes to sea on a mizzenmast is a fool and deserves what he gets, which will, if I'm any judge of it, be a deep and watery grave."

Escargot stared at him. The man was obviously mad. He'd sailed all his sense away. Every last pennyworth of it. Humoring him, Escargot could see, would accomplish more than raging would. "Why did you save *me*?"

Captain Perry smiled. "One might suppose that a man committed to warring against all that dwells on land and that ventures out onto the sea is a wicked man, a man without pity and compassion and remorse. But one is an ass. That's the long and the short of it. In you lies the proof. You floated helpless there, adrift, food for the creatures of the sea. And I took pity on you, didn't I? I fed you. And a very nice meal it was. What do you suppose the meat was? Pork shoulder? Veal?''

''One or the other,'' said Escargot.

''Hah! Neither. Shark belly steeped in seawater and dried scrapings from the underside of beach rocks. Clever, these deepwater chefs. And that broth that you consumed by the bowlful—that was bisque of feather crab, the most delicate creature that ever scuttled across the sea bottom. And the bread. Two days ago it swam in the shadows of the great southern shelf, until I caught it in a dragnet and extracted by chemical processes the natural fibre of its skeleton, which, when pulverized, yields a flour so fine that even the most meticulous dwarf baker would blather over it. And do you know who baked it? *I* did; that's who, just as another man, if he was inclined, might wash the feet of a stranger. Humility is my very nature. Humility and regret, my good fellow. Do you know regret?''

Escargot nodded. He looked across at the porthole windows where a great long fish peered in at them. The seawater had lightened. It was morning, apparently, and the ocean was awakening. Leafy strands of kelp wisped past, and a school of silvery fish hovered for a moment without, catching the rays of the watery sunlight, then turning and slipping away astern.

Escargot found himself wishing it was him who had been playing deep and sonorous tunes on the organ, that it was *his* submarine that plied the seas, sounding to black depths, angling up through kelp forests toward the shimmering surface. He looked at Captain Perry, who paced up and down, wringing his hands, still thinking of regrets. It seemed to be a good time to revive the issue of the survivors of the *Flying Scud*, but Escargot hesitated lest he set the captain off again. And if they *were* forty leagues from the island, it would be futile to think that he could sway the captain to such a degree that he would turn the boat around.

Escargot patted his chest. There lay his truth charm in its bag. It had profited him nothing so far. It was time, perhaps, to put it to use. He plucked it out and held it in his hand.

Captain Perry shuddered, as if he'd been struck by a heavy wind. Escargot clamped his teeth shut and waited. The elf staggered, clutching his head and knuckling his brow, moaning like a man tormented by devils. He turned toward the great eye of the narwhal and reeled back shrinking from the thing's horrible gaze. "I'm a tormented soul!" he cried suddenly. "A murderer. There's no crime I haven't committed. It's greed is what it is. Miserable greed. Look at this!"

Captain Perry tore open the lid of a seachest that lay on the floor against the wall. In it was a salad of gold coins and jewels. Upended seashells lay among them, heaped with pearls and gemstones. "Watch this!" cried the captain, and he ran his hands through the treasure, letting rubies and emeralds and pearls slide through his fingers, his eyes glowing with satisfaction and horror, as if a great battle were raging behind them.

Escargot wanted to bait him, to fuel the remorse, but he knew that if he opened his mouth to speak he'd say something about the treasure—admit that he wished it were his own. So he jammed his mouth shut and held on.

Captain Perry stopped suddenly and cast the lid down. He stood up and gasped as if a devil had clutched his throat. "Those poor sods on the mast," he said, tearing at his hair and looking around wildly. "I surfaced under them. That's what I did. I smashed their puny mizzenmast to splinters. They cried out. It was horrible, horrible." He collapsed into the chair he'd been using as a ladder. "The mate was right. Sharks ate them, every one. And I, my good, good fellow, am doomed by it. More than any of them, I'm doomed. You think me an elf, don't you?"

Escargot nodded.

"I thought so once too. But now I believe myself to be a man like yourself, shrunken by years of wickedness. Not another living soul knows that. My diet of fish and weeds has kept my body alive, but my soul has withered like the dried carcass of a sea squirt. I'm a horrible wretch."

Escargot nodded again. He'd have to act. The truth charm had softened the villain up. "There's hope," said Escargot, surprised at himself for saying it, then doubly surprised by its apparent truth. "Abandon this ship. Lead yourself out of its bondage. It's this infernal machine, which I'd very much like to own, that has led to your troubles."

"What's that?" asked Captain Perry, looking at him shrewdly.

"An island, I'd guess," said Escargot, pointing toward the portholes and changing the direction of the discussion.

Captain Perry looked too. There, passing along by them,

was a steep wall of rock across which grew a garden of pink and blue sea fans and water grasses. "You're right. It is an island. Dry land is what it is. I've longed for solid earth beneath my feet for years. All the rest of that was a pose. I cut foolish capers in order to blow myself up. To inflate myself. Have you ever done that?"

"Absolutely," said Escargot. "I believe that you should put ashore here. On this island. You and the rest of your crew. How many crewmembers does it take to operate this vessel?"

"One," said the captain, beginning to weep. "Do you suppose I might? What will the rest think of me? All my philosophies will seem like so much sand, so much dust."

"There's the thin chance they'll respect you," Escargot replied, choosing his words well. There *was* a thin chance, anyway—frightfully thin. "Then a man could pilot such a craft alone?"

"Easily. The ship almost runs itself. It was built by elves, light elves. A child could navigate her in a tub." He gripped his forehead again, bent over, and yanked open the door of a cupboard. He plucked out a cork vest and hauled it over his head. "I'm going to swim for it!"

"Take your men with you, Captain!" cried Escargot, clamping his mouth shut afterward.

"They deserve better than me, sir. They're renegades and pirates, both of them, but it's been me who's led them down the spiraling path of decay. They'll follow me no longer."

"Oh, but they must. They too are the victims of this undersea boat. Aboard her they'll pursue the evil ways. On land, at least, they'll be forced to turn to more honest work. They'll be woodcutters and glassblowers and chimney sweeps. The world will envy them the grime beneath their fingernails, the smudge on their foreheads."

"And me," cried Perry. "What of me? My forehead is indelibly smudged, isn't it?"

"It's a different sort of smudge, my man. The smudge I'm talking about is honest, hardworking smudge. The sort that brings a smile to the face of the old vicar."

"Church! I'll pay a visit there, build a shrine. My crew is my congregation. Shall I keep my organ?"

"We can't get it out through the hatch."

"You're right, of course. But the treasure. That I'll give as a gift. To an orphanage. That's it. To the Maritime League. Compensation is what it is, and nothing less. A man can buy back at least a fraction of his soul.''

''I'm not certain . . .'' began Escargot, but Captain Perry was caught up in the idea, and had begun to drag the chest across the floor toward the companionway.

''I'm as greedy as he is,'' said Escargot, thinking aloud.

''Of course you are. This treasure would mean the end of you.''

''But I want it very badly.''

''There's a home for widowed missionaries in the Isles that wants it more. I'm going to take it there. Now.'' He pulled the chest through the door, then stood still as a heron, a look of puzzlement on his face.

Escargot leaped across waving the truth charm and pushed the chest entirely into the companionway. The look of resolve washed over Captain Perry's pinched face again. There was a fervid, committed light in his eyes. Escargot determined to stay by his side until he was off the ship. If it cost him the treasure, so what? He'd always insisted that he had his code; well here was a chance to exercise it.

The captain pushed his way into the navigation room at the front of the ship. The dwarf with the striped hat sat before the window, piloting the submarine past the island. ''Surface!'' cried the captain, nodding toward Escargot as if to call attention to the solidity of his resolve.

''Yes, sir,'' said the pilot while pushing against a short lever that protruded from a panel before him. The vessel canted up, sailing into the growing sunlight, until with a great swishing and splashing it nosed from the sea, then settled once again with a sigh.

''The sun!'' shouted Captain Perry, as if he were seeing it for the first time in a twelvemonth. The light of it shone through the water-washed windows. ''Enough, by heaven, enough!'' he cried, and with that last confession of remorse clutched the pilot on the back of the shirt and endeavored to haul him from his seat. ''*Follow* me, man!''

''I don't at all know that I want to,'' came the reply. Then the dwarf stood up and cast an eye at the treasure on the floor.

''You can't speak in those tones to your captain,'' Perry blustered. ''I'll have you keelhauled.''

"Aye," said the man agreeably. "Where goes that there chest?"

"Ashore, man. And you with it. Where's Spinks?"

"Aft," came the reply.

"Fetch him up then. We go ashore now. At once."

"Aye, aye. Yes, sir. With the treasure, sir?"

"That's the case entirely. Now fetch Spinks. Roundly!"

The sailor disappeared down the companionway, hollering for Spinks.

"Can't reveal too much of this, can I?" asked the captain, grinning at Escargot. "Already I feel relieved. And the men, I'm certain, will see the truth of it in time."

"They surely will," said Escargot.

The two returned almost at once. It was a crew of three, including the captain. "I want some of that gold," said Spinks instantly.

"Hold your trap shut, man," cried Perry. "There's more than gold I'm a-going to give you. Out the hatch now. Hop to it, lads."

Escargot followed them up, a step behind the pigtailed Spinks. The sun shined over the ocean like midsummer, and off the starboard bow lay a low island, wooded and with a broad stream cutting the beach and a single, high, smoking cone of a volcano rising out of the middle of the forest. The captain probed with a foot midway down the deck of the vessel, and, to Escargot's astonishment, a little trap slid open to reveal a rowboat. "Hoist it over, lads," said the captain, standing by his treasure. The boat, in an instant, floated on the calm sea. Spinks climbed aboard, followed by the dwarf. Captain Perry went over next, telling Escargot to hand the treasure down to them before getting aboard himself.

"I'm not going," said Escargot, the words slipping out before he could get a grip on them.

"What?" Captain Perry looked at him in puzzlement. "You've saved us, man. Save yourself too. Follow me into salvation. These men have." And he nodded at his two companions.

"We didn't do nothing of the sort," said Spinks with a malicious grin. "We're a-going to fetch you ashore and bang your head in, then share this here treasure."

"*I'm* setting in to kill you both," cried the dwarf.

"Animals!" shouted the captain, grappling with Spinks, who attempted to haul himself back up onto the deck of the submarine.

Escargot cast a glance at the island and another at the treasure. He put a foot into Spinks' face and shoved, toppling the pirate over backward into the sea. Then he grabbed the leather handles on either side of the chest, heaved it into the air, and dropped it onto the rowboat. It punched through the bottom like a stone through rice paper, and vanished into the depths. The rowboat foundered, spinning away from the submarine and sinking almost at once beneath the water, where it floated, submerged and useless.

"You can swim to shore easily enough," shouted Escargot at the sputtering trio in the water.

"It's what we deserve!" hollered Captain Perry. But as the submarine drifted seaward and the gap between them grew, the look of intensity on the captain's face played itself out. He peered suddenly at Spinks, as if he'd just then taken off a pair of shaded glasses that had been obscuring his vision. "What the devil?" he said, casting a meaningful glance at Escargot, who had climbed by then halfway through the hatch. As it banged shut above him he heard an impressive string of curses, and caught a brief glimpse of Captain Perry, retired owner of the submarine *Omen*, tearing at his hair as he floated upon the sea, yanking and shrieking as if he would pull himself to fragments.

8

Into the Abyss

A dozen maps and charts lay scattered around the floor of the pilothouse. Escargot regarded them darkly. Navigating the submarine wasn't so very difficult. As Captain Perry had promised, a man by himself could do it, if that man had any earthly idea where he was bound. Reading a compass was easy enough. There was north; here was south; over that way lay north by northwest. But so what? He had needed no destination when he stood on a street corner in Seaside, watching a man spear up sausages with a fork. There was food and drink in either direction, and a man might wander as far as he was inclined, out of the city and into open country; there'd always be a bit of ground for him to sleep on at night. The open sea was a different matter entirely.

By plunging a lever forward he'd descend sharply. By easing off, the submarine would level itself. Another lever activated the rudder, and yet another altered the vessel's speed. There was nothing to it, really, save that one had to be always on the watch for smashing up against a cliffside or for tearing into the rubbery foliage of a kelp forest. One couldn't be map reading or napping or cooking up dinner.

In the first giddy hour following his successful marooning of Captain Perry and his crew, Escargot had sailed back and forth beneath the waves, now surfacing, now diving, chasing schools of fish, and generally learning his new trade in open water. When he stopped to have a look around he was off the same island, some few miles to windward. A breeze seemed to be blowing up, and scattered clouds bumped across the sky. The sea was chopped with little wind waves that tossed to and fro.

The truth charm lay once more beneath his shirt. He could understand at last why Uncle Helstrom had given it up. It was nothing for a villain to own, not unless he'd become so fearfully evil that the truth about himself could no longer make him flinch. It was certainly no wonder that the dwarf had warned him against hauling it out of its bag that night on the meadow. Heaven knew what he would have had to say about his devious plans. All in all, despite the charm having gotten round Captain Perry successfully enough, it wasn't worth much. If there was one thing that a man didn't want to be continually reminded of, it was the truth about himself. It might, however, fetch a considerable sum on shore. And in a pinch a man might set up as a spiritualist of sorts with it, and have moderate success working a carnival crowd or a church meeting.

When he had put it back into its pouch and slung the pouch around his chest, it was as if a rush of voices in his head had fallen abruptly silent, as if he'd been hearing the faint sounds of a distant crowd of squabbling orators, all of them exhorting and warning and reminding and haranguing and generally shaking their fingers and heads. He'd wondered at first if his—what was it?—"borrowing"—of the submarine wasn't an act every bit as loathsome as some of the thefts committed by Captain Perry. And although he worked at priding himself on having pitched the treasure into the sea, one of the voices whispered that what he *probably* intended to do was sail back and retrieve it. But he'd silenced the voices by putting them in a bag, so to speak, and then he had hummed happily around the sea bottom for an hour until the thrill of it wore thin and he began to wonder in earnest exactly where he was going and what he was going to do for supper.

So he surfaced, no great distance from where he'd set out an hour earlier, and with wrinkled maps and charts strewn everywhere. He'd even unfolded the dried-out G. Smithers map—a flowery, extravagant sort of map compared with the more seaworthy charts aboard the *Omen*. It seemed to him that every inch of ocean within a thousand sea miles of the Oriel River delta had been charted, and that it would take a man a lifetime to unroll each and every chart and study them long enough to come to conclusions. He searched among hundreds of islands, though, until his eye picked out one in particular—Toyon Island. It had been double luck that the biscuit sailor had seen fit to put a name on it, and even more luck yet that Escargot had been listening.

He discovered that he could lay the charts out, one beside and above the other, in order to piece together an increasingly larger picture of the top of the ocean. There was Seaside; there were the Isles of the Seven Pirates, clustered off the delta; and there was Toyon Island, a speck on the map some fifty miles beyond that, far enough to be over the horizon and lost on the broad sea. What had Captain Perry said, or had it been Spinks?—that they'd sailed forty miles from Toyon Island. But forty miles in which direction? If it was west, then the volcanic island off the port bow might be one of the Pirate Isles. But then surely another of the same islands would be visible; the air was clear as rainwater.

He tied a bit of string—forty miles worth according to the scale on the map—around his finger, and, covering Toyon Island with his fingertip, drew an imaginary circumference around the gathered maps. Four islands, roughly, fell anywhere near the line. Two of the islands were part of clusters. The island inhabited now by Captain Perry and his men was solitary. A third island was itself nearly twenty miles across, and was dotted with three villages. Captain Perry's island couldn't have been five miles from end to end, and if there were any villages on it, they were lost in the forests of the interior. It had to be the fourth island, a flyspeck on the chart, almost as small as the eye of the captain's gummidgefish. Lazar Island, it was called.

Escargot rooted around in the captain's quarters until he found a pen and ink, then renamed the island on the chart "Captain Perry's Salvation." It seemed to him that the island must have been named by some intrepid explorer or another—somebody named Lazar, probably—who had been dead these long years since and so wouldn't mind if Escargot, setting up as an intrepid explorer himself, meddled with the name.

But as he sat and studied the map it began to occur to him that there was something curiously familiar in it all. It was suggestive, perhaps, of something he'd heard or read. He took a look at the Smithers map. There it was—the Isle of Lazarus.

It was possible, surely, that the two were the same. They sat in the same far-flung corner of the ocean. He folded Smithers in half and carried it along down the companionway, shoving out through the hatch to have another look.

Smoke lazied along from the volcano, soaring straightaway skyward until the wind caught it and drifted it to the south, losing it in cloud drift. The picture on Smithers' map wasn't at all a bad representation, once one got around all the spirally writing and the here-lies-this-and-thats. There were the cliffs along its westward-facing shore. There was the tumble of rock at the far end. And there was the cone of the volcano, slumped and crumbled along one edge as if an earthquake had thrown half the rim into the sea.

It had to be the same island. Why shouldn't it be? Smithers had access to the same charts that cluttered the floor of the pilot room of the submarine. It would have been the most natural thing in the world to merely muck up his own map by glorifying what he had in front of him. Off the end of Smithers' island, in the depths of what must have been an oceanic trench, lay the "door," such as it was, to Balumnia. How there could be a door on the ocean bottom was a mystery, an impossibility. Surely that was where the truth left off and the storytelling started. But then why should it? Smithers seemed to be full of curiosities that at least cast a shadow into the real world, why not another one here?

And what had Escargot to do with his time anyway? Even with his charts, with his certain knowledge that he lay south of here and north of there, there was no one port that attracted him more than the others. He'd certainly have to save his wanderings along the Seaside coast until things had simmered down in that quarter. There was no good reason to stride back in grinning after he'd made such a lucky escape. And it *had* been a lucky escape, all in all. There had been a tight moment or two, but in the end he'd inherited a submarine as well as a great lot of books and a pipe organ, which he couldn't begin to play.

He strode into the captain's quarters and searched out Smithers' books from among haphazardly shelved volumes. Captain Perry hadn't, apparently, given a rap for order of any sort. Escargot had piled forty volumes on the top of the sideboard before he found, finally, buried beneath an account of the culinary practices of the marvel men of the Wonderful Isles, *The Stone Giants*. It appeared to have been unread, as if Perry had bought a job lot of Smithers books, then immediately shoved them into whatever gaps presented themselves in the stacks.

He hauled it back to the bow along with a plate of cold fish and two bottles of ale. His pocket watch had gone to the sea bottom along with his pants, and search as he might, he couldn't discover any sign of a clock on board. But then what did it matter, really, what time it was? In the depths of the ocean day and night stopped amounting to quite so much, and at the moment he was feeling bucked both by the excitement of piloting his vessel and by the possibility, however thin, that the entrance to Balumnia, Smithers' magical land, lay somewhere beneath the waves off the tip of the island.

In moments the submarine slipped under the bright waves and angled toward the west. Escargot navigated slowly, with one eye on the account in Smithers. Smithers was full of descriptions of grottoes lit by enchantment and of sunken cities and vast treasures, but there wasn't more than a handful about whether a navigator ought to angle down into this trench or ought to pop over that heap of rock or ought to be navigating sixty yards to the south beyond the craggy ledge that cut off his view of half the ocean.

So the hours slipped by. Escargot, very soon, decided that he ought to plot a course so as to avoid cruising in and out and around the same bit of sea bottom. He headed due east for the count of eight hundred, then angled around to the north for the count of two hundred, then west, then north again, on and on, wondering at every turn if he mightn't have missed what he was looking for by having counted to two hundred instead of one hundred seventy-five, or one hundred twelve. After hours of it he knew that he'd developed a navigational system that was no real system at all, only a way to trick himself into thinking that he was proceeding very logically and sensibly like a submarine captain might be expected to do.

It must be growing late. He was hungry again. What would he do if he found nothing—no sign of Smithers' enchanted door? He could hardly surface and anchor the submarine off the island, not with Captain Perry and his lot marooned there. They'd swim out in the night and cut his throat. The truth charm wouldn't avail him much—not a second time. And if he simply floated atop the sea, what then? The submarine didn't seem to be the sort of craft that would be satisfied bobbing on the ocean, not in heavy weather, anyway. It seemed to work more like a deepwater fish that slept as it swam.

The color seemed to have gone out of everything, even near the surface—a pretty clear indication that the sun was setting or else had drifted behind heavy clouds. It grew darker and darker until nothing could be seen out the windows beyond the circle of lamplight generated by the fire quartz. Searching became nearly impossible; the bright light of the fire quartz seemed to make the darkness roundabout even more impenetrable. Great fish came looming out of the black water, gaping into the light, then vanished again in an instant. Angular rocks humped up as if to surprise him, and Escargot was forced to shake the weariness out of his head and to remind himself over and over to keep a sharp eye out lest he end his journey once and for all.

He'd long ago stopped counting. That sort of thing couldn't go on forever. The two hundreds had stretched themselves into twice that because he lost count forty times or so and had to start over or at some guessed-at number. The eight hundreds were utterly impossible. So he found himself wandering aimlessly once again. Then, purely by accident, when he supposed himself a mile or more offshore, he hove into sight of the steep side of the island. He was back where he'd begun. It was too late, certainly, to venture out again. He'd have to take his chances with Captain Perry.

He followed the sweep of shoreline around, thinking to run into a bay. There had been one, he remembered, shortly after he'd rounded onto the leeward side of the island earlier that day. Captain Perry and his men had swum ashore to windward, and had, quite conceivably, murdered each other there out of general villainy and idiocy. Certainly, thought Escargot tiredly, they hadn't trudged across the island to the other side. He'd be safe enough. There must be a way to lock the hatch, and they could do him little damage if they couldn't get in.

The rocky sea bottom gave off suddenly into a little, sandy slope. Escargot navigated shoreward, across the ripples of sand on the sea bottom, awakening no end of flatfish and rays. The water brightened a bit, the consequence, perhaps, of moonlight. But it seemed strangely as if the bright water was mostly away to seaward where the slope steepened and fell away into the depths. Unless he was completely turned around and befuddled, the shallow water toward shore was as dark as ever. There was nothing to do but surface and investigate.

He found himself fifty yards offshore. He was in a bay, all right, some quarter mile across. A dark line of rock sheltered it from the sea to the north. There was no moon to be seen, only the silvery lightening of the edge of a great mass of cloud, blown by the wind. Treetops along the shore bent and tossed, and the surface of the bay scudded with little windwaves. All in all the night was dark enough for murder; certainly there wasn't enough moonlight to explain the little patch of illuminated seawater that swirled as if by magic a hundred yards farther out.

And now that he payed particular attention to it, the light was quite clearly emanating from *beneath* the sea, not from the sky. It seemed as if a great chandelier had been lit in a deep-sea grotto. Escargot was reminded abruptly of the jack-o'-lanterns glowing through the fog on the meadow. There would hardly be witches gathered beneath the sea, though. This was something else. It was what Smithers had promised. Of course Escargot hadn't seen it when he'd set out earlier. In the morning sunlight the watery glow hadn't been apparent, at least not to a person who had no idea it was there. He'd passed it at the outset of his search and had been venturing uselessly about the sea ever since, counting his way past it a half dozen times.

He stood gazing at the glow, his head poked up through the open hatch. The wind was fearsomely cold. The trees on the forest edge lashed in the darkness, swishing and moaning. The moon appeared briefly, as if to shout a warning through a rent in the clouds, and then was swallowed utterly, and the night grew doubly dark. A splintering crash sounded along the shore, followed by the solid whump of a tree flattening itself along the beach. It was no night to be anchored on the surface, and it was becoming less so by the moment.

Escargot closed the hatch behind him and strode along back into the pilot's room. He rolled his scattered charts and stowed them away. If he was setting in as captain, he'd best start by making everything shipshape. In ten minutes he was dropping into the abyss, down and down and down toward the source of light that grew brighter, fathom after fathom, until the sea was lit like a tidepool at midmorning.

It was just as Smithers had described it. He could see nothing at first, beyond bright water and bubbles and an occasional drifting fish. Then, in the distance, there were the shadows of rock ledges that grew distinct, vanished, and then leaped again into clarity, as if the trench into which the submarine fell was narrowing. Soon he crept along a rocky precipice on which a whole nation of sea life carried on in perpetual brightness. Oddly shaped fish like sidewise plates and inflated balloons and long bits of stick hovered above the pink and violet branches of corals and sea fans.

The wall was shot through with caverns and grottoes and long cracks into which Escargot might easily have piloted the vessel. It seemed to him entirely possible that through any one of them might lie submarine lands peopled by mermen or by talking fish that lived in palaces. Someday he'd have a look into it all. He'd search through Smithers to see if there wasn't a reference to such places. But for now he'd press on. Whatever it was he searched for couldn't be far below, for the trench threatened to narrow into nothing, and the light had grown dazzling.

The wall of the trench along the port side fell away, revealing a long sort of plateau on which were heaped the ruins of an ancient city: broken columns and toppled statues, all of it wound in waterweeds and covered with sprouting polyps. A thousand nautili darted across the ruins, as if searching for something one of them had lost, and the long, cylindrical shadows of cruising sharks passed over them now and again and then disappeared into the darkness of the ruins. Beyond, where the ledge narrowed again, there was a sprinkling of lights, like starlight bright enough that it shone at midday despite the sun. Escargot hovered along beside them. Fire quartz is what it was.

The trench was shot through with fire quartz, tiny crystals at first, just chips that shone against the darkness of the rock ledge. But as the vessel fell even deeper, the light outside grew even more intense, and quartz crystals thrust from the wall like spikes, casting rainbows of shimmering iridescence as if the crystal itself were dissolving in the seawater.

Escargot slowed and stopped the submarine, allowing it to drift slowly downward. If a man could break off even two dozen such crystals, that man might be able to trade them for—what? Anything. There would be no more bartering for boots and jackets and marbles and pies. He could buy what he chose. He could ride upriver to Twombly Town and buy up Stover and Smeggles and just about anyone else he was inclined to buy and then have them all pitched into the river. There must be some way to accomplish the task. Captain Perry's bottled whale eyes and octopi, after all, must have been harvested from the bottom of the sea. How did Captain Perry go about it? It might, of course, be a little bit mad to attempt any such experiments at such depths as these. But then Escargot wasn't in any terrible hurry. He was just launching out, after all, and here was an indication that he might do much better at the submarine trade than he had any reason to hope for.

He'd dropped past fifty feet of crystal—so much that the fiery gemstones had begun to seem just a bit commonplace—when he saw, waving out from the face of the ledge, a succession of single strands of broad-leafed kelp that seemed to have been secured to the stones not by the fingery holdfasts with which kelp clung to wave-washed rocks, but by rope of some sort, or wire, or thread-like filament. They'd been tied there, it seemed, and were pulled surfaceward by a host of bubbles that clung to the leaves. The strands of kelp seemed to be almost crawling along the face of the ledge, nosing along like eels.

Escargot angled the submarine in for a closer look. It was a curious business, kelp at that depth. And the bubbles themselves seemed to be creeping about, or rather something within them was creeping about. They quite clearly weren't empty. He squinted through the glass, imagining that he heard a distant tinkling sound, like glass windchimes in a feeble little breeze. One of the kelp strands lazied along through the water toward the window of the submarine, as if the kelp were as interested in him as he was in it. It bumped gently against the glass, and a bubble that clung to one of the leaves seemed to hop along toward him, very slowly, elongating itself with each jump, flattening when it touched, then springing back into shape. It edged up against the window, and Escargot found himself looking into the tiny face of a henny-penny man.

The hands of the little man were thrust through the sides of the bubble, as if he wore the bubble as an altogether suit with the pantlegs cut off at the knees, and in one hand he held a tiny rock hammer. He was altogether human, tiny as a field mouse, but with a jowly, elongated face that seemed to owe a good deal to fishy ancestors of one sort or another. And he was clothed. Escargot had always wondered if henny-penny men wore clothes. There was no reason to suppose otherwise, really. Everyone else did. It made it seem about twice as ghastly, however, that the horrible Uncle Helstrom smoked the bones of these poor devils in his pipe. It was like smoking an elf. He'd heard—or rather he'd read in Smithers—that henny-penny men lived in the sea, and that they migrated upriver to spawn, then drifted back down again on leaf boats and on pieces of bark. But he'd had no idea that they mined fire quartz.

Another dozen kelp tendrils lazied along toward him, not drifting on currents, but propelled, somehow, by the tiny men. More bubbles pushed up against the window, looking in. They seemed to be unhappy henny-penny men. There wasn't a one among them who didn't have a scowl on his face. And who could blame them? It was a fearsome life they led, wasn't it? Escargot waved cheerfully. Little men, after all. A person might carry such a thing in his coat pocket and hold conversations with it in his idle hours.

He heard the tinkling again—just the echo of it—tink, tink, tink, very slow and very close. Then another tinkling joined in, and another. They were tapping on the glass of the window, tapping out a greeting, perhaps. Escargot waved again, then sat up horrified in his seat to see a little star-shaped bit of glass chip out from beneath the hammer of the first little man who'd come to investigate him. Three more joined him and set in at the chipped spot, hammering away now in a fury. Escargot slammed the propulsion lever downward, canting away into the abyss. Henny-penny men whooshed topsy-turvy off their kelp leaves and spun round in the sudden current. One, his bubble having burst, clung somehow to the window for a few wild moments, his face pressed against the glass, his hair roiling wildly about his gaping eyes, before he catapulted off and disappeared.

The submarine careered off a jutting rock with a clank that made Escargot wince. He held his breath, fearing that the window might burst and that he'd ripped a hole in the hull, certain that in moments the sea would rush in on him and he'd drown, a victim of vengeful henny-penny men. What in the world, he wondered, did they want to attack *him* for?—savage bunch of little boggers. Did they think he was after their fire quartz? As if they didn't have enough and to spare. Perhaps they thought he was Captain Perry and held a grudge against him from some earlier villainy.

Then he realized that he had his pipe in his mouth. Maybe that was it. They thought he was going to smoke a bowlful of them. The mere sight of the pipe might have set them mad. Perhaps the dwarf had mixed so many of them into his water-weed blend that the entire race lived in fear of being smoked. Stealing their quartz, it seemed, would take a bit of doing, beyond the problem of venturing out of the submarine a thousand fathoms beneath the waves.

There was no time to study it. Something loomed ahead—a vast, domed shadow—a wall perhaps, that would signal that he'd come to the end of his journey, that Smithers was wrong. But it wasn't a wall. It was merely the edge of the broad vein of fire quartz. Beyond was darkness—a shadow so deep and vast that the glow of the gemstones dissipated in it like steam into the sky.

It wasn't solid; it was the vast arch of an open door, and beyond it Escargot could see a jumbled coral reef and a scattering of fish, startled, apparently, to see him suddenly appearing there out of the light. There was something about the darkness of Smithers' door—for that's what it had to be—that seemed to be the product of enchantment, ominous enchantment, as if he might drive into it and simply vanish.

But he'd come too far in the last days to hesitate. He plunged along at full speed. The door seemed simply to disappear, puffo, into nothing. No shadow had passed over the vessel. There had been no moment of darkness. He turned the craft about, and there in front of him, a wash of light from the fire quartz glowing through it, was the dark, arched doorway again, hovering on the sea bottom as if someone had hung black muslin from seahooks. He'd gone through it, whatever it was. It had seemed to have been nothing, and yet the water surrounding the submarine now was lit by sunlight, not fire quartz. But it couldn't be. It must be the middle of the night, and the submarine had been immensely deep.

He was struck with the certainty that he had found exactly that land he'd hoped to find. He was in Balumnia, or at least he was on the bottom of one of the Balumnian oceans. He had to be. He'd certainly gotten to somewhere inexplicable, and there could hardly be such a passel of magical lands lying about on the sea bottom that he'd stumbled into one he hadn't anticipated.

A sea turtle, vast as the side of a house, swam lazily past, paying him no mind, and so Escargot set out to follow him, worrying idly that among all the charts in the ship, there wasn't one that mapped Balumnian oceans. They were all worthless to him. He had quite likely lost himself entirely, and he'd wander round and round in uncharted waters, fishing out of the hatch, unable to find the shadowy door back into his own world, and he'd have to satisfy himself with the knowledge that Smithers had been right again and that Wurzle, regardless how vast his knowledge of salamanders might be, knew nothing of the nature of books.

The sea turtle was quite evidently bound for the surface, and he reached it, with Escargot in his wake, in minutes. The submarine nosed out of the water and settled down onto a rolling, overcast sea. He cast his anchor and pushed out through the hatch, pausing for a moment to breathe the cool, salty air and to pack tobacco into his pipe. He lit the tobacco, puffed once or twice, lit it again, and took a look around. Ahead of him was trackless ocean. He very slowly turned, tired, all of a sudden, of being a submarine captain, and there, humping up on the horizon, was a dark shoreline. If it was an island, it was a vast, low island, for the ends of it were lost in the gray distance. Balumnia; that's what it had to be. Escargot slammed shut the hatch, leaped along the companionway to the pilothouse, and set a course straightaway. He was bound to be in port by nightfall, and to be in the position once again of being able to *choose* his friends rather than falling in among lunatics and murderers by happenstance.

9

At Landsend and Beyond

A great city stretched along the coast. Like Seaside, it wrapped around a shoreline formed by the merging of a river and the sea. The river, however, was several times the size of the Oriel, and the mouth of the delta was a confusion of islands and long, empty sandspits and vast bridges that humped up like the back of a sea serpent, connecting one island to the next. On the shore beyond the last of the islands and bridges was a forest, shady and dark beneath the midafternoon sun, spreading away into the distance and creeping down almost to the rocky beach. It was a wild and uninhabited coastline beyond the city, and long windblown wisps of low cloud, gray-purple in the distant sky, made it seem as if it were the painting of some ancient wildness, and that at any moment a giant might appear, striding along the trackless strand.

Escargot floated some two miles out, a spyglass cocked to his eye. Along the mouth of the delta a dozen fishing boats worked the ocean with nets. A scattering of pleasure boats tilted before the wind, driving along in a cluster toward the city. It mightn't, of course, be a good idea just to go sailing in among them in the submarine. Like the enraged henny-penny men, they might suppose him to be some sort of nemesis, and bang at his submarine with hammers. It was possible even that Captain Perry and his men had ventured into Balumnian waters, playing pirate and then disappearing into the depths. If so, the Balumnians wouldn't be likely to be in a welcoming mood. He'd take a lesson from the entire Seaside fiasco, he decided. Stealth would profit him most.

The fishing boats either clustered together at mid delta or struck out north into the open sea. None sailed south along the forested shore. Escargot, then, angled toward the last few lonesome bridges and surfaced in the still water beneath a vast and stony span. The tide was out. Wide mudflats stretched away up the shore, revealing clusters of oysters in the silty delta sand and scallops on exposed rocks. Floating on the sunny ocean was the shadow of a bridge-tower, the pinnacle of its roof shorn off and a turret on the side crumbled and decayed, as if the city had, years past, held out against an enemy that had stormed the bridge. Escargot had vague memories of such a bridge in Smithers, but in a Smithers he'd read as a boy, for the memory was as decayed and deserted as the bridge-tower above, and it served only to make him wonder once again about the books. Smithers, quite clearly, had been to Balumnia. No other answer would do. And if Escargot was smart, he'd spend a few weeks rereading Smithers, from end to end, since it seemed he was doomed to stumble into mysteries that Smithers in some lost chapter or another had warned of.

He seemed to be comparatively safe there beneath the bridge. Not another living soul was visible—a fact that was unsettling. Why the local fishermen shunned the southern shore was a mystery worth thinking about. It seemed to him that the sooner he learned something about the world he'd found, the less trouble he would fall into. He'd swim ashore and walk into the city, trying to make it seem as if he hadn't strolled in from the south—there was no use arousing suspicion—and, if nothing else, he'd find some way of buying or borrowing a rowboat to replace the one demolished by Captain Perry's treasure.

Entering the city was simple. Unlike Seaside, Landsend hadn't any gates or guards. It was too big, perhaps, to be easily enclosed. There was a ragged seawall that held out the tide along the oceanside, but it was a defense only against the sea. Broad meadows and tidal flats, cut with placid canals and hedgerows of willow, separated the city from the seawall and from scattered fishermen's huts that stood on stilts among the shore grasses. Hulks of rowboats lay gray and rotting and curled through with trumpet flower vines, and here and there a fisherman sat on a tilted stoop mending a net, none of them showing the least bit of surprise as Escargot trudged past smoking his pipe.

The occasional huts gave off into a shantytown of plank lean-tos and tents made of old patched sails. Cooking fires burned beneath cast-iron pots, and a score of ragged children raced and shouted, whacking a wooden ball along between the shanties with curved pieces of driftwood. It wasn't at all cold. In fact the breeze that blew at Escargot's back was a warm breeze, scented with the muddy smell of marshland and the deep, silent smell of warm evening ocean.

Beyond the shantytown was the city proper, a lacework of streets and alleys that ran along down toward the river and the harbor. The houses were two and three stories high, many with wrought-iron balconies that fronted the street, overgrown with bougainvillea and trumpet flower that seemed to grow out of any little bit of ground that presented itself. The streets were cobbled, but the cobbles had been laid a hundred years since and were crumbled and broken. Scree, swept out or washed out of the street, clogged the gutters, and here and there a vine trailed from a silty heap of it, as if one day the entire city, streets and houses and all, would vanish beneath flowering vines. Escargot rather liked it.

He wandered into the first likely looking public house that appeared, one that sat next to a shop, closed for the evening, that advertised herbs, philtres, potions, and surgery. In the window of the shop was a dusty display of coiled snakes in bottles. In front of them was a heap of dried newts, all, it appeared, strung together on thread. A scattering of fish skeletons, decoratively displayed among the dried tendrils and bladders of kelp, completed the display, and in among them, wizened and shrunken but with the tiny rags of a shirt and trousers still clinging to it, was the papery shell of what had once been a henny-penny man. It lay in a glass jar, corked and with a high enough price to make it seem that henny-penny men, in Balumnia anyway, were almost as scarce as they were in the Oriel River Valley, and that they were put to uses equally as odious.

The entire display, however, made it seem to Escargot that, henny-penny men aside, he might quite likely make a living from the sea. That afternoon, while waiting for the sun to descend, he'd found Captain Perry's underwater suit, a loose and rubbery affair—trousers and a waistcoat—entirely seamless, and with an enormous seashell helmet, which had been trimmed and turned so as to screw onto the brass neck ring of the suit, and into which a glass faceplate had been set. A cannister-shaped contrivance hung on the back of the rubber waistcoat and generated air at the pressing of a lever.

The science of the thing was a mystery to Escargot, but no more a mystery than was the mysterious enchantment that drove the submarine itself. He'd decided to trust to the apparatus of the vessel when he'd marooned Captain Perry and launched out. He might just as well take the underwater suits into the bargain. It wasn't worth looking too sharply at elfin marvels anyway. In Smithers, at least, they sprang as often as not from a handful of crystalline elf silver, a spray of emerald dust, and an incomprehensible incantation mumbled in the middle of a lot of wild-eyed hurrying about by elves who had forgotten their lunch or their hat or what exactly it was they were building that morning. Elves, for the most part, were a frivolous lot, who went in for larks as much as for any sort of seriousness, and, if Smithers could be believed, their inventions ended in spectacular muddled failure as often as in success. Fortunately, Captain Perry and his men had tried the suits out more than once and had lived to spend the treasure they'd accumulated—or at least to watch it sink to the sea bottom.

Escargot was halfway through a stewed chicken when into the tavern stepped a thin, bearded man in a robe. He'd come through a door that opened in the connecting wall between the tavern and the herb emporium. His robe was tied round the middle with a length of hempen rope, and a little cluster of bird skulls hung at his waist, rattling as the man walked. His beard was of the pointy sort, laboriously cut and combed, but hardly worth having for all the work it obviously required to keep it in trim. The man's nose resembled the fleshless beaks of the birds that hung from his waist, and his eyes were dark and sunken from too much poring over ancient tomes in the lantern light. He seemed to want very much to seem worldly-wise and mysterious, as if he engaged in mystical hocum that the common man only heard dark rumors of. But the effect was ruined by his hair, which had been greased back in a gray hump, as if he'd gotten out into a stiff winter wind and his hair had been blown back and frozen there. He ran his hand over it nervously, patting it into place even though it didn't need patting. Mussing it, Escargot decided, would have profited him more.

He called for a pint from the tavern keeper in a voice that was too loud and too hearty, and he quaffed off an inch of the ale with a great smacking of lips, as if it took a man like him to *really* appreciate a glass of ale. Then he held the glass up to a lantern, examining it, squinting his eyes. He took another gulp, smacked his lips over it again, and declaimed a half dozen lines of loud poetry—his own, quite clearly.

Escargot noticed that scattered patrons cast looks at each other, as if they'd tolerated such a show any of a number of times before and had failed to be impressed. Escargot himself didn't much go in for heartiness. He distrusted it like he distrusted any sort of flamboyant emotion. Talking to the man would be tiresome. He drank up his ale, picked the last few bits of oily meat from the bones of the chicken, and then stepped across to where the robed man stood orating in a too-loud voice to a small tired man who looked about ready to collapse from the conversation.

"A pint of ale for my two friends here," said Escargot to the tavern keeper, "and one for myself, thank you." The robed man stepped back and squinted at him in suspicion, but rushed for the ale when it was sloshed down onto the counter. The second man picked up his glass, tipped his hat to Escargot, and fled, searching out a table in a dim, distant corner.

"I haven't had the pleasure, Mr. . . . ?"

"Escargot. Theophile Escargot, of Twombly Town."

"Where was that?" asked the man, squinting again as if suspicious that Escargot were fabricating things.

"Distant place," said Escargot quickly. He'd forgotten himself already. Twombly Town didn't exist in this world. He'd have to mug up a map in order to find a reasonable place to be from. Place names on Smithers' maps might be risky—only half authentic like Lazarus Island.

The man eyed Escargot, waiting.

"That's two and six," said the tavern keeper suddenly, swabbing at the counter with a dirty rag.

"Of course," said Escargot, hauling out a scattering of coins. He handed a gold sovereign to the publican and turned back to the herb merchant.

"What's this?" came the publican's voice in his ear, a bit

louder than it had been a moment before. "We don't want none of this trash, do we?"

Escargot looked at him and grinned. "What trash?"

The man dropped the coin onto the bar where it spun to a stop.

"Gold," said Escargot.

"Is that it? What kind of gold? Who's this fat bogger on the front, some kind of joke?"

"King Randolf of Monmouth," replied Escargot, understanding as he said it that the information would cause him more trouble than it would solve.

"You ever hear of such a thing?" asked the publican of the robed man.

"Not entirely," he said, coughing into his fist. "That is to say, not in recent memory. Let me see it."

The publican handed it across and watched while the herb man scrutinized it officiously. The man shoved the coin into his mouth and bit it, wincing just a little, then hauling it back out. "Highly doubtful," he said at last, shrugging his shoulders as if sorry to have been forced to come to such a conclusion.

"That's two and six," said the publican again. "Now."

"That's the best I can do," said Escargot truthfully. "There's nothing doubtful about the coin. It's gold through and through and it's worth a dozen stewed chickens and change left over."

"I don't want no foreign coins, mate. I don't want no foreigners neither. King Who-is-it! It's two and six I want or I'll sweep the floor with your head."

"Come now. Buckeridge, my good fellow. We shouldn't take on so, should we?" The robed man laid a hand on the publican's wrist, and the wrist was immediately jerked away. "The coin is doubtful, perhaps, but this man's integrity might be sound. Let me pay the two and six. Out of my own pocket. There it is, Buckeridge—two and six and a penny for yourself, my man. No, let me pay you for two more pints. I can scarce afford it, but I can lighten up the rest of the week. Dry bread and the rinds of old cheeses will suffice for supper."

The publican gave the man a disgusted look, then gave Escargot a disgusted look, then took the man's coins and turned back to his rag.

"Very provincial, these tavern keepers," said the man to

Escargot after they'd found a table. "Great mistrust of foreigners. There's been trouble, you know, down south. And upriver there's been no end of upheaval and ruination. Ships scuttled, robbers on the high road. All that sort of thing. Heaven knows Landsend is full of strangers, but they're mariners, mostly, and come from lands on the map. Yours isn't on the map, is it?"

"Of course it's on the map," said Escargot. "But it doesn't amount to much. Very small. A few cabins and a general store. It's a metalsmith across the mountain who mints the coins. It didn't strike me when I came down that there'd be any trouble with them, but I can see now that I was wrong. They're gold, though, like I said."

"Of course they are. They aren't in the least doubtful, actually. I thought it best to step in there. Buckeridge is too quick with a truncheon, to tell you the truth, so I wanted to avoid prolonged discussions and accusations and such that might work him up. Pay the man his two and six, I said to myself, even though it's dear to you, and your man with the odd coin will be happier for it. Another man's happiness, I've always felt, is to be valued as much as your own."

Villain, Escargot thought, eyeing the herb merchant. The truth charm, if he were to pull it out of its pouch, would convince the man to sing a different tune. But perhaps there was no call for that. Perhaps a certain amount of pitching in and playing along was what was called for here. He'd been hoodwinked by smooth talk before. That wouldn't happen again. "So you own the herb and philtre shop next door, do you?" he asked of the man.

"That I do. I've owned it for years, and trade with all manners of men. It's not, alas, a profitable business, for it deals as often as not with things of the spirit, things that can't be bought or sold for gold coins."

"The fish in the window, and the kelp—get those hereabouts? Easy to come by, I imagine, living on the ocean like this."

"Oh, vastly more difficult than you'd suppose. Just any sort of fish won't do. Deepwater specimens, of course, fetch the most money, but they're scarce. And the lilac kelp in the window. There's not a hatful of it in Landsend. It's worth a fortune to the right man."

Escargot scratched his forehead, arched his brow, and said,

"What if I told you I could put you in the way of six hatfuls of the kelp?"

"I'd say you were a man with a vivid imagination. Lilac kelp grows at sixty fathoms. That in the window was combed from twenty-eight miles of beaches.

"I can have it by day after tomorrow."

The herb man began to squint again. He shrugged. "I believe you," he said. "You have one of the twelve honest faces. Bring it round, then, and we'll do a spot of business. There's a man staying at the Vance Hotel on Royal Street who will buy the lot if it's fresh enough. But he moves quickly; we've got to get it to him by Sunday at the latest."

Escargot blinked at him. "I've been on the road," he said, "for a week and a half. The days just slide by. You know how it is. I'm afraid I've rather lost track."

"It's Friday."

"Of course it is!" cried Escargot, and he struck his forehead as if marveling at his own foolishness.

"What will you do for coin in the meantime?"

"I don't know," said Escargot. "I haven't had time to give it any thought."

The man rummaged beneath his robe. After a moment he stopped rummaging, as if, try as he might, he couldn't find a thing worth removing. He shook his head. "I wish I were in a way to help you more, my friend, but, as I said, the herb trade isn't as lucrative as one might think. I have almost nothing." And with that he rummaged again and hauled out his coin purse. Escargot half expected to see moths fly from it when he pinched it open. There were three coins inside. "I can give you these," he continued, "which ought to carry you across until we meet again. If you'll trust me with your coin, I'll see what I can do to get you a fair exchange. Heaven knows they'll fleece you if they get the chance. I'm an old hand at it though. I see a lot of foreign coin, as I say, and I've got certain connections, if you follow me."

"Of course," said Escargot. He eyed the man for a moment, fearing that if he turned over his coins they'd go the way of his marbles. But they weren't worth much, after all. They wouldn't even buy him a stewed chicken. They'd nearly gotten him beaten up, hadn't they? And this robed man—unlike the situation with Uncle Helstrom, at least Escargot knew how to find the man again. There was his herb shop, after all. If he played Escargot false, Escargot could at least have the satisfaction of taking it out of his hide. He hauled out his own pouch and handed over most of his coins, saving three sovereigns on the off chance that he'd find himself in the near future back in the land of Seaside and Twombly Town. The robed man gave him three thin coins in return.

"I'll do what I can," promised the man, dumping the handful of gold into his purse and stowing the thing once again in his robe. He smiled broadly at Escargot, favoring him with a look of trust and compassion.

"Two more pints here," said Escargot to the innkeeper who swabbed a nearby table, and he thrust out one of the three coins. The innkeeper squinted at it, then plucked it out of Escargot's open palm, satisfied, apparently.

"That's the spirit!" said the robed man heartily, happy to be stood to a pint regardless of how the pint was to be payed for.

Escargot wondered at first whether the innkeeper might demand more. He had no idea what the coin was worth, in terms of pints, and was relieved to get change back with the ale. The innkeeper plunked the glasses down and dropped four coins onto the tabletop—broad copper coins stamped with the likeness of what appeared to be an ape. The transaction had netted him another pint, but it hadn't given him much information about the coins, since he had no idea what the coppers were worth.

An hour later he trudged back out along the sea road carrying bread and cheese and a chunk of ham, and having spent half his money. By the day after tomorrow he'd be on his way to becoming a comparatively wealthy man, if this fellow at the Vance Hotel on Royal Street was ready to pay a fortune for a hatful of lilac kelp. He'd sailed through a stand of it a mile offshore, and it oughtn't to be impossible to find it again, either that or another patch, and hack off a shipload of it.

At the base of the third bridge was tied a scattering of coracles and canoes, pulled well up onto the shore. Escargot studied them from atop the bridge. There was enough moonlight for him to be sure that no one tended the little flotilla, unless, of course, they were far back in the shadow cast by the span.

But that didn't seem likely, so Escargot stepped down a stone stairs that wound round to the foot of the bridge.

"Hello!" he called cheerfully, and in a loud enough voice to awaken any sleeper. There was no one there. A dozen scurrying crabs fled away at the sound of his voice. Water lapped at the stones of the bridge, and in the pale starlight Escargot could see the humped tracks of moonsnails cutting the mudflats in little interlacing ridges. He found a coracle with oars slid beneath the thwarts. It wasn't worth much, as boats went, and could use some scraping and some tar. The back thwart was cracked through and the oarlocks were rusted. That made it easier, certainly, to borrow it. He would leave something in return—one of Captain Perry's sea creatures, perhaps, or a pair of the captain's shoes. But his shoes were too small, actually, to do anyone any good. Escargot would think of something.

Of course it might easily be that the boat's condition indicated that it was owned by a poor man, a man who hadn't the means to own a newer craft, who hadn't enough, perhaps, to keep his meagre boat in repair. Borrowing a boat from a man like that wouldn't entirely do, regardless of what he left as payment. He looked around and straightaway found the sort of craft that would answer—a freshly painted boat with a carved pig as a fiddlehead. It was worth vastly more than the first boat, but borrowing it was less awkward, all in all, since the man who owned it was quite clearly a man of means.

Escargot untied the boat, tossed the line into the bow, and pushed it out into the shallows, then hopped aboard and rowed out from beneath the bridge, the boat humping up over the little dark swells that rolled in to sigh on the shore. Hauling payment back before morning would be a tiresome business, but there was his code to think about. He'd find something adequate—more than adequate. Maybe the eye of Captain Perry's gummidgefish—that and the whale eye both. Whoever had owned the boat would possess the greatest and the smallest fish eyes in the sea. He could retire on that, perhaps tour the coastal cities in a cart, displaying the relics. He'd be a happy man, all in all, when he found his boat gone.

The next day but one, Escargot rowed north along the shore again, toward the city. In the bottom of the coracle lay a sizable basket of lilac kelp, moist beneath a layer of wet rags. If it was fresh kelp the man wanted, it was fresh kelp he would have, and at a price that would satisfy him. Escargot's journey on the sea bottom had been a simpler matter than he could have wished.

The rubber suit with its seashell helmet and aerator box had been nothing to don and doff, and the only anxious moment had come when Escargot had turned the taps and flooded the little antechamber with seawater. The leaden soles of his boots clamped him to the deck, and he could do nothing but stand there transfixed as the dark ocean swirled up around his knees. What if his helmet should leak? What if the seal at the neck was imperfect? He had regretted in a rush that he hadn't put the suit on and submerged himself in a tub of water by way of trying it out. But it was too late for such thoughts, and he found himself, suddenly lightened, stepping out through a circular trap and landing in a little spray of sand on the sea bottom.

At first the rushing of air in his helmet and the press of cold seawater against his rubber suit had been bothersome reminders that there was little between him and a watery grave. But the suit didn't leak, and though the air smelled tinny and damp, it breathed just like any other air, and Escargot found himself eighty feet beneath the surface, looking out at a vast garden of lilac kelp, shoulder high and undulating melodically in the soft current. Among the holdfasts crept chambered nautili and sea lemons, grazing on the kelp. The colors, muted by the depth, were ultramarine and violet, and a hundred feet or so away they faded to shadowy green where the seawater, finally, was obscured by distance.

He could have harvested kegs of lilac kelp, but he quickly determined that such a thing would be foolhardy. Here was a man's livelihood, after all, waiting on the sea floor to be plucked up and put in a basket. If the man at the hotel was desperate for kelp, why Escargot would oblige him—half a day would do it. If kelp wasn't in that sort of demand, then he wouldn't have gathered a mess of worthless vegetation only to have to dump it overside when it began to smell.

So it was with the air of a man who had newly stumbled upon success that he rowed north along the shore, bound for Landsend. He was vaguely troubled by the idea that the man who he'd traded the coracle out of might catch a glimpse of him and try to make an issue of the transaction. The best thing, perhaps, would be to seek the man out, and pay him for the boat with the profits from his latest venture. He'd let the man keep the eye of the gummidgefish, of course, into the bargain. Call it interest. He could afford to be generous.

Things were looking up. Here he was with a basket of kelp. It might as well be a basket of money, after all. And the herb man, whatever his name was, owed him for the gold too. Who could say what the profits of all this transacting mightn't finance? Kelp, certainly, couldn't be the only profitable crop on the sea bottom. He mused on for a bit, imagining the wealth that lay scattered in the oceans, waiting for a man like him to sail in and take it.

Then he thought suddenly of Leta, burning atop the pyre in Seaside and his happy thoughts were spoiled. He knew, and *had* known for the past week, that he had come to the end of nothing in Seaside. There was something in him that was dissatisfied with loose ends, with unsolved mysteries, and he felt suddenly as if he were living in a house with one wall unfinished, and that even though he sat in a chair facing the three finished walls, every once in a while he'd glimpse out of the corner of his eye, when he turned his head just so, the unplastered posts and beams of the half-constructed wall.

It was a bothersome business, this Uncle Helstrom nonsense, and he knew that he was better off rid of it. If he was. Somehow he wasn't rid of the image of Leta's face, which had become clearer over the past days rather than fading. He felt, when he thought about it, that he'd let someone down, that he'd failed in some way that he couldn't at all explain, that he wasn't the only innocent party involved in the mystery, and that he'd been so anxious to save his own fleeing hide that he'd given little or no thought what the whole business implied. Heaven knew, though, what it *had* implied. He honestly hadn't been given much opportunity to find out.

He ran the coracle up onto the shore below the shantytown, hauling it into the midst of half a dozen other boats, and set out into town. The herb emporium was dark. The same dusty debris cluttered the window, and it seemed, when he peered in past it, as if it were impossible that the store had ever been illuminated, that it had ever seen any customers besides mice and bugs. Escargot pounded on the door, then pounded again. He tried the knob, but it wouldn't turn.

He stepped into the alehouse next door carrying his basket of kelp. The tavern keeper slouched against the bar, his chin on his hands. He didn't seem happy to see the door open. "Say," said Escargot to the man and laying his basket on a table, "when is the herb store open?"

"Next door?"

"That's right. Next door."

"About two weeks."

"Excuse me?"

"Two weeks. He's out of town on business. Gone upriver after some sort of weed. He's *supposed* to be back in a couple of weeks, but don't wait up for him. Last time he was a month late. He don't care. He don't have no business anyway."

Escargot felt his stomach sink. This, quite clearly, couldn't be the case. "When did he leave, yesterday?"

"No." The man shook his head, cocked his head down, and spat past his shoulder onto the floor behind the bar. Escargot blinked at him. "Been gone for days—nearly a week."

"The tall man, in the robe. With the hair?" said Escargot, brushing his own hair back in an effort to ape the style of the man he'd given all his gold to. "The man with the bird skulls on a rope?"

"Oh, him. *He* don't own the shop. He don't own nothing. That's your man's cousin. I don't know where he is and I don't care to. Nothing but trouble in a nutshell, if you want the truth of it."

"He *said* he owned the shop," Escargot insisted, but knowing that he'd been taken once again.

"I don't wonder. He thinks he owns just about everything, and if he can get his hands on it he does, too."

"I gave him a good bit of gold coin—you remember it—and he promised to exchange it for local coin. So if he lives near here I'd like to know."

"You gave him gold coin, you say?"

"Almost all that I had."

"Expensive lesson then," said the tavern keeper, swabbing away at the counter and grinning. "It's drank up by now—and you can quote me on that—and spent in one of the houses up in Fern Hill."

"Fern Hill?" asked Escargot. "Where's that?"

"I'd leave Fern Hill alone," said the man, shaking his head.

''You won't find him there anyway. A man don't spend but one night at a time up on the hill, and knowing your man Kreslow he spent all the gold you gave him just about that fast. You're wasting your time is what I'm saying. You're from outside, ain't you?''

''That's right,'' admitted Escargot.

''Then you fell in straight off with the wrong man. That's the long and the short of it. If I was you I'd move along. There's work enough down toward the harbor, if you've a mind for work. Be happy you didn't lose the gold at the end of a knife. There's plenty around here who has.'' With that the man fell silent and set in to wiping out pint glasses, eyeballing the bottom of each before setting them upside down on a shelf behind him.

''Which way to Royal Street, then?'' asked Escargot.

''Three streets up, mate.'' The man shook his head tiredly, as if resigned to the foolishness of travelers like Escargot who failed to take a man's advice. Escargot walked along back toward his boat, mulling over this latest defeat. The needle of luck had swung round the other way; there was no denying that. The man in Royal Street was probably a lie, cooked up to lend some detail to the general fabrication. On the other hand, maybe he wasn't. And if he wasn't, then what did Escargot need a middle man for anyway? He could sell the kelp to the man himself and keep all the profits. The loss of his gold wouldn't amount to so very much then, would it?

He found himself on the outskirts of the shantytown when he finally had his mind made up. He'd return to town and find the Vance Hotel. He hadn't any idea what the man's name was, but he could go from door to door—pretend to be a vendor of some sort. Perhaps he ought to go back to the ship and work up a disguise or dress a bit more like a merchant. He'd bring around a gift for the manager of the hotel; that's what he'd do. It might quite likely save him from being tossed out onto the road.

When he heard the lapping of the ocean on the shingle he looked up, realizing suddenly that for the last mile he'd been gazing continually at the toes of his boots as they swung along beneath him. Three men stood in the little cluster of boats, watching him, it seemed. One had his hand on the pig fiddlehead, not as if it were resting there, but as if it were laying claim to it. "Damnation!" Escargot said to himself, forcing his feet to continue, steady on, toward the three. He'd brass it out, that's what he'd do—claim he'd bought the boat from a man in town. The robed man, what was his name? Kreslow, that was it.

He glanced up at the men, forty feet away now, and grinned. They didn't grin back. One, he could see, carried a truncheon. Another had his hand inside his shirt. The man with his hand on the fiddlehead hadn't any weapon, but he was the size of a wagon—and not a dogcart, either, but a coach. His mouth was bent over almost sideways as if he'd been trying to chew up an entire stalk of celery and gotten it jammed into his cheek. It was the look of a man, Escargot thought, who had something stuck in his craw.

They weren't police, that much was certain. Escargot stopped and pretended to examine the sole of his shoe. The entire affair was monstrously plain. The big man owned the boat and hadn't been happy with the gummidgefish eye. He was hardly likely to believe that Escargot intended to look him up and share with him the nonexistent proceeds from his basket of weeds. They were going to beat him silly, that's what they were going to do—Kreslow or no Kreslow. What did they care for Kreslow? Nothing.

Escargot lowered his foot to the pathway, turned on his heel, and bolted, the sound of running footsteps behind him lending him a certain amount of energy. He was through the shantytown in moments, pounding along toward the alleys that skirted the city. He glanced over his shoulder. They were shouting and roaring, stomping along waving their hands. Gathering behind them was a knot of shantytown dwellers, who shouted in chorus, racing at the men's heels. Cries of "Murder!" and "Thief!" rang out as Escargot ducked away down the first alley he came to, praying that it didn't dead end.

The alley wound sharply upward, and although Escargot could hear the sound of pursuit, he was invisible from his pursuers beyond a curve of wooden fence. He heaved along, breath tearing out of his throat, the cries diminishing behind him. He held the basket against his chest and wondered if he shouldn't throw it away. His own greed, it seemed, would be the end of him. But he held onto it. He'd lost too much already to be hasty. And if worst came to worst he could always pitch it at the mob, who, like the goblins along the river Oriel, would likely fall upon it and leave the chase to the three bullies.

Ahead was the carcass of a flatbed wagon with only one wheel, the bed canted over on its axles, facing the alley. He angled across, counting on the mob's being far enough behind him, and in three leaps pitched his basket over the fence beside the wagon, vaulted up the sloped bed, and flung himself after the basket, coming down in a tangle of fern. He scooped up the basket and scuttled across the lawn, creeping in under vines in a corner where he wheezed for breath, his hand over his mouth, certain that they'd hear through the fence his heart laboring and his lungs inflating. The sound of the mob surged toward him, led by particularly heavy stomping, then surged away again. If he was lucky the alley would wind along for miles. He hunched out from beneath his vines and made for the street, preparing to run again if the owner of the house caught sight of him. He was too winded to think of any lies.

The Vance Hotel loomed above the rest of the Royal Street residences. It was four stories high—a white painted building of cornices and columns and corbels and great mullioned windows wreathed in flowering vines. A man in a tight red suit opened the door for a woman who, despite the warm afternoon, wore a fur coat, and whose husband followed along behind her, his face pinched into a countenance of perpetual condescension. The red-suited doorman shut the door in Escargot's face, giving him a look that suggested that Escargot was most likely lost.

"Excuse me," said Escargot, realizing all of a sudden that his clothes were a rumpled mess because of the chase. He was sweating, too, after the exertion of it, and his pantleg bore the stains of the ferns he'd slid through. "This *is* the Vance Hotel?"

The man stared at him.

"I mean to say, I've need of a room. For the night. Nothing too delicate, you understand. Something with a view, though."

The man pursed his lips and shook his head, not in such a way that it seemed he was denying Escargot a room, but as if he simply wasn't in the mood for jokes, however well intended. A gentleman with a pince-nez approached, having stepped out of a hansom cab with a dog the size of a pony. "Stand aside, sir!'' said the doorman in a stage whisper. And the man from the cab pushed past, dusting at his sleeve when it brushed Escargot's basket. The kelp, it seemed, had somehow sloshed itself over the side, past the rags. It had begun to ripen in the heat. Escargot jammed it back in and covered it up, smiling weakly at the doorman and shaking his head. ''Very nutritional,'' he said, ''kelp.'' Then, seeing that things had once again gone awry, he turned and strode away down the street.

He stood in the shadows of a shuttered house across the way for an hour before the doorman disappeared, then he sprinted to the hotel before another officious guard took the first man's place. Inside was a tremendous, high-ceilinged lobby, overgrown with potted plants and carved mouldings and heavy pastel carpets thrown higgledy-piggledy about the marble floors. His basket was almost wondrously odorous, as if he were hauling an overheated tidepool along behind him in a wagon. People turned to scowl at him as he skirted wide of the long counter and headed for the stairs.

The futility of the whole business was apparent. There probably wasn't anybody at the Vance Hotel who was interested in lilac kelp in the first place. That must have been a lie. And if there was, what then? There must be two hundred rooms in the place. The hotel stretched on for half a block. What in the world, he asked himself, was he doing there besides wasting his time? He could put out to sea tomorrow and collect no end of rare seashells to hawk to perfectly reputable curio shops in the harbor. But here he was chasing down a will-o'-the-wisp that was a product of a man who'd swindled him.

He trudged up the stairs to the second floor. He couldn't just knock on a door, could he? He'd be out in a moment. He could claim in a surprised tone to have knocked on the *wrong* door if whoever opened it didn't look like the sort who would be interested in kelp. But what would such a person look like anyway? Like Professor Wurzle, frazzled and rumpled? The third floor loomed into view. He strode across the landing and up the stairs toward the fourth, thinking to get as far away as possible from the lobby.

At the top lay another landing that opened on either side onto a long hallway. In front of him and across the back of the landing itself stood a pair of glass doors, thrown back, letting in the warm afternoon breeze. Standing before them, leaning against a balcony rail with his back to Escargot, was a dwarf in a long coat. Smoke billowed above his slouch hat. Escargot walked toward him with a slackening step. The fragrant reek of pipesmoke wafted toward him on the breeze through the window. It smelled just a bit like the kelp in his basket and just a bit like the ground bones of henny-penny men. The dwarf turned and squinted at him, cocking his head. Then he took his pipe out of his mouth and looked harder. Escargot gaped back, dropping his basket of kelp to the floor. It was Abner Helstrom who stood before him, dressed in tweed trousers and a necktie fixed to a ruffled shirt with a stickpin, the pin crowned by what was either a cleverly carved bit of ivory or a miniature human skull.

10

Along the Tweet River

Escargot couldn't speak. Nothing in the world could have prepared him for this—not even Smithers. Even if he could speak, what would he say? Would he ask for his marbles back? Would he ask after Abner Helstrom's niece? The dwarf, it seemed, was no more inclined toward speech than was Escargot, and he returned Escargot's look gape for gape, puffing furiously on his pipe so that his head was enveloped in smoke.

"There he is!" came a voice from up the hall, and two men hurried toward them, the first one being the red-suited doorman, who seemed intent upon pitching Escargot into the road. The man with him wore a similar suit. "Is he bothering you, sir?" asked the doorman of Uncle Helstrom.

"That's exactly what he's doing," said the dwarf. "He's got some filthy thing in his basket there, a dead thing, I believe. It smells awfully."

"Take the basket," said the doorman to his associate.

"Not a bit of it," cried Uncle Helstrom, snatching the basket up from the floor. "I'll just take this myself—as evidence, won't I? Some sort of kelp, it looks like. Quite conceivably poisonous. I'm a naturalist, you know. I'll have this analyzed. The hotel will hear from my solicitor within the week. Meanwhile, see this gentleman out." The dwarf peered beneath the rags, then looked up and winked at Escargot as the two hustled him toward the stairwell, walking along beside him till he was out the door and on the sidewalk. He headed south on Royal Street toward the harbor, his boat gone, his kelp stolen, and his hopes stove in and sinking in deep water. But the embarrassment at the hotel was forgotten in half a block, and his money and kelp along with it. There were far more pressing and peculiar issues to confound him.

Abner Helstrom, for instance. Thank heaven he had been surprised. That signified, certainly. If he *hadn't* been, what then? What if he had *expected* Escargot to arrive? What would Escargot do then? Life on the sea bottom? There'd be nothing for it but to return to Twombly Town and apply to Beezle for a job washing windows. The expression on the dwarf's face had been genuine, though. He'd mustered the wink, finally, but it had taken him a good while to come up with it.

All of that, of course, meant that the dwarf hadn't been expecting such company, and that Escargot had stumbled into a monumental coincidence of some sort. All in all it was a turn for the better. For weeks he'd been in the grip, or so it had seemed, of Uncle Helstrom—harried out of Twombly Town, chased about the streets of Seaside. Now it was Escargot who loomed out of nowhere to confront the dwarf. It must have given him a certain amount of pause, turning around to see Escargot striding toward him. Damnation! If only he'd had a look of determination on his face. If only he hadn't been so apparently surprised to see the dwarf standing there. If only he'd managed the wink first, for heaven's sake. But he hadn't.

This, certainly, wasn't the end of anything. Things were afoot, it seemed. It was inconceivable that Uncle Helstrom was simply in Balumnia on holiday, and that the marble business and the witch in the alley weren't part of some big, unfathomable affair. Where had Leta gone? One moment she sat atop the pyre, and the next she vanished. And here was Uncle Helstrom, wasn't he? Things were afoot all right, and Escargot, no longer in the kelp business, was bound to follow them. He hadn't anything else to do. He crossed Royal Street to a sidewalk cafe, sat down at a table in the shade, and spent the last of Kreslow's coins on a pint of ale.

Abner Helstrom appeared on the sidewalk opposite a half hour later, striding along at a good clip, as if he was on his way to somewhere in particular. Feeling like a detective, Escargot drained his glass, stood up, cast an appraising squint up and down, and followed the dwarf on the cafe side of the street, keeping as much as possible in the shadows, which were long and deep, since the afternoon was fast declining into evening.

The dwarf didn't appear to be at all worried about being followed. And why should he? He'd have to suppose that Escargot's sudden appearance was nothing more than coincidence. But coincidence or no, it had put the fear into him. Perhaps, thought Escargot, a man like Helstrom was so full of plots and machinations that he naturally assumed that everyone else was too. Who would be more suspicious of others than a guilty man?

It was night when Abner Helstrom reached the harbor. The sky had been swept clean by a soft wind off the ocean, and a nation of stars shined overhead, crowding each other for space. The sea lay dark and silent with here and there the shadow of a moored boat riding atop it, one or two of which had lights cheerfully aglow in their cabins, as if their owners slept aboard at night. Away east toward the open ocean the long arch of the first of the thirteen bridges shone in patchy lantern light cast from stone lamps atop the bridge.

The harborside was a warren of decaying buildings, clapboard warehouses, canneries, and old, turreted mansions that had seen their day and had been let out to rats and cats and lodgers down on their luck. Many houses sat atop pilings, the sea lapping in beneath them. Running out to sea were broken-down piers, some no more than a dozen or two sinking pilings with here and there a mossy, barnacled timber attached with rusty bolts. The smell of fish and tar and dry seaweed washed across the evening—not a bad smell, altogether, although somehow it lent the creaking darkness of the place a musty sort of soul that made it far more threatening there in the moonlight than it would have been in the light of day.

Escargot hunched along, his hands in his pockets, vaguely unsettled by the neighborhood. He watched the dwarf a half block ahead, and he stopped once, ducking back into the shadow of a decayed stoop when his quarry paused for a moment and turned suddenly around, as if he'd heard the echo of following footsteps. He went on, though, crossing over to Escargot's side of the street, stopping in front of a tilted, darkened house, and glancing again up and down the road. Escargot watched from his doorway, determined to follow the dwarf into the house, but wishing that he had a candle with him, that and the club he kept promising himself he'd acquire.

He stepped up to the recessed entryway of the building and

peered in through the crack where the door had been left ajar. There was no closing it, in fact, since the entire house had sheered sideways over the years, the foundation sinking in the wet, sandy soil of the harborside. There was scarcely a window in the front of the house left unbroken, and what had once been an elegantly carved frieze between floors had been disfigured by years and years of hard weather and salt air and had cracked and fallen away so as to expose here and there darkened wall studs and wood lath. No one, certainly, could be living in the place aside from tramps or criminals.

He listened at the open door. There was the sound of mumbling within—people talking secretly, perhaps, in a nearby room, or as easily, people talking openly farther along, in the second story or in a back kitchen. The door pushed open with hardly a creak, and Escargot stepped in on tiptoe. Moonlight, enough to see by anyway, shined in through dirty windows. The mumbling continued, and then a shuffling of feet.

A ruined stairway angled away into the darkness of the upper floor, and Escargot debated climbing it, but gave the idea up. The darkness of the house and its general gloom seemed to make it more sensible to merely crouch into the little alcove beneath the stairs and wait, listening. There was no use blundering into some sort of horrible activity like he'd blundered in among the witches in the Widow's windmill. Stealth was what he wanted here. He'd think things out this time, and bolt for the door at the drop of a pin.

But crouching beneath the stairs wasn't worth much either. After a minute or two of listening to his heart beat and of squinting at shadows while wondering whether things weren't stirring in the darkness, he bent back out, then immediately ducked in again, banging his head on the low ceiling, as he heard, from above him, the sound of footsteps clump, clump, clumping down the stairs. He held his breath, smashing himself back into the darkness. If they passed him, heading toward the harborside of the house, they'd have to turn and look back to see him, and he'd be prepared for that. He'd jump for the front door. He could outrun anyone on such a night as this.

There was Abner Helstrom, carrying his stick now. Escargot could see his pant cuffs and the shod tip of the stick and his pointed shoes as the dwarf waited in the hallway for someone else coming along after him. Escargot knew who it would be before he heard her speak. It had to be Leta, even though her appearance there in Balumnia after her strange odyssey in Seaside made little apparent sense. But it was she, following along down the hallway in the wake of her uncle. They seemed to be in a sizable hurry—quite likely a fortunate thing, since it had seemed to Escargot that the witch had been able to sense his presence in past encounters. Perhaps their haste veiled her powers. But why the haste? Escargot grinned. They were hunted all of a sudden, weren't they? Despite the dwarf's winking, he feared that Escargot was a more powerful nemesis than he'd given him credit for. He must wonder how in the world Escargot had come to Balumnia. How in the world, for that matter, had the *dwarf* gotten there?

Escargot crouched out once again from his hidey-hole and stepped down the dark hall toward the rear of the house. The two had already gone out a rear door. Escargot hurried. There was no point in losing them now. The back door was a windowless wreck, cracked and teetering. Escargot pushed it open slowly and nearly stepped out into empty air. It was fifteen feet to the black mud of the harbor below. A stairs tilted down along the side of the house, supported on stilts, but the stair landing, right beyond the door, had broken away and fallen into the muck below years past, so the door swung out over nothing at all. Escargot jerked it shut to cut his momentum and save himself a certain fall. Then he pushed it open again, more carefully this time, and peered around it to discover that if it was thrown all the way back, he could step across to the floorboards of that part of the landing left whole—or almost whole anyway—and by grabbing the shorn-off bannister, pull himself out onto the stairs.

Leta and the dwarf had disappeared. There seemed to be nothing below him but mud and flotsam and the shadows of canted pilings. Then, fifty feet beyond, moonlight glinted off what had to be the polished brass tip of the dwarf's stick, and he heard a low curse and the sound of shoes sucking up out of mud. There they went, scuttling away like crabs beneath the docks and the open, trestled basements of houses. Escargot followed, careful of the mud, stepping from stone to stone and here and there in the footprints of the two in front of him. He'd lost them again. He paused and listened, but he heard nothing. It occurred to him in a rush that he'd been fooled. What if they'd known all along that they'd been followed? What if they'd lured him out into the dark, deserted harborside for the purpose of cracking him on the head? But he had to go on, hadn't he? If he gave off now he'd curse himself when the sun came up in the morning.

Fifty feet farther along the piers and houses ended abruptly at the edge of a long curve of mudflats that ran up into a seawall. The view was clear for two moonlit miles. No one walked along the mudflats or atop the seawall. He'd lost them. They'd slipped up into the cellar of one of the old canneries they'd passed. That had to be it. But which one? He turned and hurried back the way he'd come, watching the ground. There was only one set of footprints—his own. He hadn't been paying enough attention. Fine detective he made, racing on blindly while the two of them had merely turned aside and let him blunder past.

There they were—two more sets of tracks, but they turned down toward the sea, not up toward the road. Escargot followed them until there was a muddle of tracks and a long depression in the mud where, quite clearly, the prow of a rowboat had been dragged through. The two had been making for a hidden boat. He listened, cupping a hand to his ear. He could hear, from somewhere to the west, the sound of a tinkling piano and the shouts and cries of revelers in dockside taverns, muted by the darkness and the distance. Closer on, somewhere out on the starlit water, came the sound of dipping oars and the mumble of conversation—Leta and the dwarf, making away up the delta.

Escargot turned and ran, back through the shadows to where the seawall began. He climbed up and looked. There they were, a bobbing bit of shadow on the water, moonlight glinting on the oarwash as the rowboat cut along, not toward the lights of town, but toward the mouth of the Tweet River, as if the two were making away for good and all. He watched until they disappeared into the night, and there was nothing but the far-off piano and the lapping of the rising tide against pier pilings to remind him that it had grown late, and that he was hours of weary walking from his submarine.

He'd follow in the morning. That's what he'd do. If they *had* flown upriver, then he could easily outdistance them, stopping in at riverside villages to inquire. People would remember the dwarf, and they'd remember Leta too. Escargot certainly hadn't been able to forget her, although this last rendezvous made it fairly clear that he should have.

If they hadn't gone upriver, then he could turn about and return to Landsend. It seemed fairly certain that they hadn't known they were being followed. Escargot could easily find his way to the abandoned house again. He could return by day and snoop around. Surely there'd be some sort of telling evidence. What it was he hoped to find, however, was a mystery to him. The mystery seemed merely to be the only thing in his life that had any substance to it—his latest destination—and it drew him now as surely as Seaside and the harvest festival had drawn him weeks earlier. It was something he had to settle, it seemed to him, before he could get on to something new.

He was up with the dawnlight, navigating past a low island in the river. Hovels on stilts lined the water's edge, and a score of fishermen waded in the low water, tossing nets into the departing tide. There were a good two miles of coastline cut by jetties and piers along which Leta and the dwarf could have moored their rowboat. Looking for it in among the quayside bustle would have been futile. There was nothing to do but press on, to assume that they'd been bound upriver and that they hadn't any intention of returning. Escargot could see, through the periscope, the long, broken-down row of canneries and old houses where he'd lost them two hours earlier. From a quarter mile out to sea some of the houses looked stately and grand, for the broken windows and cracked doors and peeling paint were masked by distance. Farther along lay the new harbor. Fishing boats were docked along the wharves, and hundreds of sailors and laborers scurried like bugs, loading kegs and bales, shouting orders, and generally carrying on.

In ten minutes the harbor was behind him, and the houses and shops along the shore thinned to nothing. Boatyards with skeletal hulks on trestles took their place, and then those too gave in to low marshy tidelands peopled by pelicans and gulls and an occasional dilapidated shack. Beyond rose a range of forested, coastal hills, covered on the lower slopes by houses. Then there was nothing but open land and trees, and the delta funneled down into a real river, broad as a lake. A wide channel cut the river in two at midstream, and it seemed to Escargot, in the glow of the fire-quartz lamps, that the channel was prodigiously deep. He sped up, taking a look through the periscope now and then just in case a village would sweep into view. There was nothing, though, but an occasional farmhouse above the river, with an acre of pasture along either side and now and then a short dock running out into the water.

It seemed futile to stop. It was no more likely that the two had put up at one farmhouse than at another, and although there were boats tied up at the docks, it was impossible to say that they were the rowboat he was looking for. Somehow he had the idea that if the two *had* gone ashore at some house along the river, it would be a particularly gloomy and uninviting sort of house, that the nice, cheerful houses with their happy cattle and smoke from cooking fires lazying up the chimneys wouldn't agree with the two.

It was late afternoon when he passed the first village. It was on the southern shore, and he'd sailed entirely past it before he spied it through the scope. It wasn't much of a village, in the shadows of the overgrown forest, only a scattering of houses along the bank, backing up onto what might have been its only real street. Escargot piloted the sub around in a big circle, looking for a place to heave out the anchor. It was almost dusk, and there was a wet smell on the wind, not like rain, but like fog—the heavy, cool smell of misty air. Away off downriver, toward the sea, the horizon was gray and dark, and a roiling bank of low-lying clouds drifted along on an onshore breeze, obscuring the river and its banks. Escargot didn't know whether to be happy about the fog or to fear it. It would disguise his movements, if it was thick enough, but it would disguise *their* movements too, and all else being equal, they seemed to have rather more of an affinity to the fog than he did.

But there was nothing at all he could do about it, after all; he couldn't wish it away. So he drifted nearer to shore, casting his anchor in forty feet of water two hundred yards out. He'd have to swim for it, now that his rowboat had been reclaimed, and he didn't at all like the idea of clambering up onto the shore, wet and with a foggy night falling fast around him. But he daren't wait for morning either. If he dawdled he'd get nowhere. Either he was on the trail of Leta and the dwarf or he wasn't, he told himself in no uncertain terms. And if he *was*, then he'd jolly well better get to it. He was ready to plunge into the cold river when he changed his mind.

Captain Perry's suit—he could don one of the underwater suits and walk ashore, then shrug it off and hide it in the weeds. And if he ran into danger, if the village was as murky and grim as it appeared to be from the river, he could slip back into the suit and walk into the river, leaving danger to rail at him from the shore. Ten minutes later he was on the river bottom, treading along through the weedy silt in his lead shoes.

River water, he found, wasn't clear like ocean water had been. It was hazy, even in the glow of the fire quartz that ringed his belt. Ten feet away from him lay darkness, despite the sun still being aloft. Escargot hurried along, planting one foot solidly after the other. Waterweeds grew in dark clumps, angling away downriver in the current, and in among them, half buried in the sand, were clusters of river clams, among which strolled crayfish and ghost shrimp. A great slab of some sort of arched stone—pale green marble, perhaps, or mossy granite, glowed in the light of the fire quartz, almost sunk beneath the river bottom and grown over with weeds. Escargot strode along toward it, watching crayfish scuttle out of the light. There were more stones beneath the first, tumbling away into a deep pool, the remnants of some sort of quarry, perhaps.

They were enormous, immovable, as if they'd been the base of a monumental bridge, one that had spanned the river and had been built, perhaps, by giants. Surely no men had cut the things, and if they had, no amount of horses and equipment could have moved them. The edges were softened as if from ages of erosion, and the stones seemed to be deeply carved with great, rectilinear runes in which river moss grew in such profusion that the runes stood out from the pale green background as if they'd been painted on. Escargot gouged into the moss with his finger, sinking in up to the third knuckle. Fish darted in and out from beneath the great heap of stones, which, piled up as they were, formed deep, black caverns that Escargot himself could have crept into, if he had a mind to. But he didn't. There was something about the stones, their prodigious age, perhaps, their having sat unmoving for so long on the bottom of this tremendous dark and deep river, that hurried Escargot shoreward. If he'd been Professor Wurzle, interested in curiosities for the sake of science and history, he might have stayed to investigate further. But he'd dawdled long enough as it was, and so he strode straight on into shallow water, looming up out of the river some fifty yards down from the first of the houses in the village.

The fog had crept along into the trees overhead, impaled, it seemed, on the branches, and already the ground was wet with it and spongy underfoot. It was possible, thought Escargot, that there would be some value in merely wandering into the village clothed in his underwater suit and seashell helmet, just to give the villagers an odd thrill. But one of them might merely beat him silly with a branch, supposing him a monster, and question him afterward.

So he pulled off the suit, rolled the helmet, aerator, and belt up in it, and stowed it beneath a heap of brush along a little bit of bank that had collapsed and fallen toward the river. He looked up and down afterward, anxious all of a sudden that someone might at that moment be watching him, but there was no one in sight, nothing but the lowering fog and the darkness and the shadowy forest. The village itself was obscured by mist.

He set out up the road that ran along the bank. It wasn't much of a road, actually, just a little dirt trail along which a cart might drive if it was a particularly small cart. There weren't any signs of carts having been driven there, though, nor were there any footprints, even though the dirt of the trail was soft enough. Bushes and vines grew across it, in fact, as if it were halfway toward disappearing, and Escargot had the curious feeling that somehow he hadn't ought to be walking there, that no one walked there except, perhaps, goblins.

The log wall of the first house loomed up out of the mist before him, a shutter over a second-floor window slamming closed with a bump that yanked at his stomach. It swung open again, then whumped closed. It was the breeze blowing it, bang, bang, bang, and it seemed as if there was no one in the house to secure it. Creeping vines covered most of the wall and had climbed along onto the roof, tangling themselves into the bricks of the chimney and forcing themselves under shingles. It seemed at first as if no lights shone from within the house, but when Escargot passed on the road he could see the flickering flame of a burned down taper on the mantel, casting a weary glow over a man who sat reading beneath, his chin in his hand.

Escargot stopped in front of the house and considered. He didn't at all like the village. There was something wrong about it, as if it were the sort of place above which the night sky would be a bit too thick with bats, or where strange ceremonies involving blood and gold were carried out in the shadows of leafless oaks. But it was exactly the sort of place that would appeal to the witch and the dwarf. It had the same atmosphere that the meadow had been charged with on the night that the witches had met in the Widow's windmill. Dark enchantment is what it was, that sighed on the breeze and settled in with the fog, and crept up the sides of houses to work the shingles loose and the shutters open.

He stepped up onto the porch and knocked hard at the door. This was no time to be timid. If he was making a mistake, he might just as well make a bold one. Through the window he could very clearly see the man's head jerk, as if someone had yanked him up by the hair. Even in the feeble candlelight there could be seen on his face a look of startled terror, as if he'd imagined all along that there would come a knock at the door on just such a night as this, and here it was at last. He reached for the candle and with his fingers snuffed it out as he rose from the chair. The room was plunged into darkness. Escargot heard a rushing of footsteps along the floorboards, and he stepped back off the porch into the weeds, certain that the door would fly open and he'd be confronted by a madman. Instead there came the sound of a bolt being thrown, then another, then of a bar banging into place. The soft creaking of floorboards followed the bang, and the tattered curtains in the window moved just a bit.

"Who is it?" came a voice, then silence.

"A traveler," said Escargot truthfully, but the phrase must have struck the man within as being particularly funny, for immediately there sounded a rush of hollow laughter, and the edge of the curtain fell. Footfalls receded into silence. All remained quiet. Escargot pounded on the door again, but he knew it was useless. Travelers were obviously uncommon thereabouts, after dark on a foggy night anyway. He stepped back out onto the road and strode away deeper into town, looking over his shoulder now and again, and into the shadows of the woods. Water dripped from the tree branches, and somewhere not too distant an owl who-whooed at intervals, sounding uncommonly ghostly and sad.

Most of the houses were dark, some obviously abandoned, and only one had enough lights lit within to seem particularly cheerful—an inn, Escargot was pleased to see, although it was probably just as well that it was dark and foggy, for it seemed to be a close cousin to The Smashed Hat, only further along in decay. Escargot jingled the bell, mildly surprised to find that its clapper hadn't rusted away.

This time the door was thrown back and a man stood in the doorway with a look on his face that seemed to imply he'd been waiting all evening long for Escargot's arrival. He grinned like an ape for the space of three seconds; then his grin disappeared, he squinted up his face, and he stepped back and slammed the door in a single, practiced movement. Escargot's foot, however, caught it before it latched.

"Get your foot out of my door!" cried the man, throwing himself against it.

"No!" shouted Escargot, pushing the other way.

For a moment they stood toe to toe, one on either side of the door, heaving vainly. But the man within seemed to see that the foot was firmly lodged there and that all the pushing in the world wouldn't budge it. He might have given off and gone for something to smash at it with, but by then Escargot would have slipped in. "What in the devil do you want, pushing into a man's house at this hour?" the man demanded, not letting up on the door but peering through the crack to see what manner of ruffian it was who confronted him.

"Isn't this an inn, then?" asked Escargot.

"Well, yes. It is."

"And it can't be above seven o'clock, can it? I need a room; that's who I am. I've just had a set-to with a party of goblins up the road and I'm about done in. Killed two of them and chased the rest into the river. Nasty little boggers. Wanted to rob me, I think."

"Goblins is it!" cried the man, his mouth falling open.

"That's just what it is," Escargot lied, assuming that the man might be more hospitable toward someone who had recently thrashed a party of goblins.

"Did you see anyone on the road?"

"Not a soul. There doesn't seem to be much in the way of travelers hereabouts, and I don't blame them. A man is set upon by goblins, and when he gets to the only village between Landsend and who-knows-where they won't give him a room."

"You've come from Landsend, then, not Grover?"

"That's just what I've been telling you. All the way from Landsend, though it isn't for pleasure. My old aunt's dying up the river, and I stand to inherit a brewery when she's gone, if only I arrive to claim it. But at this rate I'll be dead myself of goblin scratches before I'm halfway there."

The man stopped pushing quite so hard and blinked out at Escargot. "I had an old aunt once," he said.

Escargot shook his head. "Heaven help old aunts." He shook his head some more, "Ah, well."

"Come along in, then. I can't offer you much, but it's dry enough and I keep the rats and bugs off as best I can. I can't stand bugs. Too many legs. And rats are worse, though not for legs. You see what I mean."

"For a fact," said Escargot, stepping in and slumping down into a chair. "I can't stand rats myself. Always chewing things up. Chewed up a Smithers novel once—very rare volume."

"Smithers!" cried the man, cheering up. "Do you read Smithers then?"

"I should say I do." Then Escargot remembered suddenly where he was and wondered that the Smithers reference had gone anywhere at all. "G. Smithers, that is."

"Of course, of course. Of Altoona Village."

"Brompton Village. My Smithers is from Brompton Village."

"Is he?" asked the man, looking as if he doubted it. "Mine's from Altoona, up the river. Wonderful lot of books he's written. My favorites are about the Pirate Isles in a magical land beneath the sea. Or at least you get there through the sea if such a thing is possible, which it's not, I suppose, unless a man is a fish."

Escargot nodded. "Haven't a pint of ale, have you?"

"Absolutely. Brew it myself. They used to cart it in from Grover, but the brewery burned and the road isn't what it used to be, and bit by bit the whole thing's just fallen apart. I'm expecting a man from up that way. A delegation. Some of us are setting in to do something about all this."

"All what?" asked Escargot, looking around.

"The whole lot of it: goblins, the road gone bad, the things in the river. Don't at all know what we can do, though, but a man has to start somewhere and there's a party up in Grover that has taken it all on. I sent up for information, but there aren't more than two or three left in this village who'll rally round, I'm afraid. Most have gone the way of the rest of it, if you follow me. The mayor went stark staring mad last month and tried to hang himself with his own suspenders. Now we don't even *have* a mayor. We've *got* to organize."

Escargot nodded. "Organization. That's the ticket, all right. Haven't forgotten that ale, have you? And a cold joint, if you've got it. Even a bit of cheese. Or a pie. Do they go in much for pies hereabouts."

"Used to," said the man, "but Mrs. Cleary's place—that's the woman who made the pies and sold them through Parker's store—has all gone to smash since the old lady . . . Hark!"

Escargot cocked an ear toward the road. In the distance came the muted sound of a wagon clattering along—wildly, it seemed—and the neighing of a horse. Both men leaped to the door, and the innkeeper threw it open, stepping out into the foggy night. He stepped back in and fetched out a lantern, trimming the wick until lantern light shone off the hovering mists. The road was swallowed up to the east and west, and only a ghostly, hovering light in the second-story window of the house next door gave any indication that there was a village roundabout.

The clattering seemed to crack through the mist, growing louder and wilder, and a shrieking could be heard above the neighing and thundering of the horse. Through the curtain of fog, looming suddenly into clarity, rattled a runaway wagon, pulled by a spooked horse with eyes wide open like plates, his mouth lolling. Escargot and his host leaped aside before the horse trod both of them into the muck of the roadway, and the wagon careered past, its driver hunched over on the seat, his legs entangled in a mess of straps and reins and bucklers, and he clinging like a bug to the rails of the wagonbed behind him while a goblin sat astride his back, tearing at his hair. Six more goblins rode behind, shrieking and hooting and slapping at each other and tugging out tufts of their own sparse hair as if to mimic the antics of their cousin in front. There was the smell of raw fish in the air and the reek of dirty goblins, and one of the little men, grinning past filed teeth, threw a handful of gnawed fish carcasses at Escargot and the innkeeper as the wagon lunged past.

Then, half out of sight again in the mists, the wagon slewed around sideways, the wheels skidded along the road, and it slammed against a pair of hitching posts that stood before a boarded up stable. One wheel cracked to bits, spokes spinning off into the night. The wagon tilted and went over in a cacophony of shrieking and flying goblins. The horse, freed suddenly from its bonds, bolted east along the river, the pounding of its hooves and the clattering of trailing tackle giving way in a moment to silence. The wagon wheels still spun like dervishes atop the fallen cart, and the goblins, strewn like autumn leaves, picked themselves up and raced away into the foggy woods, howling with lunatic laughter, as if they'd accomplished exactly what it was they'd set out to accomplish.

Escargot raced across to where the driver lay in a heap, rolled up against the wall of the stable. He seemed to be tangled up—contorted into all manners of unnatural positions. He flopped over onto his back, his eyes wide and staring, his mouth pried open as if in the midst of one last silent shriek. Escargot shook him. The innkeeper listened at his chest. "Dead," he said slowly.

"Dead?" asked Escargot, not wanting to believe what was so clearly written on the man's face.

The innkeeper nodded, goggling at Escargot and looking roundabout slowly, as if wary that the goblins might still be nigh, waiting, perhaps, to pounce on their backs and clutch at their throats with their fishy little hands.

"Scared to death," muttered Escargot, closing the man's horrible staring eyes. "We can't leave him here in the fog. They'll take him for sure. We can't have that."

"We'll bring him to the inn. I'll ride to Grover in the morning if this damned fog lifts. And I'm not sure but what I might stay there. This is the corker, this is. Poor bogger. Coming down at night was the mistake. Up in Grover they don't half know how bad it is down here. Lift his legs. He's light, this one is. They've scared the stuffing right out of him."

With that the two hauled the man across the road and into the open door of the inn. It seemed to Escargot that fog had crept in while they were outside, and that the room was heavy with mist and cool, dark air. He wished that the innkeeper had thought to shut the door. They put the dead man on a low table in the larder, and covered him with a sheet fetched from the linen closet.

"The ale," said the innkeeper, shaking suddenly as if a chill had swept up his spine. "Maybe a bottle of brandy wouldn't be amiss."

"Not at all amiss," said Escargot, slumping in his chair. And in a moment there were glasses out and the two men sipped in silence, each of them glancing out the window into the swirling fog, half expecting to see some new horror—a leering goblin face or a lurching, hooded skeleton—appear suddenly in the weeds and peer back in at them.

11

The Highwayman

"So you say it hasn't always been so, living on the south shore of the river?" asked Escargot finally.

"No, not at all. This village was a fine place to live, once. There's always been goblins about, of course, and a man wouldn't want to travel much in the deep woods beyond the hills. There's been trolls and sprites since before any of *us* settled here, but they kept to the woods, mostly. There was the occasional cow disappeared and fishbones in the well and such, but nothing like now. And it's moved in toward Grover, too, a sort of darkness drifting up from the coast."

Escargot nodded and stared into his brandy glass. He didn't too much care for local peculiarities, beyond an idle curiosity about why fishermen sailed north out of the delta and why the south road over the bridges hadn't any travelers on it. But none of that *really* concerned him, after all. "Haven't seen a dwarf come through along with a girl, have you? Very pretty girl, with black hair. He might have given his name as Helstrom. Devious fellow; some sort of magician, maybe."

The innkeeper peered at him for a moment as if he was pondering something, as if the question struck him as particularly strange. "I've seen your dwarf for sure, more than once."

"And the girl," asked Escargot. "Have you seen the girl?"

"Haven't seen any girl. Are you sure it was a girl?"

"Tolerably. Traveling upriver, maybe in a rowboat."

"In a cart, actually. They came through here this afternoon. The dwarf driving."

"Alone?"

"No, not alone. There was an old woman in the back, all wrapped up in a dirty shawl. Blind woman, I believe, from the look of her. They stopped long enough to water the horse and drove on. Seemed to be in a hurry."

"The old woman!" cried Escargot, about half baffled.

"*Some* old woman, anyway. I can't say it was *the* old woman. If I was you, though, I wouldn't have anything at all to do with this dwarf. He's from down south, on the coast, they say."

"Do they? What's he doing up this way then?"

The innkeeper shrugged. It seemed to be a subject he wasn't fond of—part of the fog and the goblins and the dead man in the road. He stood up suddenly, strode across the room, and began to wipe with the side of his hand against the white-washed plaster of the wall. "Look at this! Here it is again. I paint and I paint and back it comes, in a day, sometimes."

"What is it?" asked Escargot, squinting at the patchy dark ring that stained the wall.

"Fungus, I should think. I looked at it under a magnifying glass. It's little black flowers, sprouting there. Grows right through the whitewash. Nothing will hide it. By next week the plaster will start to soften up, and it'll gouge right out with your finger. Whole wall will be a mess. It's part of this here business, is what I think. That and the bugs in the floorboards. And the toads. There's no end of them. My dog ate one and died, right there on the floor, poor devil. Toad kept right on croaking from inside his stomach. I buried him back of the shed, and I'd swear that late at night I can hear the damned thing croaking still."

Escargot poured himself another half inch of brandy, entirely at a loss for words.

"And I'll tell you something else. There's things in the river now that come up from somewhere. Things that haven't been seen since there was nothing but elves and brownies and goblins living hereabouts. Things that died out a thousand years ago. Laslow, down the road, caught a thing in a net last week that was nothing but teeth and scales as big as the palm of your hand. It looked ancient, all black and warty. Tore his net to bits and nearly took his arm off. Things are going back, is what I think. Paint don't stick to the houses no more. Glass cracks in the windows for no good reason at all. Shingle nails rust through in the night and half the roof's on the lawn by morning and there's bugs gnawing at the rafters. Then this fungus—nothing but rot, rot, rot everywhere, and goblins on the road. You saw that. Then there's ghosts—nothing but howling on the wind, moaning coming up out of the ground wherever anyone's been buried. There was graves broken open all up and down the road, all of them empty. Grave robbers, was it? Not a bit. There wasn't nothing in them but skeletons—skeletons that left footprints in the mud when they walked away into the forest. Poor Mrs. Cleary, the pie woman. Just like our man in the road tonight . . . Heaven alone knows what it was she saw, but I hope I never see the like.

"What does it mean? It's like the clock hands are spinning round backward, is what it's like. Things falling to bits, people moving on. There's been earthquakes upriver, too—things stirring in the earth, things that been sleeping there for ages, if you ask me. And your man the dwarf. It follows him, is what it does. There's a little wind devil of decay at his back. Steer clear of him."

This last bit struck Escargot as good advice, but he knew he wouldn't take it. He had something to prove by now, something he couldn't at all explain or define, something that had to do with Leta and with the marbles and with being hoodwinked more often than he was comfortable thinking about. But it had to do with more than that too—with Annie and with Stover and with running away. That was it. He wasn't running away from anything anymore. He was running *toward* something. And if he turned around now, if he gave into fear, he'd never be able to look back again without despising himself. Besides, how much of the innkeeper's tale was exaggeration? Half of it anyway. It was late in the evening, and it was a foggy, haunted night, and a man had died shrieking in front of them. Things were bound to look frightful and bleak, weren't they? He had it on good authority that *his* dwarf lived below Hightower Village, not on the beach south of Landsend. If he'd been through that very afternoon in a cart, then Escargot would catch up with him tomorrow. The affair, for better or for worse, would end soon enough.

"I'm done in," said Escargot suddenly, realizing that the brandy bottle was emptier than it had been and that when the sun came up in the morning it would herald the start of a long, tiresome, and quite possibly dangerous day. The innkeeper led him upstairs to a room that was a far cry from the room he'd enjoyed at The Smashed Hat.

There had been an effort made at keeping things tidy and clean, and the bed, although soft as a sponge, would serve nicely. The innkeeper brought up a plate of cold beef and pickles and bread ten minutes later, and Escargot ate alone, looking out the window into the fog, and wondering at the leafy vines that had crept in under the sill and were curling around the rusting hinges, as if to jerk the window out of the frame and drop it onto the lawn below. There was a patch of darkness on the wall, a shadow deepening, it seemed, even as he watched, and in the late silence he could hear things gnawing away in the attic above and the sound of distant moaning out over the water, like the wind through tree branches or the sighing of ghosts that wandered above the misty, haunted river. Once, when he awoke hours later, he could hear the faint croaking of toads and the echo of goblin laughter on the wind, and he fell asleep thinking about it, drifting away into a long dream involving his bag of marbles and a pool of what might have been dark water or might as easily have been blood and him running and running and running from a mountain that was stirring and yawning and rising out of the ground and peering at him through ancient, hollow eyes that had only moments before been dark and empty caves.

He left the inn at dawn. The innkeeper, who was in the midst of packing his own bags, was happy enough to take one of Escargot's remaining gold pieces, despite its foreign look, and told Escargot that most of the rowboats pulled up along the bank of the river had weeks and months since been abandoned. Escargot wasn't powerfully anxious to venture back into the river in his underwater apparatus, not since the innkeeper's story of the black fish.

By the time the mists had burned off it was midmorning, and Escargot slid along somewhere upriver from Grover, which he'd apparently passed in the fog. The dwarf and his companion had the jump on him, and they seemed to be in a hurry. They would have made Grover yesterday evening and might quite easily have pushed on through the night, the ghosts and the goblins and the dark foggy woods bothering them not a bit.

On the north shore, visible in the hazy distance across the vast river, there seemed to be no hint of the haunting that was arising in the deep woods of the south shore. Farmhouses sat amid pastures and fields, with now and then a stand of trees along the riverbank, and scattered villages running along the low-lying shore. Twice he was passed by steamships, broad paddlewheelers making toward the coast along the opposite bank and well out of his way. It struck him that it might be fun to drive along toward one, on the surface and at a good clip. Then, just when the thing began tooting and blowing and things began to fall to bits on deck, drop mysteriously beneath the surface of the river and pass along beneath, surfacing, to their collected horror and wonder, on the farther side. But he hadn't any time for games, and the idea of it smacked, somehow, of Captain Perry. So he gave off idle thoughts and kept his eye on the river trail, sometimes having a look under the water for a change of pace.

Below the surface all was dim and silty with here and there a little pool of clarity where the water was slack enough to settle out. He glimpsed in one such pool what seemed to be an enormous wheel or a great millstone, cracked asunder and rising out of the black depths. The river bottom had a weird, enchanted atmosphere to it that Escargot could feel right through the walls of the submarine, a dark sort of enchantment that seemed to be held off only by the elf magic that was part of the very bones of his undersea boat, or by the light of the fire quartz glowing through the portholes and the bowlamps.

It was warmer, it seemed, and a little less troubling to navigate on the surface than beneath it. The boat seemed to want to drift toward midriver and farther, as if it were attracted to the north shore, or, perhaps, as if it were repelled by the south shore. But he had to keep an eye on the road. When he found another village he'd pull in and ask after the dwarf. If no one had seen him, he'd wait, and let the dwarf stumble upon *him*, in a cafe, perhaps, or merely standing beside the road. That would put the wind up him. Precious little winking he'd do then. What would happen would happen. He seemed to be astride a charging horse, running full tilt onto a darkened battleground, and there was nothing to do but hang onto the reins and keep his head down.

It was past noon when he saw the ship in the sky. The weather was turning. Clouds, gray and puffy and threatening rain, humped up out of the sea behind him, rolling in to obscure the sun. The pressure seemed to drop, as if the air roundabout him were waiting for something, and off over the forest on the south shore he could hear the rumble of far-off thunder, sounding like the rolling of drums. The sky was lit on the horizon by flashes of lightning, and it seemed that on the heavy air he could feel the ground shudder and heave, as if the arcing tridents of yellow lightning were somehow charging the distant hills with electricity.

He stood with his head through the open hatch, smoking his third pipe of the afternoon. Rain squalls chased each other up the river toward him, and in a moment he'd have to pull the hatch shut and get in out of it. The sky was so low that it seemed to be pressing all the wrinkles out of the river, and it had gone from gray to black, the clouds whirling and charging and threatening, getting ready to burst.

Through them, from out of the sky and slanting in on a ray of the departing sun that shone through a momentary rent in the dark ceiling, came a ship, a three-masted galleon, sails billowing along the mast, its bowsprit heaving on currents of air. It seemed as if the galleon were racing along the sun rays like a log down a chute, little wisps of cloud swirling across its bow like spindrift. Thin and distant on the wind came what sounded like the cries of a sailor in the crow's nest. The clouds closed behind it, the river of sunlight winked out, and the galleon disappeared behind the tree line, on beyond a distant swerve of the shore.

Escargot puffed at his pipe until it smoked like a chimney. Elves, it seemed to him, were a mixed sort of blessing. They were good to have around; that was sure. There was rarely a bad one among them, and they traveled in wondrous ways—in airships and sky galleons and gliders—and carried along, as often as not, magical treasures, for no reason beyond having them, to mess with now and then. On the other hand, elves rarely *were* around, only when something odd was in the wind, when trouble was brewing and had begun to boil over. There was a nagging at the back of his mind—at the front of it, in fact—that whatever trouble had attracted elves had something to do with him. But he didn't have the foggiest notion *how* it had anything to do with him.

What he did know was that the rain was serious. Sheets of it seemed to be falling, blown along on gusts of wind, and the clouds had thickened to a solid, gray-black mass, low enough overhead so that it seemed he could reach up and plunge his hand into the murk. He was halfway down the hatch, closing it above him, when he saw a cart, moving along the river road at a canter.

He hurried to the periscope and fiddled it back and forth. The road had run off into the trees on the edge of the woods, and through them he spied it, rattling along at a good clip through the rain. From out on the river, through the haze of rain, it was impossible to say who it was that drove it. It might, surely, be some local farmer driving upriver, but it might as easily be the dwarf, or Leta for that matter. Experience suggested that riverside travelers would be rare, especially in the fog and the rain, and there was no doubt that the two he followed were *somewhere* about, close enough certainly to make it highly likely that this was them. He'd have to have a closer look.

As he motored upriver, though, the road bent farther inland, hidden much of the time by dense foliage and high, crumbling cliffs that ran with rainwater. One moment the cart appeared, rolling along in plain view, the next moment it blinked away into the shadow of the forest and was gone. Escargot ran along ahead, outdistancing it. He could easily enough pick up a couple of miles on it, break out the rowboat, and be ashore to wait for it on the road, in a cloak, perhaps, and with a hat pulled down over his eyes to shade his face. He'd take along a brace of Captain Perry's pistols, charged with shot, and fire a round over their heads to show them what a dangerous nest of bugs they'd uncovered.

He put together a speech as he cast the rowboat off into the river and clambered in after it, relishing the idea of the coming confrontation all the more because it was Leta who would witness it. If the old woman sat in the back, of course, it wouldn't amount to so very much. Leta, though, would make it his grandest moment. Her eyes would shoot open. There he'd be, got up like a highwayman with his cloak and pistols—a desperate highwayman, to be sure. He'd loom up out of the foliage, tossing his cloak back over his shoulder, folding his pistols across his chest. "Halt!" he'd cry, or some such thing—there had to be something better than halt. Avaunt, maybe, or avast. He was a sea captain, after all. But avast would muddle the effect. He could see that. He rowed in long strokes through a drizzle, hoping that the rain would let up long enough for the whole episode to play itself out. If he was all frazzled with rainwater it wouldn't be half as grand.

He had to row downriver to find enough shore to run the boat onto, and then scramble up the muddy bank to the road, listening all the while to the sound of the approaching cart. There it was, a moment behind him, clattering along. A great oak grew twisted and gnarled half into the road. It would be the work of a moment to clamber up into it and drop like an ape into the cart itself as it lumbered past beneath, and he brandishing his pistols and laughing, as if he'd been toying with them all along. He grinned, picturing it. But there wasn't enough time for dropping out of the sky. The tree would be slick with rain and he might twist his ankle anyway, and here came the cart, around a bend, the cantering horse splashed with mud.

Escargot stepped out from behind his tree, shouted an oath, and aimed a pistol into the air, firing off such a blast of spark and brimstone that it nearly deafened him. The horse half reared, slewing around and running his flanks against the steep, cutaway hillside that walled the opposite edge of the road. The cart skidded sideways, its driver's face set in a grimace of fear and surprise, half at the sight of the gun-waving Escargot, half, it seemed, at the idea of the cart rolling down the brush-covered bank into the river. It wasn't the dwarf.

It was a terrified man in chin whiskers and with a long, clay churchwarden pipe in his mouth. Even as the cart jerked to a shuddering halt, one wheel against the oak, the man bit through the stem of the pipe, and it dropped like a stone into his lap. He slapped at it wildly, trying to knock the wad of burning tobacco off his trousers, but watching Escargot all the while to see what he might do.

"I got nothing!" he shouted, trembling, giving up on the tobacco. His teeth chattered like marbles shaken in a bag.

Escargot was horrified. He lowered the pistol. The man has bit through his pipe, he said to himself sadly—all on account of nonsense. "I say," he started, but the man yowled and leaped up.

Surprised, Escargot raised a pistol involuntarily, to gesture at the man, to wave him back into his seat. But the man danced there inexplicably. It was the burning tobacco, Escargot realized. He hadn't scared the man witless, after all. He saw suddenly the pistol in his own hand and lowered it again, tucking it away beneath his coat and then fumbling to do the same with the other one. The man found the tobacco and dusted it onto the roadway, sitting down again in trembling silence. "You're Jack the Lad, ain't you?" he said, eyes wide, cocking his head.

Escargot wanted suddenly to say yes. That, certainly, was who he would have *liked* to be at the moment. But saying so would lead to complications, so he shook his head. "Sorry about this," he said weakly, grinning a little. "I took you for someone else."

The man stared at him and quit quivering and chattering. "You ain't Jack the Lad?"

"No, I'm Escargot, the sea captain. I took you for a dwarf, I'm afraid. That is to say . . ."

"A dwarf!" interrupted the man, squinting now and frowning. "Yer a blind beggar, aren't you? I got three feet on any dwarf I ever seen. I have half a mind to thrash you. Look at my pipe!" He pulled the bitten-off stem out of his mouth. There was about an inch of it left.

"Nasty shame," Escargot admitted. The rain was setting in again—not so hard this time, but steady and solid. "Here." Escargot reached into his cloak to pull out one of his two remaining coins. It would half break him, literally, to give it to the man, but circumstances called for it. And it would go some way toward teaching himself a lesson too, about masquerading around waving pistols and ducking out from behind trees to surprise innocent men. "Here," said Escargot, handing it up.

The man took it and bent his head even more in evident puzzlement. "You're paying *me*?"

"The least I can do. Buy yourself a pipe and a fill of tobacco. And a pint of ale too, to keep off the damp. Forgive me this little treachery. It wasn't what it seemed."

"What's this?" asked the man suddenly, peering at the coin.

"This ain't money. This is some sort of joke, isn't it? What's your game, giving me such a fright like that?" He pitched the coin contemptuously into the woods and made as if to scramble down onto the road. "I'm a bit tired of this, I am," he cried, working himself up. His horse capered back a step or two, driving the cart behind it as if to give his master room. Escargot stepped back toward the oak tree, thinking about the disappearance of half his fortune.

The man rocked back onto his heels and spit into his hands, rubbing them together in the manner of someone who had some really serious business to attend to—business that involved Escargot's nose. The rain slanted into Escargot's face now. The forest was a blurred gray curtain. Abruptly, the man rolled back onto his heels and launched a fist, but the punch whirred past a foot from its mark, infuriating the man, who stepped forward and ripped loose another one, leaning into it too and nearly pitching forward with the exertion. Escargot stepped back, embarrassed. "I mean to say," he said, reaching in to take the man's arm.

"Brigand!" the man shouted, flailing tiredly away at Escargot's shoulder, then standing there heaving and puffing. Escargot felt worse than ever: poor man, trying to regain his lost dignity and having no luck at all.

"No need for that, old man. Really. It's all a mistake."

"I'll say it is. Yours. I'll beat the dust out of you!" With that promise the man launched in again, catching Escargot in the chest and spinning him half around, then coming on again with the air of a man looking to get back his self-respect. He stopped suddenly, lunged toward the bushes, and came up with a stick. "Now I have you!" he cried, waving the thing and twisting his face into a menacing leer. "Rob me, is it! Smash up *my* pipe! We'll see what it is that gets smashed up now!"

Escargot turned to bolt for the river. Things had turned serious. The man had gone mad, clearly, and wouldn't be satisfied until he had his way. He felt the stick whistle past his ear. "Hey!" he shouted, sliding three feet farther and catching himself on a bush. He turned, ducked a wild, arm's length swing, and hauled his second pistol from his belt. The man seemed to be blind to it. He stepped in carefully, hauling the stick back, his mouth working as if he were talking to himself. Escargot cocked the gun and fired overhead, blinking the rain out of his eyes. The report boomed like cannon fire, another fountain of sparks hissing out, and the man, stricken with fear, dropped his stick and bolted for the road, where his horse was leaping upriver with the empty cart, whinnying and tramping in a fury of mud and rain, the thudding of its hooves and the cries of its master hanging in the misty air long after the two had disappeared utterly from view.

Escargot stood heaving on the bank. Heaven knew what sort of story would be told in the nearby villages. He'd have to give up the cloak and hat business, that was sure. He hauled himself up the bank to the road once more, tucking his pistol into his belt, realizing that his hand was trembling mutinously. Rainwater ran from the brim of his hat in a steady stream, and his coat hung from him as if he'd swum from the submarine fully clothed.

Up the road twenty feet was a pair of oaks larger, if anything, than the one he'd hidden behind ten minutes earlier. One was hollow. He crouched into it out of the rain, watching the slanting drops fall outside. His own pipe, thank goodness, was in a single piece, and was dry, as was his tobacco. In a moment he was puffing away, watching the rain through a haze of smoke.

He *had* put the fear into the man, stepping out like that in the mist. He stroked his chin. He hadn't shaved since the last day on the road outside of Seaside, and a serious beard had set in, giving him the look of someone who might quite likely haunt lonely, wooded roads with a brace of smoking pistols. It was a dirty shame it *hadn't* been Leta and the dwarf. The thought occurred to him that if his sea captaining came to nothing he could set up easily enough as a highwayman, although doing so would require robbing people, of course.

Perhaps a man could learn such a thing. Or perhaps he could rob only people who deserved to be robbed—landlords, say, or politicians, or lawyers. But how would he work it?—quiz them first? Let them go if they did honest work? He'd as likely be shot by a carpenter or a writer or a farmer, come to think of it, before he had time to bow graciously and let them off. *They* wouldn't know that he wasn't going to rob them. He'd have to develop a reputation first—send out faked-up tracts, perhaps, carrying news of a desperate but benevolent bandit, complete with a craggy-faced likeness of himself, all shadowy and squinty-eyed. *He* couldn't draw it, of course, unless it was a stick-man, or a man with a head shaped like a pie.

He grinned, gazing through the rain at nothing, warm enough in his hidey-hole and seeing no immediate reason not to smoke another pipe. The dwarf was as easily behind him as before him now. This whole chase, in fact, had gotten ridiculous. He hadn't had a moment to himself since he first arrived in Seaside. He was awfully hungry, he realized. Being a highwayman pretty much took it out of you. This Jack the Lad must give the local inns some business.

He focused on the hillside across the road. He'd seen something—a movement in the brush, a color that oughtn't to be there. Was it his man in the cart, come back around to finish him off? He waited, watching the heavy shrubbery and the little rivulet that swept out from beneath it, obviously running down out of a cut in the hillside. There seemed to be a trail there, disappearing into the woods, a trail that was of no earthly interest to Escargot, except that through the pattering rain and the lazy pipesmoke there was something almost magical about it. The foliage was green as emeralds, and in among it, when the leaves would shift in the breeze, a brushstroke of bright red shone for a moment, then winked away.

He smoked a second pipe. There was something there, beckoning. It was mystery, is what it was—the sort of thing he'd set out to find those long weeks back, and unlike the other adventures that had befallen him, this one hadn't been thrust upon him. This one he'd merely happened upon, and he could do with it as he pleased. He could leave it alone, easily enough, turn his back on it like a man so wealthy in adventures that he could *afford* to turn his back on them.

So he pulled his cap down and crouched out into the thinning rain. There was indeed a trail—just a game trail, it seemed, traveled by the occasional deer or bear or raccoon ambling along down to the river for a drink in the evening. The shadows of the trees closed around him, and the leaves and grass smelled musty and wet and sighed almost soundlessly underfoot. It would take a good pair of ears to remark his presence. Water plinked down onto the broad leaves of the bushes and onto the brim of his hat. The hillside steepened and opened into a little canyon cut by the rivulet, the trail winding along by its edge. Escargot peered about him, looking for the telltale trace of red, and saw it briefly, on ahead, farther into the woods than he had thought it to be from his lair in the hollow tree.

He trudged on, puffing on his pipe, stepping carefully and slowly like a man who had no intention of rushing into trouble. He peered back over his shoulder and was surprised to see that the road had disappeared, that the canyon had wound far enough around to obscure it and that he had been swallowed up utterly into the woods and had left his river and rowboat in a different world. For a brief moment it occurred to him to turn around, to slide back down the path, clamber into his rowboat, and set out. But the notion passed, dissolving in the enchantment of the shadowy, wet woods and the afternoon silence. He fancied himself a forest wanderer, perhaps with a log hut beside a river in the deep woods, and the magic of the turning seasons in his blood. He would live in a house that changed with the weather—diamond-paned windows glinting with tree-filtered sunlight on summer evenings and running with dark rainwater in an autumn downpour. Smoke would tumble up through a stone chimney and lose itself in the low, gray sky. Animals would know him. Trolls would wander past, perhaps steal the stones from his wall for supper. But they'd leave him alone, paying him little more heed than they'd pay the morning dew or the deepening color of autumn leaves. A Smithers story would have nothing on him. He'd *be* a Smithers story.

There was the color again, nearer now—the red of Christmas glass or of a jewel in sunlight. He bent beneath a canopy of leaves. In a depression in the wall of the canyon, half hidden by branches, stood an iron pot, rusted and with a heavy wire handle that had been bent into the shape of a triangle. Within the pot, heaped up in such a mound that it seemed as if not another would balance atop it, were diamonds big as river stones, watery red even in the shadow of the hillside.

Escargot stood listening to the silence. He blinked, half expecting the pot and its contents to be spirited away. But there it sat, looking as if it had sat so for ever so long—as if years past someone had hauled it there, laboring to drag it up the trail, but had left it, finding the task impossible, and had never returned, and in the empty, wild woods no one else had stumbled upon it—no one but Escargot, who was, after all, the sort who might quite likely wander in woods as wild as those.

He climbed in under the outcropping and picked up a gem,

hefting it in his hand. Then he grasped the handle and tugged, but the rusted wire snapped loose and he very nearly jerked the whole pot over onto its side. The sheer quantity of uncut stones made Captain Perry's treasure seem like nothing at all—so much costume jewelry. He held one of the diamonds to his eye and squinted through it at the sky. It was like looking into an almost bottomless pool of pink water, beyond which shone, distant and shifting, the mountainous landscape of a dream-world.

He pulled his hat off and heaped it full. Then he set the hat down and filled his pockets. The pot seemed easily as full as it had been, and diamonds lay now on the ground roundabout. He was determined not to leave a single gem behind. They were doing no one any good hidden away there in the woods, and would finance any of a number of capital adventures along the river. *One*, in fact, would finance such adventures, but the thought of leaving a single gem lying in the wet grass was impossible. He'd haul his hatful back to the rowboat, dump it in, and come back carrying buckets. He blinked at the pot. There, thrusting up from the middle of the tumbled gems, was the jagged corner of an immense stone, big as his fist—big as his head maybe. It made the rest of them seem like sandgrains. He grabbed the great stone with both hands, and pulled on it, hauling it free.

It shimmered there, the reflections of clouds passing across it, the red color swirling and whirling and spiraling out slowly, seeming to stretch the jewel until he held in his hands not an immense diamond, but a great piece of stick candy, like a barber pole. His hat, too, was filled with stick candy: rootbeer and licorice and cinnamon and orange and cherry, all thrusting out and snapped off at the end as if broken from long cylinders. The iron pot was stuffed with it. He reached for it, unbelieving. Stick candy was well and good—magical enough in its own way—but it wouldn't finance adventures. He thrust several sticks aside with his hand, reaching deeper into the pot, where he felt something fleshy and cold, like a fish just hauled out of a river.

He jerked back with a shout, but whatever it was had gotten hold of his hand. Something bit into the fleshy part of his palm, fingernails or sharp little teeth, and he cursed himself for not having seen the truth of the thing all along. He yanked his arm out, and in a shower of stick candy there appeared the head of a goblin, eyes wild as pinwheels, teeth champing, dressed in shreds of clothes, holding onto his hand like a child afraid to cross a street alone.

It shrieked at him—threw back its head and shrieked past filed teeth, gobbling along like a conversation in a barnyard. It clambered up his arm, hand over hand, eyeing his neck, drawing itself out of its goblin pot like a serpent out of a basket. Escargot hit at it with the great piece of stick candy in his free hand, smashing it along the ear, then again atop the head. The stick candy shivered to bits, falling into the muck, and the rain set in again furiously, the wind whipping it in under the rocky ledge above.

A hand grasped his ankle. Another caught him by the throat from behind. Suddenly there were little men everywhere, creeping out of bushes, dropping from the hillside overhead, appearing through a crack in the wall of the canyon and half hidden by foliage. He clutched instinctively at the goblin at his throat and tore it loose, pitching the thing bodily at a pair of his cousins who chattered along toward him, waving toasting forks. He stepped back toward the stream, dragging three of them out into the rain, and he fell over hard onto his back, smashing a goblin beneath him and rolling away down the canyon with the other two hanging on like monkeys. He leaped up, kicking and flailing, seeing that his way down was blocked by a score of the creatures, half of them carrying lit torches that spat and fizzled in the downpour.

Up the canyon was another score, and still more slipped out through the crack in the hillside, yowling and bleating and dressed in all manners of outlandish clothing, obviously stolen from riverside villages and farmhouses. Some wore hats, stove in and torn and with fishbone ornaments thrusting out at random angles. In moments there was nothing but goblins front and back. He remembered suddenly the pistols in his belt, but the guns weren't loaded, and even if they were, what would they avail him? Goblins hadn't sense enough to fear a pistol, and if he shot one of them point-blank, it would just excite the lot of them to see it, rather than cause them to run in fear. He was lost. He gave off struggling, and the creatures stopped leaping at him, though they seemed very much ready to set in again if given half a chance.

They pushed him along, through the crack in the cliffside and into the hill itself. The sound of the rain was replaced with deep silence and the echo of scuffling feet. From below him, somewhere in the rock and earth, came the sound of a distant rush of water, of a cataract tearing along through subterranean caverns like blood coursing through veins. It was dark as pitch, save for the light of a dozen flickering torches that threw the shadows of the goblins across the cavern walls. At first Escargot concentrated on remembering the twistings and turnings of the tunnel and counting the number of adjacent tunnels they passed, but it was like the counting he'd attempted in his first submarine outing; it soon came to nothing and he lost all track of direction and distance.

12

Bleakstone Hollow

The tunnel opened out finally into a great, high-ceilinged hall. Bats swooped and darted in the light of a bonfire, smoke curling away overhead into dark crevices. Torches ringed the walls, and the hall was alive with shadows and lights and goblins. The greatest of them wasn't above three feet tall, and all were skinny and disheveled and dirty and with hair that seemed to grow in tufts and sprigs and needed cutting.

A great iron tripod sat square in the center of the fire, and from it dangled a pot not at all unlike the cauldron full of diamonds and stick candy, only this one was many times the size of the other—suitable for stewing up a horse. Or a man. Escargot looked around. There must have been a hundred of the creatures, none of them engaged in anything that made a lick of sense, except one, who kept pinching at Escargot's legs as if to assess how meaty those legs might be. Others gabbled and spit and wrestled and threw fishbones at each other in a continual wild fury, and it was a restful few moments when at least one of them didn't have his hair set on fire by a prankster messing with a torch or by rolling straightaway into the bonfire. They'd rage back and forth shrieking, wisps of hair sparking and flaming, until by sheer wild effort the fire was beaten out.

A throne made of sticks and dried bones and with human skulls as ornament sat in one low corner. On it slouched a tremendous goblin—fatter than the rest and less given to burning off his hair. He grinned past filed teeth, eyes rolling. He yelped and stood up when the lesser goblins hauled Escargot toward the throne, and he clapped his hands together like a child who's been told there's something wonderful, perhaps, for dessert. Escargot didn't at all like the look of it.

He considered for the tenth time the likelihood that he could kick his way free, that he could bowl enough of the little men over to get some running room. But they would trip him up for sure. He'd have to wait and watch. If they tried to pitch him into the stewpot . . . He'd heard stories about what goblins ate—fish and river trash mostly, but now and then a lost traveler as a delicacy, and his horse too, which they'd consume hide and hoofs and head. The great goblin sat himself down on the throne once again, picking at his teeth with a sliver and smacking his lips as if in anticipation. He reached idly down the side of his grisly chair and came up with a clump of weed, which he thrust into his mouth and champed away at, shreds of the stuff raining across his chin.

Escargot stared at him, unbelieving, as he stuffed another clump between his teeth. It was kelp that he chewed—lilac kelp, a little heap of it that sat half dry and half rotten in a basket next to the throne. Escargot had been out-trumped and wildly so. Apparently when Uncle Helstrom had a running start he could do far better than a wink. This beat the highwayman pose all to smash, and it suggested, suddenly and finally, that Escargot had muddled along into the middle of some trouble far more vast than he'd bargained for. It appeared from just about every angle that he'd quite likely come to the end of that trouble at almost the same moment that he'd realized he'd come to the beginning of it. The stew pot, it seemed, was meant for him.

A trio of goblins shuffled past, bent beneath the weight of double buckets on sticks stretched across their shoulders. They clambered up onto a rickety platform beside the fire and dumped the contents of the buckets—water, it looked like—into the cauldron, then crept away after more. Others tossed in fish, tearing out mouthfuls on the way, and still others appeared with heaps of waterweeds and cave snails and dead bats, tossing the lot of it into the pot. The fat goblin giggled the whole time, smacking and nodding and, Escargot was astonished to see, gnawing on a piece of stick candy in between handfuls of kelp, letting the sticky drool run down over a leather jerkin that had been stitched up out of hastily tanned bat skins.

"Your lordship," Escargot began, thinking that there was nothing to be lost by exercising some diplomacy.

The goblin grunted and looked at him through eyes reminiscent of Captain Perry. He ran the back of his hand across his mouth, then licked it, then, apparently forgetting himself, bit it with a certain amount of satisfaction before howling and jerking it away, then giving Escargot a hard look, as if to blame *him* for the treachery. Escargot tried again, bowing this time and saying, "I've journeyed far, O goblin king, and . . ." before the goblin stood up and spit—not at Escargot, but at one of the goblins that flanked Escargot and who had, apparently, fallen asleep as he stood there. The spitting, however, had no effect on the creature, so the fat goblin reached across, twisted his nose, and pulled out a great tuft of his hair, at which the sleeping goblin awoke with a shout and bit Escargot on the arm.

"Hey!" cried Escargot, surprised. His cloak and jacket and shirt kept the teeth from reaching his skin, but the whole idea of it was ghastly enough that Escargot picked the little goblin up and threw him spinning into a knot of water carrying goblins, buckets and bats and snails cascading away across the stone floor of the hall and a general shouting and tumult arising. I've had it now, Escargot muttered, and he set his feet, fearing an onslaught. But the goblins howled and raged, beating each other with empty buckets, scratching, and biting. Even the fat king, who'd gone back to eating kelp and stick candy and squinting suspiciously past his nose, didn't seem particularly put out with Escargot's having misused one of his subjects.

Escargot reached into his shirt on an impulse and drew out the truth charm. It had worked Captain Perry over fairly thoroughly, and it seemed to Escargot that Captain Perry was only a step or two removed from being a goblin himself. It couldn't hurt, he reasoned, to try it on the goblin king.

The king arose, slowly, staring at the truth charm, like he was setting in to address the multitude before him on a particularly weighty issue, a saddening issue, perhaps, and he knuckled his brow with the back of one filthy hand. He seemed to reel there, remembering past treacheries, past sorrows, and he stepped down onto the floor of the cavern, gabbling suddenly in a rush of nonsensical jabber. He strode back and forth before Escargot, who clutched the truth charm in his hand, hiding it as much as possible. Then, bursting into sudden tears and leaking away like a faucet, he howled and shook his fists at the distant, smoky ceiling, and he stomped his feet as if he'd just as soon pound the whole place to dust as to go on living in it another moment.

The goblins in the hall went back to filling the cauldron and squabbling among themselves, as if that sort of theatrics was entirely in keeping with daily routine. Pitiful lamentations and shrieks were nothing to such creatures, who seemed, in fact, to oppose any other sort of behavior. In moments the king had played himself out. He shook his head and sighed, then sat back down, clapped a particularly fresh-looking hat onto his head, and chomped away at a bulging mouthful of kelp. There hadn't been much remorse on his part, quite possibly because he wasn't able to remember anything that had happened longer ago than the week before last. One way or another, Escargot hadn't understood a word of it. The truth charm was worth nothing here, save, perhaps, to bean the king over the head with when it came down to it.

Escargot was struck suddenly with the hat. He'd seen it before—a flat-brimmed crush hat with a feather. A blue feather. It had been the hat worn by the man in the wagon, the man who'd called him a brigand and chased him with a stick. Around the throne were greasy, recently gnawed bones, any number of them, and behind, in a dim corner half hidden in shadow, was a slumped figure. Escargot couldn't say for certain that it was a man, or that it had once been a man, because the darkness was too deep there to say that it was anything more than a heap of something—old rags, perhaps. If he'd peered more closely, adjusted his eyes to the shadow, he could have told for sure. But he didn't. He was suddenly sickened, and the stupid squinting look on the face of the fat goblin, who worked at his teeth again with his sliver, sickened him even more. Come what may, he decided, it would go hard on them when they came for him. It was entirely possible that the poor driver of the cart, with his foolish chin whiskers and his bitten-off pipe, had given Escargot a reprieve, if only a momentary reprieve, by taking the edge off the king's hunger. The stick candy was dessert. What, or rather who, the next meal was to be seemed monstrously clear.

The king of the goblins grunted suddenly and waved Escargot away, as if he were tired of looking at him, and the little band of goblins that still clustered around hurried him away to a corner, where they left him sitting, unbound, watching the preparations for the coming feast. His thoughts kept coming back around to the slumped whatever-it-was in the shadows and to the basket—his basket—of kelp by the throne and to the self-satisfied dwarf who, by now, was safely gone. He looked around, blinked, stood up, and began to stroll away. Immediately a host of goblins rushed down upon him, gnashing their teeth in such a way that it seemed as if they'd eat him then and there, without salt. He sat back down and they gave up, a shade disappointedly, it seemed to him. Now and then a goblin or a knot of goblins made another rush at him, just for sport, anticipating, probably, that he was going to have another go at escape.

He waited until such interest died down, then set about priming and loading his pistols. At best he'd get two of them, although given his lack of familiarity with pistols of any sort, it was unlikely that he'd hit anything farther off than ten feet or so. Then, of course, they'd be upon him and would be very unlikely to leave him in peace. He managed to spill powder down the front of his jacket, and he lost the first ball when he dropped it and it rolled away out of sight. Crawling around and searching for it would do nothing but attract attention. The spilled gunpowder, however, gave him hope. He knew nothing about gunpowder except that it was wonderfully explosive. A man with a bag of it might cause some concern in a party of idiotic goblins.

He finished loading the pistols, tucked one back into his belt, and jammed the barrel of the second into a little vein of stiff clay that ran along the cavern wall, twisting the gun and digging it into the clay until the barrel was packed with the stuff. Then he stood up. Immediately a half score of goblins turned toward him, ready at the slightest movement to rush at him tiresomely once again. He nodded at them and waved cheerfully at the goblin king, who had slumped on his throne until most of him was on the floor and only his head, neck, and shoulders were still seated. His face had drooped into a jowly frown, like he was thinking of having been cheated once or having been served up a bloody haunch, perhaps, that was tough and needed another hour's boiling.

Escargot slowly removed the bag of powder from his coat and opened the top. He shouted and rushed toward the bonfire, bowling goblins out of the way to the left and right. With a wild flourish he pitched the bag end over end into the fire so that the powder spiraled out of it, then dove sideways toward the throne of the goblin king in order to be out of the way of the blast when it came. There was a sparking, he could see, and a breathy little whoosh and a bit of blue flame. That was all.

Goblins stood staring, first at the fire, then at Escargot, understanding even in their cheese-like minds that so much capering and throwing and diving must herald *something*. But when nothing at all came of it, they advanced upon him, wary this time. The goblin king waved his stick candy and danced atop his throne. Escargot stood up, pulled a pistol out of his belt, calculating and recalculating whether or not he'd gotten the right one, and fired almost point-blank into the half-empty kelp basket, which catapulted backward, throwing its contents over the floor.

The king looked at it in mild surprise, happy, it seemed, with the noise of the thing and the magic that attended it. He peered warily at Escargot, stepped down off his throne, and snatched the pistol. Abruptly he pointed it at Escargot and shouted, "Boom!" then tilted his head warily at the absence of any further development. The lesser goblins stood fearfully roundabout, chattering among themselves, while their king discovered the moving parts of the pistol and set in to experiment with them. He cocked, then uncocked it, peered down the barrel, and shook the whole works at his ear. Then he cocked it again and pulled the trigger, effecting a click when the hammer fell, but little else save general approval from the gathering goblins, who hooted and yowled and fell upon each other tearing and gouging. Escargot pulled the second pistol from his belt and handed it across, smiling broadly. The goblin king snatched it up, cocked it immediately, and yanked at the trigger.

A terrific explosion crashed off the walls of the cavern, sending the goblins into a wild rout and toppling Escargot over backward in surprise. He had hoped to be a bit farther off when the report came. He rolled toward the fire, dropping the remaining, empty pistol. He was up and running straightaway, not waiting to see what had happened to the fat king, but sprinting toward the entrance to the cavern, which was choked by maddened and befuddled goblins, who rushed down upon him even as he turned and ran in the opposite direction, deeper into the caves.

He cast off his cloak as he ran through torch-lit halls, deeper and deeper, sliding now and then along scree-slippery declines, tripping and falling and jumping up and step by pounding step leaving his pursuers farther and farther behind. What he'd do if he came upon another crowd of them he couldn't say. Finally the torches gave out and he ran in darkness. He fell once and then decided to slow down. Then he crept along, one hand on the cave wall, one in front of him, conscious in the sudden darkness that the sound of a river filled the passage.

Muttered voices sounded behind him, but very distantly, and he could hear the echo of gobbled laughter once, followed by a shriek and more laughter. Then there was silence except for the rushing water. The air grew suddenly misty and cool and he stepped along slowly, feeling his way, sure with each step that he would pitch off a precipice or run head-foremost into the end of the passage and find that he was hopelessly lost in the darkness. Above him, he knew, was a rainy afternoon and tree branches blowing in a misty wind and clouds moving in a familiar sky.

The underground river sounded suddenly as if it lay right before him. He bent along, feeling the ground with his right hand and stepping forward in a crouch, determined not to simply stride into the river and be carried away. He stepped again, his left foot coming down on a round stone, and he found himself sliding suddenly, down and down and down, hands scrabbling at the gravelly slope. With a shout and a hail of pebbles he splashed into the dark river, fighting his way to the surface, coughing and struggling and popping up finally only to be borne under again with a wild whump that somersaulted him like a rag doll and sent him gasping once more for the surface.

He righted himself finally and shot along through the roiling water, cold and breathing hard and cracking his knee as he swirled round a half-submerged rock. Ahead was a growing crescent of light that widened out in moments into the mouth of a cave. He found himself in broken sunlight, tearing between oak trees and alders and hemlocks straight into a snag of tumbled logs and brush, where he clung, puffing and blowing until he realized that he was fearfully cold and growing colder by the moment.

When he clambered down along the stream to the river road a quarter mile below, he was soaked through and through, and what's more had a stone in his shoe that nearly crippled him. He sat down, finally, on a fallen tree, pulled off his shoes, wrung out his socks, and discovered that the pebble wasn't a pebble at all. It was a marble—a red marble, slightly out of round and of the color of blood. The idea that it was one of *his* marbles, one of the lot cheated out of him by the dwarf, was farfetched. This was something similar, to be sure, something he'd picked up by accident when he'd been tumbling along down the river.

His rowboat was upriver. It had to be. But how far upriver it was he had no earthly idea. Goblins were probably rowing it up and down at that moment, beating each other senseless with the oars. A sign nailed to a nearby tree insisted that he was in the town limits of Bleakstone Hollow, and below that listed any number of things that he ought not to do, including traffic with goblins, lounge about idly, and tread in flowerbeds. But the village that sidled into view as he wandered around the bend in the road was years removed from the days when it boasted flowerbeds, and as for idling about, there wasn't anything else to do, really, Bleakstone Hollow being to all appearances utterly deserted. If anyone lived there now it *was* goblins, and it seemed, from the scattered fishbones and river trash in the streets, that such was fairly likely the case, though not a living soul was about. The air was almost void of sound, and the withered trees were as empty of birds or squirrels as they were of leaves. There was the slamming of a shutter somewhere up the street, and the breeze kicked up dust and swirled it round and round, this way and that, pointlessly, like a capering goblin.

Escargot found a suitable stick along the river and took a couple of cuts at the air to see how it felt in his hand. Satisfied, he set out to explore the village. Everything was overgrown and falling to bits. Toadstools sprouted from rotting clapboard on the sides of houses, and even as he stood and looked about him, wondering at the decay, a brick chimney on an old half-collapsed mansion crumbled across the roof in a cloud of mortar dust and shingles. Escargot was certain, for a moment, that someone had pushed it over, but it wasn't so. It had merely given out, and within days, it seemed, the heap of brick on the weedy sideyard would be lost beneath sprouting vegetation. Windows were boarded up as if people had hurried away to avoid a siege, hoping that they'd return in a better day. But better days, quite clearly, were still a good ways off.

On the very edge of the village lay a three-story farmhouse, fallen to ruin. Atop it, canted over and rusting and twisting in the wind was a weather vane. The mournful creak, creak, creak in the afternoon stillness made the empty village seem twice as empty as it was. There was an inn—two of them, in fact—sitting directly opposite each other on the main street. But neither had seen a customer in a good long time, not a paying customer, anyway, and the skeleton of a horse, its bones picked clean, lay across the threshold of one, as if it'd been too tired to step entirely inside and so had fallen asleep on the doorstep. It was a morbid and silencing thing, that horse, and Escargot decided suddenly that it wouldn't be such a bad idea after all to hoof it back down the road to his rowboat before dark. The submarine seemed suddenly as hospitable as a firelit parlor. He turned then, and saw, standing ten feet in front of him, Leta, with a ribbon in her hair.

She peered at him as if in wonder. She didn't grin eerily or cackle with laughter or turn into a cat. She seemed quite simply astonished. "You," she said, then stopped.

Escargot swallowed hard. He hadn't expected this. He'd hoped for it, true enough—half because he'd been pursuing her out of love, and half because he wanted to say a few things to her while he *wasn't*, for once, hanging from the vane of a windmill. "That's right," he said now, yanking himself together and wondering suddenly what he must look like—unshaven, his clothes wet and rumpled, his hair awry. He was half tempted to blurt out that he'd become a submarine captain, that he'd traveled, that he'd found treasures and lost them again, that he'd become, in short, a sort of Smithers hero, and all of that in under a month.

But he'd be working hard to impress a witch, wouldn't he?—a witch who'd gone a long way toward delivering him to a nest of goblins, who, by this time, would have eaten him right up if he hadn't given them the slip. "Where's my Smithers book?" he asked instead, feeling foolish.

"Heaven help us," she said, shaking her head. "You've gone mad too."

"Too? Madness isn't what *I* call it. *I* don't know if you're twenty-five or a hundred and twenty-five and I don't care, not anymore. But I want what's mine, and I've come up this river to get it—the marbles, the book; I'd be asking for my basket of kelp, too, but I've shot holes through it and the goblins can have it, for all I care."

"What in the world," she said, seeming to shiver with cold, "are you talking about?" And with that she burst into tears, cried for the space of ten seconds, then twisted off the tap and quit crying.

Escargot regarded her warily, looking roundabout himself, suspicious that the dwarf uncle might just then be stepping out from behind a building, packing his pipe with henny-penny men. He thought for a moment and said, "I don't understand a bit of this—nothing except that I've come to the end of it, or will soon."

"I wish I could say the same," she said, wiping at her eye, "at least about that last. What's that?"

"Nothing," said Escargot, pulling out the truth charm. This was no time for guessing at anything. If there were tales being told here, if he'd wandered once again into the soup, then someone was going to get a crack on the head with a stick. He tossed the charm into the air and caught it. "Recognize this thing, do you?"

"No," she said, looking suddenly up the river where the sun was settling in for the night. The clouds had broken up and flown, and only a few scattered puffs clung yet to the sky. She seemed suddenly frightened, as if she weren't at all anxious for the sun to set.

"You've seen it before, I daresay."

"I haven't seen any such thing before. Who *are* you, anyway, prowling about the streets here with a stick in your hand? I wasn't at all unhappy in Twombly Town until I ran into you and your magicians and witches."

"*My* magicians and witches? You're a fine one to talk, after that business at Stover's—taking my side and all. What was that but the worst sort of hypocrisy?"

"Hypocrisy!" she cried, beginning to weep again. There was almost no light left. Shadows had disappeared. The sky, it seemed, was moonless and dark and the dim shadows of bats could be seen reeling among the rooftops and the trees. Leta stood still, as if listening, and then, as Escargot watched, she very slowly disappeared, until there was nothing before him on the street but a wraith and something that sounded like a moan, then, very distant, a fall of brittle laughter and the tap, tap, tap of a stick on the road.

Escargot had started to run before he thought of running. But while he was running he did a bit of thinking, or rather realizing, and what he realized was that he'd been holding the truth charm in his hand while Leta had talked. She'd been telling the truth. Perhaps, he thought, the charm didn't work on witches. But then why shouldn't it? And then why would the dwarf have been so obviously frightened at the idea of his pulling it out of the bag that night on the meadow? Perhaps its powers were weakened out of doors. But they hadn't been—had they?—on the day that Captain Perry and his men had watched their treasure sink in the sea. He slowed to a walk. Something was dead wrong. He'd somehow never convinced himself that Leta was evil. She was up to *something*, for sure, or rather, someone was up to something with her. But that business in Stover's tavern and the talk on the street afterward—that hadn't been a put up job. *Why* all the rigamarole with Stover if she was a witch? How had she hidden it so well for so long and then been so completely incapable of hiding it since? It didn't wash. He stopped, took another couple of cuts at the air with his stick, and turned around to look again at the village.

Before him, a half mile up the road, lights blazed in Bleakstone Hollow. Smoke tumbled from chimney pots as if suppers were being cooked, and there was the plinking of piano keys on the wind, as if through the open door of a tavern. He stood in the road for a full minute, his heart thumping noisily, before he set out.

13

All Kinds of Pies

The empty silence of the afternoon had given way to an unnaturally loud evening. It wasn't that there were noises on the air that oughtn't to be there, only that the sounds of slamming doors and shouted greetings, the creak of wagon wheels and rusted gate hinges, the plinking of an out-of-tune piano, and the tossing of tree branches in the wind were somehow strange. Each one was clear and distinct, and Escargot could tell at once exactly what sort of a noise each was. Here was the neigh of an unseen horse; there was the disembodied crunch of footsteps on gravel. It reminded him of the time that Beezle had produced a play in the Guildhall, and Escargot, to please his wife, had undertaken to provide sound effects, thundering on a piece of sheet metal one moment and drumming out raindrops on a board the next. It hadn't the sound of an authentic storm, but was a sort of piecemeal effort put on to fool a willing audience. The noises roundabout him now were strangely similar to that, as if they weren't real noises at all, but were enchantment, conjured up one after another, side by side, instead of tossed together in a salad of sounds like real noises.

He sidled along the street, looking over his shoulder as often as he looked ahead. Through one window he saw a family gathered around the dinner table, and the smell of roast beef and pudding, followed by happy laughter, wafted through the lit window as if there were no window there at all. Through another window was a parlor with a fire burning in the hearth and shelves and shelves of books behind leaded bookcase doors. He could see the back of a man's head nodding over a volume, and on a table beside the man's easy chair sat a pint glass half drank. Another cottage, with geminate windows and painted bright white, rang with the shouts of merrymakers, a dozen of them at least. Escargot could see them milling about a sort of dining room, dipping hot punch out of a wooden bowl.

The lights burned silver, like moonlight. They hadn't the yellow glow of gas lamps or candles, although it struck him suddenly that his memory of clean and well lighted places was hazy and dim, as if he had to wander far and wide through the corridors of his memory to glimpse such a place at all. His own house was veiled in hazy muslin, deep in the shadows of his mind, and although he squinted, he couldn't quite bring it into focus.

He tried, though. There was the kitchen with the table made of oiled pine slats pushed up against the square bay window with its window seat covered with—what was it?—leather? Or tweed? It was leather. He could just picture it. He pressed his eyes shut with the effort. Suddenly it was unspeakably important that he picture it. It was dark, latigo leather. He'd covered the cushion himself with a piece cut out of a half hide he'd bought from a tanner up in Monmouth. He'd left the brand on, a circle with a moon on it, even though the leather around it was stretchy and thin. There it was. He could make it out now, way back there in an antechamber of memory, like a piece of furniture in an otherwise empty house. Something seemed to be odd about it, though, that cushion by the window. Abruptly he could see it absolutely clearly, as if he'd removed a pair of fogged spectacles. It was all stitched together and moldy and stained up like the hides of bats with the heads left on and knitted up into a vest for a goblin king.

Escargot shook his head and reeled back against a tree. He blinked out the vision of the window seat. He'd suddenly pictured the goblin king sitting there, gnawing on a bone. He watched the horrible face dissolve away in the night air. He suddenly couldn't say with any certainty that the stove in his kitchen had stood opposite the pantry or that loaves of bread had been kept in a drawer or in a bread box. Both, it seemed. He could vaguely remember the smell of a bread drawer, with its scattered crumbs in the bottom and new loaves just bought that morning from the baker's. But he couldn't quite see it, any more than he could see his Smithers collection lined up one book after another, or his pipe collection, all forty-six of them. Stover was probably smoking them now.

He thought of little Annie, but her face was lost in shadow like the rest, and for a moment he feared he'd strangle with the effort of recapturing it. There it was for a moment. She was smiling, playing with the hem of her little blanket, looking at him through eyes unaware of his weaknesses and his faults. Then she was gone, as if snatched away, and he was left in the weirdly lit street, listening once again to the scattered night noises, above which, so thin and distant as to seem imaginary, he could hear the shrill peep of darting bats and what sounded like goblins banging on copper gongs and an ebb and flow of wind in the sky above that reminded him overmuch of the breathing of the sleeping earth.

He shook his head clear again and turned to look behind him, fearing suddenly that something was crouched there in the darkness, waiting to spring on him. But there was nothing—only a street that stretched away, it seemed, blocks farther than he'd already walked. Smoke poured furiously through chimneys, churning up into the starry sky in billowy, writhing phantoms. The lights of the street behind were dim, as if they'd only that moment blinked on, but as he watched they seemed to brighten and shimmer until, finally, they were abnormally bright, like sunlight reflected off a mirror. He found that as he turned to look this way or that, the lights directly behind him dimmed, and along with them, the noises dimmed too. The piano tinkled into obscurity, just a plink, plink, plink on the night breeze, almost like water dripping into a pan in the sink, and the gay laughter of the revelers in the house he'd passed a quarter of a block down, and that he was facing now, broke out again renewed, as if someone had just that moment gotten round to revealing the punchline of a particularly long and tedious joke.

He stepped into the road, unsure of himself. He was certain that he hadn't come farther than a block or so into the village, but the lights of the farmhouse he'd passed on the outskirts glowed now as distant as the moon. He turned and started down the long street once more. The piano set in to banging away again, but he seemed to be no closer to the tavern it sounded from than he had been fifteen minutes earlier when, standing on the river road, he'd first heard it.

There was something vaguely familiar about the store he found himself standing in front of. It was closed for the evening, and, squint as he might, he couldn't make out a thing beyond the dusty, dark windows. The boardwalk he stood on, though—he'd stood there before. He rubbed at the layer of obscuring dust on the glass, uncovering the words, *Beezle's; Dry Goods and Produce*. He blinked, confused. There was Stover's six doors up. And there was the Guildhall beyond it, lit like a Christmas cake. He could hear the round, foolish guffaw of Mayor Bastable's laughter and the clinking of glasses being set down on wooden tables. There was the smell of beer in the air and of chocolate and of lamb stew laced with sage. Above it and around it, spreading through him and filling him up like water seeping into a sandy hole in the bed of a dry river, came the smell of pies cooling on a windowsill. Cinnamon and nutmeg and ginger and hot apples and butter crust filled the night abruptly, washing down a little rise that angled away toward the river. A house sat atop the rise, glowing and cheerful, a fire in the grate, a child's high laughter riding on the cool evening air.

Escargot set out toward it. He knew that he shouldn't, that there were things in the night that he couldn't at all explain, that couldn't be explained without hauling in enough enchantment to light up a carnival. But that didn't matter to him. His quest was abandoned. What had it been anyway but a lack of anything better to do? It was *his* house that sat on the hill, and enchantment or no enchantment, he'd see what there was to it. He'd come too far along strange and watery pathways not to see this adventure through to the end. There was something in him that whispered that the night was full of mystery, and that if he searched hard enough, if he could see just right—put on, so to speak, the right pair of spectacles—he could stay there in that enchanted village and let the dwarf and his goblins go to the devil.

The wind was cold atop the rise, and it made the cheery interior of the house seem all the more cheery. There was his wife, in the kitchen. She was whistling—something she was given over to when they'd met but which she'd abandoned in the two years of their marriage. And she was prettier than he remembered, with her hair pulled back in a sort of knot and a swipe of baking flour on her cheek. He pulled his coat around him but the wind cut right through it. The river sat dark and silent and still beyond the trees. Was it the Oriel or the Tweet, he wondered briefly, but he gave off his wondering when he saw, on the sill of the back window, an apple pie leaking cinnamon-laden steam like a tea kettle. He tiptoed toward it. His stomach was suddenly empty—not simply because he hadn't eaten in hours, but because he hadn't eaten a pie like that ever. It was the pie he always imagined he might eat, with great slivers of apples in it, heavy with spiced, brown sugar syrup.

He peered roundabout. There was Bastable's house on the next hill, and for a moment he imagined that he saw the mayor's head, with its unlikely spirally hair, peering out at him past a curtain drawn aside. But he blinked and the face was gone. He turned, reaching, and looked up into the face of his smiling wife, who seemed to be monumentally happy to see him, as if he were the hunter home from the hill and she were the loving wife who'd baked him up a pie. He grinned. He had a lot of apologizing to do.

"H'lo, Clara," he said, taking off his cap.

"Hello, Theo. Back are you?"

"That's right. How's Annie? Well, is she?"

The back door swung open, creaking on the broken hinge that he'd swore he would fix a month before he set out that day—when was it?—months back. Where had he been bound, anyway? He couldn't remember any destinations, only that he hadn't had any choice in the matter. But here he was home again, and that was what was important, wasn't it? Home at last, and an apple pie cooling on the window. There'd be coffee too. He'd make it himself and bring Clara a cup in the cobalt blue mug that she'd bought—when? He couldn't remember. A long, long time ago, to be sure.

The kitchen was heavy with oven warmth. He slid in behind the table on the leather-covered window seat, glimpsing, out of the corner of his eye, a movement outside, beyond the glass. There was no noise to accompany the movement save, perhaps, just the echo of muffled laughter, but it seemed to him as if someone had been peering in out of the night. He looked out but all was darkness, and up through the darkness he could just make out a wash of stars in the sky. He cupped his hands across the sides of his face to block the light from the room behind him, and he squinted in order to see better. There seemed for a moment to be a pale figure receding into the night, down toward the village. He could hear the tapping of a stick on the road. The tapping terrified him. It seemed to haul his heart up into his throat, and for a moment he couldn't breathe or speak. But then there was nothing beyond the window but darkness, and the aroma of the pie was like a down comforter on a cold night or a bottle of ale at bedtime. He smiled at his wife and discovered that Annie had crawled up onto the cushion and stood regarding him, half accusingly, half happily. He wanted to say something to her, but he couldn't remember what it was that so desperately needed to be said, and there was a lump in his throat that made it impossible anyway, so he shrugged and shook his head.

There was the sudden smell of waterweeds in the air. The glow of the gas lamps fell and rose again. The tinkling of the distant piano sprang into sudden clarity, as if it were being played in the living room. For a moment he was certain that he sat alone on a hilltop in the weedy dirt and that a glowing jack-o'-lantern hovered in the air grinning at him where his wife's face had been a second earlier. Then he was in the kitchen again, sitting by the window.

He was astonished to discover that the outside of his pantleg was dripping wet, and on the cushion beside him lay a clump of tangled waterweeds. Annie had gone. What in the world, he asked himself, brushing the stuff off onto the floor beneath the table. He looked up, hoping that Clara hadn't seen him sweeping debris onto the floor, but where his wife had stood a moment earlier slicing him out a quarter of a pie, Leta now stood, smiling, regarding him slyly, like she'd caught him at some childish, endearing prank. The small hairs on the back of his neck stood up and he jammed himself back into the seat. He fumbled at his chest for his truth charm, but gave up almost at once. He needed no truth charm. He was enmeshed in a web spun of lies and deceptions. Something lay suddenly beneath his hand, and the seat beneath him felt uncomfortably lumpy and strange. When he pulled his hand away and peered at the cushion he could see that what had lain beneath his hand was a bat's head, dried, its eyes vacant, little teeth grinning out past shrunken gums.

He was suddenly conscious that a cold wind blew through the window behind him, and that his clothes had only half dried since his journey down the subterranean river. The panes of the window were broken now or were missing altogether, and those fragments of glass that were left were covered with such a layer of dust that they were opaque with it. His oiled pine table had become dry branches, broken and scarred and lashed together with brown grass and uneven strips torn from animal hide. Leta grinned at him malevolently, and handed to him a cracked plate on which sat a slice of pie from which had cascaded a little heap of blackened bones and gristle. Escargot slammed to his feet, kicking the table at the blind old woman who materialized suddenly in front of him.

The house roundabout was a ruin of dust and cobweb and fragments of furniture and fishbones. There was the smell once again of waterweeds and of burnt bone. The fog was rising along the ground outside when Escargot broke through the hanging back door at a run and found himself not on the hill opposite Mayor Bastable's house, but once again on the main street of Bleakstone Hollow, running now toward the distant farmhouse that marked the edge of the village. He could see the weather vane atop a high gable spinning and spinning and spinning in the wind. Lights brightened and dimmed around him, and as a counterpoint, the suddenly mad piano music and the laughter and talk and night noises of the town rose and fell with the lights, all of it caught up in the dark, inside-out rhythms of enchantment.

There ahead on the road stood a horse and cart, tethered to a hitching rail. Uncle Helstrom stood beside the horse and puffed merrily on his pipe, surprised, it seemed, to see Escargot leaping toward him like a man chased by ghosts. The dwarf widened his eyes and took his pipe out of his mouth. "Quick!" he cried, "the wagon!" And with a single tug he pulled loose the line that tethered it and gestured broadly to the puffing Escargot, who leaped into the cart, shook out the reins, whipped up the horse, and clattered away upriver in a panic. He'd drive the horse all the way to Landsend if he had to—to Seaside if the horse could swim. It was wood plank he was sitting on, sure enough, not stitched up bats, and the horse that pulled the cart was a flesh and blood horse that seemed every bit as anxious as he was to quit the haunted village.

The cart clattered and careered up the road, hammering over stones, creaking and bouncing and threatening with each swerve and jerk to crack to fragments. Escargot realized as he bounced along and clutched at the bare wood of the seat back behind him that he wasn't driving the cart. The horse was running away with him, wild with fear. He hauled back on the reins to slow the beast down. Lying slack in his hands were two broken straps of rotten leather. The horse plunged along, snorting and blowing and dragging the cart beneath the low, overhanging limbs of riverside oaks. Escargot slid onto the floorboards, hanging on, tree branches flailing across his head and back.

He was aware suddenly of the weird and heavy smell of fish, like the odor of a broken bottle of cod liver oil. A snatch of idiot laughter accompanied it, and, amazingly, instead of branches dragging across him, he found himself pummeled by small kicking feet. He hauled himself partway up from the floorboards as the lurching cart pitched him this way and that. A half score of goblins raged and screamed above him. Two sat on the seat, kicking him with wild glee and abandon. Two others sat astride the galloping horse, their little, taloned hands curled into the horse's mane. In the back of the cart rode a half dozen more, who raged and jabbered and gobbled out snatches of giddy laughter.

The wagon bounced toward the top of a hill, and as Escargot hauled himself up along the footrail, shoving both goblins across the seat with one hand, he could see the river stretching out like a broad, black ribbon far below to the left. On his right the hillside angled away, a mass of tangled brush and grasses, hurtling past as the wagon crested the hill and rolled headlong into the decline. The horse stumbled, trying to control its headlong flight, and the wagon seemed to rush up upon it suddenly.

The goblins astride the horse pitched off with a shriek. Escargot, his feet set on the floorboards and his hands gripping the footrail, threw himself after them, rolling and tumbling through the brush. He found himself lying stunned and scraped against the bole of a great tree. His jacket was shoved up around his shoulders and neck, and his right pantleg hung in tatters, as if someone had been at it with a scissors.

He shrugged his shoulders, just to see if they'd shrug, and

he heard, at that very moment, a cracking of wood and yowling of goblins somewhere below in the night, followed by the sound of galloping hooves that receded into silence. A brief spurt of goblin laughter followed. He steadied himself against the tree, wiggling his arms and legs one after another. He seemed to be a wonder of scrapes and bruises, and blood ran freely along his calf and into his sock, but nothing, as far as he could tell, would prevent his limping back down to the river and searching out his rowboat. Goblins, apparently, were intent on either his capture or his death or both, and if they could find something to laugh about after their charge down the hill, then they were still dangerous opponents, and might come lurking back around in order to find him.

His rowboat lay where he had left it, undisturbed, and in a moment he was in it and spinning out onto the silent river. He was beset by the unaccountable fear that his submarine would be gone—spirited away by the insidious dwarf. But it wasn't. It lay as he'd left it, safe and secure. It was his single trump card. Uncle Helstrom, sly and clever as he was, couldn't know that he possessed it. If he *had* known, it would be piloted by goblins now, or by the dwarf himself, more likely. How he'd use his trump card he couldn't say, but he was determined to use it.

On the peaceful river, though, when he had time to catch his breath, it occurred to him that it would be easy enough to turn around and just sail away. He could be free of the dwarf entirely—right then, if he chose. His goal upon leaving Twombly Town had been freedom and adventure, hadn't it? Well, there was no better time than now to launch out onto those waters. He had his submarine; he could go where he chose. He could be his own master for once.

But he could see after wrestling with the problem as he drifted off to sleep that night, that sailing away wouldn't do. The dwarf was meddling with things that he shouldn't meddle with—causing vast trouble, it seemed, for no end of innocent people. The Leta who had served him the pie of broken meats in the house on the hill hadn't been the Leta he had met earlier in the street. He could see that now. The difference was apparent, like the difference between soda glass and crystal, between a halloween mask and a smiling face, between a bird and a bat.

* * *

The sun next morning found him on the river again, well above Bleakstone Hollow and idling along slowly. He wondered whether the cart he'd been given by the dwarf had been the cart that the two had ridden upriver on, or whether it had been a different cart—perhaps the cart owned by the poor traveler Escargot had tried to rob. If it were the dwarf's cart, then it argued that he and the witch had reached their destination, or had very nearly done so. And yet Bleakstone Hollow, when he had moored offshore at dawn and studied it through the glass, seemed to him utterly deserted again. There had been no roads thereabouts that led inland, or at least none that he'd seen. And why on earth, he wondered, would they have made such a hasty dash of it upriver just to arrive at a long-deserted village? They must have gone along, he had determined, and very shortly he'd done the same, studying the river road when he could see it, dipping occasionally into the depths of the river, half fearful and half curious about what he might find there.

Once, in a depression some hundred yards offshore, lay a scattering of what appeared to be more of the strange blood-red marbles in the weedy shadows of the river bottom. He was inclined, at first, to break out the rubber suit and gather them up in a net. But there was something about the darkness of the river and about the cold silence of it that dissuaded him. This was no time, after all, to be out after trinkets. And even if the marbles, if that's what they were, amounted to some sort of very powerful magic, so what? What did he want with magic? Nothing. Less than nothing. When he finally won free of the dwarf and his snares and plots, there was nothing he wanted to meddle with less than magic. Just last night he'd had enough of it to last him two centuries and with some left over.

But there was nothing else to meddle with, apparently. The morning came and went and then the afternoon did the same. He hadn't seen a single thing to convince him that he wasn't chasing shadows now, and by three o'clock he began wondering just how far up the river he'd sail before he'd call it quits and turn around. He had intended, when he set out from Landsend, to stop now and then at a village and inquire, and had guessed, wrongly, that there would be any number of such villages along the way. But there had been nothing but danger in stopping along the shore—nothing but goblins and stewpots and scattered, terrified, untalkative people, all of them going somewhere in a passion. Upriver from Bleakstone Hollow there were no villages at all, just miles and miles of forest and river bottom and backwater, all of which would have served him very well if he were a sightseer, but which wasn't worth a penny under the circumstances. He'd stick it for two days, he said to himself, puffing on an afternoon pipe, and then he'd come back downriver slow and have another look. If there was nothing to see, then he'd quit worrying about it and go home, wherever that was.

A half hour later the pressure seemed to drop. The late afternoon air was heavy, as with storm clouds, but the sky was blue and empty. The wind gave off and a calm settled over the river and the shore as if someone had lain a pane of glass over everything. The dipping swallows and insects that swooped and hovered over the river simply disappeared, and the water grew calm like the still surface of water in a cup.

It was a very curious business, and if the sky had turned gray and black he would have been reminded of the tornado weather he remembered as a boy, when he lived on the plains beyond the City of the Five Monoliths. But the sky stayed blue. And then, almost imperceptibly at first, the shoreline seemed to wriggle like a snake, or like a throw rug being shaken out from one end. There was a sort of rippling wave that ran across the hills. Trees, very slowly, as if surprised at themselves, toppled over and smashed into the river. Then the land grew calm again. Silence descended, although Escargot hadn't been aware, until then, that there had been any noise. With the silence he recalled the distant rumble that had accompanied the tremor, something between rocks cascading down a hill in an avalanche and the overloud beating of a human heart. He puffed at his pipe and watched little dust clouds settle where trees had gone down.

He patted his pants pocket, looking for his matches, which he'd tucked away with his marble. His matches were there, but the marble, to his surprise, was gone. He had the habit of lounging around with his right hand in his pocket when he smoked his pipe. He could haul out matches and pipe tools that way. It had become a habit with him, and, as had happened in the past, he'd probably pulled his hand out of the pocket and accidentally hauled the marble out with it. He'd lost a gold piece that same way once and had gotten into no end of trouble from his wife.

He noticed that the outside of his pocket was sticky with something, as if he'd left an unwrapped bar of chocolate inside and it had melted through. He drew out the matchbox and it was covered with dark, ochre-colored goo that smelled coppery and vaguely sickening. What had gotten onto his pocket he couldn't say—some insect, perhaps, that he'd managed to squash by leaning up against the edge of the hatch.

The river ran placid and silent, and once again it seemed to him that the air thickened and hung still. He braced himself against the open hatch. This time it was more than just the toss of a throw rug. This time the rug was having the dust beaten out of it. The landscape shifted and groaned. Hillsides heaved up in a swirl of dirt and debris and uprooted trees. A cavern appeared suddenly in a mountainside where there had been no cavern moments before, exactly like an immense mouth yawning open. As if to complete the illusion, a long ridge of stone angling down from it arched up suddenly like the arm of a giant who had just that moment waked up and stretched. He heard the noise of it this time—the tearing and the moaning and a thump, thump, thump, slow and rhythmic like somebody whacking against the trunk of a hollow tree with an immense rubber mallet.

He dropped down the hatch and slammed it shut over him, just before the wave hit. He'd seen it coming, tossed up along the shore and growing as it surged toward mid river. It had sprung out of nothing and was on him in an instant. It swept the submarine onto its side, and a great green mass of frothing river washed across the bow, the shock of it throwing Escargot onto his back in the companionway, waiting for another wave. When it didn't come he scuttled forward into the pilothouse and hauled away on the rudder, angling the ship down into deep water. In moments he cruised along beneath the surface—twenty feet down, then thirty, then forty. A submarine, he told himself, was the sort of ship a man wanted when the top of a river decided to shake itself out.

The river bottom had been stirred to life. Waterweeds tore loose and tossed in sudden currents, and as Escargot watched, a long, dark crevass split the sand and muck, and no end of debris and startled fish and water plants rushed into the widening hole. The submarine itself seemed to falter, as if the engines were suddenly paltry things, and Escargot could almost feel the ship slipping sideways and backward, being hauled along in an increasing rush, as if the entire river were being sucked into the earth like water down a drain. There was nothing at all he could do but hold on and watch. He'd end up someplace, sure enough, and he could easy enough navigate up out of a hole. He'd navigated *down* one without too much trouble when he'd come to Balumnia in the first place, hadn't he? But he could imagine, all the same, the crack in the river bottom swallowing him up and then slamming shut, cracking the submarine like a nutshell.

Then the rushing water slowed and stopped and he seemed to eddy there for a moment, as if the river couldn't make up its mind to quit fooling away the afternoon and get back around to the business of being a river. He found himself, as his craft surged forward once again, staring into the face of an enormous fish—a great, dark, finny monster that had been drawn out of the mid river channel by the quake and the fissures in the river bottom. It eyed him through the glass ports, illuminated by fire-quartz lamps. It was vast and seemed to be armored instead of scaled, as if it were the invention of a deranged blacksmith. It floated goggling at him, deciding, it seemed, whether to swallow the submarine at a gulp or search for more substantial prey. Escargot throttled forward, watching out of the ports as the creature turned lazily and followed, then fell away astern. In the shadows beyond it things were moving—not just swirling flotsam stirred up in the quake, but great gliding fish and eels; many-armed, octopus-like beasts that crept across the sandy river floor; and finned lizards, their hooked teeth glinting in the light of the fire-quartz. Lamp-like eyes stared at him out of the darkness. One passing shadow glided past for what seemed like an age, as if it were long as the river itself. Whatever creatures inhabited the deepwater grottoes and bottomless river caverns had been shaken to life by the tremor—awakened, it seemed, from ages of stony sleep, as if the quake were a summons, were a door creaking open onto a primeval landscape, and the ancient creatures that had slept there were stirring and blinking and angling up out of the shaded depths toward daylight.

14

Boggy Speaks Up

The sun looked uncommonly good to him when he surfaced—like an old friend or a comfortable hat. He hadn't been threatened, really, by any of the river creatures, although heaven help him if he had been. They'd seemed to be half drowsy, surprised to find themselves there at all. Escargot wondered for the hundredth time, as he idled along upriver, what, exactly, was going on. The innkeeper's fears, the goblins carrying on as if there was some design in their capering and howling, the enchantment at Bleakstone Hollow, things stirring in the river, the elf galleon—there could be little doubt that he was sailing into something.

He nibbled at a long strip of jerked beef and uncorked a bottle of ale. His food supply was meagre, and it certainly seemed as if there was little likelihood of replenishing it at riverside villages. Hunting in the woods was out of the question. If his ale and water gave out, he supposed, he could drink river water—boil it up and filter it first. And he could always catch fish, if it came down to it. But somehow it seemed a bad moment to start eating things out of the river; the water was too oddly murky, too full of the unsettling dust of magic.

A broad plume of smoke appeared beyond the tree line a half mile upriver. Trouble, he said to himself, throttling forward, grinning to think that he was running straight into it by choice. It was broad daylight, and would be for a good three hours yet—time enough to have a glimpse at the goings on. It might very easily be a farmhouse afire, torched by goblins. It might as easily be the dwarf and the witch. They needed a good thrashing; that's what. The idea appealed to him immensely, with the sun overhead and evening still hours away. He felt bucked up suddenly, perhaps because his bottle of ale had been an uncommonly good one and because sailing along there out on the river he was in a position to feel less threatened than he had yesterday evening, when he was alone in the dark and stumbling through an enchanted village.

The submarine rounded a long curve, hugging a high, alluvial bank and taking care not to run aground. Escargot realized that he had developed an aversion to deep water, and for very good reason, he told himself, and he was anxious to be in toward shore so that he could move quickly if it was necessary.

Tucked away in a broad cove a hundred fifty yards ahead was the elf galleon—the one that had flown from the sky—riding at anchor, and off through the trees, almost obscured by foliage, was a burning farmhouse, just as he'd guessed—a vast and roomy mansion with steep slate roofs and about a dozen chimney pots that rose above the tops of the oaks. Flames and smoke coursed out of an attic gable, and through the open hatch of the submarine Escargot could hear shouts and cries and the yammering of goblins.

Leta appeared from behind a stand of trees, running along the road toward the farmhouse as if *she*, at least, *was* determined to throw herself into the middle of things. Behind her, running along and holding onto their pointy hats, were two elves, obviously chasing her.

Escargot couldn't tell then whether she was running from the elves or toward the burning farmhouse or both, but the mere sight of her running at all sent him clambering after his rowboat. Something within him knew that it *was* Leta running along the road; it wasn't the witch. Perhaps he'd rubbed up against so much dark magic over the past days that he could sense it finally, or at least could sense its absence.

When he bumped up onto the sandy shore of another smaller cove, out of sight of the galleon, and hauled the rowboat up out of the river, Leta was gone and the elves with her. The air was full of shouting and smoke and mayhem. Three goblins, their heads bobbing from side to side, eyes whirling, came raging out of the shrubbery at him, as if they'd been on the lookout for him all along and had worked themselves into a frenzy through anticipation. Escargot had had enough of goblins and their dangerous pranks. He was out of sympathy with the little men. He plucked an oar out from underneath the thwarts and slammed the first goblin in the side of the head with the flat of the paddle. It was too long for any serious swinging, though, and the goblin was up and after him along with his companions, all of them capering along behind as Escargot charged up the bank carrying the oar like a spear.

He stopped abruptly, picked up a rock the size of a bread loaf, and threw it with all his strength at the head of the goblin nearest at hand, then leaped in after the next one, jabbing the creature in the chest with the handle of the oar and knocking it over backward into the weeds. The first goblin lay where he fell, his mouth still working feebly, the stone beside him. The third goblin hesitated, looking at his fallen comrades, then tried to heft the stone himself, shakily, with skinny little arms, baring his filed teeth at Escargot as if to throw a fright into him. The rock was far too heavy, though, and the creature dropped it on his own bare foot, howling in pain and rage, then turned and jammed a taloned finger into the ear of the goblin still sitting in the weeds. His companion howled, grabbed the offending finger, and bit it twice, only to have a clump of his hair yanked out in turn. The two fell upon each other in earnest then, and Escargot, wondering that such a thing as a goblin could exist in an otherwise rational world, turned and trotted up toward the road, at which time both the scrabbling goblins leaped up and chased after him, hooting with rage.

It was clear that there were goblins aplenty to smack with the oar. The elves, a couple dozen in all, dressed in their gaudy foolery, were outnumbered by a margin of ten to one, and it was only their sanity that evened the score against the mad goblins, who were every bit as likely to tear off the ear of one of their fellows as to attempt the ear of an elf. Swords whirled in the afternoon sunlight, wielded by the capering elves, who seemed leery of actually skewering goblins, but were waving their weapons in a theatrical show, poking the occasional goblin that achieved any real mischief. It was suddenly clear to Escargot that the elves intended to gain entrance to the burning house, and that the goblins weren't in the mood to see them do it.

He watched Leta snatch a goblin up by his trousers and toss him head over heels down the hill toward the river, then latch onto another one and sail him off too. She kicked a third in the same general direction, and although the goblins raged and spat and did little threatening dances roundabout her, they seemed loathe to hurt her. A half dozen elves rushed in at her all at once, pounding goblins out of the way as they ran, but Leta pushed the first of them in the face and sent him sprawling downhill too. There were no end of elves and goblins, both crowds set against each other, and Leta, apparently, set against the both of them. All of them scurried around her as if they had designs on her, but daren't hurt her.

Above them on the hill the house burned. The third story and attic were full of flames, which roared out the broken window and licked the eaves. In the second-floor window, peering past lace curtains that hung like cobweb, stood the old woman, the witch, as if gazing at the turmoil that raged below her. Escargot dropped his oar at the sight of her. It was clear that she *was* watching, blind or no; but she wasn't merely watching the turmoil, she was watching Leta.

Escargot picked up his oar, held it in both hands before him at waist height as if it were a fence rail and he were about to vault over it, and ran up the hill, knocking goblins aside in a wide swath. He didn't want to clobber any elves. Whatever the nature of the struggle on the hill, being elves they were quite obviously on his side—that is to say, against the dwarf. They seemed surprised to see him, which of course they would be, and were doubly surprised when he latched onto Leta's arm, kicked loose a goblin that had her by the leg, and set out at a run downhill toward the river. His goal was simple. He'd haul her to the rowboat, cast off, and make straightaway to the submarine. They'd come about and lay on full steam, as it were, for Landsend. They'd leave the lot of them behind—elves, goblins, dwarf, and witch—to sort out the mess. They could bite and poke at each other until doomsday.

A resounding crash sounded behind them, and Escargot couldn't help but look back. Half the roof had caved in, dumping burning lumber onto the ground, the flames leaping almost at once up the shingled wall, and even as the two of them watched, it seemed that the entire farmhouse, from cellar to attic, was suddenly aflame. The door burst open and the dwarf and witch tumbled out like penny gumballs out of a machine, gasping and bent and pawing the air, then stumbling to their feet and making away toward the trees. The elves, having raced downhill to avoid the collapsing roof, raced up it again, chased by goblins and in the wake of the fleeing dwarf. All the better for them, thought Escargot, smiling at Leta and winning a smile in return, and without a word they set out once more, concerned only with flight.

As they ran a fog rose off the river. It was dense and gray and heavy, as if it were the ghost of the river itself, and a chill breeze sprang up before it, swirling the mist this way and that in little tendrils. Leta jerked Escargot to a halt, twisted loose, and turned as if to run from the fog. "Quickly!" she cried, out of breath and in deadly earnest, but the swirling reek, like a little wind devil spawned of the enchanted river, soared up the hill on the freshening breeze and engulfed the both of them.

"Leta!" shouted Escargot, grabbing for her. But he found himself holding nothing at all, and her answering shout floated half uttered in the mist. She was gone. Vanished. Just as she'd disappeared yesterday evening at sunset. Sunset, Escargot muttered. Fog. Sunset and fog. All of this had to do with sunlight, didn't it? He turned hopelessly back toward the river, slouching along through the thinning murk toward the rowboat. He wouldn't see Leta again, not that day. He was sure of it. In an hour the sun would set, and he'd bet dollars to doughnuts that if he scoured Balumnia with a lawn rake all night long he'd find no trace of her—quite simply because she wouldn't be there.

When she'd appeared with Uncle Helstrom—that had been at night. It had been the witch then, not Leta. And again, in the Widow's windmill, Leta had vanished when the setting sun had struck her face. She had become the old woman. The same thing had happened in Seaside—hadn't it? He'd chased her through the streets until night had fallen, and with evening she'd vanished, winked away, and there was the old woman, again. The house in Landsend—he'd found her there at night again; that was the old woman, not Leta. The pattern was clear. It was like goblin gold, exactly like goblin gold—enchantment that dissolved in the sunlight. Darkness and fog would mask it, but sunlight would expose it. Somehow, for some unfathomable, monstrous purpose, Leta was snatched away by night and hauled along upriver, possessed by the witch. Leta's wraith, heaven knew, might be hovering roundabout him in the air at that moment, crying out in a voice that only spirits could hear. He slumped onto the center thwart of the rowboat, returning the oar to its place underneath.

The boat still sat high and dry on the beach. It seemed to him suddenly as if he had no place to go, not really. Once again he was left without a destination. The urgency of his quest had redoubled—the touch of Leta's hand and the smile on her face had done that. But all of that made it even less impossible to go on. Where would he go? Where, for heaven's sake, had the elves gone? He brightened a bit. Perhaps the elves had gotten hold of the dwarf. They'd lead him up, his head in a noose, his hands tied. Together they'd force him to release Leta. Escargot would twist his arm for him if he didn't like the idea.

There was the sound of voices behind him, growing louder by the moment. It was the elves, returning. The fog had lifted. It had risen up the hill and obscured the forest now, seeming to roll very slowly upriver, as if following the progress of a cart, say, that was making away along the river road. Escargot knew before he saw the elves that they'd have no dwarf in tow. And they didn't.

The elves—about a dozen of them now—slouched along toward him as if they were tired out. One walked before the rest, dressed in a waistcoat and buckler and with a gaudy, frilly shirt underneath. He wore cuffed boots with the toes curled back around in little pigtail points, and he dragged his unsheathed sword along in the dust of the roadway, as if he were contemplating some grand failure and could think of nothing else. Unlike his companions, he wore a cocked hat, yanked down over his brow and shading his face. A turquoise peacock feather, once grand and dashing, hung from the hatband, broken in the center and shredded to pieces. The tip of the feather lurched down into his face with each tedious, clumping step he took, and he swatted at it as he walked, as if it were an insect buzzing round his nose. His fellows weren't vastly more cheerful.

All were dressed in piratical clothes. If it had been midnight it would have appeared that they were dragging home from an exhausting masquerade, where they'd all, perhaps, drank too much punch and danced too furiously and now were tired and filled with regret. They perked up, at least for the moment, when they saw Escargot sitting in his beached rowboat. The elf in the cocked hat bristled and flourished his sword, as if he weren't quite sure whether to run Escargot through on the spot, or hang him in order to avoid soiling his blade.

"We'll have a word with you, sir," said the elf in a voice intended to be gruff.

"Theophile Escargot," he said, standing up on the wooden slat deck of the rowboat, "at your service."

"Step ashore, sir."

"Gladly," said Escargot, bowing to the lot of them and clambering out of the boat. A great moaning erupted a few yards down the beach, and the goblin whose head had stopped Escargot's rock stood up groggily and looked around him. He rubbed the top of his head gingerly, caught sight of the elves and of Escargot, and ran straightaway into the river, howling and moaning, and was borne away on the current, his head bobbing atop the water like a cleverly painted melon.

The elf captain blinked several times at the disappearing goblin, watching until it vanished beyond the edge of the cove. "Who are you, sir, and what did you mean by spiriting away the woman?" He looked around then, suddenly aware, it seemed, that Leta wasn't in Escargot's company. "Search the area!" he cried, waving his sword in such a way as to have clipped the heads off his companions had they been any closer. The elves darted off, beating the bushes and peering behind trees. One climbed up into the branches of an oak and then couldn't climb out again. He appealed to the captain for help. "Did you see anything?" asked the captain, standing under the tree.

"No," came the reply.

"Then you can stay in the damnation tree!" the captain thundered, in his way, and the elf in the tree clung to a limb and looked shakily at the ground.

"I say, Captain," said an elf in gaiters and a satin shirt, "you can't just leave poor Boggy in the tree."

"Who says I can't, now?" asked the captain, exercising his authority.

"Poor Boggy!" cried another elf, as if in reply. And Boggy himself began to moan and to hug the tree as if he were in danger of pitching off into the dirt. His cap slipped off his head, and he lunged for it, very nearly losing his balance. He caught himself, hooting with fear, and immediately began to cry.

The captain shook his head tiredly, as if to lament having to put up with such a crew as this. Then he turned to Escargot and, winking at him, asked to borrow his jacket.

"Of course," said Escargot in reply, and he pulled the jacket off and handed it over. Four elves attached themselves to it, clinging to sleeves and to the bottom seam, and, stretching it below the tree limb, shouted at the unfortunate Boggy to leap into it. They'd catch him, they promised. He wouldn't be hurt. Not a bit.

Boggy leaped, slamming into the coat and bearing all four elves down into the weeds, shouting and flailing and causing Escargot to wonder whether, taken all the way around, there was such a vast difference between elves and goblins after all. But they *had* built his submarine, of course, and his truth charm, and any number of other wonderful devices, including the galleon they had flown in on. How they got any of it done, though, was one of the world's great mysteries.

When Boggy was dusted off and comforted, and the captain had been the victim of more than one hard look, as if he had conspired to have Boggy put through such tortures, Escargot was given his jacket back and once again became the center of attention.

"Where is the girl?" asked the captain, not mincing words.

"I haven't the earthliest idea," replied Escargot, entirely honestly.

"She was with you not fifteen minutes back."

"That she was. But she's vanished. The fog came up off the river and she was gone. Into the air. Puff. One moment she was speaking, the next she evaporated and her voice along with it. I thought that you might tell *me* where she'd gotten off to. It's impossible that you know less about this affair than I do, because I know nothing at all."

The captain squinted at him, obviously disbelieving. Here was Escargot, miles from any habitable village, out wandering alone and connected in some unknown way with the girl. It made no sense that he knew nothing at all. "Who are you, then? You don't live along the river."

"Of course I do," said Escargot. "I've got an old aunt up-river from here on the north shore who's dying. Quite likely already gone, bless her heart, and she's left me a brewery. Hale's Ales. You might have heard of it. There isn't a better ale, not along the river anyway. I'm bound for there now, but I saw the house burning so I rowed ashore to lend a hand."

The captain squinted at his rowboat and then winked at him again. "Where did you set out?"

"Grover," said Escargot, smiling.

"You *rowed* all the way upriver from Grover? Why didn't you row to Hansen's Island and take the steamship. You'd save about three weeks time."

"Steamship's down. Hansen's Island was flooded in the last rain and the steamship won't be running again till Tuesday."

"Hah!" cried the captain triumphantly. "Hansen's Island! Damn Hansen's Island! There *is* no such place. I trapped you with that one, lad. You'd best make a clean breast of it now. Out with it." And with that he looked about him, grinning at his companions and nodding in appreciation of his own cleverness. Boggy's sniffing and mumbling undermined it, though, and the captain gave him a look.

Escargot thought about it. There was no reason, really, to pretend, to lie. They'd caught him at it already, and if he cooked up another one, they'd quite likely catch him out there too. He'd tell the truth, is what he'd do, for the most part, and he'd at least end up with two score of allies that he hadn't had earlier in the afternoon.

"I'm a sea captain," he said, eyeing the elves. "I've come upriver from Landsend and beyond. This dwarf has stolen my goods, insulted my person, and has played some sort of villainy on the girl Leta, who, I might add, I've taken a vow to rescue." With that he bowed to the captain again, thinking that he'd made a fairly pretty speech of it all the way around—the sort of affected talk that the captain would approve of.

"Upriver from Landsend now, instead of Grover, is it? A sea captain?" The elf slapped the fiddlehead of the rowboat with his open palm and grinned at his crew, one or two of whom cried, "Sea captain!" or "Landsend!" as if they, too, doubted Escargot's tale, but the feebleness of their taunts made it seem to Escargot that their purpose was rather to support their captain than to embarrass Escargot. The captain was very satisfied with himself. "Where's your ship?" he said with a suddenness that made it very clear he was trapping Escargot into another confession.

"In the river," came the answer.

"Ho! In the river!" shouted Boggy, restored now. The captain frowned at him.

Escargot rose, motioned to the captain, and set out around the curve of the little half-moon cove until, stepping out onto the rock and sand headland at the far end of it, he could see the submarine riding at anchor. He gestured at it and kept silent.

"Quite a device," said the captain, nodding in approval. "I know it. It belonged to a renegade, a blackguard."

"Captain Perry, that would be?"

"Yes indeed. He was a megalomaniac. There aren't many bad ones among us, sir, but he was an exception of the first water. How did you come by this boat?"

"He sank a trader I crewed on. Killed any number of men but took me aboard the ship. He had ransom in mind, perhaps . . ."

"Maybe he was after your aunt's brewery," said the captain, interrupting.

"Maybe," said Escargot, momentarily confused over whether the aunt's brewery lie had been exposed yet or not. That was the problem with lies, actually—they tended to tangle themselves up. "In a word, I overcame him and his crew and marooned them, is what I did, and now *I* pilot that boat, as I said, in search of the dwarf and the girl he's mistreated."

"Hooray!" shouted Boggy, won over, apparently. But his cry evaporated in the afternoon stillness as the captain stroked his chin in contemplation.

"And with whom," asked Escargot in an effort to get the upper hand, "am I honored to be speaking?"

"Captain Appleby and the crew of the *Nora Dawn*," said the captain very politely, as if a little ashamed of himself for having overlooked introductions. He led the way back up the beach to where the rowboat was moored. "It's no go, I'm afraid."

"What is?"

"Your meddling in this affair. It can't stand it. It *won't* stand it. Your foiling the efforts of my men to rescue the girl can be excused. *You* didn't know you were caught up in affairs beyond your ken. But now you know, and it's off down the river with you. Go home. That's my advice. It's more than that. It's my order. I'm commissioned to give them, you know, to civilians as well as to my crewmembers.''

Escargot stood blinking at him. It would be a shame to lose his temper. As officious as this elf captain was, he was more humorous than irritating. ''What about my property?''

''I'll compensate you for it. At once. That and more. I'm a generous man. I've been commissioned to be a generous man. What sort of property did the dwarf steal from you? Gold?''

''Marbles.''

''Marbles is it?'' Captain Appleby stared at him. ''You've come upriver . . . Wait a minute—Captain Perry's device! You've come from where? Seaside? The Isles? You've come through the gate, by golly, after a bag of marbles? It can't be so. Don't trifle with me, lad; I'm not in a trifling mood. Send your bag of marbles to keep your drunken aunt company. How much will it cost me to see your diminishing self atop the river?''

''A bag of very odd marbles. Red—the color of blood. And not entirely round. Even the most amateur of marble spinners could have done better. They're enchanted marbles is what I think, and . . .''

But Escargot stopped in wonder at that point, for Captain Appleby's mouth had dropped open, as if he'd just that instant had his jaw muscles severed. ''Red, did you say? About as big as what, pigeon's eggs? Where did you get these marbles?''

''From a bunjo man. Not many months back, either. And I'm fairly sure now that they'd been giving me the most astonishing dreams.''

''I daresay,'' muttered the captain, stroking his chin again. ''And you say the dwarf has them now?''

''That he does.''

''All is explained then.'' The captain turned to the elf beside him, who had been eyeing Escargot shrewdly throughout the exchange and looked to be some sort of officer, a first mate, perhaps. ''The earth tremors,'' he said.

''Of course,'' came the reply.

''It's later than we think.''

''It is that.''

''But he got sloppy with it and lit the house afire.''

Escargot eyed the two, catching most of the words that passed between them. "The earthquake earlier today. That wasn't one of your standard earthquakes hereabouts, I take it."

The captain looked up at him, grinning suddenly. "Oh very standard, I should think," he said hastily. "Wouldn't you say so, Collier?"

Collier admitted that he'd rarely seen an earthquake so all around standard.

"It weren't standard at all," shouted Boggy, unfortunately standing well behind the captain and so unaware that the captain had screwed his mouth into a sort of pickle frown and was winking rapidly at Collier. "I seen a giant head open up in the mountainside and yawn, like it had been woke up, almost, and . . ."

"And you can shut your gob, Mr. Boggy . . ." began the captain.

But Escargot, remembering the mountainside that *he'd* seen, cried, "I saw it too! Just like a mouth, wasn't it? And you could swear that there were eyes above, clamped shut, but trembling, like at any moment they were going to spring open and some great stone giant was going to stand up and gape."

"Ha, ha, ha," laughed Captain Appleby, nudging Collier, who laughed too. "Prime lark, sir. Very prime. But we've important work to do, and, as I say, you've stumbled into something that you'd got no business stumbling into. If it's a bag of marbles you've lost, you'll have another. And elfin marbles this time, not the goblin trash you lost."

"Goblin!" cried Escargot, wondering at this new development.

"Well, in almost every sense, yes. They weren't marbles at all, you see, they were droplets of blood—petrified blood, frozen blood, whatever you like."

Escargot stared at him, uncomprehending yet not entirely surprised. Evening was falling. The river flowed dark and smooth behind him, and all at once he was anxious to be away. He had no real desire to go out rowing on the river at night, and less desire with each passing moment. Captain Appleby, quite clearly, wouldn't fancy having Escargot along. The elves were on a mission, sent out by heaven knew what sort of power. And Escargot was nothing more than an interloper who had, so far, served no end but trouble. A lie, it occurred to him suddenly, would answer here, and the simpler and more bold-faced the lie, the better it would answer. He heaved a sigh, like a man tired, suddenly, with confusions that he can't begin to penetrate. "This is all a bit too much for me, I'm afraid."

"I warned you of that—didn't I, men?"

"Aye!" cried some few of the elves, nodding to one another.

"It ain't so complicated as *that*," said Boggy, shaking his head in quick little jerks, as if *he*, perhaps, if given a go at it, could explain the mystery to Escargot's entire satisfaction.

"No, sir," said Escargot, pushing his rowboat two feet closer to the water and rolling up his pantlegs, "I can't fathom it. Blood, you say, and not marbles. I've been chasing this villain across two worlds in order to get my hands on—what? It makes me sick to think about it."

"Just so," said Appleby, "just so. Cut and run, that's my advice. And as I say, I'd be in a way to advance you a bag full of elfin marbles that would make your goblin filth seem pretty rugged. Have you seen any of Mazlak's marbles?"

"No," answered Escargot truthfully.

"Well you ought to have. *If* you're a marble man like I am, and I think I can see that you are."

"It's a tempting offer, a tempting offer." Escargot pulled at his nose once or twice, as if consulting that article about the puzzling choices that lay before him. "You've convinced me," he said finally, nodding and squinting and looking downriver as if he were suddenly anxious to be off. Boggy, peering past the captain, snorted and giggled until the elf next to him nudged him in the ribs. "Just to satisfy a man's curiosity, though," Escargot continued, "tell me about this marble blood business."

"Giant's blood," said Appleby, shrugging his shoulders. "Not marble blood." He sighed and thought for a moment, considering, perhaps, how to make a long story short. "There was a time when the land was overrun by giants, to whom this broad river would have seemed a trout stream . . ."

"Stone giants?" said Escargot.

"That's right. If you know about it already, why did you ask?"

"I've read G. Smithers, is what I've done. That's all. I've wondered how much of it was true."

"Oh, Smithers is your man for the truth. That he is. He's an uncommonly good friend of ours, is Smithers, and what he writes in the book is what he writes in the book, and don't let anyone tell you anything else."

Escargot thought about Appleby's assurances for a moment, unable, entirely, to grasp his meaning, but the captain went right along without him.

"These giants then, they died out ages ago—long, long ages beyond the memory of any elf alive. Ten times beyond it. There was a struggle, you see—far too vast to reveal here—and the long and the short of it was that the giants fell afoul of powers greater than their own and were cast down, into the earth, where they've dwelt since. And not to put too fine a point on it, they weren't dead, either, but were petrified, if you follow me. If you stroll back up into those hills there you'll find cave mouths more particularly like mouths than the caves you're used to seeing, and you'll hear noises, too, like the beating of a stone heart."

"The earthquake, then?"

Captain Appleby shrugged and grinned. "You're a good man, and have an eye for marbles . . ."

"And you already figured it out anyway," shouted Boggy, grinning at the back of the captain's head. "That was a mouth, it were, what yawned in the mountainside. And the dwarf's setting in to jerk it up out of there."

"Jerk the mouth up out of there?" asked Escargot.

Captain Appleby turned and smiled at Boggy, blinking his eyes very rapidly as if a bug had flown into them. "Into the tree with him, lads!" he shouted abruptly, and made a grab for poor Boggy, who collapsed at once in tears and said that he couldn't bear to be put into the tree—not again; which was curious, certainly, since he hadn't been *put* into the tree yet at all. Captain Appleby said he'd give him another chance, then said very plainly that he would stuff Boggy's shirt into Boggy's mouth if Boggy's mouth wouldn't give off and rest. He turned back to Escargot and shrugged again, as if to say that there was no accounting for a frivolous elf like Boggy. Then he continued:

"These marbles, then, in a word, were giant's blood, shed in the great war, blood that spilled into the Tweet, into the mountain lakes and springs and froze there, like . . . like . . . What is that stone, again, Mr. Collier?"

"Obsidian, sir. Troll tears."

"Quite right. Good man, Collier. Troll tears. Have you heard of such an article, sir?"

"Indeed I have," said Escargot. "Molten rock, as I have it, cast from volcanoes into water and hardening there."

"That's it in a nut. These stone giants, you see, are much more evidently products of the earth, of clay and stone and crystal, than are you and I, and their blood, you see, runs like liquid stone. Agate, you know, is the flesh of giants. Polish a specimen, sir, and you'll see very clearly within it the blues and reds of veins and arteries and the fleshy brown of sinew and gristle and . . . well, you understand."

Escargot nodded, vaguely appalled at the idea, but finding it rational enough.

"Our dwarf, I fear, would use these 'marbles' to enchant the sleeping giants into wakefulness, and very nearly did so this afternoon. But he overreached himself and set the house afire. Hasty sort of a fellow. He knew we pursued him. We've thrown the fear into him. But he'll try again—tomorrow afternoon, if I'm any judge of this sort of thing, which I am, and I can assure you he won't set himself afire a second time."

Escargot considered Appleby's words for a moment, then said, "Weeks ago, on the meadow beyond Twombly Town, there were three witches melting the marbles down in a pot. Perhaps this dwarf doesn't have the marbles after all. Perhaps he's not the threat you take him for."

"They were *ripening* the things, lad. He's got them, all right, and if we could discover a way to get them back we'll knock a hole in his boat for sure. It wouldn't sink him, maybe, but he'd be foundering."

"The girl," asked Escargot, nodding as if satisfied, "what about the girl?"

"I was rather hoping that *you* could shed some little light on that subject."

"Me?"

"Don't tell me, sir, that you saw her for the first time this afternoon and that you took such a sudden fancy to her that you risked your hide scrapping with my men? You were in frightful danger there, my man, frightful danger."

Escargot shrugged. "Any gentleman would have done the same."

"I daresay," snickered Boggy, imitating the captain's voice and hinting, through the tone of it, that a gentleman like Escargot might quite likely be interested in more than mere chivalry.

Now it was Escargot's turn to give Boggy a look, and he considered suggesting that they put Boggy into the tree again, but he held off. The conversation was cockeyed enough as it was.

"What do you know of her?" asked Captain Appleby. "Come, man. It's been good faith all the way along. Now it's your turn to spill. There's more riding on this, I tell you, than you can conceivably suppose. Far more. The girl's life hangs in the balance. At least I think it does. If you'd save her, speak."

"Her name is Leta something-or-other. I don't know what. The witch, as I understand it—the old blind woman—holds her in thrall, and steals her body whenever the sun fails to shine. At night, or in a fog, Leta becomes little more than a wraith. I've seen it happen. It did just now, on the hillside in the river fog."

"The fog," said Appleby, nodding. "That's no common fog. The dwarf, you see, is a necromancer from the Dark Wood. He's what Smithers would call a fog dwarf—a dweller-in-the-mists, to put it more artistically, which is usually his way."

"That must be in a Smithers book I haven't read."

"My good fellow," said the captain, "there are no end of Smithers books you've yet to read. No end that he hasn't writ yet. He's in no hurry, is Smithers."

"Who *is* Smithers?"

"Just a fellow from up in the village. You wouldn't have seen him, I think."

"*Which* village, exactly?"

"Any village you please, I shouldn't wonder. But this is all smalltalk, my man, and smalltalk must wait. About the girl—where does she come from?"

"Seaside," Escargot said promptly. He didn't have to think about it. He had reviewed in his mind the little bit he knew about Leta's history so many times that it had become as familiar to him as his name.

"When?"

"Don't know. She's eighteen, nineteen."

"That don't help. The day is what I need."

"Just before the harvest festival. She was what they call a harvest maid."

Captain Appleby's jaw dropped again, even farther this time than it had when he'd heard about the marbles. "I knew it," he said in a low voice. "And we're fooling away time here. Back to the ship!" he cried suddenly, taking Escargot by surprise.

"What on earth are they going to do with her?" he asked, frightened by the captain's sudden seriousness.

Appleby shook his head grimly. "Nothing at all if you don't keep us here with your empty talk. The dwarf, as I say, is going to roust these giants out of bed, and he'll awaken heaven knows what sorts of creatures in the deep water of the Tweet. There's no bottom to that river, as you and I know river bottoms. Its waters flow out of antiquity. Things of dirt and stone will reign again. We'll save the girl—don't be afraid of that—but I'll tell you that the girl won't be saved for the sake of the girl, not that alone, but for the sake of . . . of . . . more than I can tell you now. I've said enough. Wait for us in Landsend, sir, at the Blue Head in Lanternwick Street. If we don't find you by the weekend, then you won't be in a position to worry about marbles or girlfriends or anything else but your seagoing hide. I bid you farewell!" With that he turned and stalked away, followed by Collier and the rest of the elves, including Boggy, who did a little ridiculing dance atop the captain's shadow, which, in the deepening gloom of evening, stretched ghostly long across the beach and out onto the river.

15

What Happened in the Oak Woods

Escargot sat once again in his rowboat, alone. "Not for the sake of the girl," he muttered half aloud. He didn't at all like that. There was nothing he wouldn't do, it seemed to him then, for the sake of the girl. And for the sake of twisting the dwarf's nose. He knew, finally, what it was that, as Smithers himself might have put it, "was abroad in the land," but the knowledge didn't bring him six inches closer to being able to do anything about it.

A sudden creaking and clatter arose in the sky behind him, and he turned to see Captain Appleby's galleon setting sail on the sky tides from its mooring in the adjacent cove. It slanted up past the trees, its sails billowing out in the wind that blew upriver, and as it looped around and made away to westward, he could see Captain Abbleby on the afterdeck and Collier standing beside him. The captain had a fresh feather in his hat, a red feather this time, and he wore a greatcoat now, to ward off the windy night chill. In a moment the ship seemed to be no more than a cleverly built child's toy, disappearing toward the rising moon.

He found them again at anchor, twenty miles upriver. The forested slopes of the south shore had given way, finally, to low, rolling hills and meadows with here and there a stand of oak and sycamore. The earth was cracked and had been heaved up in ages past and shaken out and shuffled and tossed so that long cuts of exposed stone angled across meadows and hillsides. It seemed unlikely that the hills and meadows had ever been the retreat of men, despite their green and sunny appearance, and there was something about the place—some low-lying atmosphere—that proclaimed, as loudly as if it were spoken through a trumpet, that the dark earth thereabouts was seeded with magic, and that when it rained, a mist of enchantment rose from the rivulets that cut the meadows and that fell away finally into the Tweet.

There was no sign of the elves, or of anyone else for that matter, although off in the distance, scrabbling across the top of a heap of shrub-covered stone, was a heavy, bent, shaggy-headed troll. Escargot felt suddenly lonely and sad in a way that he couldn't at all explain. He could hear the papery hum of dragonfly wings and the occasional splash of a fish somewhere off over the water. Far away, unseen in the cloud-drift sky, geese passed along above him, and their honking, distant and faint, reminded him of something—something he'd lost, perhaps, or something which had been promised to him and would never appear, but would be always pending, waiting, just out of sight beyond a clover-covered hillside or a stand of trees or a broad bank of cloud that obscured the horizon. He scratched his head and wondered at it all, listening to the silence.

Way off across the river, a mile or more away, the smoke of a steamship lazied up into the morning air and the thin blast of the ship's whistle sounded. The presence of a ship-load of people, playing cards and eating and leaning on rails to watch the river flow past, increased the feeling of loneliness, as if they occupied a world too distant for him to return to—a world which he had occupied for a time but had been cast out of, largely because of his own laziness and pigheadedness. In a melancholy mood, he dawdled there, smoking his pipe and calling up memories which were as much a product of the morning stillness as of anything else.

After twenty minutes of that sort of thing he realized that he was powerfully hungry and that he had almost nothing left to eat. He held a glass tumbler in his hand, half filled with the contents of the last skunked bottle of ale. When he'd opened it, it had seemed to him better than nothing, even though he wasn't normally given to breakfasting on ale—especially bad ale. But even the jerked beef was gone. He had nothing else. There were a half dozen apples, but he was sick of apples, and these had so thoroughly gone to mush anyway that he couldn't bear the thought of eating one. He'd been too caught up in revelations yesterday evening to remember to ask the elves for food, which, without any doubt, they would have given him generously. He'd eaten elf chocolate once, heavy with coffee and brandy. And he'd drunk elfin ale at the fair in Monmouth several years back. He remembered it as being sharp and sweet at the same time with the tang of very cold mountain water about it. Then there were elfin pies, of course, which weren't, perhaps, quite the equal of the pastries baked by field dwarfs, but were easily worth a journey on foot of several hundred miles and half a dozen other sacrifices thrown in.

He decided to fish. It seemed as if it had been an age ago that he'd wound up his trout and squid lines and left them beneath the log along the Oriel. He wondered if they were still there—if they would be there when he got home finally, and whether the hooks would have rusted themselves to nothing. He'd catch a fish and eat it, is what he'd do, then set about the day's heroics. If Captain Appleby could be believed, and it *seemed*, at least, that he could be, then the afternoon might tell the tale. He'd have to look sharp then, and for that he'd best have a full stomach. If he caught some sort of prehistoric monster out of the river he'd throw it back; that was all. He wouldn't be *forced* to eat horrors.

Somehow it seemed more sporting to fish from the rowboat than from the open hatch of the submarine, so holding his ale glass between his knees, he rowed carefully in toward shore, into the slack water of a shallow little inlet, and cast his anchor. Almost at once there was a nibbling on the line, as if about twenty tiny fish were reducing his bait to nothing. He jerked it once or twice to discourage them and to catch the eye of something bigger. Then he let the bait sink to the bottom and lie there while he filled his pipe.

Clouds drifted across the sun, now casting the river into shadow, now clearing out and letting the sunlight turn the river into diamonds and glint. In the passing shadows the river seemed to darken and deepen, and Escargot could see way down into the moving water where waving tendrils of weed grew in clumps. He could make out the stones of the river bottom, vague and indistinct below him, disappearing utterly in the sunlight, then reappearing, dark and mysterious, as if they were a product of cloud shadow. He watched, looking for his bait, which lay hidden under there somewhere, and he saw the silver glimmer of a long fish nosing along the sand. They were down there all right. One of those would feed him for a week. He could salt it up and stow it in the larder. He squinted, trying to find it again, and he jerked on his line to see if he could spot the baited hook.

He peered at the scattering of stones on the river bottom, nearly putting his face into the water. The sun looked out briefly from behind the clouds and then accommodated him by hiding itself again. The rocks—or whatever they were—were long and curved, and were laid out far too regularly to be the product of chance. They looked for all the world like ribs in a rib cage, and above them, lying off to one side, was a tremendous weed-strewn boulder of such strange and suggestive shape that he was certain at once that it wasn't a boulder at all. He poured the warm ale overboard, rinsed the glass in the river, and shoved the bottom of it into the water, leaning over and squinting into the open end of the glass.

Now the shadow worked against him, and what lay below seemed to be nothing but a peculiarly arranged jumble of rock. He waited, swinging round in the current, until the sun shone once again and the river bottom was illuminated. There lay almost directly below him now the rib cage and skull of a giant, the skull half obscured by waterweeds. In its lower jaw clung half a dozen stony teeth. Escargot gazed at it in wonder, seeing suddenly the drooping curve of his fishing line, faintly aglow in the sunlit water, descending into the weeds that grew in profusion roundabout the skull. With a suddenness that nearly toppled him from the tilting thwart, the silver fish darted from the mouth of the great skull, jammed itself into the waterweeds, and darted back into its weird hidey-hole.

Escargot's fishing pole jerked out from where it was pinioned beneath his leg. He dropped the ale glass into the river, lunged at the pole, and caught it and himself before falling overboard. The rowboat was half awash with the effort, though, and Escargot found himself pulling and tugging and sloshing around, utterly unable to reel in even an inch of line.

He pushed the pole in under the thwarts finally, grasped the line with both hands, wrapped it twice around his palms, and yanked, throwing himself back, determined either to have the fish or break the line. When it went suddenly slack he thought he'd done just that—broken the line. But almost as soon as he thought so there was a ferocious pulling, and the line went weaving away, as if the fish had abandoned the skull and were running for deeper water. Now the line was caught on nothing but the fish. He pulled and reeled and reeled and pulled, and slowly, in shrinking circles and with the fish making occasional little darts toward the bottom, he hauled the great fish alongside the boat. He shoved a hand in under its gill and heaved it over the side, into the six inches of water that covered the deck. The fish flapped there, gasping in the shallow water. It was three feet long if it was an inch, but there was nothing in the least monstrous about it.

He pulled in the anchor and rowed back to the submarine. The entire fishing venture hadn't taken more than an hour, but somehow it had made him fearsomely hungry, as if he'd added three or four hours worth of hunger to the hunger he'd started the day off with. He dragged the fish through the hatch, letting it fall to the floor below where it flopped tiredly, and he stowed the rowboat before climbing in himself.

He was whistling in the galley two minutes later, whisking a carving knife across a stone. He'd never much liked the idea of cleaning fish; in the past, he'd as often as not let his wife do it. She'd cooperate, unnecessarily frugal as she was, because she knew that if it was left to Escargot it might easily not get done at all until it was too late and the fish was ruined. He was vaguely embarrassed to think about it. But it was fishing he liked—that and eating. Cleaning the fish and hacking them up had never seemed a part of either of those two pastimes. So he'd get home with his catch, wave them at Clara, and promise to get at them in an hour or so. But then there'd be Smithers to read or Annie to play with and he'd find, as often as not, that the hour had come and gone and that Clara, frowning silently, had taken care of the fish.

Could you find time, she'd ask with manufactured politeness, to throw these carcasses to the cats? But when he'd agree, feeling badly that once again he'd neglected duty, she'd snatch up the fish remains and throw them to the cats herself, not in a huff, but calmly and deliberately, as if she knew that he couldn't be depended upon for even so much as that, and that busy as she was, and overburdened with cares, she'd undertake the job herself and see that it was done right.

It was that, perhaps, that made it seem to him now that cleaning fish was such a satisfying activity. He took particular pains to clean the scarred wooden board and to keep any muck from the fish from smearing the place up. He had no cats aboard—a deficiency he'd correct once he was out of the current mess—so he'd have to pitch the bones and the head and the innards into the river. If he had more provisions he'd boil them up into broth and make fish stew, but he wasn't equipped for that.

He squinted at the leftover debris on the board and poked at it with a knife. What the cats saw in it was something he couldn't very easily imagine. Goblins were the men for fish innards, not cats, who in every other way were sensible creatures—testy at times, but sensible. Professor Wurzle, certainly, wouldn't throw the guts into the river, or to the cats either for that matter. He'd investigate them first, study them, write them up in his notebook until he'd got his understanding of their mysteries honed to just the right edge. By then even the goblins wouldn't want them.

What in the world, wondered Escargot, fiddling with the mess of little tubes and bags and glop, was there to study? A man like himself, planning to make a living by selling oceanic mysteries, ought to know just a little about the creatures he intended to sell, and he certainly ought to get over his squeamishness about such things. He peered suspiciously at the mess, noticing through a slit he'd cut in some organ or another, round, red balls, suspiciously like the marbles he'd given Uncle Helstrom. He cut the thing open entirely, and there, globbed inside, were a couple dozen of the things, so exactly the right size, shape, and color that for a moment Appleby's tales of giant blood seemed questionable. Had he traded from the bunjo man a bag of cleverly preserved fish eggs?

It certainly seemed unlikely. And why would Captain Appleby lie? There *was* a giant in the river, wasn't there? Then there was the yawning mouth in the mountainside—Boggy had seen that too. This was coincidence, is what it was, and, once he thought about it, not a very grand coincidence either. There were probably a dozen things in the wide world that resembled his marbles, including real marbles. He scooped up the debris, suddenly surmising that he'd learned enough about the insides of a fish to get him through the rougher trials of his career, and he set out for the companionway with the thought of pitching the mess into the river. Halfway there, however, he changed his mind for no reason he could define, and he stepped along to the library. He pulled down the jar that contained the eye of whatever fish it was that was second in minuteness to a gummidgefish, and dumped in the eggs. The eye had floated there contently enough for heaven knew how long; he could keep the eggs there too for a time, just in case.

A half hour later, dressed in dark trousers, shirt, and jacket, Escargot crept along through a long, dense stand of broad-leaf oaks, which wound uphill from the river and fronted a meadow. He had no real idea that there was anyone or anything on the meadow, but there must be *someone* about, elves anyway, since they quite clearly weren't aboard the *Nora Dawn*. He worried vaguely about the troll he'd seen earlier. Twice he found little heaps of broken stones—all of it agate, from the look of it—which had been gnawed and chewed and then cast away. He picked up a stone to have a look at the long tooth marks in it, but the thing smelled foul, so he pitched it into the shadows and hurried on.

He was anxious not to be seen by anyone except Leta. It seemed to him that if she was so astonishingly crucial to the dwarf's venture, then the best way to foil his schemes was simply to spirit her away. He had decided that he didn't give a rap about his marbles—the dwarf could have them. And his desire to tweak the dwarf's nose had diminished until he felt it just a little less strongly than his desire to be quit of the dwarf for good and all.

The sky was clear at last of clouds. An autumn wind, cold and brisk, had scoured them away and hurried them off to more urgent business elsewhere. He would have liked a sweater under his jacket, for the wind, diminished by the trees as it was, still slipped in under the collar and sleeves and made him think, with a double pang of regret and terror, of the house at Bleakstone Hollow in which the man sat before his hearth, nodding over ale and a book.

Leaves dropped from the oaks and drifted along on the wind,

now swooping groundward and almost settling, then whirling aloft again and charging along past him, the wind tugging at his coat all along as if mistaking it for a leaf. He hunkered over and crossed his hands in front of his chest, stepping over a heap of deadwood and peering ahead of him in an effort to make out where the woods ended and the meadow began.

It seemed to him suddenly that he was surrounded by a sort of leafstorm. Thousands of leaves careered past, changing course, rising and falling and hovering and capering as if they were propelled like him with the desire to reach the meadow. One floated around the side of his head, and, drawing near to his nose, gave a quick flutter and shot away. Escargot leaped, and shouted in spite of himself, covering his head with his arms suddenly and ducking down into the weedy humus underfoot. Riding atop the leaf had been a henny-penny man, dressed in a black hat and the tatters of tiny clothing. He'd had the beard and eyes of a prophet, and he'd shouted something incomprehensible as his leaf rose on the wind and bore him away.

All the leaves weren't ridden by henny-penny men, Escargot was relieved to see, only every tenth leaf or so. Still, there must have been hundreds of them—thousands, perhaps, sometimes solitary riders, sometimes two to a leaf. He could hear singing on the wind—a high, piping song that resembled the tone of one of those silent dog whistles that's really not silent at all. He crouched beneath a tree, watching the flotilla pass. He had no desire to get mixed up with henny-penny men who might take it into their heads to set about him with rock hammers. And he certainly didn't want to hurt any of the little folk. He could wait; their passing wouldn't take a minute, he told himself, starting to pull his pipe and tobacco out of his pocket and then thinking better of it and putting it back. The fall of leaves had already begun to diminish, and he could see the last dense swirl of them disappearing through the oaks. Leaves still fell, but they wafted their way groundward like sensible leaves and were ridden by nothing at all.

The woods fell silent, disturbed only by the distant humming of bees. He set out again in the direction taken by the henny-penny men. In ten minutes he stood on the edge of the meadow, looking across clover and lilies strewn with red and brown oak leaves. A stream meandered across it, spilling over a stone embankment and angling toward the edge of the woods somewhere behind him. On beyond the meadow, rising up into the misty distance, were rolling hills softened by water and time, hills which seemed to be marbled with caverns. It was easy to imagine that one hill might be the thigh and knee of a fallen giant and another might be an upturned skull, half buried and with eyesocket caverns staring down toward the woods.

Escargot waited there, not sure what to do. He had the feeling that adventure was about to be thrown at him like a stone, that he had only to wait there ready to catch it. He heard, or thought he heard, deep below him, the beating once again of a stupendous heart, mingled with the sighing breaths of a sleeping giant, or of hundreds of sleeping giants, breathing as one in an enchanted, stony slumber. It might as easily be the wind, of course, rustling the treetops.

He stood just so for minutes, listening and waiting until he was rewarded with the sight of a group of elves, a half dozen in all, that appeared two hundred yards out over the meadow, as if having marched up from the river. He smiled when he heard what was most likely Boggy's voice, lamenting something, and then another voice, completely out of patience shouting at him to shut up.

The elves scrambled atop a rocky prominence, and one of the elves—Boggy again—was hoisted complaining into the branches of a dead and gnarled tree that stretched two bare limbs over the chattering stream. There was a shout. Boggy snatched off his hat and waved it wildly, standing up and whistling, then shouting as he tumbled from his perch, falling into the stream below. Boggy's shipmates scampered along the meadow, rushing at the stream as if to save him, making a hash of the effort, and then rushing along again, as Boggy was borne away on the current.

Escargot stepped out from the cover of the woods, thinking to help. But there was nothing, really, that he could do for Boggy that the elves couldn't do, and it was unlikely that the little fellow would drown in such a stream, so he paused and had a quick look up and down before stepping back into shadow.

Even as he did so two things happened. Another party of elves crested a little rise and stormed along toward the stream, shouting a warning to Boggy's party, which had stopped the runaway elf by then and was hauling him up onto the clover.

There was a scream that tore across the open meadow at that same moment, and it became suddenly clear that this second party of elves wasn't rushing in to help save Boggy at all, but was angling down toward the woods, toward where the stream fell away into the shadowed tangle of vines and creepers and scrub.

Escargot edged into the sunlight once again, shading his eyes, hoping that the elves, all of them engaged by one tragedy or another, wouldn't notice him. What he saw was a troll, humping fearfully along in a sort of two-legged gallop, its ape-like arms, scaled and mottled, dragging along on either side like rudders. The troll's head came to a sort of point on top—not a horn, exactly, but like he wore a little pyramidal hat, and he seemed to be swatting at himself as if he were plagued by bees. He wore a garment of some sort that was ripped and draggled and dirty and hung in tatters. Through it shone scaly, green skin, dull as unpolished jade except here and there where the sun glinted on shiny patches—water, perhaps, or blood. Leta ran along six paces ahead of the troll.

The beast took a swipe at her with a taloned hand, but was wide of the mark by several feet. Then it stumbled, rolled, and got up—groggily, it seemed. Escargot looked around as he ran, searching for some sort of weapon. There was nothing but stones. He threw one at the creature, hollering, his shouts lost beneath the roaring of the troll itself and the calling of the elves, who brandished swords and pistols now, firing random shots into the air.

The troll fell again, crept up onto his knees, leaned on the meadow grasses, and howled one last trumpeting groan before collapsing onto its face. Leta continued to run, not looking back. The elves rushed past her, certain, perhaps, that she'd stop, and danced roundabout the fallen troll aiming their weapons and threatening. But the thing lay dead, and obviously so. Leta slowed her pace, looked back over her shoulder, and stopped, undecided. At the sight of Boggy's party running toward her across the meadow, though, she slogged through the stream, leaped up the opposite bank, and ran straightaway for the forest.

She was in among the trees and shadows in moments. Boggy and the elves with him slowed and hesitated, perhaps wondering if there mightn't be more trolls in the woods. They wandered across toward where Captain Appleby and the others still bent over the fallen creature. Appleby looked up, as if surprised to see Boggy's band. "Where is she?" he cried, snatching off his hat, and Boggy, soaked and bedraggled, started to answer, gesturing toward the woods. Escargot slipped in through the trees himself, leaping over a rock and scrambling through heavy brush. In the tangled woods he'd make better time than the elves. It might be simplest to start shouting for her. She was quick and clever and might easily give him the slip at the same time she was hiding from the elves. Why she was so set on avoiding the little men was a mystery, but it was very obviously the case. All of that was to his advantage, for he would seem to her the only ally among the entire odd lot of them.

Shouting, though, would alert the elves. They'd know that he hadn't gone to Landsend at all, that he wasn't waiting patiently in Lanternwick Street at whatever ridiculous inn it was that Captain Appleby had recommended. And who knew what sorts of things lurked in the forest? The dwarf himself might be nigh, or the witch. This was no time to go shouting.

He stopped and cocked his head, listening. There was momentary silence, then the sound of elf voices away behind him, then silence again. He hurried on, clambering over a fallen log and stumbling out onto a trail that wound between the oaks. A whistle sounded behind him, and then the voice of Captain Appleby: "What!" it said first in a sort of stage whisper, then, "Fool!" followed by a flurry of muttering that Escargot couldn't make out. After that Boggy's voice cried out, "I can't! It's too high to jump!" and then a string of elfin curses from Captain Appleby, out of patience with poor Boggy.

The idea of it appealed immediately to Escargot, who pulled himself up into the low branches of an oak and scrambled as high as he dared. Back when he was twelve years old he happily perched in the uppermost branches of a great alder in back of his house near Monmouth, but now, somehow, he wasn't quite as surefooted. He climbed very carefully and held onto the trunk, appreciating Boggy's fears. He found himself suddenly above the forest, looking down through the half-leafless oaks. Out on the edge of the woods lay the troll where it had fallen. Two elves still stood beside it, ready with their swords if the thing should attempt to get up. Boggy and Captain Appleby and the rest of the crew were hidden by layers of foliage.

Ahead of him though, not fifty yards up the path, a shadow slipped along silently, making for the river. It was Leta. It had to be. She leaped across a broad patch of sunlight suddenly, hurrying back into shadow. Where she was running Escargot had no idea. Perhaps she was just running. She had to be utterly unaware of the nature of her plight, the reason she was hauled in leaps and bounds up a strange river through an even stranger land.

Escargot clambered out of the tree and set off at a dead run. She'd hear him coming, of course, and would try to outrun him, not knowing who it was that pursued her. But by then he'd have the jump on her, and they'd be far enough ahead of the elves for him to risk calling out. Suddenly, there she was. She turned and held a broken-off oak branch in her hand, thinking, as likely as not, that it was a troll that raced up behind her. Escargot stumbled to a stop, grinning and gasping and waving at the stick, miming wildly that he'd rather she didn't hit him with it. She lowered it slowly, puzzled to see him there.

"Come on!" he wheezed, nodding toward the river. "They're right behind us. I've got a boat on the river. You'll be safe there."

"Safe!" she said, laughing at the idea, but she ran along just the same, carrying her stick with her, and the two of them didn't stop until they'd broken from the river edge of the woods, flown across the meadow, and hauled the rowboat out of the mouth of the creek. Then they were off, pulling for the submarine, Escargot watching the edge of the forest for the issuance of the elves. It made precious little difference now, of course, for he and Leta could be aboard ship and sunk out of sight beneath the river long before the elves could rally round and set out in serious pursuit. They *were* safe, in a word, and the sudden realization of it made Escargot laugh out loud.

"Care to share the joke?" asked Leta, smiling at him.

"It just occurred to me that we've made it. We're safe as babies."

She stared at him, looking round her at the wide river. "Are you suggesting that we row to the other side?"

"Not at all," said Escargot, grinning at her as she caught

sight, for the first time, of the submarine, floating like a behemoth in the current. Her eyes widened. Escargot grinned some more, then forced the grin to relax a bit, and not look foolish. He could hardly contain himself though. This was more like it. He'd imagined, weeks past, finding her in Seaside and slipping up behind her unseen to tap her on the shoulder. That would have been fun, of course, but it would have been nothing to this. The ruined Escargot she had taken a fancy to in Twombly Town had not only journeyed mysteriously to this faraway, exotic land, but he'd appeared like a phantom in the oak woods, and had led her out safely, outwitting two dozen elves, snatching her, as it were, from the grip of the dwarf, and spiriting her away to an astonishing submarine. It was all very satisfactory.

She looked thin and hunted, although the hollowness that the weeks of turmoil had bestowed upon her cheekbones made her rather prettier than otherwise. It was a daunting sort of prettiness, though. She regarded him coolly, with a look of suspicion in her eyes. He tried another grin, but got none in return. The rowboat bumped against the hull of the submarine with a suddenness that almost pitched him into the river. He barely noticed it, though, and was so clumsy at securing the rowboat to the submarine that they nearly slipped away downriver before he could get it right.

Leta wasn't smiling at all. She sat as if in deep thought, and he was afraid for a moment that she'd decline to come aboard. If she did, he was lost. He couldn't very well demand it, could he? But why *wouldn't* she want to come aboard? He'd come halfway across two worlds looking for her. He'd fought goblins and outfoxed elves and harassed a very dangerous dwarf, all on her account. Well, that wasn't true either. To a degree he'd done it on his own account. But he *had* done it, and she'd appreciate that, surely. He started to speak, but the words seemed to run up against each other in his neck and wedge together there, so that he croaked like a frog with a throat condition.

She followed him up the ladder, though, and watched as he stowed the rowboat; then she climbed down the hatch, looking wonderingly roundabout—at the fire quartz and the carved companionway. She peered in at the pilothouse, oohing and aahing at the sunlit river that pressed against the windows and at a school of river squid that happened, at just that moment, to be passing by in a wide-eyed rush. She turned toward him, pointing at them. Thank you, squids, Escargot said to himself, and he gestured roundabout as if to say, "Well now, how d'you like it?" But actually he said nothing, for Leta was frowning at him again and looking at him sidewise, as Captain Appleby must sometimes look at young Boggy when he suspected the little elf was up to some sort of trouble.

"I'll take it down a ways, if you don't mind," said Escargot, slumping into the pilot's chair. "I'd rather the elves didn't know I'm about. The less anyone knows about my presence the better." He felt satisfied with that; it had the right air of mystery to it. And it wasn't boasting, either; it was true enough.

"Surely," she answered, moving across to watch through the windows. "What is it you're up to, anyway?"

"Up to!" cried Escargot, taken aback. "I'm not *up to* anything. Really. My only interest is to . . . to . . ." He faltered there, not being entirely able to define his interest in so many words. He was blushing, he knew, but Leta wasn't watching him, so it didn't matter so very much. "The dwarf, you know, stole my bag of marbles."

"Marbles?" She looked at him curiously.

"That's right. You remember the marbles. In the leather bag. I showed them to you at Stover's that day. It turns out that they're enchanted in some way, and that the dwarf is going to use them to . . ." At that point a grim thought occurred to him. It was possible, barely possible, that this wasn't Leta at all. Or was it? She'd been in full sun—hadn't she?—and the sunlight hadn't turned her into the witch. And yet the whole sunlight and fog and darkness theory was only a hunch, really. What if he'd stumbled into a trap of some sort here? What if this *wasn't* Leta, but was the old woman. He hadn't been able to tell the difference between the two on the meadow that one evening. He messed in his coat for a moment and pulled out the truth charm, very nonchalantly, as if he were hauling out a pocket watch or a pipe. He didn't want to seem to hide it, and yet he didn't want to make an issue of it either. He grinned at her and started in again.

"What is that?" she asked suddenly, interrupting.

"A truth charm," he found himself saying before he had a chance to force himself to shut up.

"A truth charm? Why?"

"I'm afraid you might be the witch."

"Why are you afraid of that?" she asked, grinning slightly.

"She scares the devil out of me, that's why. I'm pretending to be some sort of hero here, posing around in this submarine, but really I've been sort of forcing myself along, you know, talking myself into pushing farther upriver."

"Why? To get your marbles back."

"N . . . no," said Escargot, struggling to hold his tongue. "I've been hoping that you . . . that is, I'm in . . . I mean to say . . ."

"What?" She was smiling now. "Could you put that charm away?"

"Yes, for goodness sake!" cried Escargot, dumping it back into its pouch. He'd started to sweat, he realized, and there wasn't any way at all that he could carry on with the conversation. He'd wait for her to speak.

"I saw one of those once. The Seaside dwarfs used to sell them—very cheap, actually. Almost no one wanted one. They were clever, but dangerous. The trick is that you only ask questions when one is exposed. You never make statements, unless, of course, you've got some particular reason for forcing yourself to be truthful. They're really rather insulting, aren't they?" she asked, suddenly serious.

"How's that? I certainly didn't *mean* anything by it. One has to be careful, though, with this dwarf. And the old lady. I almost believe she's worse than he is."

A shiver seemed to go through her right then, as if she were reminded of something. She grew abruptly irritated and gave him a stern look. "You've come upriver after *me*?"

Escargot grimaced, but nodded, feeling like a child who'd been caught creeping through the watermelon patch carrying a carving knife.

"I'm grateful for that," she said. "Really. It's a chivalrous thing. But I'm afraid you've presumed a lot, haven't you?"

He shrugged.

"What did you have in mind, spiriting me away to a safe port, kissing my hand and saying good-bye?"

"Something like that," he mumbled. "I guess."

She smiled at him. "I tried it already. Two days ago at sunrise I stole a canoe, right below a town called Grover, and paddled across the river and hailed a steamship. We were four hours downriver when a fog came up. It rose off the water and seemed to chase me from deck to deck, and I even tried to climb up the handholds on one of the stacks to stay in the sunlight. But it was futile. I found myself next morning outside that deserted village where I ran into you. What that means, unless I'm mistaken, is that we'd sail away, you and I, until the sun went down or the fog came up, and I'd be gone again. I'm afraid this thing has to be seen through, although I don't know how."

Escargot watched her. He wished he could say that *he* knew how it was going to be seen through, but he didn't; he couldn't. He hadn't gotten half enough information out of Captain Appleby. What did the dwarf intend to do with Leta? What did the elves intend to do with Leta? Shoving her below decks and locking her in wouldn't answer. He nodded his head and squinted his eyes in a knowing fashion, but the only thing that he knew for certain was that his squinting and nodding wasn't going to fool her one bit.

He'd half imagined that Leta would be overjoyed to see him. But he could see that such an idea was built largely on fancy—on the incident in Stover's tavern and the few words they'd exchanged on the street afterward. He wished, for the twentieth time, that he'd thought all of this out long ago. He'd come to no end of trouble in his life because he failed to think things out. Ten minutes of good, hard, squinty-eyed thought might have saved him from a doomed marriage, and from the pie and cream trick and the midnight fishing, and he might have done something about his having been swindled out of his house and out of his marbles . . . and, well, it was all in the past, wasn't it? There were more immediate troubles, to be sure. He couldn't at all read the half smile that played across Leta's face. It wasn't, entirely, the look of someone filled with irritation at another person's presumption.

"How did you kill the troll?" he asked, tacking onto a new course.

"I didn't kill him. He dropped dead. There were little men in the woods."

"Elves?"

"No. I think they were henny-penny men. They were riding leaves, anyway."

"Henny-penny men saved you from the troll?" Escargot was astonished. Here was an unlooked-for mystery.

"I don't think they killed the troll to save me. They were killing the troll when I walked into the clearing. The troll looked like he was buried in a leaf pile, but he wasn't. The leaves were swirling around him, thousands of them, and henny-penny men riding them, sticking the thing with little spears. You wouldn't think that a henny-penny man spear would amount to much when it came to trolls; they must be dipped in poison of some sort. The thing saw me, I ran, it chased me, and not fifty yards out onto the meadow it dropped. And I saw a curious thing, too, when I made for the woods again. There was a party of goblins, I don't know how many, and the henny-penny men were after them too. There was a goblin dead already, lying in the stream, and another that was dying."

"Vicious little things," muttered Escargot, mystified.

"Goblins?"

"Yes, them too. I meant henny-penny men. Lucky they didn't get onto you."

"They might have easily enough. The goblins might have drawn them away, though; they must have been following me, and have been, off and on, since we started upriver. They're all minions of the dwarf, you know, are goblins."

"But not henny-penny men. That's good, isn't it?"

"I suppose. What do you have to eat?"

"Fish!" cried Escargot, brightening. He was happy, for once, to be able to do something for Leta, even if it was simply to cook her up a piece of fish. They went off to the galley together by way of the library and captain's quarters. Escargot was mightily proud of the enchanted quality of his craft, although he knew that such pride was foolish, since the building and outfitting of the ship had had nothing to do with him. So he kept himself from saying anything that sounded boastful, although he did point out that he might quite likely possess one of the largest G. Smithers collections in two worlds, counting those he'd left with Professor Wurzle.

They ate fish, but Leta was quiet and moody, thinking, no doubt, that at any moment a fog might rise or that evening lay only a few short hours away. Escargot didn't say much about his conversation with Captain Appleby. He knew only enough about the mysteries that were afoot to alarm her, not enough to explain much. She, however, told him a thing or two that *he* didn't know, and that set him to thinking that whiling away the afternoon talking over fishbones mightn't be wise, even though somehow or another he couldn't think of a more satisfactory way to while away an afternoon. Not that he was particularly fond of fishbones.

Leta had, indeed, been fleeing from the elves. They'd slipped up on her early that morning and had hauled her off to their galleon and locked her away below decks. Captain Appleby had been full of assurances that they'd see to her safety, that she wouldn't be harmed, that within the hour they'd be airborne and they'd carry her beyond the reach of the dwarf, who intended, they claimed, to kill her. The dwarf needed a blood sacrifice, and the blood must come from a harvest maid. The dwarf was a necromancer, said Captain Appleby, an enchanter from the Dark Forest, and was bent on launching—or finishing, as it were—a battle that had been partly decided millennia past. He would destroy the elves if he could. He would bring the moon plummeting out of the sky. He would cast the land into darkness. There was a certain collection of what seemed to be marbles, oddly enough, that he needed in order to accomplish his task. He had those now, due to the stupidity of a man named Escargot. He had his harvest maid too. He'd arrived, finally, on the meadows where the last great battle had taken place. That very evening might spell doom for them all.

Captain Appleby had winked at her in a fatherly way. She'd see reason, he knew. She was a bright girl, considering that she wasn't an elf, and she wouldn't mind spending an hour or two below, would she?

Yes, she would, as it turned out. She'd asked where they were bound, and he'd grinned and winked again, as if his winking explained heaps and heaps of things and made everything just fine. She hadn't any choice, really, and below deck she'd gone. She hadn't been there an hour when a little elf arrived with a plate of food, and had whispered to her that the captain was a horrible evil elf, who intended, in fact, to take her far away—to the moon, he said. Forever. The elf, whose name was Boggy, had taken pity on her and she'd pretended to overcome him and had tied him into a chair and had fled, but hadn't been gone minutes before there was a hue and cry and she'd taken refuge in the woods. The elves had gone round along the meadow, it seemed, and would have gotten her, too, if it hadn't been for the appearance of the troll. Then she'd run into Escargot, or rather he'd run into her, and here they were, eating fish and fooling themselves that there was something they could do.

Escargot shook his head. "Better you'd gone to the moon," he said with a sigh. "Captain Appleby was right. That's the only way. Boggy the elf isn't to be trusted. He was acting out of spite for the captain, not out of gallantry."

Leta shrugged. "It doesn't much matter, does it? I'm not going to the moon with a shipload of silly elves."

Escargot pondered for a bit. "I might just pay a visit to those elves, myself," he said. "I can pretend to bargain for you with them. I don't know exactly what I'll ask for, but as far as they know I'm just an adventurer. There's got to be another way round this, seeing as you won't live on the moon. I might be able to get onto something by talking to Captain Appleby."

"And what am I to do?"

"Wait here."

"I'll wait," she said after a moment, "but I'm a little tired of all this bargaining, of decisions being made by people who haven't consulted me and don't care to. I'm tired of waiting, too. I'm smart enough to know that I haven't got anything better to suggest, but if something occurs to me while you're gone, I won't be here when you return."

Escargot hesitated. "That's fair enough," he said. "I . . . I hope you haven't mistaken me in this business. Captain Appleby told me that he was intent on saving you from the dwarf, but that he wouldn't be doing it for your sake. *I'm* doing it for your sake, though. I just thought I'd tell you that."

"Then you're a fool, aren't you?" she said, standing up from the table and stepping across to gaze out through the ports. The sun's rays still slanted through the green water outside, and in the hazy distance fish glided past, going about their business, caring nothing for the troubles of elves and giants. She turned when she heard Escargot leaving, and she smiled at him and said, "I think you're a very nice sort of a fool, though." And Escargot grinned at her and strode off down the companionway like a man with a purpose, already wrestling in his mind with Captain Appleby and with Uncle Helstrom, thinking now that he might tweak both their noses before this business was through.

16

Henny-penny Men Again

Escargot stepped along through the shallows, carrying his shoes and with his pantlegs rolled. He'd hidden his rubber suit and helmet beneath dense bushes some quarter mile downriver, having taken a circuitous route into shore in order to throw any watching elves off the track. The sun shone warm and cheerful in the early afternoon sky, as if it were determined at last to brighten the landscape and chase off shadows. He could almost have convinced himself that it was a sign of some sort, that it marked an end to the dark, enchanted clouds that had hovered over the entire Uncle Helstrom affair for the past weeks. Escargot grinned to think that Leta's parting words could have had such an effect on him, and he began to whistle merrily and out of tune, as he usually did, thinking to himself that it was high time that Theophile Escargot made his presence officially known.

He would watch no more from the wings. He would vault onto the stage and announce his presence. He had, for the first time, a real interest in the piece, was no longer being dragged about against his will. Captain Appleby had been right, no doubt. This was an affair that was beyond his understanding. But what of it? Captain Appleby's understanding wasn't all that spacious either, was it? And the dwarf, certainly, was acting out of some sort of greed, out of self-interest. Well Escargot would have a part in the drama himself, and not as a second, either. It was top billing from this point on, he thought, skipping a stone out over the smooth river, and he tramped around the edge of the cove, watching the *Nora Dawn* appear from behind the thick trees.

They'd be frantic. They wouldn't have any idea where Leta had gotten off to. The dwarf, in fact, might have her at that moment. They'd expect earthquakes, awakening giants, heaven knew what sorts of cataclysms. Escargot would stroll in among them, bowing. He'd pause to light his pipe and to puff on it for a moment with the air of a man who has studied things out and wants to phrase things particularly carefully in order not to be misunderstood by a precocious, but, perhaps, slightly scatterbrained audience. He stood for a moment, wiggling his toes in the sand, his arms crossed, trying to think up a really remarkable bit of something to impress Captain Appleby with. A quotation would be nice—something profound. A snatch of verse from Ashbless, perhaps.

He found himself, abruptly, looking at the galleon through the crossed cords of a fishing net. He shouted and flung his arms up, but they were borne back down to his sides and he was suddenly surrounded by a very serious lot of elves, including Collier and Boggy. He felt like a fool, with his nose pressed through the mesh of the net and a dozen elves grappling at him as if they expected him to cut up rough. He squinted through the net at Collier and said, "I was just coming along to see you fellows."

"That's exactly what you're doing," Collier replied staunchly.

"This net, then . . ."

"No trouble!" the elf shouted, cocking his head at Escargot.

"Not a bit. Trouble from me? I've got to talk to Captain Appleby."

"Tie him up!" Boggy shouted enthusiastically. "He's a bad one. He didn't do what we told him."

"Mr. Bogger," Collier said, giving Boggy a look.

"Well he didn't, did he? We told him to go on back. That's what the captain said. The inn at Lanternwick Street. He was to wait there. And here he is. I told you he was a rum one, but no one listened. And here he is, come back with an eye to the girl. It was him that conked me on the head and let her loose. That's what I think."

"Silence, Mr. Bogger!" Collier shouted, grimacing at the elf, who at once fell silent but continued to nod and to raise his eyebrows and glare at Escargot until Collier turned away. Then Boggy crossed his eyes and thrust his tongue out.

''Bring him along,'' commanded Collier, at once setting out down the beach.

Escargot walked along, encumbered by his net, happy that Leta, at least, wouldn't see him in such a costume. As a sort of lark he wiggled his hand up to his coat, pried his pipe and tobacco out, and set about filling his pipe, which, if he twisted and turned it just right, he could push through the net. Boggy insisted immediately that Escargot was trying to ''burn his way out,'' but Collier apparently couldn't see the harm in it, for he told Boggy once again to hold his tongue, and they led Escargot, net, pipe, and all onto the ship and into a low cabin where Captain Appleby sat glowering at the wall, apparently lost in deep thoughts.

Escargot sat down, working his hand out from under the net. He took the pipe from his mouth and said good day to the captain. Captain Appleby looked up slowly and nodded. He blinked twice very slowly and said, ''Why are you wearing a net?''

''That was my doing, sir,'' offered Collier.

Captain Appleby stared at him. ''Remove it, then. I won't speak to a man wearing a net. I don't care who he is.''

Collier helped drag the net off, then bowed himself out of the room, taking the net with him and grinning weakly. ''Where is the girl?'' asked the captain.

Escargot widened his eyes and shrugged.

''One of my men saw you on the meadow this morning when the girl eluded us. It was your doing. Don't deny it, man.''

Escargot shrugged again, by way of answer, wondering idly how a G. Smithers character would react. Dignity, of course, was called for, as was cleverness. There would be a bit of verbal fencing here; Escargot could see that. He smiled at the captain. ''I won't deny that I've had a hand in the girl's escape.''

''A hand, is it! You've sold us all, sir. That's what you've done—hands and feet and all, right up to our noses and with our hats thrown in on top. You've quite likely had a hand in the girl's death, is what you've had. She'd be aloft in the heavens now, if it weren't for your getting your hand in. She'd live in comfort, in luxury, forever, in a place where the dwarf has no power. She'd have been beyond his grasp. Where is she now?''

Escargot shook his head. ''There must be another way around this business. She won't go to the moon. She's said as much. She'll . . .''

''The moon! Who have you spoken to? If it's Boggy, by heaven I'll tie him into the crosstrees until he weeps us a river broad enough to float home on.''

''Not a bit of it. I've got sources, as I've said. Have you seen one of these?'' And Escargot pulled out the truth charm, tossing it up into the air and catching it so that the eye carved into the stone seemed to be peering at Captain Appleby.

''Of course I've seen one of those! They were given away at penny carnivals for years. Are you waving it around because you suppose me to be lying, or because you're particularly fascinated by a child's toy? If it's the truth you want, I'll give it to you. Soon, very soon, the dwarf will enchant the sleeping giants out of their age-old slumber, and he'll do it by *killing the girl*! Can you grasp that? There'll be mayhem that you can barely imagine, and your marbles and your truth charms and the girl will be swept beyond your grasp forever. They'll pluck your undersea device out of the river and comb their beards with it!'' Captain Appleby paused and glared at Escargot, who couldn't tell whether he was blustering because he was honestly worked up or whether he was merely trying to be impressive. Escargot started to speak, but the captain interrupted him abruptly and asked again, ''Where's the girl?''

''Aboard the submarine,'' Escargot replied without being able to stop himself. ''That is to say . . .''

''That she's aboard the submarine.'' Captain Appleby grinned at him. ''Put away the charm, Mr. Escargot. Better yet, throw it into the river. No man wants the truth too often.''

Escargot, smiling weakly, put the charm away. He wouldn't throw it into the river, but he wouldn't be quite so hasty in pulling it out of its pouch either. And he'd have to be a bit more on his guard than that, or Captain Appleby would get round him in a moment. ''Of course she's in the submarine. That's what I've come here to tell you. How can she save herself? That's the problem, isn't it?''

''In the submarine, do you say? Below the surface? If she's under water she might be safe. Enchantment doesn't travel in deep water as well as it might. The witch mightn't even be able to find her.''

''Ah. Well, yes, she *is* in the submarine. I thought it best to keep her out of sight, you know, until I'd talked to you. She's thirty feet down—safe from goblins, and safe, as you say, from enchantment. Perhaps we can come to some sort of agreement here. I'll say once again that she won't go to the moon. I'll kill the dwarf myself to keep her here.''

''Huh!'' grunted Appleby in a tone that made it seem as if he thought it unlikely that Escargot could accomplish such a thing. ''I don't understand talk of striking bargains. The long and the short of it is that if he gets hold of the girl there'll be trouble, and all the bluff talk in the world won't have the slightest effect on it. Thirty feet of water, do you say?''

Escargot looked at him warily. ''At least.''

''Come now. Is it thirty feet, or is it more? If she's too shallow she might as well be sitting on the shore waiting for them.''

''Thirty-six feet, then.''

''Mr. Collier!'' shouted the captain, thumping his fist on the table. The cabin door opened and Collier stuck his head in. ''Take her out fifty yards, Mr. Collier, and cast anchor. Send all hands into the rigging. First man who spots the submarine gets triple pay. Except Bogger. He gets double pay, and if he don't like it he can cry. She's down six fathoms—should be easy enough to spot in this sunlight.''

''Wait a moment!'' shouted Escargot, leaping to his feet.

''Wait nothing! If this man interferes, lock him in the hold. Lock him in the hold anyway. Put Boggy in there with him. Don't let Boggy into the rigging or there'll be nothing but trouble. And tell Boggy that if this fellow escapes, Boggy'd better go with him.''

''Aye, aye, Cap'n,'' said Collier, shutting the door. Moments later there was shouting on deck and hurrying about, and then the door opened again and six elves pushed through with drawn pistols, ushering Escargot out into the sunlight briefly and then down the companionway below decks. He found himself finally in a cramped cabin lit by sunlight slanting through three tiny portholes along the starboard side. There was a chair in the cabin and a little table with a book on it, as if the book had been left there to entertain captives. *Window-*

ledge Gardening for the Homebody it was called, and was full of smudgy illustrations penned by an artist who might have been cross-eyed. Escargot thumbed through it and then put it down, wondering whether they were under sail and drifting out onto the river. He shoved his face up against a porthole and watched. They hadn't even gotten underway yet. Captain Appleby assumed, quite likely, that there was no very considerable rush, as long as Escargot was safe below. Leta, he'd assume, would wait for Escargot's return. The more he thought about it, the less he liked the idea of being a prisoner of the elves.

He pounded at the cabin door, and almost at once Boggy's voice answered from the other side. "What?" he asked.

"Let me out of here!" shouted Escargot.

"You prisoners always say the same thing," said Boggy.

"For heaven's sake, Boggy. You let Leta go. Why won't you let me go too?"

"She's prettier than you."

Escargot rushed back across to the porthole, but the little circular view of river and shoreline revealed nothing at all. There was the sound of footfalls on the deck above and more shouting, but from his prison he could make nothing of any of it. He paced up and down the small cabin—three steps this way, three steps that way—accomplishing nothing at all beyond working himself up. He felt like he'd explode if he didn't get out. Shouting and crying would merely make him look like a fool. Waiting would mean allowing the elves to snatch Leta from the submarine to haul her away forever. He struck his fist into his hand. Boggy or no Boggy, he was getting out.

He slid the chairback under the latch on the door, so that the front legs of the chair angled into the air. Then he climbed up onto the table, brushing his head against the ceiling, and leaped down onto the front of the tilted chair. The door latch broke loose and spun away into a corner as the chair slammed down onto all four legs. The door flew open and Escargot threw himself after it, rolling out into the companionway and springing to his feet. Boggy lay curled up on the floor, holding his head.

"Boggy!" cried Escargot, worried at first that he'd hurt the poor elf.

Boggy looked up at him, grinned, and said, "I didn't mean nothing by saying she was prettier than you."

Escargot started to speak, saw the futility in it, and leaped away down the companionway instead. There was almost no chance that the elves above hadn't heard the crash of the door flying open, and none at all that they'd fail to hear Boggy, who, as soon as Escargot ran, set in howling and hooting and shrieking in such a way that half the crew was likely to be on them in a second.

Sure enough; as he topped the companionway stairs, there were three elves, Collier in front, far more surprised to see Escargot leaping up at them than Escargot was to see them. Escargot bowled through them, scattering them onto the deck. He shouted a hasty "Sorry!" as he vaulted the deck rail and fell on his back into the river. Before the hue and cry was sent up, he had struck out for shore, and he wasn't three minutes getting there. He could hear Boggy's shouts even as he loped away down the river road, and he could hear Captain Appleby shouting back. He felt a little like shouting himself. He'd done very nicely, and the best part of it was that the elves hadn't the vaguest idea how he intended to get back aboard the submarine. They quite likely wouldn't chase him, assuming that he was merely making good an escape, and that they could still sail out over the river and find the submarine and somehow drag it up out of there.

In ten minutes he was on the river bottom, slogging along in his rubber suit. He smiled at the occasional fish that swam by, wishing that he could say something to them, and he was half sorry that some deepwater monster didn't poke its nose at him so that he could hit it. But no monsters appeared. He slipped aboard the submarine and tore off his seashell helmet and suit, leaving them in a heap on the wet deck. Then he dashed out into the companionway, threw open the door to the library, and shouted, "They're after us!" to a startled Leta, who was reading a volume of Smithers.

In the pilothouse minutes later he navigated the craft upriver toward the *Nora Dawn*. It would be fun to give them a bit of a thrill. They'd be out of the cove by now and onto the open river. Leta watched him, saying little. There they were, at anchor, right at the edge of the deep channel. They could see him too; there was no doubt of that. He sped forward, angling to starboard into the channel, dropping to twenty, then thirty, then forty feet, until he was certain they could see him no more. He could imagine the faces that Captain Appleby would make. How he'd yell at Boggy now! Escargot grinned. He angled the ship up toward the distant surface. The dark shadow of the *Nora Dawn* floated suddenly above. He drove beneath it, close enough almost to scrape it, and burst from the water at the far side, the nose of the submarine hanging in the air for a moment, cascading water, before slamming down again into the river and settling there. Then slowly and deliberately, as if out on a Sunday outing, he made away upriver, leaving the elves to their astonishment.

He turned to smile at Leta, but he found that she wasn't there. She'd returned to the library to read her book. Escargot immediately felt foolish. He'd been showing off; that's what he'd been doing. And Leta wasn't the sort of girl who cared for showing off. Still, the idea of Captain Appleby standing on the quarterdeck, a spyglass in his hand, about to say something weighty to Collier, and then the submarine, shooting beneath him like that . . . Escargot grinned, then wiped the grin away and headed for the library.

Leta was cheerful enough, it turned out. He half expected her to say something about his prank, but she didn't, which made him feel even more foolish.

"Well," he said, pretending to look at the books on the shelves, "we've eluded them again."

"That we have," she said, simply, still reading. "Why?"

"They locked me up when they discovered you were aboard the submarine. They intended to get you back, I think, and then heave away for the moon."

"So Boggy was right."

"Boggy was right. You'd be beyond the dwarf's grasp there. But you could never return. I told Appleby that we'd find another way, but he wouldn't hear of it. Kidnapping you would be the safest and quickest way to foil the dwarf. But I learned one thing anyway. Appleby tells me that you're safe here. The witch can't reach you here like she did when you were aboard the steamship. Her magic won't work through water."

"So I live beneath the river?"

"Well," said Escargot, pausing to tamp tobacco into his pipe. "No. Only for the moment. The dwarf, according to

Appleby, intends to strike soon now—this afternoon, perhaps this evening. We'll scuttle the lot of them, then, by spending some time under water."

"We?"

"Actually, I'm going back out to have a look around. Something might suggest itself. I have a curious notion that there's more to this than Appleby lets on. It's not just a feud between the dwarf and the elves. The whole land seems to be alive with enchantment, and I intend to spy it out this afternoon."

"I'm not entirely sure that I like the notion of you spying things out while I sit around safe and wait."

Escargot shrugged. "You'd step ashore and a fog would come up and you'd be gone. That would be the end of it, wouldn't it?"

Now it was Leta's turn to shrug. What Escargot said was true. She had no choice but to let him play the hero. That was entirely satisfactory. It was what he'd been aching to get a chance at for weeks. And now with Leta safely aboard the submarine, aboard *his* submarine, he could wade away in his rubber suit and turn his attention toward the dwarf without worrying about her safety. He could slip in and out of shadows, peer at the dwarf from treetops. Something *would* suggest itself—some way to slide in and ruin things for the posturing Uncle Helstrom.

He stepped across to where his fish eggs reclined in their jar, uncorked it, and plucked out the red eggs, setting them along the valley between the pages of an open book and blowing them dry. They were squishy, to a degree, but not soft. Leathery was the word. If he wrapped them carefully enough he could haul them around in his coat pocket without smashing them.

"Well, I'd like to be off," he said. "Why don't you pilot us in toward the cove. Captain Appleby won't be half quick enough to catch us even if he sees us—which he probably won't. He won't expect us to come cruising around now. Then you can take the boat out into deep water again until, what?—say five o'clock—then swing back in and pick me up. Don't come up above thirty feet, though, especially on toward evening."

"Aye, aye, Captain," said Leta, saluting stiffly. "All hands to the pilot room."

Escargot smiled back at her, altogether satisfied with himself, and already starting to daydream about how he would put an end to the dwarf's deviltry, then stride into the river in his seashell helmet, knocking on the hull of the *Nora Dawn* as he trudged along beneath it to the vast amazement of the elfin crew that would be lined up goggling along the railing.

"There's a big piece of that fish left, but not much else. When we get out of this maybe we can head across the river and round up some sort of lunch. I asked once before—do you remember?—that day after you quit Stover's. You said that you wanted to wait a bit. Things have changed now, though. That was about a hundred years ago."

"At least," she said, sighing. "I wouldn't mind lunch, actually."

"Right. Lunch it is, then. It's a date, isn't it? I'll just be away for a few hours." In half an hour he found himself once again on the river bottom, striding along through the sand in weighted shoes.

He skirted the woods this time. He was fairly sure that wherever the dwarf was working his enchantments, it wasn't within the oak woods. Besides that, he hadn't any real urge to run into henny-penny men, not after the episode with the troll. Evidence seemed to indicate that through some odd fate he and the henny-penny men fought the same battle, both of them in league against the dwarf and his minions. But that was just a hunch. They hadn't hesitated to come after him with rock hammers when he was under the ocean, had they? It was best to wait for them to declare themselves one way or another.

The afternoon was unusually fine for a late autumn afternoon. There was a chill on the breeze, but it had to work so hard to cut the radiant heat of the sun that by the time it set in on you it had already worn itself out. And there was just the hint of smoke on the air, like pruning fires burning miles away on the grassy floor of an orchard. It was unlikely, though, that there were any orchards nearby, not unless they were tended by goblins, who would as likely as not burn the orchard and leave the prunings lie about. Then they'd burn their hair off into the bargain, in order to avoid haircuts, perhaps.

Escargot strode along through the shadows, watching the river road for elves and the woods for goblins and trolls, and wondering at the smoke on the wind. If it wasn't from pruning fires, what was it from?

Dry leaves, newly fallen from the trees, scrunched underfoot, muffled by the moist, decaying leaves beneath them, and Escargot expected to see on each drifting leaf a frowning henny-penny man, navigating on windy currents. He half wished he was small enough to ride on leaves. He could make a boat out of a piece of bark and sail the day away in a rain puddle.

He reached the woods' edge, finally, stepping in among the last scattered trees and peering out onto the meadows beyond. There was the stream that had undone poor Boggy. There were no elves on the meadow now. They weren't out searching for Leta any longer. They knew she was beyond their grasp. Escargot wondered what they *were* doing. Holding powwows, probably. Captain Appleby was threatening, no doubt, and Collier was correcting him and Boggy was sticking his tongue out and generally ruining the effect. Every sort of person had his job to do, he thought, taking the long view of it. Henny-penny men mined fire quartz beneath the sea; elves built marvelous contraptions for people like Captain Perry to steal; goblins raged around in an effort to see that nothing ever ran particularly right for anyone, including themselves; dwarfs dug out rubies and emeralds and baked bread and acted very sure of themselves; and men—what did they do?—made fools of themselves, more often than not, while putting on airs. Escargot felt as if he saw things particularly clearly right then, as if the whole world and all its strange caper-cutting was laid out in color in a G. Smithers book on one big, illustrated page.

He shook his head and realized that he'd been standing there daydreaming in the shade of the woods. It was a dangerous sort of daydreaming too. He recognized certain symptoms in it; he had been feeling self-satisfied and clear-headed. It was a smug sort of attitude that seemed always to lead to disaster or humiliation—to goblins coming up out of a hole in the ground and grabbing his ankle, to someone hitting him with a stick, to his talking very solemnly and having a bug fly into his mouth.

Suddenly he heard, very low and distant—as if it were wafting in on the breeze off the river, or as if it were the river itself singing across the stones of its own bed—a sort of deep and tuneful humming. He cocked his head and listened. It had the tone of a church choir about it, and it brought to mind a sentence in Smithers about enchanted breezes drawing tunes out of the willows and cattails along river banks. Could this be part of the dwarf's magic? Were things starting to stir? But that didn't seem altogether likely. There was something solid and good about this; it was utterly unlike the random cacophony of noises that had surrounded him that evening in Bleakstone Hollow.

It seemed to be drifting downwind toward him, from somewhere deeper in the woods. He crept along toward it, hunched over, taking cover behind occasional trees and shrubs. Caution seemed to be worth riches to him just then. The music grew louder shade by shade, until it became a separate thing from the sighing of the wind in the trees and from the crick and crackle and rustle of the woods.

There was a movement among the leaves just ahead. He crept toward it, squinting, realizing all of a sudden what it was that was singing; it was henny-penny men, a gathering of them, rank after rank of them sitting atop pebbles, lounging back against leaves propped on their own stems as if the little men sat on hammock chairs.

Escargot lay on his stomach, peering through the brush. One wild-haired henny-penny man seemed to be leading the choir in the last strains of the song. It was a hymn, and no mistaking it. The song trailed off, replaced by the silent afternoon and the lonesome calling of a whippoorwill. There was the sound of henny-penny men clearing their throats and shifting round on their leaves, and Escargot could see some few of them tugging at their shirt collars like bored parishioners seated on Sunday afternoon church pews. The little man before them waved the tiny book in his hand and began declaiming.

Escargot had to cock his head and cup a hand to his ear in order to hear, and even then most of the oratory escaped him on the breeze. The speaker wore a black frock coat, the skirt ragged and tousled in the breeze. His face was fringed with a monumental beard, black and stiff, and easily as long as his hair. This last thrust away from his skull like rays from a dark sun, and all in all he had the look about him of a man who had a fizz bomb concealed in a parcel. Escargot was reminded of Stover, somehow. It wasn't the man's appearance that did it; it was the starched and holy way he cut up and down in front of the crowd, thumping his book and carrying on. He would have made a first-rate pirate, Escargot decided, if he were about eighty times as big and had a glass of rum in his hand and a parrot on his shoulder.

Listening to the man's oratory was useless; Escargot couldn't make anything of it. They were there for some compelling reason. This was an army, is what it was, and the man in the frock coat was firing them up. He waved his volume in a passion, his beard wagging, and from the crowd there came scattered shouts of assent. Finally he fell silent, turned, and seemed to look straight into Escargot's face. He stood scowling. There was something about the angle of his chin and the roundness of his face that made him seem vaguely aquatic, and brought to mind the Professor's description of homunculus grass and the old story of how in the dim past henny-penny men had ridden to battle on the backs of trout.

For a moment Escargot considered leaping up and running. It would be a grim thing indeed to be swarmed over by the little men, and there was a good chance that if he ran for it he'd escape them before they had a chance to mount their leaves and follow. But in the time it took him to think about it, it became clear that the frock-coated minister hadn't seen him after all, for the man set his book down upon a stone and turned back to his congregation. Escargot squinted at the book, trying to make out the tiny lettering on the cover. It was a three-word title, and the author's name below it was an initial and . . . Escargot blinked and nearly shouted in surprise. It was G. Smithers—*The Stone Giants*. The henny-penny men read G. Smithers too. Who *didn't* read G. Smithers? Did the goblins have copies of Smithers, torn and greasy with fish slime and shoved beneath stones in the woods?

His wondering at it was interrupted when the henny-penny men, through with their camp meeting, began filing away out of the clearing. Some of them dragged their leaves after them; others abandoned them. Escargot watched them leave, waiting until long after the last one had disappeared so that his own leaving—which must sound to a henny-penny man like the crashing of a bear through the forest—would go unremarked. He trudged away toward the meadow, finally, puzzling over the whole business, but vaguely happy with it, and wondering if, when the business with Uncle Helstrom was finished, he mightn't be able to trade the henny-penny men something for a miniature copy of Smithers. It would be something like the eye of the gummidgefish and would be the start of his own collection of wonders. Perhaps somewhere out in the hills there was an ancient volume of *The Stone Giants* that was big as a house.

He saw the smoke clearly from the edge of the forest. It was off to the east, rising in curly little spires from beyond a jumble of rocky hillocks, looking for all the world like the smoke of an enormous pipe. It no longer reminded him quite so much of pruning fires. It was a weedy, muddy smell, weighted with the sharp chalk smell of burnt bone—an unmistakable smell, and one which a henny-penny man might easily find offensive. Escargot took a long, careful look about him, then set out at a run toward the nearest shelter a hundred yards off in the direction of the hills. He was bound to have a look at the source of that smoke. If he could do it, he'd settle the dwarf's hash then and there. Uncle Helstrom, surely, wouldn't welcome a rock in the side of the head any more than the next man would.

17

The Thing From the River

The temperature seemed to drop as Escargot crept up into the low-lying hills. The sun hung above the horizon, and its rays had grown thin and feeble, as if they wanted little to do with the deserted, rocky landscape and much preferred the open meadow. There was something strange about the hills, too. It might quite easily be a trick of his imagination or of shadow, but the rocks and fissures and humps of rising hills looked for all the world like bits and pieces of dismembered giants, heaped about the meadows and left, over the years, to petrify and to settle into the earth. Here was a ridge that looked overmuch like a half-buried leg, perhaps. And there was the top of a great, hummocky stone that might easily be a bald pate scoured by ages of weather and wind.

Escargot felt as if he were creeping through a graveyard, and he avoided stepping on rocks that his imagination might turn into old giants—if it *was* his imagination that was doing the turning. There were shadows aplenty, cast from the rocks by the declining sun, and Escargot stuck to them, crouching in the comparative darkness, stopping to listen once every minute or two, fearful that the dwarf, or more probably the witch, could sense his approach, could feel his own shadow passing over the enchanted ground.

The smell of smoke had almost disappeared from the air. The wind had turned around to blow from off the river. But he could see the smoke still, rising above the hills before dissipating like steam in the breeze. And he could hear a low chanting now, the voice of a single person, starting and stopping, rising and falling, somewhere just ahead. He looked behind him over the meadow, and was surprised to find that he stood some few hundred feet above the river. There was the *Nora Dawn*, riding at anchor, and there were the oak woods, a dark patch against green. The body of the troll still lay where it had fallen, and above it, circling slowly in the sky, were a half dozen great birds.

Above him lay a castle-like rock, canted over as if it had once taken a notion to tumble onto its side and then given the idea up. It was split nearly in two, and through the split shone blue sky and distant mountains. The base of the rock was cast in deep gloom, and Escargot crept in between the two halves, wafering himself against the rock and listening to the chanting that was quite obviously proceeding from the other side. He slid along the crack, avoiding loose stones, smashing himself against the shadowed wall that rose sheer and black above him. At the far end of the fissure he stopped and peered slowly out, holding his breath.

There below stood the dwarf—Abner Helstrom, whatever his name might be—laboring over a fire that burned in a dish. Beside him was a heap of bone. There was his own basket, still holding waterweeds, although they didn't appear to be lilac kelp; they seemed to be fresh weeds out of the river. The dwarf mumbled over the smoke, waving his staff through the spiraling reek, then bent and plucked up a bit of dripping, muddy weed and dangling a tendril of it into the flame.

The dwarf had tethered his horse and cart on a grassy swath of meadow at the base of the rocks, and the horse chewed moodily there in the shade, raising its head now and again and looking around itself suspiciously as if it sensed an impending storm. It seemed to like the smell of the curling smoke even less than did Escargot, for each time the dwarf dipped the weeds into the flame and a dense, steamy cloud went up, the horse seemed to shudder, as if it had seen a ghost ride by on the wind.

Not ten feet in front of where Escargot crouched lay a heap of leather bags, no doubt full of potions and philtres and maybe a spare pair of trousers. There was no getting at them, though, without revealing himself. If he'd had one of Captain Perry's pistols with him he might have tried to shoot the dwarf where he stood. But both the pistols had fallen into the hands of the goblins, and even if he *had* pistols, his aim wasn't good enough or his hand steady enough to accomplish anything. He'd do better with a rock, although a rock, unlike a pistol ball, would serve merely to make the dwarf mad. He could rush out at him, perhaps, and try to crush his skull with a really big rock, but it seemed, now that he gave it some thought, that such a plan would be doomed to failure. The dwarf would dodge the rock and then turn him into a toad or something, and he'd have to go hopping back to the submarine to try to apologize to Leta for having boggled things up again. He'd watch and wait; that's what he'd do. Rushing in hadn't served him very well in the past.

So he crouched there in the shadows, watching the horse fidget and whinny. The smoke, as it billowed and blew and rose skyward, seemed to take on strange and unlikely shapes, and now and then one would swirl and thicken and coagulate into a foggy, stretched spirit, its mouth agape as if frozen in a silent howl of remorse. The horse could see them too. It wasn't Escargot's imagination. But while Escargot could at least partly explain the terrible phenomenon, the horse couldn't, and the poor beast jerked on its tether, which was trapped beneath a rock.

Uncle Helstrom poked at the fire, then carefully laid a skeleton hand atop it. Escargot watched in horror as the hand twitched and hopped and the fingers closed over the coals as if the hand intended to squeeze them into powder. A monumental cloud arose, tumbling and writhing and looking for all the world like a grinning, smoky skull champing its teeth and tearing itself to bits in the wind.

The horse whinnied. Escargot cocked his arm and threw a lemon-size stone at the horse's flank, hitting the beast on the starboard side of its tail. The horse shrieked and bolted down toward the broad meadow, yanking its tether free and heading downriver at a gallop.

The dwarf cast a fresh weed onto the fire, shouted, and set out in pursuit, whistling and commanding and thumping on the dirt with his staff. Before both of them had disappeared beyond the rocks, Escargot found himself leaping down toward the dwarf's bags. Kicking the fire to bits and scattering the weeds and bones would probably accomplish nothing. The dwarf would merely light it again. But there might be something in the bags . . .

He yanked one open and found nothing within but more bones. In another were dried herbs and the half-decayed head of a carp. In the third, down among a couple of old books and a cap smashed flat into a disk, lay a little wooden box with a clasp lid. Inside were his marbles—Escargot's marbles, that is to say. Quickly he emptied the marbles into his pocket and hauled out the fish eggs, counting out the same number and dropping them into the box. Then he slipped the box back into the bag and yanked it shut, scuttling away into the little divide moments before the dwarf came puffing back into sight, his horse, apparently, having eluded him.

The dwarf beat on the ground two or three times with his staff, mumbling half aloud, and then bent over and blew on his fire until the skeletal hand, balled up into a fist now, glowed red. Escargot crept away, step after silent step. His heart thundered, and he felt suddenly like shouting at the dwarf, laughing wildly at him, ridiculing him. But it was something like hysteria that made him want to do that, and so he forced himself to be slow and silent and careful until he was out of the rocks and onto the meadow, at which point he turned and ran, coattail flying, toward the distant oak woods.

He didn't care who could see him then—the dwarf, the elves, the henny-penny men—it didn't matter a bit. He had the marbles and he had Leta, and the dwarf had nothing but a bit of foolish smoke. He didn't even have his horse anymore. He would not only fail to work his deviltry, but he'd have to walk home into the bargain. Escargot muffled his laughter and kept up his pace. He looked over his shoulder. The dwarf hadn't seen him or heard him, apparently, for the smoky phantoms still rose over the rocks one by one as the dwarf fed his waterweeds to the coals, unaware that Escargot had dealt him a blow.

Stealing the marbles had been better than hitting the dwarf in the head with a rock—heaps better. It was better than a wink or a basket of kelp in a goblin cave. All else being equal, it might have been more to the point if he had merely stolen all three bags and kicked the fire to bits. Then he'd have the bones and the herbs and the marbles and all, and Uncle Helstrom wouldn't have the price of a piece of pie. But that wouldn't have been quite as clever, quite as subtle. Subtlety was what would turn this business into an art. The dwarf knew that, and Escargot respected him for it. That's why it was so much fun undoing him. Captain Appleby was blind to it, though. Steal the girl and flee; that had been Appleby's method.

What would they all do next? They would understand, suddenly, who it was they were meddling with. He'd settle the witch next; that's what *he'd* do, although how he'd do it he couldn't say. He'd trust to his luck again and something would turn up. Then, when he was done with them for good and all, he'd sail across the river, find a cafe, and order about a dozen pies—*whole* pies, he'd say to the astonished waiter—and he'd watch the man's eyes shoot open. Then he'd eat every one of them with a spoon; he wouldn't even slice them up. He'd start in the middle and work out toward the edge, and every now and then fill the hole in the center with heavy cream. He'd leave the crust, too. He grinned when he imagined the look that would appear on Leta's face when she saw the retrieved marbles. "It was nothing," he muttered half aloud, shaking his head a little bit. "I spooked his horse is all, and then rifled his goods." He winked and nodded. That would make her put her book down.

He found himself stepping out of the shadow of the woods. He'd traversed them hardly realizing what he was about. He'd been daydreaming again. He looked around him and listened for a moment. Then he listened again, and thought he heard somewhere up the river road the sound of shouts and cries, pale in the distance. He strode along toward them straining to hear, then broke into a run at the nearby sound of a gabble of goblin laughter cut short by the distant boom of cannon fire.

The *Nora Dawn* stood out into the river some hundred yards. Her chase guns still smoked, and as Escargot leaped down the decline toward the sandy bank, spark and flame erupted from both cannon at once, and there sounded a hollow clang, the ring of cannon shot off the hull of the submarine—his submarine. The ship was half beached, like a dying whale, and clinging to the stern was a vast creature from the river, black and scaly and ancient. It had the tentacles of a squid, and it turned the *Omen* this way and that as if to shake something out of it. Its head writhed from the water, too heavy and rubbery for the beast to hold it erect. It had the beak of a parrot, which it gnashed against the side of the submarine, as if to tear the ship in half, and it spewed out air through blow holes in a hoarse slobbering of river water and air.

The cannon aboard the elf ship fired off another twin round, one of the balls geysering into the river, the other smashing into the back of the mottled creature and disappearing like a stone in a pudding. It threw itself sideways, splashing a great sheet of water across the edge of the cove, and for a moment seemed to relax its grip on the submarine.

The hatch flew open and Leta appeared, hoisting herself out and rolling across the steep deck. She clung for a moment to one of the forward fins, then slid across the brass and copper hull and into shallow water, out of the reach of the thing from the river. It seemed not to notice her escape, but tore once more at the submarine, lifting the stern free of the river. Water cascaded from the screw and hull and fins, and the brown and orange metal, turquoise with verdigris and lined around the ports with silver, glinted for a moment in the sunlight before the beast shook it out like a dog worrying a rat, and then dropped it into the river again and disappeared. The ship swung round into the current as Escargot ran along the bank, fearful that he'd lose it entirely, that it would wallow out into mid river and fill with water, sinking dead and silent in the deep channel. But it scrunched up into the shallows instead, driven farther onto the beach and canting half over onto its side.

Leta stood on the beach alone. A longboat full of elves put out from the *Nora Dawn*, and rowed furiously shoreward, anxious both to settle their account with Leta before she eluded them again, and to avoid running up against the monster that had dealt so handily with the submarine. Before either party could reach her, though, goblins broke from the cover of a little grove of trees upriver and rushed toward where Leta stood on the bank.

Escargot shouted, forgetting about his submarine. One of the elves stood up in the bow and pointed, urging the rowers to haul on the oars. Leta spun round and knocked two goblins aside with the back of her hands, but then the rest were upon her, chattering and cackling and swarming like rats in a cellar, and she went over backward in a tangle of writhing little men, the lot of them rolling down toward the water as goblins dropped off and hollered and tore at each other like mad things.

Escargot found himself plucking them up and sailing them into the river before he stopped to think what he was about. There seemed to be nothing else to do with them. Hitting them in the head made them cackle even louder with laughter, if such a thing were possible. More goblins appeared now, rushing toward them down the road, their sharpened teeth gnashing and their sparse hair wild and blowing.

There sounded a great splashing from the river all of a sudden, like a dozen great serpents beating the water. Rising in a mass of bubbles and steam stained pink by the thing's blood, the river monster plucked up floating goblins and whirled them skyward, throwing some of them into deeper water, holding onto others and slapping them down onto the roiling surface of the river.

The elves in the longboat rowed more furiously than ever, but downstream now, away from the thrashing, blowing creature. The *Nora Dawn*, her anchor hauled abeam, drifted in the current as sails unfurled along the masts, Captain Appleby wisely seeking to put some distance between his ship and the carnage atop the river. The monster, in a gulp, ate a goblin, shoving it past its beak and into its horrible tearing mouth. Then another goblin, limp as a cloth doll, followed it. Another crowd of goblins that had been rushing along furiously toward him and Leta had slowed and stopped. They stood gabbling in low tones, blinking in wonder, then broke and ran toward the meadow. Escargot tumbled the last two of their brethren in the same direction, opening his mouth to shout a warning, just for good measure, at the retreating mob.

Then he saw, standing beneath the mossy, overhanging limbs of a barren and twisted oak, the old woman, very still and with her head bent slightly sideways as if she were listening to the wind.

Escargot's shout died on his lips. He knew at once why it was that the witch hadn't been with her master a half hour earlier. He'd sent her after Leta. The river monster had been doing her bidding, had delivered the submarine to her with Leta inside. There wasn't anything in the least bit subtle about it; the thing had picked up the submarine as if it were a salt shaker and had dumped her out.

Escargot grabbed Leta's hand and hauled her along the sand, toward the beached submarine. The sun, he realized suddenly, had vanished beyond the river, and the misty gray of evening crept across the beach even as they ran. He pressed her hand in his, as if clutching it tightly would keep it from evaporating, from slipping away into nothing, and he glanced once into her face, which was lined, it seemed to him, with terror and resignation.

And then suddenly he was holding nothing at all—only a handful of fog that his fingers closed over, just as the skeletal hand that the dwarf had thrown into the fire had closed over a powdery heap of ash. She was gone again, and he fancied he could hear on the wind the faint echo of her cry, but he couldn't quite make out what it was she'd said.

He turned in a fury, forgetting about the submarine and about the thing in the river. He ran toward the lone oak tree, leaping across a driftwood log, thrashing through a stand of willow scrub, then stopping and staring when he realized with an abruptness that nearly knocked the wind out of him that it wasn't the old lady who stood now beneath the tree, listening at the wind; it was Leta. The shadow of the oak, dim in the dark of evening, spread out before her along the ground, looking for all the world like a vast black cat with its back arched and front legs stiff. And then, as quickly as he understood what it was he saw and set out once again at a run, Leta vanished, or rather the witch vanished, and there *was* a black cat, sitting on its haunches beneath the tree. By the time he'd struggled up the hill, the elves racing and shouting up the river road behind him, the cat was gone, lost on the shadowy meadow.

"Well," said Captain Appleby, drawing slowly at his pipe and regarding Escargot through squinting eyes, "you've rather made a hash of this one."

The complaint infuriated Escargot, even though it was largely deserved. But then what could he have accomplished if he had stayed behind in the submarine, if he hadn't left Leta alone and gone out after the marbles? His presence there wouldn't have confounded the river monster in the least, and he certainly wouldn't have been capable, when it came down to it, of jerking the sun back into the sky and warding off evening. There was nothing that he could have done. That was clear. He'd told himself that about a dozen times and he found himself ignoring Captain Appleby and telling himself again, replaying in his mind all of the possible scenarios that *hadn't* happened that afternoon, and finding that none of them would have ended any differently.

He'd been outfoxed again; that was the long and the short of it. He'd trumped the dwarf on the meadow, but the dwarf had had cards in his hand that he wasn't showing—aces in his sleeve. Now evening was drawing on and they sat uselessly in the captain's cabin, either or both of them standing up now and then to peer out of one of the portholes. Smoke rose again from beyond the first rocky hills. Appleby had sent out calls for help, but what more could they hope for than another galleon or two of elves? Even that was hoping for too much.

"What can they do without the marbles?" asked Escargot tiredly.

"They can kill the girl. They don't need marbles to kill the girl."

"But *why* would they kill the girl if they don't have the marbles? You told me they needed both."

"They need both, perhaps, to defeat us utterly, at a blow. But they don't need both to turn the valley upside down. Better we'd kept the girl and left him the marbles, which are nothing but blood anyway, like I said. They've got blood enough in the girl to wreak no end of deviltry."

Escargot winced. "Aren't your men ready yet?" Hurrying feet clumped along over the deck above. Shouted orders rang out. Collier stuck his head into the cabin, started to say something, then hastened away leaving it unsaid. The night was dark and clear outside, and in an hour a full moon would have risen above Landsend. Escargot decided that he couldn't wait for Captain Appleby. Elves or no elves he was setting out.

"My men are ready," Appleby said. "I haven't decided yet what it is we're going to do. Steady-on, is my motto, and you'd do well, lad, to take heed of it. Waging war is something like playing chess. Drink another bottle of this ale."

"No, thank you." Escargot shoveled cold fragments of a meat pie into his mouth and drained the last half inch of ale from his glass. Steady-on was right. He'd had enough sitting about. He'd lost a battle that afternoon; there was no denying it. But he'd won another, hadn't he? And so far Captain Appleby had done little about the menace save lobbing a cannonball into the head of the squid. The time for waiting and planning was past. "I'm setting out." Escargot stood up and put a hand on the door latch.

Captain Appleby nodded, apparently satisfied. Escargot had been vaguely afraid that the captain would attempt to lock him up again. He'd think, perhaps justifiably, that Escargot had been working a bit too often at cross purposes with them, and he'd decide that Escargot was better off out of the fray. But that wasn't to be the case, apparently.

"Good luck to you, then," said the elf.

"Thank you. I just can't wait about, you know."

"Of course you can't. I wouldn't either. And it might easily be best if we had a go at this villain from different angles—confuse the issue a bit. Do you want company? I could sacrifice Boggy, perhaps."

"No, thank you anyway."

"I thought not," said Appleby, sighing. "Cheerio, then."

"Bye." Escargot let himself out and left Captain Appleby smoking alone in his cabin. He wondered what plans revolved in the elf's mind. Something was up, certainly, but there was no guessing it out. The captain was troubled. Most of his bluster and drama had left him—ironed out by the spectre of doom that had risen with the night. Escargot rather liked him better for it.

The moon, when it rose, glowed like an illuminated pearl, and it seemed to Escargot as he stepped along the path through the dark woods that it was a heavenly lantern, hung on a hook in the sky for the sole purpose of lighting his way. It disappeared behind dense foliage and then appeared again in a wash of silver and then was gone once more, and he had to pick his way like a blind man over deadwood and half-exposed rocks. Then suddenly there it was in the sky again, seeming to hover between the waving, upper branches of great trees and casting its cool glow across the trail.

The pale lights playing over mottled trunks and patchy, sun-starved grass were like so many flitting ghosts, shifting and sighing and entrapped, somehow, within the silent depths of the moonlit woods. He wondered if there were henny-penny men about, perhaps watching him from tree branches through black, brooding eyes and combing the tangles out of their beards with thin fingers.

But soon he stepped out of the tree line and onto the open meadow, and the clutching darkness fell away and disappeared. The moon smiled down on him like the face on the clock on the wall in little Annie's room, and once again it seemed to him to be the face of a friend. He remembered again having sat by the riverside weeks back, thinking that Annie might ride along with him on adventures. All that business about her learning elfin tongues and deciphering the gabble of goblin talk—all of it was nonsense. He could see that now.

Almost nothing, it seemed, went along according to plan. You could spy everything out from a thousand lofty hilltops, could peer through telescopes fitted with elf glass, until you convinced yourself that you saw everything clearly, that the future, surely, could be mapped with a quill pen and the ink dusted and dried. But it would turn out that there were *two* thousand hilltops, half of them invisible beyond the crests of the others, and that beyond them were ten thousand more, and that all the telescopes in the wide world, strung end to end and twisted into focus by the steadiest hand, weren't enough to spy them all out. And then, marching out from beyond those hills would come a bank of rainclouds, hidden moments before, and the sudden downpour would reduce your little ink and paper plans to a wash of blue haze.

But you'd make another map—wouldn't you?—thought Escargot, hurrying along across the meadow. You'd patch one up out of the fragments of the others and you'd convince yourself that this time, surely, what you held in your hands wouldn't go to bits in the rain. You might just as well do that or stay home. You couldn't admit, ever, that your hopes and dreams were just goblin gold, turning to bugs and trash in the light of the noonday sun.

One day he'd reach Twombly Town again; the winds would blow him home. But for the moment the winds blew elsewhere, and there was nothing for him to do but to trim the sails and drive with a will toward shore.

Ahead of him now lay the stony hills, dark and jagged against the gray, rolling meadows. From beyond them glowed a light. It wasn't the pale radiance of the moon; it was the yellow, dancing flicker of firelight. Escargot felt suddenly exposed out there in the open night, and it seemed to him as if half a hundred goblins watched him from hidey-holes among the rocks. The dwarf, surely, would expect trouble. And it was trouble he'd get.

No one accosted Escargot on the meadow. No goblins appeared; no trolls hunched out to chase him. No leaves navigated by henny-penny men tilted toward him. He found himself in minutes among the moon shadows cast by the scattered rocks at the base of the hills. He could hear the dwarf's chanting now, much clearer than he'd heard it that afternoon, as if it carried better on the empty night air. It seemed to him too that far away and all around him sounded a peculiar straining creak, like the slow closing of a screen door on complaining hinges. The night, he realized suddenly, was alive with noises, most of them mysterious. They weren't the scattered, random noises that had drifted on the air in Bleakstone Hollow; they were noises made by the stirring landscape, by the shifting, it seemed, of the hills themselves.

Whatever the dwarf was about, he'd gotten underway, and in earnest, too. A thin thread of moonlight glowed through the fissure between the great, tilted rocks. Escargot made for it, wary of goblins, and peered through at the sloping meadow on the far side. There was Abner Helstrom, conjuring with his bones and his weeds. Beyond, bivouacked on the meadow, were no end of goblins, clustered around fires that burned with the brightness of metal glowing in a forge, but which cast almost no light at all beyond a very small circle. The goblins nearest the flames were almost white with the radiance, but some few feet away they were cast in shadow, so that it was impossible to say how many goblins were massed there. In among them were the great, humped shapes of trolls, sitting stupidly in the darkness. Overhead, flitting and wheeling, flew thousands upon thousands of bats, as wild, it seemed, as the goblins themselves and swooping and darting above the flames with unnatural energy. The goblins danced and leaped and wrestled and cackled, and it seemed certain that the dwarf had situated them a distance from his conjuring so that they could cut their foolish goblin capers without spoiling his work.

Why he'd encamped them there was impossible to say, but it seemed reasonable that they were the dwarf's army, waiting, perhaps, for the arrival of the elves. Captain Appleby and his men would be sorely outnumbered, even if they were joined by a flotilla of elf galleons. The dwarf would be very happy, most likely, to merely waste the elves' time away in pointless battle with goblins and trolls, in order to allow him to work his mischief unencumbered.

With a suddenness that threw Escargot onto his face, the ground heaved and shook and then grew still. Uncle Helstrom skipped before his fire, laughing shrilly, delighted with himself. He pounded on the earth with his staff, blasting sparks out of dirt and setting off more rumbling in the earth. A great cheer arose from the massed goblins, who almost certainly had no idea what it was their master was about, but happy with the idea that the night was filled with first-rate confusions.

Escargot pulled himself farther along through the defile, crawling on his belly into the open shadows. He could see the witch then, stooped among some stones below and to the left. She seemed to be asleep, or in some sort of muddle, and there hovered roundabout her head what seemed to be a little misty cloud, torn by the night breeze but continually re-forming, only to be torn to shreds again. He wondered momentarily if the cloud was Leta, or rather was the wraith that was all that was left of Leta at the moment. His wondering was interrupted when, as if he were lying atop a rug that had been jerked out from under him by unseen hands, he found himself rolling and bumping across the stones, smashing finally against the wall of the sheer rock, which was tilted now at an even more precarious angle than it had been moments before. The rumbling beneath him in the earth grew louder, and the echo of the beating heart, which he'd first heard downriver days before, seemed to be the sound of someone beating with a tree trunk on the stretched hide of the hollow earth.

There was a movement behind him—not the punchy capering of goblins, but the slow, creaking heave of moving ground. The half-buried ridge of rock that had seemed to him to resemble a leg hours earlier shifted and tilted and thrust up suddenly, cascading dirt and pebbles. There could be no question now about imagination. It was an awakening giant, is what is was, and almost as soon as he realized it and leaped away so as to get out from under the towering rock, he saw the smooth hummock of stone that he'd taken for the top of a giant's head stir itself suddenly, shift, and jerk over sideways, revealing a deep and cavernous eye that seemed to stare up at the moon.

Escargot suddenly had no further desire to hide among the rocks. He stepped down in a crouch, keeping well out of sight of the witch and well to the back of Uncle Helstrom. He threw himself into the high grass of the meadow, rolling down a little decline and then scuttling up again until he could just see over the top of a rise. He expected that at any moment the ground would heave and he'd find himself standing on the shoulder of a giant, or that the goblins, seeing him suddenly from below, would come cackling up toward him.

The dwarf meddled in his bags, yanking out the little wooden box. Escargot smiled. He had no idea what would happen, but he smiled anyway. The hills that hid the southern horizon seemed to have come suddenly to life, and where moments before there had been a valley, now there was a precipice, and then the precipice would shake itself and seem to become an elbow and the mountain rising beyond it would become the hunched back of a crawling giant. The goblins and trolls capered in wild abandon below, and there arose the sound of great copper gongs being beaten, and the noise of a multitude of flutes blowing in weird harmony. It was as if the night and the countryside had been animated by the dwarf's enchantment and that even the trees standing in little copses roundabout the meadow would in moments begin dancing in slow circles.

Escargot squinted at the firelight above. He could see that the dwarf held in his hand a little heap of marbles—or rather of eggs. The witch had struggled to her feet and waited there as if in expectation. The fire leaped and died and leaped again, and in the sudden glow the dwarf held in his hand not a half dozen marbles, but a tangle of little wriggling creatures. Fish! Escargot cried, half aloud. The dwarf shook his hand as if he'd just then discovered a spider on it, and he leaped back grimacing, dumping the little fish into the fire. Nothing at all happened. The goblins continued to cackle and dance and whistle on flutes, but the hills and rocks seemed suddenly to slump. Half-risen giants collapsed in heaps, whumping up clouds of dust, and the rising heartbeat dimmed as if a door had been shut in front of it.

Uncle Helstrom raged around his fire in an absolute fury, stomping and kicking and scrabbling in his heap of dried bones. Escargot could hear him cursing and railing as he piled fuel onto the coals, flinging on a tangle of river weeds and fanning the whole smoking business with his hat. He beat with his staff against the ground and shouted incantations, and once again the heartbeat filled the night air and the mountains shifted and moved.

The piping and gonging fell off, and was replaced by the bellowing of trolls and wild gabbling of goblins. The multitude on the meadow seemed to surge up toward the hills, but Escargot couldn't at first see what it was they were rushing at. Then, rising above the rocky prominence, their tattooed sails illuminated by moonlight, three elf galleons scoured along on the wind, and following them in formation sailed three more, the cannon of the first trio already thundering brimstone and sparks as they came around in a line and fired a broadside into the surging army on the plain, driving toward the massed goblins and trolls, elfin archers firing from the rigging, pistols blazing along the rails.

18

The War on the Meadow

Escargot cheered in spite of himself, then fell silent and dropped flat onto the grass. When he looked up the dwarf was still at it, working furiously now, but the witch seemed to have stirred. She stood some few feet farther along in his direction, and she stared straight at him. He stared back. Some little part of her, he knew, was Leta. The two of them—he and the witch—had a score to settle between themselves. Maybe she knew that too. Even as he thought about it, the moon edged out from behind a rocky hilltop, and moonlight illuminated her. For a moment it was Leta who stood there, but only for a moment, and Escargot realized, when he saw her, that he'd been thinking that he might, if he moved very quickly, dash across the few yards that separated them and bowl the witch over—knock her down, bang into the dwarf's fire. But the glimpse of Leta, false as it was, evaporated the idea.

The witch seemed to stumble, as if she'd been pushed from behind by a ghost, and she waved both arms before her, waggling her fingers in the air as if wrestling with a spirit or conjuring wildly. Escargot could see what appeared to be a swirling little cloud above and behind her, pale against the dark stone and almost opaque in the moonlight. And the moon, just then, seemed to Escargot to be many times its usual size. It filled a quarter of the sky—maybe a trick of the dwarf's enchantment, or maybe the doing of the elves.

A stone the size of a grapefruit banged down next to his head, and he shouted in surprise, cutting it off instantly for fear of being heard. But of course the witch already knew he was there, and what she knew Uncle Helstrom knew, or so it seemed. It was time to move. If he'd been serious about taking center stage, well, here was the curtain call. He leaped up, feeling at his belt for his pistol and dashing toward the comparative shelter of the rocks, where the witch still grappled with spirits.

The meadow, suddenly, was bright as day. The moon seemed to have *become* the sky. It spread across the sky from the treetops of the oak woods to the southern hills. Silhouetted against it, their sails billowed and their bowsprits cleaving heavenly seas, three more elf galleons drove toward the meadow. There sounded a flourish of trumpets that sent a thrill through Escargot. Here was something to see. They'd have the dwarf now for sure. They'd sail over his head and douse the boneyard fire with a hose. They'd drop a piano on the head of Uncle Helstrom and smash him into pudding. The goblins would flee; the witch would melt into syrup.

But just then, just when one of the galleons—the *Nora Dawn*—seemed intent on doing just that, the awakening giant in the rocks behind the dwarf stood up and shook itself out. It towered above the meadow, gray in the moonlight, its face creased with fissures, its head swiveling on a creaking, stony neck. The dwarf cast handfuls of sparks toward the four corners of the compass. He stretched his hand into the fire, plucked out heaps of glowing coals, and pitched them this way and that. The *Nora Dawn* swept down upon him, running before a wind that seemed to blow straight out of the face of the moon. Elves lined the rail, archers and marksmen, waiting for Captain Appleby's command—waiting until they couldn't miss.

The dwarf paid them little heed. He pounded with his staff, flinging hot coals at the moon now, and just as Appleby shouted, just as the archers drew their bows taut and the dwarf looked up at his fate, the stone giant stretched out a vast, crumbling hand and plucked the *Nora Dawn* from the sky. He looked at it wonderingly, like an enormous baby peering at a windup toy. The elves, still on deck, stared at him in frozen horror, hearing, no doubt, the wild laughter of the dwarf below them.

Escargot shut his eyes, thinking of Boggy and Collier and the captain, and when he opened them a second later, the ship was gone, disappeared behind the pinnacle of stone. The giant had set them down on the meadow, and stood now looking at his hands as if mystified by them, as if he hadn't seen them in a long, long time. Then he opened his mouth and croaked, like two stones being rubbed together. He looked at the moon, and a frown of sudden hatred crossed his face, as if he remembered an old grudge. His arm swept out, striking at it, and a hail of rock rained down over the meadow, scattering goblins in a wild panic.

Uncle Helstrom danced before his fire. More giants loomed up from among the distant hills, creaking and moaning. The elfin ships scattered before them, anxious to avoid the fate of the *Nora Dawn*, whose crew appeared from beyond the rocks, running along onto the meadow to engage the goblins. A half dozen crewmembers, Captain Appleby among them, rushed in at the dwarf, weapons upraised, but the stone giant swept the lot of them onto their backs like nine pins, then set about trying to squash them with the tip of his first finger. The elves, though, were quicker than he, and they scuttled away after their companions, who by now were into the thick of the goblins, and were shooting and hewing and shouting.

The galleons above swept along beyond them as close as they dared, firing into the goblins, chasing down trolls. But even as Escargot watched, two of the ships collided, one of them splitting open and tilting sideways, spilling elves onto the heads of the throng warring on the meadow. The broken ship sank heavily in their wake, and cracked asunder when it struck the meadow grass. The other galleon limped toward the woods and the river, intending, perhaps, to set down in the cove.

An explosion of spark and flame erupted from where Uncle Helstrom conjured at the feet of the giant. The dwarf himself crouched behind the great foot of the creature, peering past the dirt and roots clinging to it. At first nothing changed, except that the moon seemed at once to have shrunk and its brightness to have diminished. The old woman ceased her struggling and hobbled toward the dwarf. Escargot bounded after her.

He could hear little above the booming of cannon and the creaking of the hills and the shouting of the multitude on the plain, but just then, in the middle of the cacophony, a voice seemed to shout into his ear. "Drop!" it commanded, and he dropped, hearing the thunk of a wooden club smash into the rocks above him. He rolled sideways, lurching to his feet and drawing his pistol at the same time. Before him, crouched and ponderous and with its mouth open and drooling, lurched a troll half again taller than himself. And behind the troll, his cutlass glinting in the moonlight, stood Captain Appleby. The cutlass clanked off the heavy, rusted chain wrapped about the beast's head and shoulders, and shivered in Appleby's hand, then dropped to the meadow, the captain grabbing at his wrist.

Escargot fired straight into the troll's face, managing to astonish the creature and to shatter its ear, but to miss doing any telling damage by a remarkably wide inch or so. The thing bellowed and raised its club, swinging ponderously at him. Escargot turned and ducked. There was no time to meddle with pistol balls. It hadn't been Appleby who had shouted the warning. The voice had been the voice of a woman—Leta's voice. He was sure of it. But Leta was nowhere around, and the troll was lurching forward even as Appleby retrieved his cutlass and took another swipe. Escargot drew his own blade and swung the ponderous thing like he was clearing brush, and though neither one of them managed particularly to hurt the beast, it was dumbfounded, it seemed, by being accosted from two sides at once, and it turned first toward Appleby, then toward Escargot, flailing away ineffectively at both.

"The witch!" shouted Appleby, spearing at the troll. "Kill the witch! Cut her head off! Push her into the fire!"

Escargot turned to do the captain's bidding, but knew at once that he couldn't. As long as he couldn't say for sure what the witch was, what part of her was Leta and what part a devil, he couldn't push her into any fires or cut off her head, not to save himself, not to save the world. Even as he thought about it Captain Appleby was gone, swept up into the battle and hollering something over his shoulder about duty.

Escargot had nothing against skewering Uncle Helstrom, though, and he turned and struck straightaway toward the dwarf. The stone giant bent toward him, cocking its head, opening and closing its hands. Escargot veered away from it, thinking suddenly that he'd attend to the dwarf later and seeing for the first time two very remarkable things. From the hills to the south, clacking along with moonlight glowing through rib cages, endless disheveled ranks of skeletons strode spindle-legged onto the meadow. There were hundreds of them—

thousands, perhaps, torn from opened graves along the river. They shone like old ivory in the light of the silver moon, and even at a distance of half a mile and over the din of the battle, Escargot could hear their bones clattering like dominoes falling in a heap onto a wooden tabletop.

At the same moment came a movement in the sky. It suddenly seemed as if the low heavens were full of moving stars—innumerable stars that slanted down past the dark oak woods, whirling along on the wind as if the Milky Way itself had been blown to bits and swept to earth in a rush. The lights shone brighter by the moment, and Escargot could see, finally, that they weren't stars at all, but were tiny lanterns, below which flew small, dark shapes on moonlit wings.

The dwarf's bats, still swooping and darting over the meadow and worrying the elves aloft in their galleons, flew in a cloud to meet the pinpoints of light, and Uncle Helstrom himself shrieked in a fury and looked around, hollering at the witch, who huddled now in a dark alcove in the rocks.

At the moment the dwarf turned his attention away from his magical fire the moon seemed to plummet earthward, once again brightening the meadow. The goblins and the trolls and even the lumbering giants paused in the middle of battle, falling back in the face of the awakening moon. Three stone giants, heavy and slow and ponderous and striding now in the wake of the skeletons, shook themselves like a man might shake his head when waking up from a long afternoon nap, and the shaking seemed to dismember them. Fingers flew off here; stony ears tumbled onto the meadow there; a great head shivered into scree and rained down onto a host of raging goblins, scattering and crushing them. One giant sat down heavily on a troll, then slumped backward, the ground shaking with the thud. It was as if in the suddenly brightened moonlight they were disintegrating, bit by bit.

The dwarf shrieked, pulling at the arm of the witch with one hand and stoking his fire with the other, and the sky, suddenly, was full of henny-penny men, each of them wearing a necklace of fire quartz and brandishing a spear. Trolls howled and fled, goblins fell onto their faces. The little men sat astride owls that swooped down onto darting bats, rending the things with their talons.

A great cheer arose from the elves, and the ships, afraid now that cannon and pistol fire might as easily hit friend as foe, swept south toward the hills to meet the advancing giants. And even as they sailed before the wind, rope ladders dangled from the sides of the galleons, sweeping along the plain, and elves scurried down them, tumbled onto the meadow grasses, and sprang to their feet, rushing up and into the fray.

Their ships drove on toward the giants, who lumbered down toward the meadow now, bellowing and lurching, awakened at last to the task at hand. Three of the galleons ranged abreast of each other once again and advanced on the foremost of the giants, a shaggy monster, hairy with trees and grasses still rooted in the creature's earthen skin. The galleons fired as one, a dozen guns in all, the ships swerving round and running down the meadow again as the monster reeled and creaked. Its left arm fell to rubble and half its midsection disintegrated in a spray of rock and dirt, leaving the creature wavering there in mute surprise until the great weight of its head and chest pulled it over and it thundered down onto the grasses in a cloud of flying debris.

Its fellows, eight in all, and more moving among the distant hills, seemed not at all to notice the plight of the first, and the galleons were among them once more, this one delivering a salvo from its twelve pounders and blowing an enormous leg into fragments, that one firing away with its chase guns as it swept past on the wind, the smoke and brimstone swirling about the heads of the giants, who staggered and swatted and lumbered forward in confusion.

One galleon, its billowed sails painted with the visage of a round-faced, bespectacled, cloud-cheeked man, came around too soon, and an enraged giant, half his granite face blasted away moments before, swiped at the ship, snapping its mizzenmast like a piece of stick candy. The ship shuddered under the blow, listing crazily as the giant struck again, sweeping the mainmast by the boards and staving a great, gaping hole in the starboard bulwark. The ship sank to the grass like a leaf drifting out of a tree on a windless day, and elves scurried out of her like bugs as the giant brought a stony foot down onto the ship, smashing her afterdeck to flinders before collapsing himself, the remains of his face breaking to smash on the meadow beyond the crushed galleon.

The night was full of booming guns and the creak of toppling giants. Goblins raged beside trolls, seeking to tear at elves with their teeth. Half the goblins had lit their hair aflame in the melee, and they capered wildly and with no particular purpose, perhaps assuming in their dim way that the mere sight of them would throw fear into the elves. But what the elves fought for lent them a bravery that a goblin or a troll couldn't fathom, and for every elf struck down with a troll's club or smothered beneath rushing goblins, two more surged in shouting, flanked by henny-penny men and sending the goblins scurrying in howling confusion.

The battle had ascended the hill toward where Uncle Helstrom tended his fire. The dwarf watched warily, casting his glowing cinders by the handful as if the little pinwheels of spark and flame were a wall against the warring armies. Escargot charged at the dwarf. The stone giant, sitting behind Uncle Helstrom like a genie waiting for a command, looked at Escargot, then raised his hand slowly, intending, perhaps, to swat him like a fly. Moonlight suddenly shone off the enormous, grass-covered hand, bathing it in opalescent radiance, and the hand broke free at the wrist and disintegrated from rock to sand to dust before it sprinkled onto the ground. Then the moon lit the giant's wondering, upturned face, and the creature fell over backward as if in a sudden faint, the ground shuddering with the impact.

Escargot, who had been anxious to avoid the threatening giant, found himself hurtling now toward the dwarf, who cast into his face a scattering of glowing coals that fanned out in a bright arc before him. Escargot seemed to smash against an invisible wall formed of enchantment, the dwarf grinning at him from beyond it and reaching once again into the coals. Another spray of sparks and embers sent Escargot reeling sideways. He fell, rolling across the grass toward where the witch stood snatching at the air again. There was the milky cloud roiling about her, more substantial now, as if the mist were turning to ice. Escargot plucked himself up, astonished. The witch spoke with Leta's voice. She *became* Leta for one startling moment, but it was Leta with the face of a cat, then Leta with no face at all, then the witch again, stumbling toward the dwarf as if she were in a terrible hurry to finish the evening's work.

Escargot shouted, and his shout was returned—not by the

dwarf or by the witch, but by Leta herself. She stood behind the witch, against the sheer, tilted rock on the hill. Escargot could see straight through her, as if she were some sort of clever, magical projection. The dwarf cast the witch aside and snatched at Leta, but his arm passed through her arm. Bathed in heightening moonlight, seemed to solidify suddenly. She swung wildly at the dwarf, who had spun halfway around with the force of his own blow, and her open hand clipped him on the ear and sent him reeling. He lurched after his staff, kicking through his little heap of bags. Escargot bounded in before him, snatching up the staff and flinging it end over end into the midst of a howling mob of goblins below, and the staff, glowing in moonlight, seemed to cleave them like a scythe through wheat.

Bracing himself to meet the dwarf's onslaught, Escargot was surprised to see his foe flee across the meadow after his staff. He didn't, obviously, care a rap for Escargot, but was intent only on holding onto as many of his magical trappings as he might. Escargot plucked up one of the bags and upended it, shaking out a dried bundle of homunculus grass and flinging it onto the fire.

The air was at once saturated with the smell of mud and waterweeds, and a great reek of smoke billowed out into the wind. The dwarf stumbled among his goblins, hacking with his staff at whoever or whatever came near him, shivering two skeletons into scattered bones at a blow. Captain Appleby appeared suddenly before him, cutlass upraised and a look of stony resolve on his face. But the dwarf smote the ground with his staff, mouthing a curse, and the captain tumbled over backward and lay still. Boggy stood over his fallen captain, slashing away tiredly at a knot of skeletons, bones skittering away across the meadow and the skeletons clacking and lurching and plucking up fallen swords which they swung clumsily with both hands.

Abner Helstrom stopped and looked about him, eyes narrowed as if he were wondering what smell it was that filled the air, and then he shrieked and ran toward the fire, carrying his staff in both hands. The henny-penny men suddenly went mad. They gave off thrusting their little spears into the sides of goblins and trolls and wheeled toward the fire, infuriated by the smell of smoke.

The air roundabout Escargot was filled suddenly with swooping owls and with the tiny scowling faces of henny-penny men, set upon murder. He would discover now, he thought to himself as he crouched and ran toward the rocks, whether he counted as friend or foe among the henny-pennies. To his vast dismay Leta seemed oblivious to the flashing spears of the little men and to the fiery thundering of the dwarf. She bent toward the fire, which leaped and roared with a fury born of enchantment gone awry. The witch fled before her, bent and hobbling.

The girl grabbed the witch's shoulder and spun her around, looking into the face of a blank, eyeless, staring thing, drooling onto the webby lace at its throat, the face of a thing dead and buried. Leta shrieked at the sight of it and then hurled herself forward, slamming stiff-armed into the witch and tumbling her over backward into the fire.

There was a great gasp of flame and reek, and the fire went out as abruptly as it had flared up moments before. The witch was gone, as if evaporated. The goblin fires on the meadow, one moment leaping and burning and winking, snapped into darkness the next like snuffed candles. The moon sailed back into the heavens and in a moment bobbed there pleasant and serene, as if it hadn't witnessed anything at all out of the ordinary that night. Goblins and trolls and clacking skeletons fled into the hills, pursued by henny-penny men. The elves threw down their weapons and cheered, their victory assured, the threat to the valley, to the wide world itself, seeming to have been doused in an instant.

The dwarf screamed and struck at the cloud of whirling owls. Hundreds of the birds winged roundabout overhead, their tiny riders watching for an opportunity to sail in and take a poke at the dwarf, who fled away down the meadow toward the southern hills where the last few giants even then collapsed back into stony, ageless sleep. The dwarf ran trailing his staff and holding onto his slouch hat with his free hand as henny-penny men flew at his back. And as he ran, a wind devil sprang up from the scree and dirt and torn vegetation that had been a giant, and scoured roundabout the meadow as if searching for something. Shouting incantations, Uncle Helstrom ran toward it. The wind devil, as if abruptly having caught sight of what it was looking for, spun toward him in a swirl of leaves and dust and making the sound of wind whistling through tree branches.

Just as the dwarf reached the whirling perimeter of the little spiraling cloud and burst into a peal of wild, conceited laughter, an owl swooped before him and the henny-penny man astride it thrust his spear into the dwarf's face. The laughter changed abruptly to a shriek; the owl and its rider were swept into the wind devil and spun round like paper whirligigs; and the dwarf seemed to turn to dust, consumed by the wind and borne away toward the south, the faint, strange sounds of moaning and laughter lingering on the suddenly still night air.

Epilogue

''You can have them with my blessing,'' said Escargot to Captain Appleby, who sat with a bandaged head on the sandy shore of the river.

The elf held in his hand the box of marbles, the droplets of giant's blood stolen from the dwarf. Escargot hadn't any use for them. He'd keep the truth charm, though. That was a thing that a man could trade, if it came down to it. It had served him well a time or two, and he was just getting the knack of using it to his advantage. He looked into his own hand at a marble Appleby had just given him. It was made of glass that was almost invisible, it looked so clear, and swirling through it was a translucent rainbow of spiraling color.

''Shake it in your hands,'' said the elf.

Escargot cupped his hands over it and shook. It felt as if the marble had gone to bits, and when he peeped in, there were six marbles, not one, and each utterly different from the rest. He looked at the elf in astonishment.

''Works on the principle of the kaleidoscope, actually, The principle of the rotund mirror, we call it. Only they don't shiver to bits after they appear, like the reflections in a kaleidoscope do. Shake them again.''

Escargot did, and found himself holding a whole handful of marbles. He emptied them into the bag containing the truth charm, started to thank Appleby, but was interrupted by a tiny voice emanating from just above and beyond his ear.

''What're they for? Are they bullets?''

''No, no,'' said Escargot, turning to the little man perched next to his head, on a tumble of driftwood. It was a henny-penny man, the orator from the oak woods. He regarded the bag full of marbles dubiously.

"They don't do anything at all," explained Escargot. "You just sort of have them."

The henny-penny man blinked at him, uncomprehending. "And you say that's why you want the book, too?"

"That's it. Exactly." Escargot had been bold enough to ask the henny-penny man for the tiny copy of Smithers, then had examined the thing with a magnifying glass, astonished to find that it was the same edition and printing as his own and had been signed, too. It was baffling, to be sure, and neither the henny-penny man nor Captain Appleby could explain it to him—the henny-penny man because he didn't know or didn't understand the question; the elf because the mystery was too deep for the minds of mortal man, or so he said. Escargot didn't press him, largely because the captain seemed to wax theatrical now at any opportunity, and the subject of his superior knowledge of the mysteries was certainly such an opportunity.

He hadn't been able to think of anything to offer the henny-penny man in trade. Unlike marbles owned for the sake of owning marbles, trade was something henny-penny men understood. In a rush of inspiration, however, Leta had folded sheets of Captain Perry's stationery into paper airplanes, and the henny-penny man had spent most of the morning aloft, planing across river breezes at speeds unattainable by mere leaves.

The submarine lay at anchor once again. There was the dent from a cannonball in her side and sucker marks the size of bucket mouths along her stern, these last etched into the brass and copper hull, too deep, quite likely, even to polish out with a pumice stone. Leta had put most of the interior right—shelving books, cleaning up the mess from spilled bottles and jars, ordering maps and charts that had fallen from niches in the walls.

A single elfin galleon floated yet on the river. In a half hour it would be gone, scaling through the heavens until it lost itself in cloud drift. Escargot could see the top of Boggy's head, almost hidden among kegs piled on the poopdeck, among which Boggy had been hiding most of the morning in order to avoid being put to work. Henny-penny men had been disembarking in driftwood fleets for the last half hour, sailing down the Tweet toward Landsend and the sea. The sun shone overhead like an orange on a pale blue plate, and the air was silent but for the hum of dragonfly wings over the still green waters of the cove. Even with the thin chill on the westerly breeze, you might have thought it was a midsummer noon—except that faint and thin from across the river hovered the smell of pruning fires, and every now and then, drifting from the woods, a leaf would come sailing and bumping and painted red and orange and brown with an autumn brush.

Escargot, for the first time he could easily remember, felt free of the webs that he had managed most of his life to entangle himself in. He felt as if at last he could stand up and stretch without cracking his elbow against something. He smiled at Captain Appleby, thinking that the elf was an awfully pleasant sort. Then he smiled at the henny-penny man, who tugged his paper airplane across the sand now toward a little crisscross raft of twigs he'd lashed together. Aboard the raft stood a paper hut, moored to the timbers of the deck with straight pins. The little man had shrugged at Leta's warning that the thing probably wouldn't last out the trip to Landsend. For a few good miles, anyway, he'd be the envy of all henny-penny men. Escargot watched the raft swirl away in the current, and although he waved, the henny-penny man didn't wave back. They weren't, apparently, much given to sentimentality.

Escargot was full of it, though. He smiled again at Captain Appleby, who was stirring and looking uncomfortable, as if being landbound didn't suit him and he thought it was high time the galleon was aloft.

''Ever visit the Oriel Valley?'' asked Escargot.

''Oh, yes. We're bound there in spring, in fact. There's a gathering in the White Mountains.''

''How about Twombly Town? Ever stop there?''

''We elves don't much meddle in the lives of men, actually, though we certainly might, if there was cause to. Why?''

''Oh,'' said Escargot. ''I don't know. My daughter's there, actually, and I'm bound for somewhere else. I just thought that if you were going that way, don't you know, you might give her something for me. But I won't even ask if there's trouble in it for you.''

"No trouble at all."

"Then give her one of these." Escargot pulled a marble out of the bag and handed it across to the captain, who nodded profoundly, as if he understood very well why delivering the enchanted marble to little Annie was important enough to compel Escargot to ask such a favor of him. "Best not to let her mother know. She won't understand it. A marble is just a lump of glass to her, and if it comes from me it'll seem like a wicked lump of glass at that. But Annie will catch on. I'm afraid that if I don't give her such things, she won't be very likely to get them at all."

Captain Appleby nodded again. He understood that too. He slipped the marble into his pocket and assured Escargot that elves were on tolerably good terms with children. Children were far more closely related to the elves, he said, than were men and women, whose vision, by the time they were grown, had as often as not begun to fail, and they saw everything through a mist, even though they were convinced that they saw very clearly indeed.

Leta climbed out of the hold of the ship just then, wiping her hands on a towel with the air of someone who's finished a substantial bit of work. "It's eleven-thirty," she said to Escargot, and then threw the towel at him. "Are you rested yet?"

Escargot grinned at her. "I was just telling the captain here that it wouldn't hurt me to polish the glass in the portholes before we launch. Wasn't I, Captain?"

Captain Appleby coughed into his hand and then nodded, widening his eyes. Leta nodded too. She wasn't at all convinced. "I won't eat another fish," she said.

"Lunch!" cried Escargot, fired by the idea. "I was forgetting lunch. Eleven-thirty, do you say? Are we shipshape—all the spars varnished and the bowlines heaved out?"

"Aye, aye," she said, saluting with two fingers.

They sailed across the water fifteen minutes later, watching the north shore where the distant spire of a church steeple rose beyond a cluster of riverside houses. A steamship was just then putting out from a dock, and they could hear the airy cheer of wellwishers ashore and see the rising billow of white, cloud-like steam from the smokestacks.

Then Leta grabbed his arm and pointed, and there behind

them, sailing into the cloudless sky, was the elf galleon, with Boggy and Collier and Captain Appleby aboard, bound for the heavens, for the moon itself, perhaps. It tacked across the wind, rising and rising and shrinking as it rose, until it was impossible to say that it wasn't merely a bird that they watched, winging its leisurely way across the sky in the warm radiance of a noonday sun.